Union Made

Eric Lotke

Library of Congress Cataloging-in-Publication Data:

Lotke, Eric, Union Made

1. labor union 2. Union campaign 3. Social justice 4. Accounting

This novel is a work of fiction. Names, characters, places and incidents are either the product of the author's imagination, or, if real, used fictitiously.

Cover art by Lara BeaudryByer

Book design by D. Bass

Published by Hardball Press, Brooklyn, New York

ISBN: 978-1-7344938-3-2

www.hardballpress.com

info@hardballpress.com

Rise like lions after slumber
In unfathomable number
Shake your chains to earth like dew
That in sleep have fallen on you
Ye are many, they are few.

Percy Shelly, *Mask of Anarchy* (1819)

ONE

Nathaniel *A Problem of Timing*

Nathaniel Hawley stirs the onions and snaps at his television. "They'll move the jobs overseas. Then where will you be?"

Nate's apartment is a tidy little space in Richmond, Virginia. The TV chatters at him from a shelf filled with books he hasn't touched in years. "You can't have high wages and low prices," he advises the strikers on the screen. He didn't catch what they're striking about. Is their factory moving to Mexico? Striking won't help.

On the stove, onions are sautéing and rice is boiling. Nate started the rice as soon as he got home from work, and left it alone while he changed clothes and chopped the onion. Now everything is two minutes from finished. He slices cheese and scrambles eggs with local news playing in the background. *Can't Survive on $7.85*, says marchers' banner. The demonstration is at the Pac-Shoppe on the north side of town. The cashiers want a raise.

Nate is thirty years old, with brown hair and brown eyes. In a police lineup, he might be picked every time because he looks like so many people, or he might never be picked because it's so easy to look past him. His hair is thinning, he doesn't wear eyeglasses and his height is the mathematical median for the American male.

He drops the cheese into the pan with the onions, then pours the egg on top. Over the sizzle he can hear the cashier explaining how little she's paid and how hard she works – at Pac-Shoppe during the day, then cleaning an office building overnight. "I can't survive on $7.85," she says, as if she's reading her own banner. She talks about her husband's disability and the age of their kids.

"Go back to school," Nate advises her. "Get a better job."

Nate doesn't intend to be mean, just practical. Her boss probably has a sob story of his own, and it includes making payroll. "Everyone has it hard," he says. "My wife is gone and dating is hard. Money might help."

Nate's ex-wife, Rose, used to tease him about talking to the television. "They can't hear you," she'd say. "They probably wouldn't listen anyway."

Nate deftly flips his omelet, and pats it flat with the spatula. If Rose were here, dinner would be finished already because Rose preferred the onions lightly sautéed, barely yellow and soft. "Practically raw," Nate used to tease. He prefers his onions browned to the point of crispy – "cooked to death," Rose would say. This dish was a staple in the household, omelets over rice, for dinner or breakfast, though not both on the same day, Rose always insisted. One of them made a salad while the other tended the stove.

The onions didn't force the divorce, of course, nor did Nate's habit of talking to the television. He did it less back then, anyway. Their four years together were more happy than sad, and last month was four years apart. As Nate gets older he appreciates why people say time flies. His friends tell him he needs to start dating again. His mother's been saying it for years.

On screen, a union representative repeats the line about $7.85. Nate looks up expecting to see a union thug, some old guy in a denim shirt who needs a shave. Instead it's a cute young woman with dark blonde hair and a striking red blouse. "Last year, Pac-Shoppe made $2 billion in profits," she says. "They can afford to pay a living wage."

Nate shakes his head at what sounds like an impossible dream as he chooses another channel at random. He slides the omelet from pan to plate, one circle inside another, then scoops rice on the side. He adds salt, pepper and Tabasco but the circle is too beautiful to leave alone. He dashes the Tabasco into the shape of two eyes and a smile.

There. Now his dinner is smiling up at him. Nate is so amused he shapes the rice into a triangle over top of the circle, like a party hat. "I can't believe I never thought of that before," he says out loud. He's having so much fun he adds more Tabasco than he really wants, just to make the smile bigger.

It all goes wrong on the first bite. Nate cooked the onions Rose's way, chewy, oniony and hard. "They're practically raw!" he exclaims, teasing a woman who left him four years ago.

Now it's so obvious even Nate can see it. He's cooking for his ex-wife and making jokes for nobody. He needs to concede what he should have known and his friends have been telling him for years. He pushes away his plate and sighs into the empty room, "I miss my bride. I'm lonely."

Catherine *Predators and Prey*

"Okay guys," says Catherine Campbell. "We have their attention. Now we need to step it up."

Catherine is in the local headquarters of United Commercial Workers Local 429. Outside it looks like a derelict warehouse district, with vacant buildings and a used car lot. Inside it looks like a bus station at rush hour, bustling with activity and littered with old coffee cups and empty pizza boxes. Catherine is in the center room, a big square space with folding tables and chairs left wherever people used them last.

Two dozen people are looking at her, Pac-Shoppe employees and coalition partners from the community, all in red t-shirts, the unifying color for the campaign. Catherine is wearing a red work shirt unbuttoned over a black tank top. Her dark blonde hair is cut short and practical. She tells the crowd, "We know we have their attention because yesterday they issued a press release calling us everything but communists. Store traffic is down nearly twenty percent since we started. Nobody wants to cross a picket line."

A few people interrupt with applause. "You can clap at that," Catherine says. That gets a few laughs and a new round of applause, so she pumps it up more. "What do we want?" she calls out, initiating a cheer they've done many times before.

"A raise!" the people cry.

"When do we want it?"

"Now!"

Catherine repeats the cheer to rally the crowd. This is her action nucleus, fired up and ready to go. "Today we have three actions," she asserts. "Both stores, plus a new third location."

"The mayor!" someone shouts. Catherine doesn't notice who.

"That's right," she affirms. "The mayor. Today we demonstrate in front of City Hall." Catherine reiterates what they know – which is that Pac-Shoppe can afford to wait them out. Pac-Shoppe has plenty of profits to cover any costs, and it can sit still for longer than they can sustain this level of exertion. The union needs to get a third party involved, and they're angling for the mayor. "He's going to step up and take our side," she declares as if her confidence makes it true.

Catherine has had countless meetings with mayoral aides. She's reminded them of the union's financial contributions and the doors it knocked during the campaign, but the mayor himself remains elusive. "A lot of shoppers like their prices," his chief of staff told Catherine. "You'd rather they leave?"

Catherine can't keep waiting. She needs to push the mayor to side with the workers, not the corporation. She's gambling that when the microphone is in his face the mayor will say the right thing. Today's action is designed to get it there.

Just then Elena Perez walks in from the street, and Catherine pauses for another round of applause. "Great job, Elena," she says as the room quiets down and Elena turns bright red. "You're our hero."

Elena is a tiny Latina woman with short dark hair who radiates energy. Today she is wearing purple pants and a red Disney sweatshirt. Last night she had her first interview on network television. People saw her on TV, so now she's a superhero.

Elena is the Pac-Shoppe employee who first contacted Catherine about starting a union, roughly six months ago. "They don't pay us right and they don't treat us right," she said at the time. "Can you help?"

"No," said Catherine, answering straight from the organizers' playbook. "But I can help you help yourselves."

Then Elena took the lead at contacting co-workers to turn disjointed complaining into a campaign to form a union.

Elena's family is in a tight spot, though. Her husband, a pipefitter, was injured when a steam pipe burst while he was working on it, burning his face and hands. Their daughters are six and twelve, and right now Elena's biggest worry isn't her raise but whether her husband will get his eyes and hands back so he can work again – as a pipefitter or anything else. Even so, she's finding time to help with the campaign.

"Is there anything you want to add?" Catherine asks her.

"Better wages aren't just for us," Elena replies. "Better wages are better for everybody. That's what we need to tell the mayor. That's what we need to say at City Hall."

"Perfect," says Catherine. "You're hired." That gets more laughter and more applause.

Catherine breaks the crowd into teams based on which action they're doing, plus a fourth team for artwork, slogans and banners. There are several common slogans and anyone who dreams up a new one is free to add their own. Yesterday's addition was "Pac-Shoppe works because we do."

As the room reorganizes itself, Elena pulls Catherine into a room on the side. "They came by again last night," Elena says.

Catherine turns in alarm. "The same men?" Strangers have been threatening Elena when she goes to her car at the end of her shift, and sometimes when she gets home at night.

"Different men. But they look the same and they said the same thing."

"They're only trying to scare you," Catherine says.

"They do scare me! They threatened me and my daughters. They said my husband can't protect me anymore." She presses back against the wall and crosses her arms over her chest, concludes in a whisper. "They know he's hurt."

This is tricky. Catherine wants to comfort Elena and tell her everything will be okay. But she can't truly promise that, and more importantly, she can't minimize or contradict how Elena feels. She reaches out to touch Elena, on the shoulder. "I know it's scary," she agrees. "But they won't hurt you." She reaches with her other hand, so now they're all but embracing. "Threatening you is against the law. But what you're really afraid of ... that would be a crime. They won't do that. Their goal is to scare you, not to hurt you."

Catherine steps back and changes her tone. "Take out your phone when they come," she advises. "Take out your camera and make some kind of recording ... or make them think you're going to. Scare them back." She hates this part of her job – putting other people at risk. Catherine is willing to put her on life on the line to help other people – and sometimes she has. What's harder is sitting safe in her office or secure in her bed while thugs terrorize Elena at night.

"They get closer every time," Elena says. "They're like wolves. I'm a little deer. They're hunting me. Hunting me and my girls."

"That's right." Catherine seizes the metaphor. "You're like a deer. You're safer in a herd. That's us. The union is your herd. That's why they don't want us to create one. Stick together. There's strength in numbers."

Nathaniel *Traffic Jammed*

"Don't worry!" Nate's boss exclaims as if he were running for the door. "This is good for you, I think." His boss explains that their little accounting firm has been acquired. Last night the partners accepted an offer from a private equity firm.

Nate's an accountant. He fusses with numbers, and makes sure two plus two always equals four. If it doesn't, he figures out why. It's easy for him. Numbers are his friends.

Nate works with businesses, not households, so the twos and fours on his desk usually have thousands or millions attached, sometimes tens of millions. Small errors can go a long way. There is a legendary story about someone who used the wrong number of zeroes.

"We'll be doing their books?" Nate inquires.

"Nope," his boss replies. "Not theirs." Nate's new job will be to examine the books of companies the equity firm invested in or is considering investing in. Is the company profitable? By how much? Do their numbers support their growth projections? It's a whole different kind of math Nate's never done before.

Nate isn't nervous, though. He's thrilled. He's just a dull numbers guy. The only reason people keep him on the softball team is so he can do the statistics. But not anymore. Now he'll be swimming with the sharks. He'll be a master of the universe. Forget the sports page, bring on the *Wall Street Journal*. He's not running for the door. If he knew how, he would dance.

Instead he buttons down a day's work and drives home at the end of the day. As he gets to the part where he daydreams of bonuses tied to investment returns, the traffic starts to crawl. It's bumper to bumper, as far as he can see. Is there an event at the Coliseum? He's pretty sure there isn't. He turns on the radio instead of fishing for his cell phone. Right now it's 5:58. In four minutes he'll get "traffic and weather together on the twos."

He turns off at the next intersection, hoping for better luck on a different street but clearly he's not the only one seeking escape. He turns to the local jazz station, thanking Rose for the discovery and reminding himself to flip back by 6:02.

With sax and piano he makes peace with his place in line, waiting two cycles of the light before making it through, but being careful not to block the box. Cool jazz is perfect at this moment, soothing not dramatic. He daydreams about company books and hopes he'll be able to figure everything out. Every now and then he advances a couple of feet. No matter. He's in no hurry. Traffic happens. He figures someone had an accident.

News comes on at the top of the hour so Nate doesn't even need to wait for the traffic report. The news is all about the union protest at City Hall. "Midtown is one big traffic jam," says the DJ on Cool Jazz 101. He talks about police and protests. A union worker talks about getting his "fair share."

"Forget that," Nate says out loud. By now his peace is ruined. He's getting hungry and going nowhere. Any sympathy he might have had for striking workers is gone, gone, gone.

Catherine *Out of Order*

Police cruisers line the street where cars normally park. At the end closest to City Hall, an armored personal carrier, like a miniature tank, sits with its engine running. *Police Tactical* is blazoned on its side and *Rescue* across the front.

Catherine parks her car and walks the last few blocks from the maintenance actions at the Pac-Shoppe stores to today's feature at City Hall. It should be in full swing by now, and the visuals should be perfect. A camera filming the crowd will show City Hall as background in one direction and the state capitol in the other. Catherine admires the Virginia state capitol building as she walks past, the grand columns and triangular pediment designed by Thomas Jefferson himself. *Yes, America, we are part of you*, the union is saying. Collective action is more like America's colonial uprising than a communist invasion. *Now give us our fair share of the profits we help create.*

Today even the weather is on the union's side. It's a crisp, cool sunny day in April, the perfect day that makes people love the spring and forget the cold rainy ones. Tulips and pansies line the sidewalks on the Capitol grounds.

Catherine can hear the protest before she sees it. "What do we want?"

"A raise!"

"When do we want it?"

"Now!"

Soon they are in view, a hundred people wearing their signature red, filling the narrow plaza between City Hall and the street. The size and energy of the crowd fills Catherine with hope. Some people are marching back and forth across the entrance, banners held high. Others gather around a speaker on a stage that Catherine knows is made from plywood over milk crates.

As she gets closer she can read the banners.

"A fair day's wage for a fair day's work," says the first.

"Pac-Shoppe needs us more than we need them," says the next.

Catherine knows that similar demonstrations line the doors on every side, so it's impossible to enter or exit City Hall without feeling their presence.

Maya Perez, Elena's younger daughter, surprises Catherine, catching her leg in a little mini-hug. "Mom said I could miss school," she says by way of introduction. Maya is in first grade, and she's dressed in red.

"Did she?" Catherine replies.

"Mom said I would learn more here."

Catherine stoops down to her level, looks her straight in the eye. "Mom's right."

"Let's go!" Maya grabs Catherine's hand and tugs her toward the crowd by the front of City Hall. Maya's red is an Applebees t-shirt, too big for her, worn over a blue long-sleeved shirt for extra warmth. "There's Mom!"

Now Catherine, too, spots Elena. She's talking to a journalist with a microphone in his hand while another films them with a camera on his shoulder. This shot will show City Hall as backdrop.

Catherine has to trot to keep up with Maya. She doesn't want to distract Elena during an interview, but if Elena wants to introduce her daughter, Catherine could facilitate.

"The police chief wants law and order?" Elena declares as they arrive. "I'll give him law and order."

She pulls from her bag today's march permit issued by the police department. "Zoom in on that," she instructs the cameraman, then turns back to the journalist conducting the interview. "If the chief doesn't like us here, he can take it up with his own people. Or better yet, he can take it up with PacShoppe. As soon as we get a raise we'll clear off the plaza."

Elena is simply fabulous. As an organizer, Catherine can make sure key people have copies of the march permit but can't speak the way Elena does.

Maya tugs on Catherine's arm. "Don't mess with my Mom," she says.

"Believe me, I won't."

They listen until Elena is finished, then the camera crew hurries to the front of the crowd. Elena steps over to exchange fist-bumps with her daughter, then excuses herself to follow the television crew. "Jasmina Barr said she would talk to them," she says. "I promised to make introductions."

"Terrific," Catherine replies. It's great that she found another spokesperson from their movement. It's better for the public to hear from actual workers than union organizers.

As Elena walks off, Catherine says to Maya, "Shall we march?"

They join hands to walk the short distance to the crowd by the front door. At this point there is little work for Catherine. She is free to be just another body in the crowd, and available for troubleshooting as needed. This is the fun part, marching with company on a beautiful day. She starts to feel like maybe they could win.

She risks a question of Maya, "How's your Dad?"

A little blue passes over Maya's sunshine. "He's okay, I guess. He still can't see. I read to him at night. He's bored a lot."

"You read to him?"

"All of my favorite stories." This brightens her up. "He can't read for himself. He can't even watch TV."

"That does sound boring."

"He listens to the radio while we're in school. Sports, I think. And he does lots of push-ups and sit-ups. He's turning our apartment into a little gym. He borrowed some barbells."

The police take over before Catherine can reply. Two squad cars zoom down the street, sirens blaring; an air horn blasts so loud it makes Maya wince. "This could be bad," Catherine says. "Let's take a look." This time it's Catherine tugging Maya toward the street.

What's happening is obvious before they arrive. Police are shutting down traffic. Cruisers position themselves in the middle of intersections as officers direct traffic to detour or turn around. Catherine can't tell what triggered the change. "I guess the police chief has had enough," she says. They'd prepared for this contingency, though they didn't expect it to happen and it doesn't really affect them anyway. It will reduce some foot traffic and the number of people who see the march firsthand, but pedestrians aren't their real audience. The mayor and city council are the target.

Intentionally or not, the police chief is probably helping. With traffic shut down and parking places taken by police cruisers and armored vehicles in the intersections, the Mayor can't act like this is none of his business. He can't dismiss it as a private dispute between private actors on the outskirts of town. He'll need to take a side. Catherine only hopes the police aren't showing which side he's on.

She walks with Maya toward the main crowd at the front entrance, detouring across an alleyway that leads to the Virginia state library.

That's where it happens. Elena is talking to a dozen protestors in a little group, probably directing them to bring their march to a different door.

A car dodging the police blockade cuts through the alley. He's driving fast, probably trying to beat the next closure. Elena's back is to the street, her attention on her crowd. She turns just as the car moves into range.

Maya sees it, too. "Moma!" she yells as she pulls away and runs in her direction.

Nathaniel *Anger and Mercy*

It's almost dark by the time Nate gets home. *Stupid union,* he thinks the entire trip, stewing in his car, never finding an open road. More than once he hears sirens coming from the City Hall area, the heart of the jam. *Can a union be arrested for stupidity?*

He pulls into the Corner Deli for a pastrami sandwich, which comes with a nice pickle. His fridge is low and he doesn't feel like cooking. Rose always told him to stop worrying and spend more money. "For here or to go?" asks the young woman at the counter.

Her question stops Nate cold. He hadn't thought of that.

Eating here means no dishes at home. There are plenty of empty seats but the people here are couples, families, or groups of friends. If a single woman were eating alone would he ask to join her? Probably not. "To go," he replies.

At home he watches a few minutes of a baseball game, the Washington Nationals versus the Baltimore Orioles, as close to a home game as they get in Richmond. "Nice catch," he says, as a Washington player grabs a flyball between the foul line and the stands. That's two outs in the bottom of the third, with Washington up by one.

It's early in the season and the game doesn't matter much. He watches to the end of the inning, then the station turns to a news update about the traffic jam and the union strike. "Enough already," he says as he reaches for the remote, but the visuals catch his attention. It doesn't look like a protest march. It looks like a crime scene.

Squad cars with flashing lights fill the background. A uniformed officer is talking about blood loss and head wounds. Strikers are in tears. The camera zooms into a *Can't Survive on $7.85* sign on the ground, covered with footprints and tire tracks. Someone's in the hospital? Dead or dying? He tunes in for the story.

There she is again, the cute union organizer with the dirty blonde hair, but this time Nate notices her introduction.

"Catherine Campbell of the UCW," says the news anchor. *Catherine Campbell* is a name he knows. He reads the name displayed at the bottom of the screen to make sure. Catherine Campbell broke Nate's heart in high school. Could this be the same Catherine Campbell?

He tunes in hard, studying her closely. She seems the right age. Nate isn't great at faces and it's been a lifetime or two, but he could swear it's the same Catherine Campbell. But at this moment she doesn't look like a crusader for the downtrodden. She doesn't repeat her line about $7.85 or lash out at the evil oppressor of the working class. She looks miserable, like it's a funeral not a protest.

"I'm sorry," she says. "I'm sad and I'm sorry."

He turns up the volume, which he'd lowered for the baseball game. *Is it her?*

"I'm sorry for the people who got stuck in traffic," says Catherine Campbell, looking straight at the camera as if she's talking to Nate personally. "I'm sorry for downtown business disrupted by road closures and traffic blockages." Nate can see City Hall over her shoulder.

She turns to look at her people before coming back to Nate and the camera.

"I'm deeply sorry for Elena Perez and her family." She doesn't look like she's faking when she wipes a tear. "And I'm sorry for the driver. He, too, is a working man, hurrying home to his own busy life, maybe children of his own. Now this. Stuck in someone else's traffic jam."

Nate can hardly believe it. She isn't angry at the guy who might have killed her colleague.

"We need to find a way to make this work for everybody," she concludes. "We're all in it together."

That line gives Nate his answer. It's the same Catherine Campbell.

Saint Mary's Hospital is on the north side of town, and the Emergency Room is easy to find, clearly marked and with plenty of parking. Catherine parks next to a giant red SUV and walks to the front door as an ambulance pulls up and paramedics unload a young man strapped to a gurney and covered in blood. *A few hours ago that was Elena,* Catherine thinks. Last time Catherine saw her she was being strapped to a gurney and covered in blood. *The same ambulance?* Could be. She follows the paramedics through the entrance but they continue through another door while Catherine stops at the help desk.

"I'm looking for a patient named Elena Perez," she says to the young woman wearing the blue hospital blouse whose name tag says *Olivia* and *Happy to Help*. Her hair is peroxide blonde and her lipstick inhumanly pink.

"What department is she in?" Olivia asks.

"Maybe the ER. She was in a car accident this afternoon."

Olivia points over her shoulder. "Right there," she says, making clear it's a stupid question.

"Somebody said something about a coma," Catherine adds.

"Why didn't you say that?" replies Olivia with a dirty look, as if Catherine hadn't just said it. "Neurology, then. That's in the Petersen building."

Catherine extracts directions to the Petersen building, along with generous condemnation that Olivia can't access patient information here at the visitors' desk. "You aren't the first person to ask, you know."

First Catherine tours the ER waiting room, looking for someone familiar. Elena's kids seem young to be here, though, and her husband is recently injured himself. Catherine probably wouldn't recognize Elena's other friends or relatives, and they wouldn't know her, either. After one swift lap she gives up and heads for Neurology.

The hospital hallways are crowded with doctors and nurses in scrubs or lab coats, and orderlies pushing carts, wheelchairs and sometimes beds. The whole spectacular diversity of humanity is on display. Catherine passes people of every race, every age and every physical condition. Half of them have IV tubes stuck to their arms or breathing tubes in their noses. A toddler in green overalls sprints past her toward an old woman in a wheelchair.

"Granma!" the toddler exclaims.

"Gently!" Granma, replies.

The machinery of healthcare is awesome and humbling. A sack of liquid connected above Granma's wheelchair drains into her arm, and another sack drains out near her feet. Computer monitors line the walls or rest on carts connected to electronics whose purpose Catherine cannot imagine. Everything is brightly lit, and no place appears private or off limits. But Catherine's awe is tinged with dread. Does Elena have health insurance? Surely not through her job as a part-time clerk at Pac-Shoppe. Her husband probably has insurance through his job, because construction jobs tend to be union. She hopes he has a plan that covers the family. And she hopes he won't lose it at the end of the month, along with his eyesight and his job.

Catherine remembers how her family lost its health insurance when her father lost his job. She was a kid. Her parents worried about many things, obviously, but health care scared them more than anything else. What if someone got sick? Why if they got *really sick*? Catherine's mother used to panic at the sound of a cough. Even when lost jobs were replaced by new jobs, worries about health insurance never went away. At a time when most children felt invulnerable, Catherine lived in fear of car accidents. Death by infection was no farther away than a stroke of bad luck. Tooth aches were no small thing in Catherine's family.

Catherine stops a nurse carrying a clipboard as she nears neurology. The nurse walks her to a computer, and informs her that Elena is now in Orthopedics, back in the direction she came from. "At least it will be closer to the car," Catherine thinks as she reverses course and walks back the same long hallways.

"How can I help you?" asks the helpful clerk at the front desk of Orthopedics, a crisply efficient older woman who greets Catherine with a smile. By some merciful coincidence of timing, the area is empty as she arrives. Waiting room chairs sit unused and magazines lie untouched on a table. The woman is practically waiting for her, and Elena's information is but a few keystrokes away.

"Room 3317," she says. "Right where that bed is .... *now.*" She points down the hallway and draws out the sentence until a bed being rolled down the hallway passes a door.

"There are people there now. You can join them or wait." She gestures toward the empty seats.

"Thanks," says Catherine. "I'll risk it." She wonders who it is, and whether she'll know them.

Two doctors walk out as Catherine arrives, but still there are others in the room. Maya lights up when Catherine walks in. She scoots across the room and hugs her like she's family. Catherine can feel fear in her hug, and longing for security.

The older daughter, Maya, twelve years old, barely acknowledges Catherine's entrance. She leans sulking against a wall, beside a curtain that probably separates a different patient on the other side.

Elena's husband, Ricardo, is the worst. He doesn't even seem to know Catherine has joined them, her entry doubtless obscured by the doctors' leaving and other bustle in the room. Finally, he turns in her direction.

His face is almost terrifying. The skin is pink and brown, and thick like it's been painted on over his real face, or like a rubber mask he'll pull off when the joke is over. His face and his neck are covered with black spots, and yellow flakes are peeling across his forehead and down his cheeks. His eyes are red, except where the pupil should be, which is covered as if by a giant black contact lens. The rim of his eyes is blacked, too, like Halloween mascara but horribly real. He is painful even to look at.

Worse still is the insecurity. Ricardo doesn't stand like a blind man, practiced at navigating without his eyes. Every inch of him screams uncertainty. He stands like he doesn't know where he is, who he's with or when he's going to fall down again. The contrast to his body makes it even more agonizing. Ricardo is trim, muscular and athletic. A body like that belongs on a soccer field, sprinting for the ball, or nimbly climbing a ladder to reach a challenging joint. Instead it is standing scared in a hospital room carrying a face like a zombie from television.

At first Catherine is literally speechless. She says nothing long after the time for introduction has passed, but she gets away with it because he doesn't even know she's in the room.

"Hi, Ricardo," she says, announcing herself and covering a miniscule uncertainty about his name. "I'm Catherine from UCW, Elena's union." She knows he can't see her, and she doesn't want to assume he'll remember her. "Do you mind if I join you?"

He reaches his hand out to shake, but he's off by thirty degrees. At least she got his name right.

Catherine steps into the correction and shakes Ricardo's hand. His right hand is fine but his left is covered in bandages.

"How are you?" she offers a habitual greeting and regrets it instantly. He's in a hospital. He's blind and burned, standing beside his half-dead wife. *How are you?* Catherine would kick herself for asking the question.

Ricardo seems to see nothing wrong. "I'm blessed," he replies.

Blessed? Catherine thinks maybe she didn't hear him right.

"Elena's going to be okay," Ricardo says. "She's out of the coma. She's going to live. God willing, she might even be able to walk."

"That's good news," Catherine says, still baffled.

Ricardo isn't finished. "I'll get my eyes back, too. The doctor says it's often temporary, and not to give up hope until next month. But God is good. I'll have my eyes back before next month."

He stands taller as he says all of this, and his confidence is infectious. Whether it's medically justified or not, Catherine starts to share his enthusiasm.

"My company is taking good care of me," he continues. "They brought me the paperwork for worker's compensation, and said they would expedite the handling. It won't be a whole paycheck but it will help."

"How's your health insurance?" she inquires. It seems odd to mix God with health insurance, but in the absence of other ideas she says what's on her mind.

"I'm still on the company plan. They said they'd pay me until the end of next week and keep me on the insurance until the end of next month. If I get better, they'll just hire me back. It'll be like it never happened."

Elena breathes out a long sigh, almost as if she, too, had been holding her breath through the ordeal but now she knows it's going to be okay. Suddenly, Catherine realizes that though it was Elena she came to see, she'd barely even noticed her. Now she sees that although Elena appears to be asleep, her face is scratched and bruised, with tubes connected to her nose. Parts of her scalp have been shaved clean to be covered with bandages. The familiar Elena Perez is barely recognizable in the residue.

Elena is attached by one leg to a framework above her bed. Her leg on the far side is covered by towels but the near leg is sheathed in a shining silver metal frame with rails and pins that's connected by cables to a framework over the bed like a jungle gym on the playground. The cables pull her leg diagonally into the air away from her body. It hurts just to look at it.

Catherine is suddenly grateful that Ricardo can't see. It's hard to be optimistic in wreckage like this.

Maya seems to know what she's thinking. She leans in against her, and Catherine reaches her arm around her shoulder, drawing her in nice and tight.

"Will Moma be okay?" Maya asks.

Catherine doesn't know. Maya is likely closer to medical information than she is. Elena is out of the coma, though, apparently not on the brink of death. "I think she'll be okay," Catherine affirms. She doesn't think she's lying.

"Will she be able to walk?"

That stumps her. Catherine has no idea what's up with her legs.

She looks to Ricardo for support but his attention is elsewhere. He's turned back toward the bed and seems to be trying to find it.

Maya goes on. "We used to play freeze tag at the bus stop. Will we still be able to play freeze tag?"

"I don't know," Catherine says. She truly doesn't. What she does know is that Ricardo is dangerously off course. His exploring hands are about to connect to a tabletop filled with instruments, not the bedtop.

Catherine turns from Maya to assist him, taking his hand and leading him the few steps to the bed, and placing his palm on Elena's arm.

Ricardo immediately recognizes where he is, and he feels down her arm to her hand, which he takes in his own. He lowers himself to his knees by the bedside. Unaccountably, Catherine's mind flashes to a child doing his bedtime prayer. *Now I lay me down to sleep, I pray the Lord my soul to keep.* But Ricardo isn't praying. Catherine can see the relief in his entire body as it comes to rest securely on the floor. His shoulders relax and his whole body seems to exhale. It's suddenly vivid how difficult it is for this wounded man even to stay upright on his feet, how courageous he is to greet Catherine normally and his heroism at navigating the hospital system. Kneeling by the side of the bed, he raises his other hand so both are now clutching his wife's. Now that he understands where he is, he raises his head and turns his blind eyes toward Elena's. Catherine doesn't need to see his face to know how lovingly he's looking at her, even sightlessly, as she turns her full attention back to Maya.

Nathaniel *Special Fun*

Nate met Catherine in eleventh grade, when she moved to his home town of Virginia Beach. Nate is certain it was eleventh grade because it was the year they studied calculus. Catherine joined a handful of girls in a roomful of boys in Frank Cox High School, and she didn't really break Nate's heart. He broke his own.

The new girl sat in class, beautiful and mathy and funny. Nate sat in class, longing for her. He could barely find the nerve or the opportunity to talk to her, let alone ask her out, and soon enough someone else had managed it. After a few months she broke up with him – Timothy Parker, to be precise – and she became technically available. But still his actions never ventured beyond daydreaming and the occasional "good morning." A few months later someone else was going out with her, and a few months after that she was gone. She and her family had moved back to Wisconsin, he believes, or wherever she'd come from.

Thus, Catherine Campbell entered and exited his life. Their single most important conversation was also their last. Nate had been holding a door open for some ancient, geriatric couple laboring toward the central office, probably the grandparents or great grandparents of a student. Nate saw the door looming ahead of them, so he raced ahead to open it for them, and stood patiently while they made their way through. Catherine had been behind all of them, and she, too, waited patiently for them to finish the move.

"We'll be them someday," Nate offered as they stepped together through the door.

"That's nice," Catherine replied. "We're all in it together." She used the same line back then as she used yesterday on the news.

Nate made sure to sit next to Catherine in math class later that day. He hoped to continue the conversation, but Catherine announced to the class that she was leaving, and everyone crowded forward for explanation and farewell.

They never spoke again. Soon after she left the state entirely.

How about now? Might he get a chance to try again? He's still a nice guy. Nate is itemizing the evidence when his boss walks into his office. "Follow me," he declares. "Are you ready for some fun?"

Nate banishes the memory of Catherine Campbell and agrees to fun as he steps away from his desk.

If Hollywood were casting a senior partner in an accounting firm, they'd pick Nate's boss. He's a sixty-two year old white guy, with his remaining edge of gray hair cropped close to the scalp. He wears wire frame glasses and a gray suit with a white shirt and a red tie, except for when he diversifies to a blue suit or a yellow tie. For comic relief Hollywood might even give him the same name – Daniel Daniels – though for Nate's boss it's his real name, not a joke. He goes by Mr. Daniels.

He's no longer a partner, though. His firm has been absorbed into the behemoth of Fitzgerald Financials. Mr. Daniels announced the acquisition like it was news, though surely he and the other partners had been cooking it up for months. Nate doesn't know how much they got for their stakes, but he expects it was more than he'll make in the next several lifetimes. All Nate got out of it was a company cell phone. Of course, he's happy to not have to pay for his phone anymore – he even kept his old number – though he's been warned that now he can be called at any time. He's also learning what more has changed, and it has him smiling.

"You've heard of Pac-Shoppe," Mr. Daniels says as they turn into his office.

"Of course."

"You know they're having union troubles."

"I see it on TV." That's not all he sees. He can't keep his eyes off Catherine Campbell.

"Exactly. Investors who watch TV are fleeing in panic. They're selling Pac-Shoppe stock like it's contaminated with plague."

"Isn't that self-perpetuating? Some people sell, so the stock price drops, so more people sell? Soon enough the company is in actual trouble."

Mr. Daniels' office is a classic executive suite complete with wooden desk and leather armchairs. Photos of his wife and grandchildren line the walls, along with diplomas and certificates of appreciation from the city, his golf club, and the Richmond Community College.

Mr. Daniels grins sarcastically. "They might get in trouble. Especially if 'trouble' includes being acquired by people like us, just because the stock price dropped so low." He pauses to make sure Nate is fully following. "But nothing has really changed. The company will outlast the unions. In fifteen minutes the headlines will disappear. The labor unrest will be resolved. The stock price will return to what it was before the headlines."

"But what if the unions win?" asks Nate. "What if they force a big raise? What if payroll cuts into profitability?"

"First of all, they won't win," Mr. Daniels replies. "Second, even if they do, it will be some trivial face-saving, two-cent raise so the union bosses can declare victory even though nothing really has changed."

Then he turns serious. The sarcastic grin fades, replaced by the serious expression that Nate associates with complex calculations on major accounts with high valuations. But this time there's something more, something Nate has never seen before, something predatory. Mr. Daniels isn't only thinking hard. He's licking his chops.

"If there is any real change," he concludes, "it will be in ownership."

"Ownership?" asks Nate. "Someone is going to take them over?"

"We are." Mr. Daniels declares. "Or we might. Not the whole thing but a controlling share. At this time Pac-Shoppe's largest shareholder holds twelve percent. If the price drops low enough, we could buy that much. Or more." He walks to his window and looks outside. "But if we are going to do it, we need to act fast. Before the dispute is settled. Before the stock price recovers. Before the next report shows the absence of an actual underlying problem."

"I get it," says Nate. "Before the TV investors start buying again."

"Exactly. But there's a catch."

"Okay."

"When this union crap goes away, profitability will be restored. But what is profitability now? What was it in the first place? Was Pac-Shoppe fairly priced before it hit the skid? Or did the union fight simply call people's attention to underlying actual problems?"

"I'm starting to see," says Nate.

"Riddle me this," Mr. Daniels replies. "Is Pac-Shoppe underpaying its workers because it's stingy and mean ... or because the profits are so low money isn't available?"

"That's the question," says Nate.

"That's one of them. In the next fifteen minutes – before the unrest is settled and the waters smooth – we need to learn everything there is to know about Pac-Shoppe. We need to learn how much they make, and how much they *say they* make. We need to learn how payroll compares to overall expenditures, and how Pac-Shoppe's staff compensation compares to its peers. We need to learn what Pac-Shoppe owns, what it owes, and who it owes it to. Everything. If it applies to Pac-Shoppe and it has a dollar sign, we need to know it."

"And we need it yesterday."

"You got it," Mr. Daniels replies. He points to a pile of colored folders on his desk, and pulls a flash drive from his pocket. "This is the fun part."

Catherine ***Wholesale Atmospherics***

God bless Loren Ibsen, chief of UCW's Department of Special Operations. Catherine knows it's him as soon as she walks into the office – or rather, tries to walk in.

The entire space is filled with balloons. Every color, every altitude, inflated balloons fill the office from floor to ceiling. There are so many balloons Catherine can't walk without squeaking and shoving through the mass. It's blinding, too. She can't see through the swarm. Eventually she invents a stroke, sort of like swimming, and sashays her way toward the only sound in the office, someone filling balloons with gas and clipping them shut.

"That's you, I trust," Catherine says toward the sound.

"Oui oui, mademoiselle. We needed a lift." Loren has a distinctive voice, a sweet baritone and an accent he calls "pure South Carolina."

He's right about the lift, too. Elena's accident was a pick-axe to their momentum. Now Catherine is smiling ear to ear in a sea of balloons. "Where are you, so I can hug you?"

"Keep your hands to yourself, mademoiselle." She can hear him smiling.

"How will we hold our planning meeting when we can't see each other? Where should we hold it"

"That's your problem, commander-in-chief. I got a deal on balloons. A thousand balloons for twenty dollars. Every color. Two of them are gold. Whoever finds the gold gets a prize."

"Are these helium?" They are floating at different levels.

"It's a mix. I brought my salvage tanks to Wholesale Atmospherics."

"Wholesale Atmospherics?"

"They sell air. They break it down into component pieces, and sell the parts. Helium costs a few pennies per cubic foot. Oxygen, nitrogen ... you name it, they sell it. Considering what they pay for raw material, their margins must be pretty good."

"Loren, you are a miracle."

"Keep your hands to yourself."

Catherine hears a squeal of delight as someone else enters, followed by more voices as several people arrive together. Even as they wriggle through the room, Catherine finds a chair and listens before revealing herself. Children. Her people sound like children. Invisible to each other and unselfconscious, they're like kids on a playground or kittens in a ball of string. They are talking and laughing, spinning balloons and sneaking up for a tickle. Simple joys long forgotten are bubbling all around. Catherine can't remember the last time she smiled this hard.

Games are invented and sneak attacks launched while Catherine waits for others to arrive. She hears more laughing and giggling and, every now and then, a pop. Eventually she calls the meeting to something like order and they do a bare minimum of work, mostly rescheduling for later.

Loren's first gold balloon yields donuts, which are promptly shared all around.

His second gold balloon yields clementine oranges, which meet the same fate.

Catherine is still smiling as she eats both her donut and her clementine. Her agenda went out the window, of course, but it doesn't matter. With people like this, she can do anything.

"What is the purpose of an SEC filing?" Mr. Daniels asks Nate, who is sitting at his desk studying official documents filed by Pac-Shoppe with the US Security and Exchange Commission.

"To meet federal obligations for disclosure and reporting," Nate replies. Publicly traded companies, like Pac-Shoppe, are required to make certain information available to the public.

The great Dan Daniels makes a farting sound with his lips. "Oh, Grasshopper," he says. "Much you have still to learn."

Mr. Daniels has become a new person since the acquisition. Formerly an accountant's accountant, caring only for clarity and precision, he has now taken to soaring rhetoric and flights of fancy, waxing rhapsodic about growth curves reaching the sky and acquisitions glowing like stars. He has assumed a persona he calls a Shaolin priest. Nate is the fledgling devotee he calls "Grasshopper."

"How did you obtain the SEC documents you are reading?" Mr. Daniels asks.

"I downloaded them from SEC.gov," Nate replies.

"And who can download from SEC.gov."

"Anybody," says Nate. The Shaolin priest is leading him toward either a lesson or a trap. Nate follows gamely.

"And if anybody can get them, who are they for?"

"Everybody."

Mr. Daniels' smile tells Nate he got it right. The guru affectation bothered Nate at first, but either Mr. Daniels has softened or Nate's gotten used to it.

"Continue with the SECs," Mr. Daniels continues. "But remember the truth of what you said. SEC filings are written for anybody and everybody. Pac-Shoppe wants investors to think it's doing great at the same time it wants Uncle Sam to think it is penniless. It wants stockholders to see its long term vision but it doesn't want competitors to see where it's going. SEC filings sing for multiple audiences."

"So pay more attention to the numbers than the words."

"Numbers don't lie," Mr. Daniels says. "People do. And people who rely on the executive summary fall for it. The only reason to read the words is to see how they diverge from the numbers." He opens his arms and bows his head as if receiving energy from the divine. "The annual 10-K is the lodestar of course, but the lesser filings matter too. The DEF-14A contains detail about executive compensation."

"I found that already."

"How about the press releases they issue when they submit their filings?"

Nate shakes his head.

Mr. Daniels doesn't need to say what comes next, the lesson fully implied, so he changes the subject. "Compare their official declarations to what you find in here." With a flourish, he places a new flash drive on Nate's desk as if it's the key to the kingdom of heaven. "These are Pac-Shoppe's internal books. They should be familiar to you from the work you used to do – statements of account, including revenues, expenses and variances. They should be complete and comprehensive, itemizing everything from payroll to utility bills. This flash drive should show how much Pac-Shoppe spends on toilet paper at its corporate headquarters."

He concludes by bowing his head and pressing his palms together, the guru entering a meditative trance. "Ask me not how I received the information."

That warning Nate does not need. "What am I looking for?" he asks instead.

"Precisely, Grasshopper," Mr. Daniels replies. "You are looking to see what you are looking for." He locks his eyes on Nate's. "Look for what seems unusual. Did outlays for toilet paper increase after the holiday party? Maybe people got sick and they sued the caterer. Are copays for cancer medications unusually high near a distribution center? What happens if they are?"

Nate joins his hands and bows his head in deference to the guru. "Pac-Shoppe gets sued for poisoning its staff and shipping carcinogens all over the country. We'd rather learn that *before* we buy them, not the next day."

"You are seeing clearly now," Mr. Daniels replies. "Attend especially to any differences between the SEC filings, the press releases, and the flash drive." He gestures toward the

SEC filing open on Nate's screen, and actually moves the flash drive from the desk into Nate's hand. "You have everything you need."

"Thank you," Nate says. He is eager to get to work.

"Needless to say, everything on this disk is highly securitized. No copying, printing or 'save as' something else. Nothing leaves the office. No replication of any kind."

"What happens?"

"Hellfire, oblivion, universal damnation. Want to give it a try?"

"No, thank you."

"Very wise, young Grasshopper," says Mr. Daniels, then mixes a metaphor. "May the force be with you."

Nate immediately checks out the flash drive. It contains an Access database with thousands of documents, classified in a way that allows them to be sorted by date, document type, location or several other useful fields. Nate clicks his mouse on 2019 and a list of all 2019 documents appears. At random, he clicks on shipping records of a distribution center in Cullman, Alabama, and closes it as soon as it appears on screen. Now he sees how it works.

This is comfortable and familiar. Nate knows Access, and these documents are well organized. One set of clicks brings up SEC 10-K filings from every successive year; a different set of clicks brings up "budget to actuals" for every retail center.

Nathaniel Hawley is as happy as a pig in mud. Forget the SEC filings. This is the good stuff.

Nate decides that his job is to understand what's happening from this flash drive. Start with the innards. Master the facts. Later he can examine how the public documents conceal or explain what he knows already.

Nate doesn't wonder how Mr. Daniels got this flash drive. He doesn't want to know and he understands why Mr. Daniels doesn't want him to know. Instead he wonders whether that union – the United Commercial Workers – has a flash drive like this.

Is this industry standard, simply par for the course? Does everyone considering a corporate acquisition or union campaign start with information like this, along with staffs of people to interpret it? Or is this information rare, special and unique.

Nate doesn't wonder how Mr. Daniels got the flash drive. He wonders what it's worth.

Leaving the database, he Googles some news stories to see if union statements suggest access to this kind of information. There she is again, Catherine Campbell. Whatever search algorithm answers his questions also drives him toward the latest news in the Richmond salary campaign, and Catherine Campbell is in the middle of it.

The temptation is too great to ignore. Divine forces are blessing Nate to do what he wants to do anyway, which is to learn more about her personally. Obviously there are many Catherine Campbells, but it's easy to find the right one, starting with her biography on the UCW web page.

UCW's Catherine Campbell is originally from Wisconsin, which lines up with Nate's memory from high school. It doesn't mention her one year in Virginia Beach, which seems fair. It says she went to the University of Wisconsin, though not what year she graduated, which would help with her age.

Catherine Campbell plays the viola. That's a surprise. The viola? Nate doesn't see her playing viola in front of Pac-Shoppe, but there's more to it than that. Why would anybody play the viola? Violin, sure. Or strum a guitar. He can imagine her jamming Bob Dylan or singing union songs around a campfire. But why the viola?

Another page answers his question. "I like to sit in the middle," she once said in a UW alumni interview in response to exactly the same question.

Well, there's an answer that doesn't say anything. Is it maybe some insider musician joke? Nate doesn't get it because he's not in the club?

At first he simply wonders if he'll ever meet her, but he soon realizes how much he wants to. They both live in the same city – at this time, anyway – and they're both orbiting the fringes of Pac-Shoppe. It doesn't seem impossible they might meet. The high school overlap gives them something to talk about, at least. Probably she's forgotten that moment in the hallway but hopefully she remembers their time together – even if she doesn't know he dreamed of her every night, while she hardly knew he existed. Can a high school crush last this long?

One more question suddenly seems important. Is she married? A survey of her UCW biography and her Linked-in profile don't indicate one way or the other. Official bios often mention "happily married with two children," or some such, especially for women. Catherine Campbell's bios do not. Maybe the information is simply omitted ... or maybe she isn't married.

That's none of your business, Nate tells himself as he closes the screen.

None of this is doing any good for Fitzgerald Financials, which needs information yesterday. Certainly it isn't answering questions Mr. Daniels posed. He reopens the Access database, starting with Pac-Shoppe's budget from last year, eager to dig in.

But still. He wonders why she plays the viola.

Catherine *Not Dead Yet*

The central meeting room at UCW Local 429 is humming with energy. Together they've recovered from Elena's injury and laughed through Loren's balloons. Now they're back to work and back in action. Catherine is certain because she designed a test to find out. She asked people to wear red to work to signal they're still standing together – and practically everyone did.

The campaign got a lot of attention the day it marched on City Hall but Catherine has mixed feelings about it. The attention didn't come from the rightness of their cause or the size of their crowd. Attention came because they tied up traffic. Even before Elena's accident they dominated the airwaves and took over the news cycle. Not because they deserved a raise but because they were inconvenient.

"Okay," concluded Ramona McNamara, the head of the campaign's informal communications committee. "If the press wants traffic jams, let's give them traffic jams."

Everyone bounced the idea around until it became the organizing principle for the week of action. "First let's hear from the Logistics team," Catherine says to the crowd in the central room.

Benjamin Winkler steps forward, head of the logistical team. "We're planning four actions," he declares. "One every other day, starting tomorrow and finishing next Monday."

"You have the locations picked?" Catherine inquires. She knows the answer because she participates on every team, but this meeting makes sure everybody knows everything.

"Yes, ma'am," Ben replies, gesturing to the map behind him on the wall. "Tomorrow, Tuesday, is action number one." He presses a yellow post-it note labeled *One* in the center of the map. "Tomorrow we move on the central business district."

Many people know this already but still Ben receives a rustle of enthusiasm.

"They've seen enough of us out front of Pac-Shoppe. We need to take the battle someplace else." Ben gestures across the map, highlighting the full scope of the city. "Tomorrow at the business district we'll remind everybody that the first purpose of Pac-Shoppe is to make money. Everything else is details."

He places a new post-it note with the number *Two*. "Action number two is on Thursday," he says. "On Thursday we mobilize by the campus of Virginia Commonwealth University. The location is bad for traffic – which means good for us – and VCU students are natural allies." He points to two people in the audience wearing VCU T-shirts.

"Young and idealistic," says one.

"Poor," says the other.

Everyone laughs appreciatively. Ben introduces them as heads of the VCU outreach committee, then he moves on, placing a third post-it note on the map. "Action number three is my favorite," he says. "Action number three is on Saturday, shopping day. We'll hit the high-end stores in the shopping district. You know. Anne Taylor, Victoria's Secret and Brooks Brothers." He describes a stretch between two bus stops that are easy for people to reach, and points out a cigar shop, a wine shop, and two jewelry shops. We'll show that nobody who works at Pac-Shoppe can afford to shop at places like that ... though we'd be happy to." He raises his hand in imitation of someone enjoying a cigar.

"Action number four is next Monday," he concludes with another post-it note. "On Monday we go back to City Hall. We'll see if we can't get the mayor, after all."

Ben and the logistical team have already obtained march permits for each location. The plan is to march on the sidewalks, and trust the police to block off enough traffic to generate some press. If the chief doesn't comply they might take to the streets themselves.

When Benjamin is finished and questions have been answered, Catherine moves on. "Communications team, what do you have for us?"

Ramona McNamara steps forward, a large black-haired, broad-shouldered woman with a fighting spirit and a knack for what media like to hear. "Press releases are drafted for each action. Each release explains what is unique about each event, and restates the overall themes. We have editorial board meetings scheduled with the *Free Press* and the *Gazette*. The big kahuna, the *Times-Dispatch* continues to dodge."

"They'll come round," Catherine replies.

Ramona explains the social media strategy, including hashtags and twitterstorms. "The key is that Pac-Shoppe get blamed, not us," she explains. "We, too, would rather not be out here blocking traffic. As soon as Pac-Shoppe pays us a living wage, we can all get back to work."

"What about the police?"

"The police are just doing their jobs. Pac-Shoppe has put them in a difficult situation, too."

"Nice move," Catherine replies. "No need to blame the police."

"Hopefully they'll keep on being stupid."

Catherine would love to bash the police but she moves on instead. "Faith committee," she declares. "Whatcha got?"

Harmon Wright steps forward, a Methodist minister with a long gray beard. Harmon doesn't work at Pac-Shoppe but his parish serves a low-income community, and plenty of his ministry either works at Pac-Shoppe or shops there. Harmon feels like his mission requires him to side with the poor against the powerful, and he's been working for months to convince other members of the faith community that they should too. "As you know, we had support during the original protests but it has skyrocketed since Elena's accident. A silver lining, I suppose, but I'd prefer she were here with us."

"How's Elena doing?" calls a voice from the back.

Catherine has no choice but to digress for Elena. She mentions her visit, and someone else says she's been meeting the girls at the bus stop in the morning. Yesterday they even played freeze tag. Nothing has changed medically, though. Elena is still bedridden and Ricardo is still blind. Progress, if any, will be measured in weeks not days.

Having given Elena the respect she deserves, Catherine changes the subject. "Shoppers team? How goes?"

The shoppers are critical. The campaign keeps them front and center, since the workers' goals arguably go against their interests. Shoppers have always been part of UCW's crowd and some of the best voices all along. Although shoppers like the low prices, shoppers have jobs of their own, and everyone wants a raise. Many are willing to support other workers, just as they would want someone to support them – or that's what the campaign finds if they are approached slowly, carefully and with friends. Besides, lifting wages at the bottom can create an upward force at every level.

Committee chair Stephanie Lerner reports the updates, then raises eyebrows by announcing the newly created "animal subcommittee."

"The animal subcommittee?" Catherine asks. She hadn't heard that before. "Do you meet at the zoo?"

"For outreach to the animal clubs," Stephanie says like it's obvious. "You know. The Elks Lodge. The Lions Club. The Loyal Order of the Moose." She pauses to let the room snicker appreciation for each entry. "There's loads of them. But there are so many clubs – to say nothing of schools and sports leagues and YMCAs – we needed to subdivide to keep things in order. So we made a separate subcommittee for animal clubs."

Stephanie's son David chimes in, "We serve animal crackers at our meetings. They get it." David is in high school. He's parlaying his mother's activism and his own volunteer-hours into a term paper for credit at school.

"The Kiwanis got jealous, though." Stephanie continues. "They nicknamed themselves Kiwis and asked if they could come to our meetings."

"They held their elbows by their sides and tottered around like flightless birds," David adds, tucking in his elbows and chicken-walking to laughter all around. "So we let them in. Mom figured we'd rather have them excited than disappointed."

"Good job," says Catherine. "Especially if the animals are bringing actual human people to our demonstrations." That's what matters. That's what Catherine needs to hear.

"You bet," says Stephanie. "Many of the animal members are getting up in years. They remember when a job paid a living wage, and raises came annually. They remember that their manager's kids used to go to the same public schools as their own. Lots of them remember their unions, too."

"I remember unions, too," Catherine replies with a chuckle. "We're not dead yet." The shoppers' committee has been working for months, reaching out to any member association that can gather a few dozen people. Pac-Shoppe workers who have a connection to the association ask to be invited to a meeting to explain the campaign and make the pitch – for sympathy, support or even volunteers. The goal is to build connections between working people – across races, neighborhoods and even income levels. Members of the campaign offer support, and often participate in other groups' events in return.

"Who's next? How about the staff committee? Anything new?"

The staff committee is crucial in the opposite way, oriented internally not externally. This committee is Pac-Shoppe employees reaching out to each other, keeping them informed about the campaign, asking their opinions, and reassuring each other that activism won't cost them their jobs. It was the first committee formed, once there was enough support to declare a campaign. Its first job was to pass out petition cards so the request to form a union could be verified, quantified and eventually advanced to a vote.

As the campaign moves above ground, Pac-Shoppe has become more aggressive, threatening to take organizers' jobs and warning everyone that "union communism" will wreck their families, their company and their way of life. *UNIONS KILL JOBS,* declared one recent flyer, printed like an epitaph on a tombstone and delivered by US Post to everyone's home. *YOURS NEXT.*

The staff committee tries to allay the fears Pac-Shoppe is trying to invoke. Employees communicate individually with their co-workers. They explain that forming a union is a legally protected right, and that Pac-Shoppe can't fire them without breaking the law. They dispel rumors, explain the rules and help people consider what actions they are willing to do and how much risk they are willing to take. It's very personal work. Catherine encourages the staff outreach committee to tell people that the campaign supports whatever decisions they make individually – from marching on the front line to staying at home with their children – while asking for more and holding themselves out as examples.

Deborah Little steps forward to report that committee members knocked on over four hundred employee doors over the weekend, and recorded two hundred conversations on site or after hours in the Pac-Shoppe parking lot. "Records and updated contact information is in the database," she concludes.

The audience is getting excited as the accomplishments pile up, and Catherine can feel people coming together as part of a movement. "Are you fired up?" she inquires, detouring to pump up the energy. They've been building toward this week for a long time. This is their answer to Pac-Shoppe disrespect and Elena's hospitalization. "Are you ready to go?"

Catherine turns it into the familiar cheer. "Fired up?"

The room shouts back in unison, "Ready to go!"

The traditional call-and-response increases in volume and velocity with repetition. Ramona has rolled loose paper into a triangular megaphone, and she leads the crowd back and forth.

"Fired up?"

"Ready to go!"

Before they adjourn they hear from the last few committees, with good news coming from outreach to local businesses and to legal support. The only bad news comes from the government affairs committee. The campaign's two faithful City Council members, Dorsey and Kristal, will speak up for workers, but Mayor Jefferson remains elusive and noncommittal. That's frustrating. Catherine wanted at least to have a meeting by now. She needs to know which side he's on, and what he expects from his police. Support from the mayor can't win a campaign but it can help. Opposition can kill it dead.

Nathaniel *Life Experience*

Another baby shower. Nate's old friends all seem to be getting married and fruitfully multiplying. A few years ago he went to weddings; now he goes to baby showers and receives birth announcements. Each one is salt in a wound.

This shower is for Sara Jameson, a friend from college who was Sara Ritland when they met on a softball club during their sophomore year at the University of Virginia. The celebration is at Kelsey O'Connor's house, a friend he met through Rose. Nate still plays softball with Sara's husband, Julian.

That's Nate's problem. Even though they were only married for four years, it was long enough for their circles of friends to overlap and intertwine.

During and after the divorce Nate stayed away from social settings with friends because they were too likely to include Rose. But that was hard in its own way, and after some lonely time he made himself live with it. Now he can be in the same room with Rose and chat as if everything is normal, even laugh at her jokes – she's still funny, after all – but he still isn't comfortable and it still doesn't feel normal. He's just being brave.

Rose has a boyfriend by now. Brent. She's likely to come to this shower, and if she does, she's likely to bring Brent.

Brent's a nice guy, at least – why shouldn't he be? Nate's met him several times. Nate's made peace with the fact that he and Rose are traveling in separate directions. At some level he still loves her and wants her to be happy. "I'm happy that she's happy," he tells himself and others.

But at some subterranean level Nate isn't at peace at all. Brent is sleeping with Nate's wife. Nate wants to tear his lungs out.

The room is crowded as Nate enters. The house is beautiful, with colorful area rugs over blue carpets. The walls are beige and decorated with artwork, mirrors and, especially today, baby shower decorations.

"Congratulations!" reads one banner tacked up the length of one wall.

The opposite wall has little ribbons, "Mom to be" with tiny pink hearts, and "It's a girl!"

That's the first Nate's heard about the gender. Pink helium balloons float around the room trailing pink streamers.

Most of the people he knows by name, though several he's never seen before. The trouble is the gray zone in between – people he knows or ought to know, but he doesn't remember their names or where he knows them from.

That, too, is where Rose always came in. "Who is that?" he could ask *sotto voce*, and she would sneak him an answer. Rose was his memory and their collective social secretary. She knew names and birthdays, and sent out appropriate notes or congratulations – even when they were more Nate's friends than hers.

Wouldn't it be nice if Nate could ask her if he knows this Catherine Campbell? Unfortunately, Rose's memory doesn't go back that far. Or at least not her memory of his memory. Their lives converged in college.

Nate and Rose met in a statistics class in their junior year at UVA. Nate was taking statistics to supplement his accounting major and broaden his kinship with numbers. Rose was taking it as a requirement of her sociology major, but math was not her strong point, and she needed help.

"If there is a fifty percent chance that something can go wrong," Nate offered when he saw her struggling with a problem, "then ninety percent of the time it will."

She looked up puzzled until she realized it was a joke.

"Murphy's Law in statistics," she said.

"63.9 percent of statistics are misleading," he continued.

"I'm Rose," she replied.

"Nate."

She took him to dinner that night at a restaurant he'd walked past many times but never noticed. After the next class, they met to discuss probability distributions; in the evening she took him to an outrageous uproarious bagpipe concert that he still remembers with a smile. Over the weekend he convinced her that bowling is always more fun than you think it's going to be, and they had a blast. That night they fooled around.

Nate was smitten, head over heels. He'd never felt that way before. Rose said she never had, either. And since she had more former boyfriends, he figured she was the expert. The summer after graduation they were married.

"Wait!" everyone advised at the time. "What's the rush?"

But they were 22 years old, blindly in love, and thought they knew everything. When Nate said "'til death do us part" he meant it absolutely. He never doubted that she did, too.

The troubles started soon after they moved in together. If they'd lived together then maybe they would have figured it out earlier. As it was, they were already married. They had what their marriage counselor later called "existential incompatibilities."

Some were trivial. Nate wanted a clean kitchen to cook in, but Rose let dishes stack up. Rose wanted a clean bedroom, but Nate left clothing hung over chair backs and bedframes.

Of course they tried to accommodate each other. Nate put away his clothes and Rose did more dishes, but they never quite lived up to each other's standards, and frustration only grew.

Then there were the deeper incompatibilities.

Rose wanted to spend. Nate wanted to save. "Retirement?!" she exclaimed. "We should live so long."

Nate wanted to sleep in on weekends. Rose wanted to go berry picking.

Nate worried about taking risks. Rose was willing to roll the dice.

Now he sees her enter the room, with Brent behind. Rose is stunning as always, blonde hair in a ponytail, like a happy little girl. People step aside as they arrive, like a parting of waters so she can proceed straight to Sara to offer congratulations.

How does she do that? Nate's been here for longer and he hadn't noticed Sara or even remembered to look for her.

He retreats to the snack table and occupies himself filling a plate with carrots and red pepper slices. While he's busy he hears people talking about Pac-Shoppe. "Those marches are killer," says a man from Rose's office whose name Nate doesn't recall. He is tall with brown hair, wearing a blue collared shirt and loading a plate with pretzels. "I heard traffic around VCU was tied up all afternoon."

"It's awful how they treat their employees," says the woman he's talking to. She has red hair and Nate doesn't think they've met before. "I hear the CEO makes 200 times as much as the line staff."

Nate goes ahead and joins them. "That's not bad in the industry," he says as he adds hummus to dip his carrots. "Over 300 times is customary."

"You're the numbers man," says the man who clearly remembers Nate. "What's new in the world of accounting? Are you working for Pac-Shoppe?"

Nate skips the unnecessary details. "Not working for them but examining their books," he says. "Their margins are slim and their profits are only so-so. I don't think they have space to give the union much more. If they did, their shareholders would come after them."

"Between a rock and a hard place, eh?" he says.

"They don't really have a choice, then," says the red-haired woman. "Investors *über alles*."

Soon they are joined by the man who instigated Nate and Rose's divorce, even if unknowingly, unwittingly, and with the best of intentions. Ethan Blumenauer had given them concert tickets. Free and clear, no payment expected, no strings attached. He couldn't use them and offered them to Nate and Rose.

Of course, Ethan doesn't know that Nate remembers him that way. He greets Nate warmly, and the Pac-Shoppe conversation drifts downstream.

Ethan looks good, as he always has. Compact and strong, Ethan's sport is squash. His apartment is filled with trophies and medals since college, maybe before, and continuing at some level even since that time. Now he wants to offer support about Rose.

"It's a shame about her getting married," he says. "I always hoped you two would pull it out."

She's getting married?! Ethan seems to think Nate already knows but this is a body blow. It hits Nate in his gut. He wants to sit down and he looks for a chair but instead he sees Rose and Brent holding hands.

Nate manages to keep his game face on. "Congratulations, I suppose," he says. "I'm happy that she's happy."

"I guess you two weren't meant for each other," Ethan offers as consolation. "Trial and error. A harmless mistake."

Nate's not willing to go that far. Nothing about their marriage was harmless. Nothing was meant as trial-and-error, and he can't let anybody call Rose a mistake. Tragedy, sure, but not a mistake. Working to sound thoughtful and casual he offers a compromise. "Call it a life experience."

Neither Nate nor Rose especially wanted to see the show Ethan gave them tickets to. Indeed, when Ethan bought his tickets they'd considered joining him ... but they decided that the location was inconvenient, the schedule was tight, and it wasn't worth the effort to see a band neither of them loved.

The difference was Nate still felt the same way. He'd have to hurry out of work, rush to the train station, eat some crappy dinner and, depending on the train, hopefully not miss too much of the concert. It didn't seem worth the trouble. The concert would bring more stress than joy into his life.

"Let's make it work," said Rose when the tickets dropped from the sky. "We can do it."

But Nate didn't want to.

Later, the counselor helped them to see that the argument showed a critical difference between them, their approach to goals. To Nate, goals ran through the question of whether they were worth it. He assessed every goal in terms of costs and rewards. Activities large and small, from life ambitions to home décor – everything had to be worth the trouble.

Rose was the opposite. Pick your goal and pay the price. Once she'd set her mind to it, she'd move heaven and earth to get it done. Free concert tickets? So what if we miss dinner and arrive late. Let's go.

Or to put it differently: what's wrong with you?

Of course, Nate doesn't say any of that to Ethan. He simply concludes, "I want her to be happy. I wish them the best."

Maybe he shouldn't be surprised that Rose reaches him before he reaches her. She simply joins Ethan and Nate together, with a plate of hummus and pita in her hand.

Nate didn't see her coming.

Catherine *Limits of Law.*

Catherine's in her office at UCW, or at least what she calls her office – one of the side rooms off the central meeting room with a desk, a computer and stacks of work waiting for attention. The only decoration is a poster of Che Guevera that looks older than she is.

Her cell phone rings. It's Jasmina Barr, who agreed to talk to the press the day Elena got hit at City Hall.

"They changed my shift," Jasmina says without introduction. "Can they do that?"

"What do you mean, 'changed my shift'?" Catherine asks. "What did they do?"

"I mean they changed my shift," Jasmina repeats, now sounding exasperated with Catherine as well. "I used to work a regular day shift, nine to five. Now I work overnight, one AM to nine AM."

"Ouch," says Catherine, buying time while she considers the options.

"Nine to five I could put my kids on the school bus in the morning and cook a family dinner. Evening is family time."

Catherine doesn't remember what Jasmina's husband does but she knows he works more hours than she does, including weekends. She also knows that they have a fourteen year old daughter and twin twelve year old boys. Jasmina believes that young teenagers tend to "tip" one way or the other, and she wants hers tipping to the family, not the streets. Those evenings are precious to her.

"Did they tell you anything? Did they say anything to you?" Catherine is stalling for time because she doesn't like what she's going to have to tell her. "Was yours the only schedule that changed, or was it a major reorganization."

"Just me," Jasmina replies. "I couldn't even tell who got my old shift."

"Can you find someone to trade with you?"

Jasmina hardly bothers to answer. "Nobody wants the graveyard shift."

Memories come flooding back while Jasmina talks. Catherine's first campaign, a few years out of college, was a terrific success. The union of Animal Control Officers – dog catchers – in Indiana wanted officers to be dispatched in pairs instead of alone. They weren't striking for money, they just wanted to be safe. Two officers working together meant fewer bites and an easier job corralling larger animals. With a few small actions, big meetings and clever press, the union achieved the change the officers wanted. The drive was so effective Catherine believed her own slogan, *The people united will never be defeated.* Her elation didn't last through her second campaign, though. She remembers humming to herself, *The people united still don't stand a chance.*

By the time she was finished at the ironically named Union Pharmaceutical, twenty people had lost their jobs and six were beaten to the point of hospitalization. The move that finished the campaign was Union Pharmaceutical assigning key organizers to duties that were toxic, hazardous and maybe deadly. *Want a union? First work sixty-hour weeks with chemicals that will burn out your eyes and give you cancer.*

Catherine's team didn't just quit, they were chased away by the people they were trying to help.

Is Pac-Shoppe turning the same corner? Jasmina might be the first casualty. Catherine asks, ""Did they mention your press interview when they changed your shift?" That's the most important thing that changed before the reassignment.

"No."

"Did they ask about the petition?"

"No."

Catherine and Jasmina both know it's union related. It's why Jasmina demurred before finally agreeing to speak out in public. "I'll talk to our lawyers," says Catherine. "Maybe we can get your old shift back."

"Maybe? When?"

"For now just start on your new shift. I'm sorry. Nothing will happen immediately."

Jasmina doesn't even say goodbye. All Catherine hears is the sound of the line going dead and a union not being worth the risk.

Rose has never looked so beautiful, maybe not even on their wedding day. Her eyes sparkle and her blonde hair sets off her pink blouse to perfection. Except that she looked at least this beautiful on their wedding day. Nate has pictures to prove it.

She dips a piece of her pita bread into Nate's hummus. "Thank you," she says with a smile.

"You're welcome," he replies. "Help yourself."

Ethan steps aside as they navigate an actual, sincere hug and kiss on the cheek without spilling the plates in their hands.

"Congratulations," Nate offers before she can open the conversation. "About you and Brent. I just heard." He wants to sound generous and sincere. "For real. I mean it." It breaks his heart, but at some level he does.

"Thank you," Rose says. "I was just coming to tell you. It's new news, and I wanted you to hear from me first."

"Thanks," Nate says, though it's not clear what he's thanking her for. They both treat it as awkward business out of the way, and they manage just to chat. It's sociable and amiable and easily taken for ordinary party conversation. Rose tells Nate about her new fitness class. Nate tells Rose about the takeover at work. Brent comes by and receives a congratulatory handshake, but then he, too, finds someplace else in the crowd. Maybe it's uncomfortable for him, too.

Nate asks, "Where will the wedding be?" Rose's parents and his own lived near enough to each other that they could pick a venue halfway between. Nate has no idea where Brent's family lives.

"It will be in town here," Rose replies. "This is our home by now. It's better for us and our friends" – she gestures around the room – "and equally inconvenient for both our families."

"You don't need to invite me," Nate declares, surprising even himself by answering a question she hasn't asked. He is certain she's wondering what to do. "It would be awkward for both of us," he explains. He meant himself and Rose, but he quickly adds, "him, too," indicating Brent, who is still in view.

Rose all but melts in gratitude. "Thank you," she says. "I've been wondering how to handle it. I truly didn't know. You shouldn't be excluded, but ...," her voice trickles off inconclusively. "It seems so recently that we ...." A little tear in her eye suggests this is hard for her, too. She touches Nate's shoulder and only now does he realize how close they've been standing, inside of what would be considered personal space at a cocktail party but comfortable for both of them. "That's very kind of you." Rose's eyes relax and her jaw loosens in a way that others might not notice but Nate remembers well.

"I hope you're perfect for each other," says Nate. He starts to feel a little tear of his own. His emotions are raw, wounds not fully healed.

Rose shakes it off before it goes too far. "Are you seeing anybody?" she asks, pulling her hand from his shoulder and inching backward. "Any progress of your own?"

Nate doesn't like that word "progress," suggesting steps and goals.

He starts to shake his head in the negative but then corrects himself. "I have a crush on a union thug," he says.

She smiles wistfully. That was another problem they had. She didn't always know when he was being serious.

This time he's surprising even himself.

Catherine *No Budget, No Injury*

Catherine summons Loren Ibsen into her office.

"Was I naughty?" he says when he arrives. Loren is lanky and blue jeaned. He is in his thirties, but he looks like he's still behind the high school gym smoking pot.

"No," she says. "You weren't naughty. I need a favor."

"Done," he says, and turns to leave as if asking him for a favor is the same as getting it done.

Catherine smiles. "Thanks. Let me know how it turned out." She closes the book on her desk as if the meeting is finished for her, too.

Now it's Loren's turn to smile. "What can I do for you?"

Catherine sits down and turns serious. "The traffic is going great. We're tying up the streets and getting loads of press."

"I sense a 'but' coming."

"But Pac-Shoppe isn't getting enough of the attention. People still basically like them. We need to do something to make Pac-Shoppe look bad."

"Like if they beat up our protestors with sticks?"

"That might work. But hopefully something else. We need something to prick their popularity. Something to put the words 'Pac-Shoppe' and 'bad' into the same sentence."

"Or the same news story."

"You get it."

"Do we have to be nice?" asks Loren with an innocent grin.

"What do you have in mind?"

"They're kind of kicking our butts off the record. They break the law while we apply for parade permits. They put us in the hospital while we have lawyers dotting our I's and crossing our T's. It's kind of unfair."

He's right. Elena can't walk, Jasmina's working overnight, and everyone's afraid of losing their jobs. Catherine needs to show that her team, too, can throw a punch.

"Don't hurt anybody," Catherine warns. "I don't want us sinking down to their level."

"When do you want me to not hurt anybody?"

"Before Monday."

"Anything else?"

"Maximum distress," she says. "With no injuries, no property damage and zero budget."

"And no fingerprints," he agrees. "Next time give me something hard."

Easy research reveals that Pac-Shoppe started as a routine retailer in Seattle, selling clothing and household goods with a slightly Asian flair. Nate supposes the extra "pe" in "shoppe" offered an old-time Anglo familiarity for people whose tastes hadn't yet crossed the Pacific Ocean. Pac-Shoppe's breakout move was early recognition of China as a low -cost supplier of an infinite range of consumer goods. While other companies dreaded communism and feared Mao's ghost, Pac-Shoppe opened a lead in classic American retail, from pillow cases to living room sets, fully manufactured in China. In a few years Pac-Shoppe grew from a single store in Seattle into a national chain.

Nate discovers that the corporation's biggest risks have nothing to do with worker wages. Pac-Shoppe's biggest risks come from disruption in its supply chain, especially from China, or US changes in trade relations or tax policy regarding offshore operations. Other major risks relate to on-line shopping, or even the ability of customers to compare prices in real-time while walking the aisles. Secondary concerns relate to "reputational risk," or simply the positive perception customers have of a clean, neat, low-cost, low-frill place to shop.

That's where the union danger comes in. Pac-Shoppe needs people to like it, not see it as a sweat shop. Customers are shopping for low prices. Their goal is to get a deal, not grind workers' faces with the heel of their boot.

Fitzgerald Financials has assembled a team of analysts. While some have been looking overseas, Nate has been living Pac-Shoppe's domestic corporate financials. He's read SEC filings, press releases, and the transcripts of investor phone calls. He's learned to disregard advisors like Morningstar and Hoovers, who have interests of their own. He sticks with the facts reported to the public and the miracles in the flash drive.

Nate's learned that Pac-Shoppe is in a pretty comfortable position. Gross margins are in the thirty percent range year after year. Earnings before interest, tax, depreciation and amortization are higher than ten percent and often closer to fifteen. Overall profits are in the eight to ten percent range, upwards of $2 billion on $25 billion in sales.

Labor is merely one of many of Pac-Shoppe's overall costs, mixed in with variables like the price of gasoline and the exchange rate between the US dollar and the Chinese yuan. Pac-Shoppe's greatest cost is acquiring products for resale, over which it has relatively little control. Labor costs have the same impact on profitability as the popularity of the "Pac-card," including its discount incentives, compared to other credit cards with "cash back" incentives.

Surely Pac-Shoppe has room to give its workers a raise. Probably it should, and likely it will. Mr. Daniels was right. The cost of the "face-saving" concession it will make to the unions is a rounding error on an operation of this scale. The stock price plummet of those few days of bad press far outstrips the risk to profitability.

"We should buy it now," Nate advises Mr. Daniels. "Buy as much as we can. Before the stock price recovers."

He can hardly believe he's saying such a thing. Nathaniel Hawley just recommending buying a $25 billion corporation like it's a pair of shoes on sale.

He's learned not to believe the attacks on TV, either. Profitability at Pac-Shoppe is strong but not extraordinary, and worker wages are low but consistent with industry standards.

No, the world isn't perfect. But Pac-Shoppe is neither the cause nor the solution.

Nate is dreaming of a cup of coffee with Catherine Campbell, woman of his past and maybe his future. Does she not know what he knows? What would she say?

Catherine *Not Too Super*

Catherine agrees to let Elena's daughter, Maya Perez, join her on Friday. Maya's feeling sick and wants to stay home from school. Her father called to say she could probably tough it out, but she's toughed out a lot recently, and she wants the day off.

Ricardo can't care for her on Friday. Catherine doesn't ask why.

Maya's mother is in the hospital and her friends are in school. Staying home alone or with a neighbor might barely be an option, but what Maya really wants is to spend the day with Catherine "where her mother used to work."

Catherine thinks it's sweet that Maya thinks of it that way. Elena never worked for United Commercial Workers. She worked for Pac-Shoppe. Elena just volunteered a heavy part-time with UCW, helping to organize the workers and leading outreach in the community. Elena created and chaired the staff committee, talking to her fellow workers, and was active on the faith committee, where she found supporters from her own church and the churches of several of her friends. More than one Sunday morning, Catherine gave Elena and Maya rides to services that were hard for them to reach.

"Of course," she tells Ricardo. "I'm doing a walk-through of the site of tomorrow's action."

But first she asks him to put Maya on the phone to agree to one condition. "It will be a long day," Catherine says. "You have to let me buy you lunch. Okay?"

"Yes, Miss Catherine."

"Then I'll pick you up at eight."

Maya lives on the opposite side of town, but nothing in Richmond is really that far away. Her apartment is low and tan brick, with a large parking lot. She's waiting outside for Catherine sharply at eight.

"Sick? My foot!" Catherine exclaims at first sight. "You don't look sick at all."

Maya is all but glowing, a first-grader dressed in purple t-shirt and yellow sneakers, ready for a field trip.

"Last night I had a fever," she says hopefully.

"How much?"

"Ninety-nine."

"That's not a fever."

"Point one!"

"Let's go," Catherine says. "Hop on in." She's happy to tease her but doesn't want Maya to think she has to go to school after all. That's a decision for her father to make.

The logistics team picked the location because of its high-end commercial image and because it's easy to reach by bus, which is how most demonstrators will arrive. Catherine knows the area and has been there many times – it's the heart of downtown, after all – but she wants to survey it herself with this action in mind.

No surprise, she doesn't find parking on the street, but she's happy to park her car in the parking lot of the Whole Foods a few blocks away.

From the Whole Foods they walk to the bus stop at the near end of the route. The street level is restaurant and retail, while the floors above are mostly offices. The street is bustling with people heading for work, though most stores don't open until nine.

On one hand, it is silly to trouble people just because they're shopping for cigars. They don't have the power to give the campaign what it wants. They aren't store managers at Pac-Shoppe retail outlets, or on the Pac-Shoppe board of directors. Why should the campaign bring its problems to people who couldn't help, even if they wanted to?

On the other hand, they too might shop at Pac-Shoppe sometimes. They may shop downtown for cigars but shop at Pac-Shoppe for breakfast cereal, batteries and laundry detergent. Catherine knows that image matters to Pac-Shoppe. It can't be good for business for people who buy cigars and orchids to consider you dirty or indecent. And who knows? One of these downtown shoppers might have a friend who has a friend in a position to be useful.

Three people are sitting at the bus stop when they reach it. Maya sprints the last few feet and starts climbing up the pole.

"Look down the block," Catherine instructs her. "What's your favorite store?"

Maya barely seems to look, as if she knew it already. "Ben and Jerry's."

Following her gaze, Catherine now sees the sign, even from street level. "Let's go."

The sidewalk is broad and clean. The store windows are tall panes of glass, sometimes with curtains but never with bars. Trees line the street, surprisingly leafy and plush for inside a city. Cars are parked along the full block, along with parking meters.

The Ben and Jerry's is not yet open, but the florist next to it is, with spectacular displays in the window. Maya marvels at purple irises, orange lilies and potted palms. Outside the door, a man in blue coveralls is sweeping the sidewalk.

Catherine spots the Victoria's Secret on the other side of the street, and steps into the gap between two parked cars for a better view.

"Be careful!" Maya warns.

"Thanks," Catherine replies. She's studying traffic, watching the flow of cars, pedestrians and buses. She wants to see chokepoints and bottlenecks, and tries to understand the area from the police point of view. Where might they block off traffic? What if they do?

She also wants to consider it from the press point of view. How will this street look to a TV camera? If the marchers decide to step into the street, force a confrontation with police. They'd rather do it in front of a jewelry shop than a liquor store. How about the Victoria's Secret?

Catherine rejoins Maya on the sidewalk and they walk until the light turns red.

"Turn green," Maya tells the traffic light in a tone of command.

"I don't mind stopping," Catherine replies.

"Stay red," Maya orders.

Catherine looks at her quizzically.

"It's called a mini-superpower," Maya says.

"A mini-superpower? What's that?"

"It's like a superpower, but not a real *super* superpower. Not like flying or Superman strength or X-ray vision."

"Like what, then?"

"Like the ability to hold a traffic light green so you can make it through, or the power to turn the other light red so you can cross the street."

"And you have this superpower?"

"No. It's just imagination. I play it with my friends for fun. We invent mini-superpowers it would be cool to have."

"That does sound fun. What other superpowers do you imagine?"

"Never having to tie my shoelaces. That's my favorite."

"It's called Velcro," Catherine replies. Maya doesn't seem to get it, though, and Catherine thinks for a moment about taking her shoe shopping. "Can I create a superpower to wish your mom well? And your dad, too?

"I tried already. It didn't work. That's too super, I suppose."

"I tried it, too. It didn't work for me, either. But I haven't given up yet." Catherine realizes belatedly that she should have left that subject buried, give Maya her morning to escape, so she keeps playing to cover it up. "How about this imaginary superpower? No tangles. Headphone and power cords never get tangled." Catherine suffered a small annoyance in her backpack mere hours ago.

"Good one," Maya agrees. "No shoelace tangles."

"Or hair," Catherine adds. She remembers how her mother used to tug out her knots when she was Maya's age and grew her hair princess long. That didn't last past elementary school. "What else?"

"Always know where you left something," Maya offers.

"Good one."

"Change a candy flavor," Maya continues, clearly having created lists with her friends, and having favorites on the top of her mind. "Imagine if you could change a candy flavor from something you don't like into something you do like."

"Convenient for Halloween," Catherine says, though she suspects that lately people have been giving her more candy than usual. "I would turn candy corn into M&Ms."

Maya brightens as though Catherine read her mind. She bows and offers like an English lady at tea, "Peanut M&Ms, if you please."

Maya is in Catherine's sweet spot for kids. Catherine has always enjoyed six-year-olds, and always known how to handle them. She's baffled by infants and toddlers, screaming baskets of needs she doesn't understand. Teenagers are impossible for Catherine and everyone else. But kids in those kindergarten years are perfect, with their eager curiosity and eyes of wonder. Catherine is having so much fun she's hardly paying attention to where she is or how long everything takes to walk, but she's happy for the company. She looks backward to the Victoria's Secret, and notices they passed a chocolatier. This would be a nice street for optics. Maybe the chocolatier is what made Maya think about the candy.

"Can I turn peas into chocolate chips?" Catherine continues. "As a mini-superpower?"

"I like peas!" Maya protests.

"Oh, sorry. Asparagus."

"What's asparagus?"

"It's a vegetable. If you eat too much, it makes your pee smell bad."

Catherine worries maybe she's being too familiar but Maya's smile tells her she's on board. "Sounds interesting," she says. "Does it really work?"

"We'll find some for lunch."

"But not too much."

"That's up to you."

Onward they wander through the streets, checking stores, comparing superpowers, and watching the traffic come and go. For the first time in years, Catherine starts to feel a pull for home. Not kids of her own – that's a universe away – but the desire to live somewhere, to make a nest, not move from campaign to campaign as UCW needs her. She expected to hate Richmond when it was first assigned. Between the confederate history and that awful year in high school, she treats Virginia like a giant black mark.

But the city has won her over, with its broad streets and elegant architecture. Back home in Wisconsin at this time of year, it might still be snowing and lakes might still be frozen. Here she's walking among tulips and daffodils. Ordinarily she would move out when the campaign was finished, but this time she might ask UCW if she can stay through the implementation phase. When Elena's legs are better they can go for a walk.

Nathaniel *Blue and Green*

Fitzgerald Financials bought twenty percent of a Fortune 500 company. "Does that put us in the Fortune 2,500?" Nate asked Mr. Daniels. One fifth of one five-hundredth is 2,500, after all.

The good news is he gets the joke. Not everybody would.

The bad news is he doesn't think it's very funny.

Mr. Daniels will be on the NBC news tonight to discuss their acquisition of a large stake in Pac-Shoppe Corporation. At 20 percent, Fitzgerald Financials will be the single largest shareholder. Nate is reviewing numbers with Mr. Daniels on the way to the station.

How cool is that? One minute Nate is a lowly accountant, helping companies with their balance sheets. Next minute he's counseling corporate raiders where to strike, and the next minute he's helping make the evening news.

Nate's never seen a TV studio before. He can't wait.

NBC sent a limousine to pick them up at their office. *Who else sat in this seat?* Nate wonders as they drive across town. Who else has gotten the celebrity treatment from the network, driven by limousine to make sure they arrive on time. Who is he rubbing butts with, even indirectly? *The mayor? The governor?*

"I'll avoid the overseas supply chains," Mr. Daniels suggests, thinking out loud. "It's too messy and too dangerous."

"And a source of actual problems," Nate agrees. A different team had researched that dimension. It weighed in the *No* column.

"Talk about the profits," Nate suggests. That was his research and a big factor in the *Yes* column.

"I want people to think we were incredibly sharp, buying at this bargain price, and to get in now before it's too late."

"That will drive the stock price back up," Nate agrees.

"If it goes too high we can sell next week," Mr. Daniels says. "If I'm not convincing, the price could keep going down."

"If they ask about labor unions?"

"I'll dodge that, too. Compensation and benefits are average for the industry. Profits are responsible but not excessive. I'll leave management to work it out with the unions. If anything, I'll use it as a chance to express confidence in current management. No need to scare them at this time."

While other cars are sitting in traffic, their driver seems to know every cut-through and the timing of every light. They're sailing downwind through the streets, impervious to resistance. They cruise past the gothic spire of the old city hall and the gleaming modernity of the Wells Fargo tower.

They chat more about the numbers that Mr. Daniels already knows. Profits and margins, sales revenues and tax obligations.

Mr. Daniels always wears a suit. Tonight Nate put one on, too. He doesn't expect to see the camera but he wants the Fitzgerald Financials team to project perfect professionalism. Soon they arrive at the studio, a modern looking office building with a satellite dish on the roof. A young woman in a blue suit greets them at the door. "I'm Mandy," she says. "I'm your producer for the evening. Right this way."

She escorts them through an undecorated lobby to an elevator and presses the button for the fourth floor.

"You're Dan Daniels from Fitzgerald Financials, right?" she says to Mr. Daniels. "You're here to talk about the PacShoppe acquisition."

"Correct," he replies.

"We're happy to have you. Right this way to the green room."

She leads them down a short corridor lined with television screens playing NBC programs to a small room that isn't green.

Dominating the room is a giant TV screen on the opposite wall. "That shows what's presently on the program," Mandy explains. "The studio is through that door and make-up is through that one," she says, pointing to the other two doors, each with its own prominent label. "Make-up will come for Mr. Daniels in a few minutes. Any questions?"

"No," says Mr. Daniels.

"Help yourself to water or coffee," Mandy says. "Feel free to arrange the furniture any way you like, and press this button if you have any questions." She points to a large red button by the make-up door as she exits the way they entered.

Mr. Daniels drags a chair toward a wall and has a seat. "I'm going to sit by myself for a minute," he says.

Nate accepts his invitation to be left alone.

The walls of the green room are light blue with a large painting on each wall, uninspiring landscapes with trees and lakes, as if they want people to be bored and undistracted. There are several chairs and a few coffee tables, all loose so they can be moved wherever people like.

Maybe three minutes later the door to the make-up room opens and Mr. Daniels is escorted inside. Nate is instructed to stay in the green room.

On screen, a Harvard economist is discussing the national debt with a member of Congress, the NBC News logo conspicuous in the background. Is that happening on the other side of this wall?

Then the door to the hallway opens and Mandy walks back in, this time escorting Catherine Campbell of the United Commercial Workers and a different woman Nate doesn't know.

"Oh my God!" Nate says to himself, nearly out loud. Catherine from Cox High School is right there across the room.

In person she is obviously the same person. She looks like she's hardly aged since high school. He wants to race across and give her a familiar hug, but he's restrained by both professional dignity and the same nervous awe he had in eleventh grade. He is equal parts thrilled and mortified. If he opens his mouth he will surely say something stupid.

How should he start? Will she remember him? Can he ask about the viola?

Mandy describes the room just as she did for Nate earlier – explaining the TV screen and the call button – but says to the unknown woman before she leaves. "Make-up will call you in a few minutes, then we'll have you on to discuss the Pac-Shoppe takeover."

Catherine Campbell has attention only for the other woman. "Relax, Jasmina," she says. "It's just like we practiced.

Be yourself. Talk about what you want to talk about. Feel free to disregard the questions."

"No matter what?" Jasmina asks.

"No matter what. Say what you want to say. Asking you a question just means it's your turn to talk."

With that, the door to the make-up room opens and Jasmina is ushered away.

Nate is alone with Catherine Campbell.

Catherine *You Can Do it*

Jasmina is so nervous! The limousine picks them up at the UCW headquarters, probably the nicest car to reach their parking lot in years.

"Is this for us?" Jasmina asks. "It's so big!" Jasmina is Pakistani with jet black hair offset by a single ruby strand her teenaged daughter colored last week.

To Catherine it's an ordinary limousine, long and black, with the back seat arranged as six bucket seats facing each other. Between them is a table decked with water bottles, *People* magazine and *Sports Illustrated.*

Jasmina looks terrified. She straightens the magazines, doubtless knowing that they'll scatter at the first acceleration. "You do it," she says.

"You're better than me," Catherine says, not for the first time. "People want to hear from you. It's your life I'd be talking about. They should hear it from you. You're the party of interest, an actual real-life Pac-Shoppe worker talking about real life in Pac-Shoppe."

"But I don't know anything!"

Catherine has briefed her on profits and earnings and she can hold her own, but she's right to be nervous. If they're talking about profits and earnings she needs to change the subject.

"Who has to live with the poverty wage?" Catherine asks.

"Me," Jasmina admits.

"Who had her shift moved without a choice?"

"Me."

"When was the last time you got a raise?"

"I got half a percent last year, nothing the year before."

"How does that compare to your rent?"

"My rent went up $90 last year. I stopped buying meat for dinner." She shakes her head and cuts herself off like she accidentally shared a secret. Never before had she mentioned the meat.

"We didn't stop entirely," Jasmina corrects herself. "But only on Fridays or special occasions."

Catherine reaches out to touch her in encouragement. “That’s the kind of story they need to hear,” she says. “That’s why they need to hear it from you.”

Catherine brings her back to easy lessons, things she’s said many times before. Stay calm. Be yourself. Tell the truth. “By the way,” Catherine concludes. “Pac-Shoppe made two billion dollars last year. They can afford to give you a few of them.”

By now they’re pulling up to the studio, third in a line of limousines picking up or discharging passengers. When they reach the front, a young woman named Mandy greets them and opens the door. “UCW to discuss Pac-Shoppe?” she inquires. “I’ll bring you up to the green room.”

There’s already someone else in there. A young man, probably from the financial trader that stands to make a killing off Jasmina’s misery. Catherine realizes the campaign did him the favor of tanking the stock price. It’ll come back up after it’s settled and he’ll make a killing.

Nathaniel *But what?*

It should be easy. Nate need only introduce himself, something he's done thousands of times. He can ask about Frank Cox High School as if he's unsure himself. See if it's true, and see if she remembers him, too. Leave the viola out of it.

He tries not to watch her as he thinks about nothing else. Should he introduce himself as being from Fitzgerald Financials or from Frank Cox High School? And what next? Should he act like seeing her is a surprise? It shouldn't be. She's been on TV, after all. He could have recognized her as soon as he saw her. In fact, he did. Or maybe he should act like he's seeing her for the first time in twenty years. Has it been that long? No, it's been fifteen.

At least his math hasn't abandoned him.

But wait! He has so many other questions, technical ones of tax and finance. Does she know that Pac-Shoppe's profitability is healthy but not extraordinary? Does she understand that Pac-Shoppe wages are industry standard, with little room to rise? How much of a raise does she need to call it a win?

Could Nate somehow be the hero who brokers the deal? Here in the green room of NBC, Catherine Campbell and Nate Hawley reach an agreement – comparing how much the investors might offer with what she might be willing to accept. They can agree today or discuss it over coffee tomorrow. Next week the rest of the world can watch it on television.

Don't be silly, he tells himself. The only thing he could give her of value would be the financials. Many of them she probably has – like the SEC filings – and the rest is hellfire confidential. Either she has the information or she doesn't. Either way he's not going to give them to her. That's nothing to talk about.

Hey, I'm Nate, he imagines himself saying. *I've got lots of cool stuff. You can't have it but trust me, it's really cool.*

No, there's nothing to say.

It happens faster than he expected. With the speakers in the make-up room and the program not yet started, Catherine walks over to shake Nate's hand.

"Hi, I'm Catherine from the United Commercial Workers," she says.

Her hand is cool and strong. Nate hopes his isn't embarrassing.

Nate states his full name and doesn't bother with his job title, hoping for recognition that never comes. Then the show begins and they turn away to watch.

Catherine *But what?*

He's so scared! So pathetic looking.

But then Catherine thinks again. He isn't pathetic. He's just nervous. A scared little boy wearing his father's suit. Sure, he works for the predator but he's a wage-slave like Jasmina. Better paid, she's sure, but far from the ruling class.

He looks familiar, too. Catherine has a good memory for faces and she thinks she's seen him before, though neither name nor place comes to mind.

Maybe he came to one of their actions, watched from the sidelines. Maybe he'd been sent out to do opposition research. Know thine enemy.

She wonders what he does for Fitzgerald Financials. He looks old to be a college intern, brought along with the boss to a TV show to add excitement to unpaid labor. Probably he's a financial analyst or some expert in the office who briefed the big-wig on the numbers so he wouldn't say something stupid and tank the stock – as if *that* would affect Pac-Shoppe's underlying health anyway.

Then she realizes he's probably a financial analyst with access to Pac-Shoppe's internal records. What if he knows something she doesn't know? What if he has something UCW can use? She decides she should at least visit with him and see what she can learn.

"Hi, I'm Catherine Campbell," she says, walking across the room to shake his hand. But they can't go farther as the show begins. A three-minute segment isn't long enough to discuss anything interesting, anyway, and up close she almost feels bad for considering it. He looks so nervous and scared, like a child about to cry.

On screen, the NBC host asks Jasmina what the merger means to her. The big TV zooms on little Jasmina's face and Catherine zooms with it to watch her reply.

"Absolutely nothing," says Jasmina. "What do I care who owns how many shares of whatever? Nobody asks me anything. Somebody's going to get rich, though. That won't make a difference to me, either."

Catherine doesn't even try to hide her smile. She turns to see how it affected the analyst from Fitzgerald Financials. Will he accept Jasmina's dare and prove her wrong? Instead she realizes how closely he's watching her even as they both watch the TV. And again she wonders, *why does he look so familiar?*

<u>Nathaniel *I wish*</u>

The show is over. Mr. Daniels comes bustling out the studio, asking how he did, and Nate needs to act like he saw everything and declare Mr. Daniels a terrific success. But Nate never really spoke to Catherine Campbell. He never asked her about Frank Cox High School. He never invited her to that cup of coffee. He's kicking himself. He wishes he had.

Catherine *I wish*

The show is over. Jasmina comes bustling out of the studio, asking how she did and looking relieved like she escaped a firing squad. Catherine gives Jasmina a giant hug and her full attention.

She never really spoke to that nervous young man from Fitzgerald Financials. She never got to explore what he does or what he knows. She should have at least invited him to a cup of coffee. She's kicking herself. She wishes she had.

TWO

It's Saturday morning and Catherine is driving downtown to the shoppers' action. She offered Maya a ride but the logistics were tough and Maya wanted to take her father on the bus, a field trip of his own. It's just as well because Catherine needs to make a phone call.

Catherine's mother answers on the first ring. "Hi, mom," Catherine says. "Happy birthday."

"Good morning, Cate," her mother replies, using a title Catherine outgrew in middle school. "Thanks for thinking of me. You must have a busy day."

"Why do you say that?"

"Because you wanted to call me before you forgot or got caught up in the bustle."

Catherine laughs loud enough her mother can probably hear on the other end. "You know me too well."

"I've known you since before you were born," her mother replies. "Are you driving?"

"Yes, I'm driving."

"Well, be careful. I don't want you to die on my birthday."

Catherine wants to laugh at that, too, but manages not to. Instead she reassures her mother that she'll be careful and talks about where she's going. She describes the shoppers' action and the "delightful six-year-old" she'll see when she arrives.

That was a mistake. "You'll borrow other people's six-year-olds but you won't have one of your own?" her mother replies. "You're not getting any younger, you know."

"I'll be thirty-one next month. You can call to wish me a happy birthday. I promise not to crash when I answer."

Catherine is the only-child of a mother who wanted more. Her mother came from a big family and married young. She was aiming for four kids, but cancer derailed those plans shortly after Catherine was born. Chemotherapy worked but she lost both the time and the ability to have more kids. Of course, she was grateful she got better, and happy to be alive – but she missed the big snuggly family she'd always longed for. Catherine's mother was talking about grandchildren before Catherine was a teenager.

"Want to give me a birthday present?" her mother asks.

"Of course," says Catherine, certain she won't like where this is heading.

"Go on a date," her mother replies. "At least one date."

"Deal. I'll go on a date. At least one." She carefully modulates her tone so it comes out as a joke. "Before your next birthday."

She hears her mother chuckle gently on the other end. *Same old Catherine,* she must be thinking.

Catherine isn't opposed to romance or sworn to celibacy. In college she had a boyfriend or two, but her career proved to be far more interesting than she expected, and certainly more interesting than dating. It doesn't help that there's nobody even on the horizon – though, when pressed she confesses she doesn't spend much time looking.

"Is anything new with Dad," Catherine asks, deliberately changing the subject.

"Dad's fine. Nothing new."

"Send him my love," says Catherine. "And happy birthday again." She truthfully explains that she's nearing her destination and needs to attend to exiting the highway, then looking for parking.

"Thanks for calling," her mother says. "I love you."

"Love you, too," Catherine says. She means it without reservation. She has a terrific family and loves both her parents. But as an only-child, weddings and grandchildren are all on her. And she has to admit she isn't trying very hard.

Nate *Outsider Trading*

On Saturday morning Nate does something he's never done before. Rose made him do it, or at least she inspired him. Rose left because he was straitlaced and boring. Frugal like a college student, risk-averse like an old man.

But now he's swimming with sharks.

Nate logs onto his checking account and his Vanguard investment account. Not bad, he thinks, as he examines his position. The screen shows him bar charts, pie charts, and line graphs all trending upward. Everything is black or green. None of it is red, proof of what frugal boring living can achieve. He scrolls up and down the screens, examining his performance history, appreciating his account balances. In a different era, with different technology, he'd be counting his gold, thumbing the coins. He almost wishes he could feel something tangible, the weight of coins in his hands. "Pretty good," he says out loud. "Well done, Nate."

Apparently he's talking to his computer now, too.

Fortunately, Rose isn't around to hear.

Indeed, nobody is around to hear. Nate is all by himself, lonely with his positive growth curves.

He clicks on the link that says *Make a Change.*

This isn't insider trading, Nate has convinced himself. Fitzgerald Financials' investment in Pac-Shoppe became public yesterday. He's responding to the same market cues any investor might, not privileged information he got on the job. Others might be placing trade-orders that will also transact on Monday morning and Nate is simply in the queue, not jumping ahead.

He places an order to sell $25,000 of his dependable moderate risk mutual funds.

"Are you sure?" Vanguard asks. "Trades are irrevocable once made." Nate looks at the picture of Rose he still keeps on his bookshelf. How long after she's married can he keep that picture? Is he doing this for her or for himself? Is he still trying to impress her?

No, he's moved beyond her, he is certain. Nate is doing this for himself.

Vanguard wants him to be sure. "Click yes to confirm," it says.

Nate clicks "Yes," then advances through a series of screens until he reaches a place for new transactions. Here he places an instruction to buy $25,000 of Pac-Shoppe stock, now trading roughly 20 percent lower than it was last week before the union campaign tanked it.

Again he is warned, "Trades are irrevocable." Again he is asked, "Are you sure?"

Nate hesitates but powers through. Yes, he is sure. He clicks the "Yes" button and lets out a long sigh.

In a millisecond it is done. Irrevocable. Irreversible. Or as the screen says, "Confirmed." He just sold his safety and bought some risk.

Nate wants to feel a surge of adrenalin. He wants to feel the thrill of the hunt, to see the blood in the water, to feel the spear in his hands or the gun at his shoulder. He's not just swimming with the sharks. He's one of them now! A predator in the open sea, stalking profit and eating risk.

That's how he wants to feel but he's nowhere close. Honestly, he is scared to death.

Nate just bet more than half his life savings. If something goes wrong, he won't feel like a big game hunter who missed his mark. He'll feel like a jerk. He skipped years of concerts, cruises and happy hours – and he will have nothing to show for it. He will become exactly what he warned Rose against – ready to buy a house, but without a down payment. Ready to retire but without the nest egg. And why not? Because for one crucial millisecond he pretended to be a shark.

He tries to reassure himself. He is taking the same risk he advised Mr. Daniels to take. Together they are betting that the union is a blip and that next week Pac-Shoppe stock will be back where it belongs, 20 percent higher than it is now.

If it was good enough for Mr. Daniels, isn't it good enough for Nate? His team of smart, capable professionals concluded that it was the right thing to do. He could make $5,000 by the end of next week.

He should be happy, right?

As Rose used to say, no risk, no reward.

Nate hopes she's right.

Right now he is sitting at home hugging himself behind his desk. Do sharks do that, too?

Catherine *Victoria's Secret*

The street is filled with horses.

Not only do the police close the roads on Saturday, but they patrol the streets with mounted officers, strong young men in blue uniforms atop chestnut chargers, wearing crash helmets and armed with guns. Some walk in formation down the yellow line while others stand like statuary in the intersections.

"Can I touch your horse?" the child asks. She looks about eight years old and her brother is maybe six. From the excitement on the kids' faces, their shopping trip sprouted a zoo.

"Her name is Bertie," says the officer. "Just be nice."

He and his partner are stationed at an intersection making sure, Catherine can only suppose, that nothing goes wrong. At some unfathomable cost to the public, they are defending Pac-Shoppe's right to keep its workers in poverty.

This is terrific.

People tend to shop on foot, anyway. The car is simply for the trip downtown, then they park and walk.

Today people can walk in the street.

They don't even need to look out for cars.

And there are horses!

Is this not heaven, from an urban shoppers' point of view? The streets are filled with shoppers on a Saturday afternoon. No cars are in the street and no clouds are in the sky. It's sunshine in every direction.

And it's made for TV.

Stephanie and her son David are holding court in front of the shoe store. They are surrounded by television cameras, and a crowd of pedestrians. Up front, Stephanie is displaying shoes with price tags converted into hours of work at Pac-Shoppe.

"This is the standard dress oxford by Hugo Boss," she says, "selling inside for $415, equivalent to a mere 52 hours of work at Pac-Shoppe wages." She holds up what looks like an ordinary men's business shoe draped with a tag that reads *52 hours*. "You can buy this shoe after 52 hours of work at Pac-Shoppe poverty wages — roughly a week of work, plus a weekend."

She sets it aside and picks up a different shoe. "Or perhaps you want the Gucci standard oxford? It costs a mere 104 hours of work — roughly two weeks of work, plus another weekend. I sure hope you don't have to pay for food, rent or health care. I definitely hope you don't have kids!"

The audience murmurs appreciation and some of the cameras scan the crowd.

Up front, David, standing next to Stephanie, pronounces, "With three more hours of work you can buy a pair of socks." He holds up a pair of black socks with the label, *3 hours*, rotating around for all to see. "Or perhaps you prefer Merino wool for only seven hours of full time work, a cost of $54.95, measured in dollars."

"How much for silk?" his mother asks.

"Eight hours for silk," David replies. "$64.95 or one full day of work. Twelve hours if you want cashmere."

"So I would need to work more than a day at Pac-Shoppe – or at Pac-Shoppe wages – to buy a single pair of socks from this store?"

"Just one pair," David replies, "though not the nice ones. Want to check out the cigar store?"

It's beautiful theater, and the cameras are taking it all in. A steady stream of marchers fills the background, wearing red t-shirts and carrying campaign posters. The standard *Can't Survive on $7.85* is matched by posters that show shoes and cigars with the price tags that Stephanie and David are talking about.

On the edge of the crowd Catherine sees Jasmina talking to a journalist who is taking notes in a small stiff notepad. "Why do you stay?" Catherine hears the journalist ask. "If it's that bad, why don't you just get another job?"

Jasmina reacts like she's been asked why she doesn't sprout wings and fly to the moon. First she looks surprised, then astonished. By the time she replies she looks frankly disgusted. "There are no better other options," she says. "Believe me. I've tried."

A mounted officer walks behind her and pauses. The horse steps sideways and turns its head as if to review the reporter's notebook. A woman walking by steps around, leaving a wider berth than probably necessary.

Meanwhile Catherine notices that David has moved toward Victoria's Secret. Stephanie left him to do this one alone, the compromise to a disagreement between mother and son.

The poster in the store window is a voluptuous female bottom wearing minimal lace panties. "All cheek panties," the poster reads. "Sixteen dollars." The panties are pink but barely visible within acres of naked skin.

David walks straight to the pantie poster, and places a sticker on each cheek, patting it gently into place. "Sixteen dollar panties," he announces, then steps aside so the labels are clear. "One hour per cheek."

His audience breaks into applause as he blushes brightly and works to keep a straight face. "My mom didn't want me to do that," he confesses. "She wanted to keep it PG."

A shopper in the crowd, an older man, takes David's side. "It's Victoria's Secret. Nothing is PG!"

Nate *Fuel on the Fire*

By now Nate has moved far beyond following the union casually in the news. If it isn't in the newspaper or he misses it on TV, he investigates to see what he's missed. Obsessed would be an overstatement, but surely he is more than concerned.

And why not? His work is counting on it and now his personal savings are caught up in it as well.

This union business needs to resolve quickly and favorably – from Pac-Shoppe's point of view, which is now his own. He needs to have bought Pac-Shoppe stock at the bottom, before the recovery, not early in its descent to zero.

Of course, he's watching Catherine Campbell, too. He knows from watching her and Jasmina back in the green room that she prefers to put workers out front and keep herself in the background, though he knows from watching TV that she doesn't always succeed. He has seen Catherine Campbell with her dark blonde hair talk about wages, talk about profits and talk about executive pay. But he's never seen her talk about competition or market forces. He's never seen her consider what would happen to Pac-Shoppe if it gave her the raise she wants.

Likewise, he has not seen her admit that Pac-Shoppe wages are typical for that type of job, nor acknowledge that there is such a thing as the bottom of the ladder. After all, *somebody* has to have the entry-level job — and her people are it. He hasn't seen her talk about people who started down there but worked their way up. Indeed, he hasn't seen her talk about progress, promotions or merit at all.

He's not thinking of any of that when it happens, though. It's Sunday afternoon and he's wheeling his groceries toward the car, worried only about whether his ice cream will melt before he gets home. He's walking across the display window of the Best Buy when the televisions light up with a breaking news alert.

Pac-Shoppe evacuated, says a screen nearby. Nate stops to look, but all he can see is a news anchor speaking into a microphone. If the sound is on, it's behind the glass.

The screen adjacent is showing a soccer game but a few steps down an even bigger screen shows the Pac-Shoppe with fire trucks outside and the parking lot filled with shoppers. It's the Pac-Shoppe on the northside of town. He recognizes it instantly by now. *Evacuated*, says the heading. *Panic at Pac-Shoppe.* Nate watches only long enough to determine that he can't learn anything more from this side of the window.

He rushes to his car to turn on the radio. The all-news station is talking about some prince in Saudi Arabia. He practically hits a mother with child as he frantically adjusts the radio looking for options. "Watch where you're going!" he hears from behind. The rear view shows a man, probably the dad.

Nate finds weather, blues harmonica and Top Forty. He finds advice about buying a new furnace and a more comfortable mattress – but he can't find what's happening at Pac-Shoppe. He's checking pre-sets, clicking *scan* and succeeding at not hitting anybody, including that asshole making the left turn on the yellow that he's racing as it turns red.

Nate changes strategy and leaves the radio on news, figuring Pac-Shoppe will be recapped at least once before he gets home. At the next red light he picks up his phone and checks his headline service.

He doesn't see anything about Pac-Shoppe. The light turns green before he can query.

When he gets home he learns that the Pac-Shoppe on the east side is being evacuated, too. The TV shows images of crowds and emergency responders in a chaotic jam outside. The news anchor is urging the city to stay calm while talking about a child who's been separated from his mother. "If you're watching this and you see Billy in his red turtleneck, tell him his mom is here by the ABC News van."

Nate fires up his computer and looks for other news. He learns that the northside Pac-Shoppe has been emptied and the parking lot is nearly clear from the earlier incident. The police have been complimented as models of order in an emergency. The mayor calls the police chief "an island of calm in a sea of chaos."

The fire marshal takes over Nate's television screen. "We have found the source of the problem," he announces. He is a large, jowly man in a uniform that looks oddly excessive and obsolete, with a bronze badge and fringed epaulettes. He holds up a small orange towel. "Someone deposited this kerosene-soaked rag into the air exchange. The odor circulated around the building and caused the impression of a gas leak."

"So there was no danger after all?" the news anchor asks, a young woman in a blue blazer. "Everyone is safe?"

"Everyone is safe. The rag is entirely harmless. It's some sicko's idea of a prank, I suppose." He goes on to explain that natural gas is odorless, so a sulfurous additive called mercaptan is added to alert people in case of a leak. "But mercaptan smells different. My officers knew it wasn't a gas leak as soon as they entered the premise. Still, Pac-Shoppe was right to evacuate," he concludes. "You can't be too careful when you're dealing with gas."

Even as the fire marshal explains the virtues and dangers of gas heating, Nate's computer is telling him that the same conclusion has been reached at the north-side Pac-Shoppe. "All clear," the banner now reads.

Now Nate remembers his ice cream and groceries out in the car. Even as he races downstairs hoping for the best, he realizes that during this entire episode he never worried whether people might get hurt. He didn't fear explosions or mass casualties. He feared a deeper crash in Pac-Shoppe's stock price.

Oh my God, he realizes as he fetches his ice cream. Maybe he really is becoming a shark. Is that okay?

Tonight's meeting is supposed to be a celebration of yesterday's success at the shoppers' action and final planning for tomorrow's action at city hall. Instead it's all about the gas leak.

"Did you see Eli Stowe during the evacuation?" declared Stephanie of the shoppers' committee. "He looked ready to pee in his pants." Eli Stowe is the manager of the east-side store where Stephanie works. He's notorious for mixing up shift schedules and making people work over-time without credit.

"How much business do you think they lost?" asks Benjamin of the Logistics committee. "More than they'd pay to give us our raise, probably."

There are about twenty people present, the nucleus of the campaign. They are tired but focused. The UCW's Richmond headquarters is looking both better and worse for this week of action. It's worse because coffee cups and art supplies are scattered everywhere, and everyone, including Catherine, has fallen behind at keeping it neat. But it's better because every item of mess is another souvenir – the pink spot where paint spilled while decorating a pig, the empty jug of apple cider where David and Stephanie calculated their price tags over dinner.

"Who do you think did it?" asks Benjamin.

"They blamed us," someone offers.

"But the rag wasn't even red. It was orange," comes the reply.

Heads shake all around. The perpetrator is a mystery.

"I bet it was one of us," Benjamin declares. "But I hope they never prove it."

"Probably the police chief did it," offers Ramona of the communications committee. "It made him look like a hero."

"The mayor all but kissed him," says Deborah Little, key for reaching out to staff and keeping the campaign together.

"The mayor should toast us for putting up with Eli Stowe," someone replies.

The big congratulations from the mayor worries Catherine, too. On the one hand, the police chief did a credible job in a mock emergency. On the other hand, the mayor's first entry into this whole Pac-Shoppe situation is on the side of the police, and quite a strong one, too. He's been quiet all this time. Why does he choose to weigh in now?

Loren Ibsen suddenly takes over the room. He's been hovering on the sidelines as usual, barely noticeable in a celebration of what only Catherine knows to be his handiwork. Now he walks to the center of the room, clapping his hands in a rhythmic one-two-three, one-two-three. Soon enough the whole room is clapping one-two-three along with him. All eyes are on Loren as he takes the center of the room.

"I'd like to make a motion," he declares when he has everybody's full attention and brings the clapping to a halt.

"Seconded!" someone shouts from the back.

Loren smiles but carries on. "I'd like to change the name of my department. No longer am I in Special Operations, a name that's old and can mean anything."

Catherine doesn't know what he's talking about. "Special Operations" was never much of a name, but it's been called that forever and it has a strategic looseness that fits Loren well.

"From now on I am the Department of Industrial Sabotage."

The room goes quiet as people consider the implications.

"The problem isn't just Pac-Shoppe but the whole system in which it operates. We need to crash the whole system down."

Catherine doesn't think of Loren as an orator but the room resounds with cheers.

"From now on I work for the Department of Industrial Sabotage. Acronym DIS. My purpose is to DIS people."

As people chuckle agreement Catherine jumps in with him. "The motion has been made and seconded," she declares. "Let us call the vote." Catherine knows Robert's Rules as well as anybody. "The Department of Special Operations shall henceforth be called the Department of Industrial Sabotage. All in favor say Aye."

The room resounds with Ayes, and a smattering of applause. Catherine sees a crowd of tired, hardworking people in a better mood than she's seen them in weeks. She knows it's just a diversion, not a true amendment of the organization chart approved by the board of directors, but she's enjoying it just as much. "All opposed, say Nay."

The room is silent for a moment, followed by one single exception. Loren Ibsen alone calls "Nay," a clear strong voice and the only person to vote against his own motion.

"The motion carries," Catherine declares, baffled but in wonderment.

"Nothing should ever be unanimous," Loren explains. "You've been DISd."

"You're not done with Pac-Shoppe," Mr. Daniels declares.

Nate is in Mr. Daniels' office. The boss is behind his desk, surrounded by photographs of children and grand-children. Nate is standing by a wall decorated with a gargantuan mounted seabass that Mr. Daniels caught in the Gulf of Mexico and that his wife wanted nowhere near their living room.

"I didn't think I was, sir." Or at least Nate hoped he wasn't, though the sale is now final. He's still looking for an excuse to call Catherine Campbell.

"You've spent a lot of time in Pac-Shoppe's books."

"Yes, sir."

"Go back again. This time look for new efficiencies. Look for costs that seem higher than they could be or expenditures that aren't producing proportionate returns. We might need to give them another look."

"You're questioning management after all?" Nate asks. "I thought you were expressing confidence. You didn't want to scare them with new ownership."

"Express confidence I will," says the Shaolin priest. "The communication of efficiencies you identify is yet to be determined. But I want to be in position to ask questions and assess their answers."

"Yes, sir."

"I have some new information." He passes across his desk another flash drive. "This one has more detail in payables and receivables, indexed by type and by store location. Much of it will overlap with the other drive, but it might have more in a few spaces and less in others. And it's current to the minute. The other drive had more history but stopped six months ago."

"I noticed."

"Good luck, young grasshopper. Return to us a golden buttercup."

"Yes, sir."

Catherine feels pretty good about today's action at City Hall. The campaign's message is starting to get through. Today's press coverage was less about the logistics of traffic and more about why Pac-Shoppe workers were out there and what they were trying to say. City Hall proved to be a perfect backdrop. Today they focused less on Pac-Shoppe wages and more on the public subsidies and what Pac-Shoppe does to deserve them.

"Wait a minute," said Paul Spaft to news media covering the day. Paul is a local businessman and chair of the campaign's informal business committee. "Why don't I get subsidies? I mean, I hire people. I pay taxes. Loads of them! Property taxes, FICA taxes, income taxes. You name it, I pay them. The government doesn't pay me to run my business. Why should it pay Pac-Shoppe?"

Tonight's agenda is nothing but celebration. The crew finished the week that Benjamin had mapped out for them, with actions at VCU, the shopping district and today back at City Hall. Workers and allies passed out fact sheets about the tax abatements and direct subsidies the city offered Pac-Shoppe to induce it to open stores in Richmond. Campaign flyers compare the cost of the subsidies to how much Richmond gains from the Pac-Shoppes, and compare it all to the budget shortfall of Richmond local schools.

Paul was the star of today's show. Paul ran his own muffler shop before his National Guard duty called him to Iraq. Now he's regional sales director at AutoZone. He speaks the language of business and connects naturally with employer's who don't like Pac-Shoppe's business model and conservatives who want to shrink government or keep it out of business. Paul's been back for three years now, but he keeps his military haircut and his all-star physique.

Now he has a little crowd around him looking at his laptop. "Watch this one," he says. He presses a few buttons and turns the laptop out to his audience.

On screen is a director of Richmond's AutoZone and a respected member of the local Chamber of Commerce. Paul's video shows him talking to CBS news earlier today. "I don't want my tax money subsidizing free-and-reduced-price school lunches for Pac-Shoppe kids," he says. "Those kids qualify for free-reduced lunch because Pac-Shoppe doesn't pay their parents enough money. That's wrong. Pac-Shoppe needs to pay them enough to buy their own lunch. I pay for my own kids' lunches. I pay my employees enough for their kids' lunches. I don't want to pay for Pac-Shoppe's lunches too."

"Great work, Paul," Catherine says. "I just want to thank you again for all the work you're putting in."

"I risked my neck trying to build a nation in Iraq," he replies. "I'll be damned if I'm going to sit back and let Pac-Shoppe suck me dry at home. I pay Pac-Shoppe when I shop. Why should I pay Pac-Shoppe to let me shop there? How about this? If we subsidize them in advance, then we can shop for free."

Catherine has heard him deliver versions of that line several times today, and he gets better every time. Tomorrow he's scheduled for some studio time at CBS. Catherine offered to join him but he said he didn't need her and she agrees. Paul says talking to press is like talking to his squadron in Iraq. Keep it simple, repeat it plenty, and add a joke.

Now Jasmina enters the hall, wearing a loose blue shirt and tight black jeans. "Hey," Catherine calls out. "I'm glad you could make it." Jasmina's schedule is tricky since she started the graveyard shift. "How's it going."

"It's going," she replies. "It's like I tell my children, 'There's always a way to make it work.'"

"But you don't sound happy about it," Catherine observes. Jasmina may be coping, but little more.

"It's okay," Jasmina says. "I get home at ten in the morning. The house is empty but I cook and eat a nice dinner. I put the rest away and go to sleep. Round about six or seven in the evening, everyone is home and I'm ready to wake up – and dinner is already made, though for me it's breakfast. But that's okay."

"You miss your kids at their breakfast and after school," Catherine observes.

"I'm looking for a different job," Jasmina confesses. "I miss you guys. I miss coming to these meetings. I feel like I'm quitting the team ... but I can't work the graveyard forever." She looks uncertain, then declares with confidence. "My kids still need me." She brushes something visible only to her off her jeans.

Catherine takes Jasmina by the hand. "Take care of your kids. Please. That's most important. We'll be okay. You've done so much already." Catherine is about to add some more, thoughts about job-hunting or sympathy for her family – when a loud thumping erupts from the front door. Loud aggressive knocks, like the police on a warrant, not a late-comer to a meeting. "Excuse me," she says to Jasmina as she hurries up front.

The door is opening as Catherine arrives.

Two strong young men in uniforms are pushing into the room. They look like police or sheriffs, though somehow different, followed by a third man in a civilian suit and tie. "Fire Marshal," announces the uniformed leader as he enters the room. "Everyone stay as you are."

Catherine recognizes the Fire Marshal from his TV time this afternoon, but she's never heard of a shock inspection. Is this revenge for Loren's prank? She steps forward, taking charge for their team. "How can I help you, officer."

"I heard you were having a gathering tonight. I just wanted to make sure everything is in compliance. I need to be sure everyone is safe."

"Thank you," Catherine says. "We're fine. There's no fire of any kind. We're not even cooking."

"Your legal notice?" he asks.

Fortunately, she knows what he means. She nods toward the door where a sign is prominently displayed in accordance with regulation, *Maximum Occupancy 75*. They are nowhere near seventy-five, though she dreams that someday their little community coalition might push that limit. Outgrowing this space would be a problem she'd love to have.

"Count off," the marshal commands.

"We're about thirty," Catherine replies. Counting off will be inconvenient, and it's obvious that they aren't seventy-five.

"I need to make sure everyone is *legal,*" the marshal continues, with emphasis on the final word. "Do you have more people *hiding* in a different room?" Now his emphasis is on "hiding."

Legal? Hiding? Is this the Fire Marshal or immigration enforcement? Catherine can feel fear rippling through her crowd. Most of them are legal but maybe not all of them, and everyone has a family.

"Space is limited to seventy-five under the fire code," he says. "I need to make sure everything is legal and everyone is safe."

Catherine can feel his words decimating their meeting. Unsafe? He has just made them so. How many of her members have a brother or sister they need to keep off radar? How many have a parent living in their home without proper documentation? Who has an outstanding warrant for an unpaid traffic ticket? Will they risk coming to the next meeting? Maybe not.

"Count off," the Fire Marshal commands again.

"Okay, folks, line up," Catherine says. The Marshal has made clear who's in charge and she concludes that the better part of valor is to assist him.

It takes only two minutes to count off twenty-seven people plus five more minutes to hold people in line while they search the premises for anybody more. When the Marshal is satisfied he says they can go back to their business, but he holds Catherine another minute while he locates a form he needs her to sign. She waits patiently, knowing that their meeting is effectively over.

She walks him to the door and watches until he drives away. When she returns she notices that their sign-in sheet – the paper with everyone's name and best current contact information — is gone.

This makes no sense to Nate. What does he know about efficiencies? He's an accountant. An accountant who works for investors. He's learning about finance, and the smart people around him already know about finance, but none of them knows anything about running a store. What's the difference between money wasted and a smart long term investment? Nate doesn't know. Ask someone who knows how to run a store! Preferably a major national chain with a wide-ranging inventory and an international supply chain. They might know. Nate doesn't.

Fitzgerald Financials also owns stakes in semiconductor manufacturers and drug companies. Tomorrow will Nate be asked to find "efficiencies" in those, too?

He asks around the office, looking for help or insight. Daniel "Shaolin" Daniels only tells him to "cut costs and increase returns." Thanks a lot for that. *Buy low and sell high.*

What he really learns is that Fitzgerald Financials understands business as financial assets, hardly more than allocations of capital with quarterly returns, more like a bank than a business. Nate always thought business was about making things, satisfying customers, and developing new ideas – not just collecting dividends. But maybe he's old fashioned. Maybe he should open a shoe store and get out of the shark tank.

He reviews the numbers until the cleaners arrive. Every evening around six, a crew of young women – mostly young women – come in to vacuum floors and empty trash cans. Nate is always courteous to them but nothing more. Tonight he takes their entry as a cue that it's time to leave.

Nate has realized two important things – that he's going to be fine, and that none of this matters anyway. Within a few days Nate will have produced some kind of report. He will have identified expenditures that have yet to generate a return and some taxes or other costs that were paid when they could have been deferred. He will dress it up in the language of liabilities and yields. He will submit it and receive thanks and kudos in return. People will think he's smart. Maybe his report will even be useful for something someday.

But does he know if money would be better going to Catherine Campbell's people for a raise? He doesn't even try to figure that out. He can't tell if money would be better spent on payroll or advertising or researching future trends. For that you'd need a store manager. He's just a shark.

Jasmina was only the first. Today was a bloodbath.

Catherine is having more flashbacks to that Union Pharmaceutical campaign. The company resistance started with threats, then firings, then more firings. While threats and firings are routine, some campaigns turn a corner and never come back.

At Union Pharmaceutical, Catherine's supervisor thought the organizers needed to nudge people along, to encourage them past the dark spot. Later he said he had disregarded warning signs. The campaign didn't need encouragement, it needed to slow down. The leaders were getting ahead of their crowd. Sometimes you need to retreat to fight another day.

Today Pac-shoppe told Stephanie Lerner her shift was being changed to the overnight graveyard. They didn't say it was because Stephanie and her son were so effective on Saturday at the shoppers' action, but surely that's no coincidence. Starting next week, Stephanie won't see David before school or, if Jasmina's experience is any guide, after school either.

Deb Little of the outreach committee, was fired straight out. She arrived at work – after making and paying for her commute – but her time card was no longer there. When she turned to look for it, security officers grabbed her arms and hauled her outside.

"This room is for employees only," they said. "You're trespassing."

Eli Stowe stood behind them to make clear this was no mistake.

Surely, it was no accident that they chose Deb Little, whose role was to reassure members and sympathizers that activism is safe. She lost her job with no notice, no warnings and no prior workplace infractions. In case people didn't get the message, two more co-workers were fired at lunch time. "The next Deb Little," management called them.

A flyer appeared in the locker room by the timeclock. "Who will be the next Deb Little?"

Underneath it was a reproduction of the petition card that people have been signing to indicate their interest in forming a union.

All day long people show Catherine postcards they'd received in yesterday's mail, cards showing a shadowy figure labeled *Union* holding a gun to the head of a brightly colored figure labeled *Worker*. "A union or your job," it says. "You choose."

Even worse was Benjamin Winkler of the Logistics Committee. Ben wasn't fired or moved to an impossible shift. Ben was promoted to assistant manager, a move that's good for him but terrible for the campaign. First, the campaign loses Benjamin as a member – because now that he's management he can't be in the union – so the campaign loses one of its most skilled and experienced internal organizers. Worse still, Benjamin's promotion invites a serious problem of trust. People will wonder whether Benjamin sold them out to get that promotion. What did he do or not do to curry that favor? If they can't trust Benjamin, people may wonder, who can they trust?

Catherine is happy for Ben, of course. He'll make extra money and have access to health insurance. Ben's parents are both unwell and she's sure he can use the money. But she's willing to bet that he would have preferred a smaller increase along with everyone else in a storewide raise. Instead he'll be the most hated assistant manager in the northside Pac-Shoppe. Congratulations.

Catherine assures people that much of this is against the law and that the union is taking legal action, but they all know that relief, if any, is far away. She's thinking harder about the work behind the scenes. Management is changing tactics and ratcheting up a notch. Somebody is probably orchestrating the change, managing the illegal mailings and the threats people receive at night. Union busting consultants are routinely hired to do the dirty work.

Pac-Shoppe is showing subtlety, though. Not just firings but artful targeting and careful selections. The latest maneuvers have Catherine thinking of Theresa Staedtler, union buster extraordinaire. Staedtler runs one of the filthiest, most hated anti-union shops around, and these moves look like hers. Promoting Ben to assistant manager – a blow to the campaign that carries no risk for the company? That's crafty but clean. The visit from the Fire Marshal looks especially like Staedtler, who always brings government in on the company side. Even the mayor's accolade for the police chief suddenly makes more sense.

That means the challenge isn't just to take Pac-Shoppe to court for its own wrongdoing, but to connect Pac-Shoppe to actions done by others on its behalf.

Did Pac-Shoppe hire Theresa Staedtler? When? Which of them is responsible for which action? Catherine needs to connect the dots.

Doubtless Pac-Shoppe will have hidden its tracks. Staedtler is a skilled professional who has done this many times.

But Catherine has resources of her own. How about that nervous young man from Fitzgerald Financials? The one she met in the green room during Jasmina's interview with NBC? He was a financial analyst. He's probably studied every one of Pac-Shoppe's books. He knows if they're doing business with Theresa Staedtler. He probably knows how much they paid her, and the date they cut the checks. Or if he doesn't know already, he has the ability to find out.

He, too, is a skilled professional of course. Probably he wouldn't divulge confidential information.

But on the other hand, maybe he'll answer an oblique question or let something slip. All UCW needs is enough to make a good faith allegation in court.

It doesn't take long to reach the only possible conclusion. There's no harm in trying. Catherine should give him a call.

Nate *Wahooo!*

Nate is at his desk pondering efficiencies when his phone rings. It's the receptionist.

"Catherine Campbell on the line," she says.

What? Catherine Campbell? Nate is thrilled and mystified. He wants to grab the phone and shout for joy, but he probably shouldn't talk to her and certainly not here. Nothing he might want to ask her or tell her can be said this close to Mr. Daniels' walnut desk or his trophy bass. Nate's been racking his brain to think of something he could discuss with her ethically, or some excuse to initiate a conversation. At least now he doesn't need an excuse to start.

To the receptionist Nate says, "Put her on."

As the lines click their connections he walks to the door and closes it gently. Closed doors are uncommon at Fitzgerald but not impossible. He can manage this for a minute without unwanted attention.

"Good morning," Catherine says, before it's even clear that the connections are complete. "This is Catherine Campbell of the United Commercial Workers. Is this Nathaniel Hawley?

"Yes," he says. "I'm happy to hear from you." He purposefully leaves no doubt that he knows who she is or what she might be calling about.

"Is this a good time to talk?" she asks. "Or a good place?"

"Not really," he admits. He's whispering into a telephone with his back to the door.

"Then let's make an arrangement."

Catherine *Taking Sides*

Catherine hangs up on Nate and calls the mayor's office. It takes only a minute to get his chief of staff on the line. She can picture him in his office at City Hall, black hair, football shoulders, a man who knows he's powerful and wants you to know it too. His desk will be piled high with papers and the conference table covered with old coffee cups.

"We're coming after you next," Catherine says.

The chief is all business and won't waste time on good morning. He takes Catherine's call because he trusts her to take less than two minutes. "What for this time?" he replies.

"Remember those Pac-Shoppe subsidies you rammed through the city council? A couple of million dollars' worth."

"Over ten years," he replies.

He knows what she's talking about.

"The mayor wouldn't return my phone calls but now he publicly hugs the police chief for overreacting to someone's prank." She's careful to avoid responsibility. "He's taking sides. Don't think we haven't noticed."

"The mayor is on the side of the working people, as always," he says.

"Pac-Shoppe's property tax abatements took money from schools," Catherine replies. "The economic development grants went to a corporate Goliath, not small local start-ups where that money could have made a difference."

"Grant decisions are made by a committee," he says.

"A committee of political appointees," she replies. "I want you to know that I won't play along when you pretend to be neutral. Starting yesterday, every pothole on every street became your fault."

"It already is."

"But the money you might have used to fix it went to Pac-Shoppe instead. Also the money you might have used to fix streetlights or repair swing sets in the park. And speaking of swing sets, property tax abatements hit schools the hardest, and class sizes are up at elementary schools. Middle schools cut art classes last year, and Thomas Jefferson High School is still waiting for its new chemistry lab. I'll discuss it with the school PTA. I'll make a chart. I'll put the cost of the new chemistry lab and an art teacher next to the amount we're giving Pac-Shoppe in property tax abatements. I'll give it a title like 'Pac-Shoppe takes money from school children.' Or maybe, 'Mayor gives money to Pac-Shoppe instead of kids.'

"Then I'll add another column. I'll show how much Pac-Shoppe made in profits last year. How much it paid shareholders in dividends. I'll add how much the CEO made, too. Maybe I'll compare that to what the workers make...."

"Okay," he says, cutting her off as he sees where this is going.

"Not yet," she says, talking over his effort to interrupt her. "We haven't gotten to the taxpayers yet. Do you know offhand how much taxpayers spend on Medicaid because Pac-Shoppe doesn't provide health insurance for its employees? I don't know offhand but I'm sure I can figure it out. I'll make a table for that, too." She pauses now to give him a turn. "You were saying?"

"I was going to ask what you want from us." He actually sounds concerned. "Your wage dispute with Pac-Shoppe is an internal matter. I don't know what Pac-Shoppe pays or what it ought to pay. We take no position on it. I want your workers to be paid fairly, of course. But I also want Pac-Shoppe shoppers to save some money. I leave it to you guys to work that out."

"And so we shall," she replies. "But it would be easier if the mayor reminded everyone what he said when he was making the case for those subsidies. He said Pac-Shoppe would create *good* jobs and that the taxpayers would get back *more than* they were putting in."

"You may need to be patient."

"Do you want to see the quotes?"

"I'm sure you have them."

"We're asking Pac-Shoppe for forty cents an hour at the bottom of the pay scale, trickling uphill proportionately. We're asking for more control over shifts and schedules, with an incentive for the overnight shifts. I can send you details but what we want from you is a reminder to Pac-Shoppe that Richmond has met its end of the bargain. We gave the grants. Say in public that you're disappointed that Pac-Shoppe hasn't met its end of the deal."

Catherine pauses for him to reply but he remains silent. She says, "It looks to me like you're taking Pac-Shoppe's side. If it's not clear to everyone else, I'll clarify it for them. If you want to take the workers' side, this would be the time to say it."

This time she waits to make clear that it's his turn. Catherine is finished. She's made her request and told him what he needs to know.

Finally comes the reply. "I'll transmit your concerns to the boss."

Catherine can't tell if that's a brush-off or a sincere commitment. "Thank you for your time and attention."

They don't meet for coffee during the day because Nate doesn't want to risk being seen with her by anybody from Fitzgerald Financials. They decide on a late dinner, not an early breakfast, and Nate chooses his own neighborhood, partly because it's convenient and partly because he has perfect confidence that nobody at Fitzgerald Financials lives within two tax brackets of his apartment. Catherine agrees so quickly he wonders if maybe she lives nearby.

Rose discovered this restaurant, of course. The menu and décor are straightforward country kitchen, but the prices are fair and the food is far better than appearances might suggest.

Nate arrives first, and early. He accepts seating at a table for two and prepares to wait. He told Catherine he'd wear a red sweater to make himself easier to spot. Only now it occurs to him that she might see deliberate solidarity with the red t-shirts her minions wear on the street. He hopes not.

"Can I get you anything while you wait?" asks the waitress. She is pretty with short black hair and looks barely old enough for high school – or maybe Nate's getting so old everyone seems like a kid these days.

"No, thanks," he replies. "Just water."

Then Catherine arrives, also ahead of schedule. Nate sees her enter and he stands to make himself easier to spot. She notices him even as the wait staff puts it together and escorts her in his direction.

Catherine looks terrific, as always, but with a healthy youthful beauty, more like an Ivory Girl than a high school kid.

"No, thanks," she says to the waitress. "Just water."

Next thing he knows the waitress has filled their waters and Catherine Campbell is sitting across from him like it's the most natural thing in the world.

"It's nice to be early," she says. "It doesn't happen very often."

"The whole world is too busy," Nate adds. "Nothing ever stops."

She raises her water glass as if toasting agreement.

He toasts his back.

"Nice to see you," Nate says. "Thanks for coming."

"Okay, then. Tell me everything."

She says it like a normal request, just a conversation opener, but it strikes him as a preposterous demand. She sees his alarm so she makes it easier. "Maybe just start with where you're from and what you do at Fitzgerald Financials. Feel free to add how you are and whether you had a nice day, while you're at it." By the time she's finished she's smiling so broadly it's clear her introduction was an open invitation, not a hold-up.

"We'll take them one at a time," Nate replies. "First, I had a lovely day. Second, I'm a financial analyst at Fitzgerald Financials. Third, I'm from Virginia Beach. I went to Frank Cox High School."

She looks like a bomb went off. A bomb at first, then a gigantic blossoming smile.

"Mr. Leibniz's calculus class in eleventh grade!" she declares.

He reaches across the table to shake her hand. "Nice to see you again."

Of course her grip is strong and secure, and of course she does a better job navigating around the glassware and table settings than he does. "You're a financial analyst? Looks like you put your math to work."

"I'm an accountant, really. A CPA. The finance stuff is new." Why does he have to retreat like that? He wonders why he wants to hide his newfound glamor. "And you? Any math?"

"Sometimes it's handy in negotiations," she says. "I've already roughed out a position while they're still typing digits into a spreadsheet." She correctly assumes that he knows what she does for a living. "But I don't use calculus very often."

He's not sure what to say next. The ultimate agenda was never clear but this is dangerously close to business. Unsure how to handle it or how to make the leap, he reaches for his old friends. "When things go wrong, what can you always count on?"

She looks equally happy to keep it light. "Your fingers," she says with a smile. "I haven't heard that one in years."

"Why is a math book always unhappy?" he asks.

"I give up."

"Because it has so many problems."

She actually laughs out loud at a joke that probably hasn't been funny since eighth grade, so he risks one more. "What do you get if you divide the circumference of a jack-o-lantern by its diameter?"

She shakes her head. She doesn't know, but she immediately holds up her hand to stop him from answering. "Give me a minute," she says. She sits perfectly still, gazing at an empty wall until spontaneously breaking out in laughter. "Pumpkin pi," she declares.

Nate can't help but admire her cleverness. He heard that as a joke followed by the punchline. He doubts he could have figured it out on his own. As he wonders what comes next, the waitress arrives to take their orders.

"What do you recommend?" Catherine asks him.

"Pumpkin pi?"

Catherine smiles in recognition and the waitress simply offers more time.

"Honestly, everything is good," Nate says.

Catherine studies the menu and settles on chicken parmesan. Nate orders a fried flounder, something he wouldn't cook at home. Not that he makes chicken parmesan very often. Not when he's cooking for himself alone. He notices that neither of them orders an appetizer or a drink other than water. It was never clear who's paying for this.

"So it's been fifteen years," she says, apparently ready to fill in the surprise. "What happened in between?"

He goes ahead and tells her about Rose and about his accounting career, or at least the thirty second version, but thirty seconds is all it takes, including the recent twist. "Your turn."

She shrugs her shoulders. "No marriage, no divorce, no kids. Work, work, work."

"What kind of work?" he asks. She, too, has fifteen years to account for.

"What you see," she replies. "Union organizing and wage campaigns. Trying to get workers their fair share."

They reach it so naturally it would take an act of avoidance to get around it. Nate plows on. "Pac-Shoppe," he declares, as if it is a subject unto itself.

She looks at him with the full attention that he remembers made him so nervous in high school. "What do you know that I need to know?" she asks. Again her expression suggests that it's an invitation, not a hold-up, but this time he wants to get it right. What exactly has he been meaning to tell her?

"I've been studying their books," Nate begins. "Fitzgerald Financials turned Pac-Shoppe inside out before we made that offer. We know everything."

She nods for him to continue.

"Retail is incredibly competitive," he says. "Margins are razor thin. Pac-Shoppe doesn't get special loyalty from its customers, like cars or clothes sometimes do. Pac-Shoppe has a good selection at a good price. Nothing more than that. If they don't compete on price they go out of business."

"But it's doing well enough that you all just bought a big piece of it."

"We think it's stable where it is," Nate replies. He's pretty happy with his straight-up delivery, using new terminology as comfortably as old jokes. "Profits are fine but not extraordinary. But it's a large franchise doing a lot of business ... small margins can add up to sizeable dollars."

She's looking at him like he's saying something wrong.

"Somebody is going to make that money. It might as well be Fitzgerald Financials."

He winces as he says it. Even he can tell that he hasn't made things better. He's back in high school, tongue-tied and stupid. "I mean. Obviously the business isn't going to operate at a loss. Somebody is going to get the profit. Why not us?" By the time he reaches the end he sounds to himself almost pathetic, begging her permission to earn a living. "If it isn't us, it will just be some other shareholder."

She says nothing, waiting him out, giving him more rope than he knows what to do with. So much for being a shark. "What I mean is, there just isn't much room to give workers a raise. Any pay increase would cut into profits. There isn't much to share. If the margins shrank any smaller, shareholders would go ballistic."

"Shareholders?" she asks. "That's you, right? Aren't you the shareholders you're afraid of?"

"Shareholders put money in and they expect to take money out. That's just how it works. Employees get paychecks, and shareholders get returns on investment. Everybody wins."

"Everybody?" she asks.

"Yes, everybody," he insists. "Everybody gets their fair share. Maybe the employees want more. But the shareholders want more, too. They can't have it, either."

"What's stopping them?"

"Math!" he exclaims. "If workers get a percent more, then shareholders get a percent less. The only other option would be to raise prices. Our competitors might like if we did that ... but our customers won't."

"So you're defending the status quo," she declares. She looks resigned to his conclusion.

"I'm just respecting the marketplace," he offers. "Competition is the key. Customers and competition. If we raise our prices, our customers will go someplace else. Probably to someone who pays their workers less than we do. That wouldn't make anybody happy."

"Except your competition," she says.

"Exactly," he agrees. "Unionize them instead."

Catherine *Gravity Bricks*

He's so sweet. Catherine remembers Nathaniel Hawley as the gentle scared kid, one of the good ones in a year that wasn't much good for anything. Now he wants to act like a financier but piracy isn't in his blood. She remembers the moment he held the door open for that elderly couple in the hallway. Most high school kids aren't that sympathetic, especially for old people who slow them down and get in their way. Probably he's forgotten all about it, a trivial moment from another life.

She appreciates that he stands when he sees her, making himself easier to spot, a courtesy to both her and the wait staff. She notices that he's wearing a red sweater but decides it's a coincidence.

Now that the Cox High School surprise has faded she's pleased to realize that she's happy to see him. It's like seeing an old friend, even if they were barely acquaintances. That year at Cox High was a terrible dislocation for a teenage girl. She left behind all of her friends and the beginning of romance. The whole move was a disaster, an effort to put her dad's career back on track. She's glad to find she doesn't hold that awful year against Nate.

He's even funny. That's another surprise, given his professional disability. As he tells math jokes she think of an old accountant joke – something about the cannibal CPA who charges an arm and a leg – but she decides not to go there.

He's locked in the financier's mindset, though. "Everybody wins," he explains. "Employees get paychecks and shareholders get returns on investment." He seems to think that explains it all.

"The key," she replies, when the capitalist model has reached its natural conclusion, "is to take wages out of competition."

"Out of competition?" he says. "There's no such thing as 'out of competition.' Competition isn't a choice. It's like gravity. We're stuck with it."

"Have you ever flown in an airplane?" She can't resist. "Or seen the spacewalks on TV?"

He starts to protest but she signals her concession. Airplanes were just for fun. "Let's start with the basics," she says. "One worker alone is powerless. If one worker alone complains about long hours or low pay or unsafe working conditions, that worker will be fired. There's always another worker desperate enough to take the job."

Nathaniel Hawley nods his head. He's actually listening.

"But all the workers together, if they all form a union, they can disrupt the work. They can close down the factory or cause the employer enough inconvenience that it's easier just to give them a raise."

"Maybe it was like that once," he says, "but ...."

She waves him off. It's obvious what he's going to say and he knows it too. He backs off to see what she has in mind.

"Suppose you're a bricklayer," she says. "Or better yet, suppose you run a bricklaying company. You run a nice small bricklaying firm. You make a nice brick wall at a good price. Your customers are happy."

"Sounds tempting," he says. "Can I be me? Is it too late?"

"But the bricklayers who work for you want a raise. Of course, you'd be happy to give them one ... but then you'd lose business to cheaper firms."

"Competition," he says, nodding his head. "Now I don't want to be me anymore."

"But wait! Now suppose a union comes to town. Suppose the union organizes all the bricklayers in the community. Suppose the union gets every bricklayer in the neighborhood to agree that they all need more money. If all the bricklayers demand a raise at once, then it's safe to give one to yours. You can pay your people more without losing business to the next company."

"Because everyone raised wages together."

"Right," she agrees. "We just took the wages out of competition. We created a baseline bricklayer wage. Companies can still compete on quality, design, timeliness ... whatever else it may be. You might choose to hire the best bricklayers, pay them more, and build the best wall in town – for a higher price – but you can't compete downward on wages."

He is nodding in agreement. “It’s like a minimum wage for bricklayers.”

“Exactly,” she says. “If you’ll support us in raising the legal minimum wage until it’s something that can feed a family – say, $15 an hour – then I promise we won’t ask for more. But until then, we need a raise.”

“But wages aren’t ‘out of competition’” he complains. “You’re only asking Pac-Shoppe for a raise. Our competition is still paying the same $7.85.”

“One piece at a time,” Catherine concedes. “We’re working backstage on some other companies and backstage on that minimum wage as well. It won’t all happen simultaneously, but hopefully it will fit quickly into place when the first brick goes down. And if I may quote a smart accountant, ‘Why shouldn’t it be you?’”

When dinner arrives Nate is glad he picked this restaurant. Catherine's chicken parmesan is so hot the cheese is still bubbling from the oven. Alongside on her plate is a rice dish with red peppers and what appear to be pinola nuts, adding flecks of color and texture to the grain.

Nate's flounder is sautéed to a golden glow. Alongside are fried potatoes with onions, nice and crispy, just the way he likes them. Sprigs of parsley add some color.

He'd forgotten something else he liked about this restaurant: the entrees come with a side salad, family style for the whole table, a simple dish of lettuce and tomatoes with dressing on the side. Nate grabs just one leaf of lettuce and leaves the rest untouched for later.

From Rose he learned to prefer his salad European style, after the main dish.

"Nice meal!" Catherine exclaims as it is all set on the table. "This dinner is five-star quality in a three-star setting and a three-star price. Good call."

"Thanks," Nate replies. He decides not to say he used to come here with Rose, but hardly ever since. He can leave that off the table, so to speak.

For a while they are silent as they each dig into their meals, though each lets on how much they're enjoying them. "Nice touch with the salad," Catherine says as her chicken shrinks to leave room on the plate.

"You're welcome," Nate replies, before realizing she hadn't thanked him.

"Did you know union workers built the pyramids?" Catherine asks.

He looks up quizzically. He always thought the pyramids were built by slaves.

"It was originally designed as a cube. Each shift did a little less work until the last said, 'throw a rock on top and let's go home.'"

Nate laughs out loud so hard it's almost embarrassing. He wipes his mouth with a napkin.

"Do you know why the orange juice workers decided to unionize?" she follows up.

This time it's his turn to hold up his hand to stop her. "Because they were getting squeezed," he concludes.

"Bullseye. Some were even getting canned."

Silence gets a turn after that. They both turn back to their dinners, enjoying a peaceful moment in a busy day.

"Okay then," he says, as his mind turns back to work. "What about the shareholders? Even if by some miracle the customers don't move to a different store ... or if by a different miracle, that store also raises its wages to take that 'out of competition.' What about the shareholders? They, too, had expectations. They need their fair share."

"Or what? They'll invest in something else?"

"Well, yes!"

"Why do I care? Let them. Investors can flee. Maybe a stock price comes down. Someone else will buy at that price. Maybe a bank will make a traditional loan. Maybe the workers will buy it out themselves. Investors only provide capital. Who cares where they stick it."

Somehow she makes that last sound almost obscene.

Okay except he realizes he's someone who now does. Suddenly he needs that stock price up high where he bought it ... hopefully higher.

Catherine continues. "So shareholders want a ten percent return on their investment? That's not 'math.' Ten percent is no more mathematically necessary than $7.85 an hour. Move our workers up to $8.85. Investors can take nine percent and be happy for it."

Nate is speechless. He always took the need to maximize profits and maximize shareholder return as a given. Everything else followed from that.

"This isn't about math," she concludes. "This is about power. Shareholders would be happy to cut our wages and take home eleven percent, wouldn't they? What's stopping them?"

Nate shakes his head.

“One worker alone is powerless. A union together can negotiate its fair share of the profits. If nine percent is what’s left for shareholders after the workers are paid a living wage, then nine it shall be. That’s math, too.”

So little Nathaniel Hawley turned out okay after all. He seems to be listening and taking it all in. He's not ready to abandon his capitalist model – not over one slice of chicken – but he seems to recognize there's more to the story.

Catherine debates about what to do next. Really she wants to ask him her questions about Theresa Staedtler. But asking too much too soon might chase him away. Her purpose in this meeting was introductions, "get-to-know-you," and show that there's another side. Their history helps, but unions are still new to him. He has to want to help before she can ask him to.

What else would it take? A whole new meeting, maybe more. A level of comfort and conversion to the cause he might never reach. Maybe she should gamble now instead of wasting the time.

"Ultimately, this is about power," she explains. "Pac-Shoppe has more of it, and they use it to drive wages down. Down to poverty now, starvation if they could. In capitalist theory, the workers push back and a settlement is negotiated – one where everybody wins. But the power is too out of balance. Pac-Shoppe clearly has a lot. What do the workers have?"

It's truly a question for fishing. She doesn't know how he will answer it.

He takes a long time to think. He serves himself some salad and looks like he might say something, but he focuses on the salad. She's happy to see him pick up a carrot slice with his fingers, like she would have done, not fuss to skewer the little thing on his fork.

Finally, he looks up. "Not much, I guess."

"Collective action levels the playing field. Capitalism needs unions to work."

He nods his head in a conciliatory way. She almost hears him thinking, *Hmmm. Never thought of it that way.*

"Information is also out of balance," she continues, pressing her advantage.

"How's that?"

"Pac-Shoppe knows everything about us. We don't know hardly anything about Pac-Shoppe." She is tossing more bait, closing in on her goal.

"But you know plenty about Pac-Shoppe," he protests. "You read the same SEC filings I do. You say it on TV all the time. How much it makes in profits. How much the CEO is paid. All of that."

"Sure, we know that," she admits. "But that's not the juicy stuff."

"Oh?"

"How much is Pac-Shoppe paying its union busting consultants?"

"What?"

"The people who follow workers home and threaten them at night. The people who distribute flyers that say 'Unions kill jobs.'"

"Who's doing that? Pac-Shoppe isn't doing that."

"That's because it's illegal."

"I know."

"That's why Pac-Shoppe doesn't do it."

"I thought you just said they did."

"No. Not Pac-Shoppe. The union-busting consultants. The people Pac-Shoppe pays so its hands are clean. Pac-Shoppe is an honorable company. Everything is legal. Everything is in order. Go to the SEC web page. Download the 10-K. Everything is fine."

"I've been there. Everything *is* legal. Everything *is* fine."

"Yes, but everything isn't there. The truth but not the whole truth, as the courts might say."

He's looking at her in surprise. He sees the point. He's taking the bait. She asks, "How much is Pac-Shoppe paying Theresa Staedtler?"

"Who?"

"Theresa Staedtler. She's a union-busting consultant. She keeps on opening new companies and creating new names. UES, Ultimate Employer Solutions. UUS, Ultimate Union Solutions. UE, Ultimate Efficiencies. Names like that, usually with a U and an E or an S. Something is always Ultimate, something is being solved. I think Pac-Shoppe retained her to do its dirty work in this campaign."

"What makes you say that?"

"Look for her in their books. Check those names. It will be odd amounts of money on odd dates. Maybe $17,376 on March sixth, then $22,344 on April twelfth. It will be tens of thousands of dollars, not millions. And it will be on odd dates, not monthly or quarterly on the first or fifteenth. It will look like just another incidental vendor payment buried in the books, not big enough or regular enough to attract attention. The check will be payable to UUE or UEE or something like that. That's her style. That's how she likes it. When UUE gets in trouble she'll close it down and open up again with a new name and a new PO Box. Oh, that's another thing. The address will be a PO Box."

"You're kidding me."

"No, I'm not. But I can't prove it. And that's why they get away with it. They're breaking the law and covering it up." She risks a final charge. "You're helping."

Chapter 38 Nate *Good Tips*

She's got to be kidding.

Catherine Campbell seemed so normal – almost convincing, about the justice of her cause or the capitalist's unfair advantage – but then she turns the corner to some crazy shadow campaign with illegal operatives on cloak-and-dagger crusades.

PO Boxes? Is this for real?

Thankfully, she changes the subject.

"Do you remember, back in college we used to get mail in PO Boxes?" She sounds whimsical, almost light hearted as she free-associates to a different place and time.

"Worked fine ... except for packages," he agrees.

Next thing he knows they're swapping stories about the college mail room. Both of them got birthday presents from their mothers that caused an inconvenient pick-up and, in Catherine's case, moldy cookies. Nate even got a chuckle out of a joke he never really understood.

> *Why did the chicken in the Amalgamated Egg Layers Union cross the road?*
> *Because she had OSHA protections and good health insurance.*

They simply split the cost of dinner. They return the check with two credit cards and ask the waitress to cut it in half.

"We need to tip her well," Catherine suggests.

It's easy to agree. Their cheap dinner without drinks shouldn't ruin the waitress's livelihood, her income calculated on a percentage basis.

No, they don't kiss goodnight. There isn't even an awkward moment when it might have been possible. But truthfully when it was over Nate had had a blast. He hadn't had that good a "date" in years.

When it was all over she invited him to look for UES in Pac-Shoppe's books, and let her know if he found anything interesting.

"They can get away with it forever," she said. "I need just a little bit of actual evidence to file for an injunction."

"Okay," he agreed. "But don't hold your breath."

Not until he's on his way home does he realize he meant about sharing confidential records from Pac-Shoppe's books. He hopes she didn't think he never wants to see her again. Next time he'd try to talk about more than just Pac-Shoppe.

Catherine *Yes or Never*

Well, that was a lovely evening. Catherine can't claim it for her mother as a date, but it was certainly more fun than she was expecting. She even learned a new accountant joke.

What happens when you lock a wild hyena and an accountant in a room?

The hyena stops laughing.

She doesn't know if she convinced him about Theresa Staedtler and she has lots of reason to think she didn't. But surely there was no harm in trying. She didn't present it as a formal "ask." She just gave him all the information and told him what she needed. He's plenty smart enough to figure it out. She changed the subject before he consolidated his position by fighting her off.

Maybe he'll check in Pac-Shoppe's files.

Maybe he'll find what she thinks is in there.

Maybe he'll tell her. Or maybe he won't.

There's no harm in trying.

And she had a lovely evening.

Unless he calls with information on Theresa Staedtler, it's a shame she has no reason to see him again.

Nate *Back to Books*

No way is Nate going to violate the fundamental ethical precept of his profession, and share confidential client information. She can forget about that. He'd lose his job, his license and his self-respect. It would serve him right if he landed in prison. He wouldn't do it for money or for fame ... and certainly not to impress a pretty girl.

He is curious, though. Does this mythical Theresa Staedtler even exist? Staedtler and her hydra-headed ever-changing corporate entity? Partly he is curious about the supposed existence of this evil being, but behind that he's curious about Catherine Campbell. Is she crazy? She looks nice and talks a good game, but maybe she's nuts. There's one way to find out.

He hurries into work early the next day, building in time to look for Theresa Staedtler and her underground company. He figures he can arrive early enough to squeeze it in without changing his honest goals on a busy day, simply including it in his search for "efficiencies."

Mr. Daniels is waiting for him as he arrives. "The early bird gets the golden buttercup," he says. "Good morning."

But instead of encouraging Nate toward his buttercup, he assigns him to a whole new project, a pure distraction of an accounting problem being considered in a different company.

At first Nate is annoyed. He had his day planned, and he was eager to begin. But he soon finds himself happy to be back on familiar turf, with a common problem of bookkeeping. Fitzgerald Financial's chip manufacturer, Phoenix Semiconductor, has multiple departments, each with its own subaccount, and something has gone wrong in reconciling company totals with the subaccounts individually. It turns out to be a long day on a short deadline, but relaxing all the same; puzzles to solve with answers that sum correctly when he gets them right. Around dinnertime he's transmitting results and packing up for the day, satisfied with a day's work in which 2+2=4. No, he didn't go hunting for Catherine Campbell ... but tomorrow is another day.

He hears the cleaning crew come in, which tells him it's later than he wishes. He hears them vacuuming in the hallway, and one comes into his office to empty his trashcan. Nate doesn't even look up as he's tidying his inbox and skimming headlines in the news.

Outside in the hallway he hears someone talking in alarm. He can tell it's a member of the cleaning crew speaking into her cell phone in a mixture of English and Spanish, probably the woman who emptied his trashcan a moment ago. He hears in English, "failing trigonometry," followed by "No tutor! No sufficient dinero. Sorry."

Nate can tell without trying what's going on. Someone – her kid? – is struggling in math. She doesn't have money for a tutor and she's desperate for alternatives.

Nate remembers trigonometry from high school. That's when math started to get hard. Even kids who were naturally good at math had to practice and pay attention. Other kids got in trouble. Regular kids who successfully memorized multiplication tables but lacked mathematical aptitude – "mathitude," as his teachers used to say – found themselves struggling.

In Nate's twilight peace he wonders if he could help. Surely he can help a high schooler –middle schooler? – with trigonometry. But would he want to? How would he even make the offer?

Even as he wonders what to do, she finishes the call and reenters his office to wipe the window sill. Nate feels some higher power clearing doubt from the path before him, Shaolin forces make his choice obvious.

"Excuse me," he says.

She doesn't even look at him. Doubtless she assumes he's talking on the phone or to someone else.

"Excuse me," Nate says again.

Now she looks up, startled, as if the furniture is speaking. He's violated the implicit contract that each of them acts as if the other person isn't there.

"Excuse me," he repeats. "I'm sorry to intrude. I heard you talking about trigonometry. Something about a tutor."

She starts to shake her head in opposition.

She seems to understand, though. Her English appears to be at least that good. "I used to be a math tutor," he says. "Maybe I could help. With the trigonometry."

Tutor is perhaps an overstatement. Back in Frank Cox High school, where he seems to be returning, he was a member of the math club. One of their projects was helping students who were falling behind. It was all done in secret, a hidden society of geeks helping students who would be embarrassed to be caught receiving it.

But she doesn't need to know all that. All she needs is a little boost. "For free," he clarifies. "I won't charge you anything." Before she can even register alarm he continues. "Truly. I'm happy to do it."

He's convincing himself even as he says it. It was fun, back then. He wonders if he still has the knack. He hopes he can remember trigonometry.

"My son," is all she says.

"Does he speak English?"

Now she brightens and stands proud, and Nate sees her for the first time really as a person, a slender woman, youthful but in her thirties, wearing a pretty yellow head band. "He speaks English for both of us," she announces. "Everything I learn English I learn from him."

"That's wonderful," Nate affirms. Soon enough they have agreed to meet right there in the office tomorrow evening. He'll see if he can help her son while she's busy with her work.

Catherine *Changing Times*

A new rule has been declared at the northside Pac-Shoppe. Starting tomorrow, people can't start the timeclock until they are in uniform and their work stations are ready to go.

People used to clock in as soon as they arrived. They would set up their work stations on company time, pulling up their assignments and putting on their aprons. Starting now they'll need to set up on their own time, and they can't hit the clock until they begin their actual work.

Catherine has been told that Eli Stowe spent the entire day walking around, pulling people aside and practically rejoicing as he explained the change.

"No more saying good morning on company time," he repeated all day. "What next? Punch the clock before breakfast?"

Poor Ben Winkler. His first job as Eli's new assistant will be to enforce the rule.

This move hits everyone hard. It's only five or ten minutes before and after each shift, but by the end of the week that's at least an hour when they're at work and working, but not getting paid for it – though it's less about the money than the slap in the face. What if they do say good morning on company time? They're people, not machine parts. Will they be disciplined if they smile? Catherine is tempted to ask her Department of Industrial Sabotage to consider arson of a private home, but she succeeds at keeping her mouth shut.

Nate spends the next day with the Phoenix Semiconductor again. Really, this is more archeology than accounting. Companies were acquired and accounts were merged with insufficient attention to file compatibility. Now he's filling in gaps and unwinding overlaps.

It keeps him away from Theresa Staedtler, but it's another day of puzzle-solving entertainment, and the day passes in an easy arc of success. Around dinnertime, he hears vacuuming outside and a knock on his open door.

"Please," he says, stepping away from his desk. "Come in."

"Hello?" says the bashful young woman, peering into a room she's entered hundreds of times without asking or even announcing herself. "Are you still okay?"

"Yes, please. Come in."

She steps fully into the room with a kind of curtsey, and gestures behind her. "This is my son, Emilio."

On the other side of the door Nate sees a brave boy or maybe – to be fair – a nervous young man. He looks maybe sixteen years old, short and slender, with the barest hint of a shadow on his upper lip, a mustache he's nurturing for all he's worth. Nate can see that he's dressed for the occasion, in freshly pressed black slacks and a blue collared shirt buttoned to the top.

Meeting someone he perceives as mother's boss is probably harder for him than it was for students to accept help from other students when they were all in high school. Nate sees a little boy mustering his courage to be a man.

This can't be easy for her, either. She has no reason to trust him and doesn't know what expectations he might be bringing to this deal. He simply assumes that she hasn't told her boss and, if she has, that she promised it wouldn't affect her work.

"I'm pleased to meet you, Emilio," Nate says, holding out his hand. "My name is Nathaniel Hawley."

He'd thought about offering some greeting in Spanish – *buenos dias*, or something like that. With the assistance of

Google he could easily pull that much off, and he thought maybe it would make the boy more comfortable, a good faith effort to meet him halfway.

But he decided not to. He didn't want to create expectations that he could talk to him in Spanish and didn't want to pretend that this is anything more than what it is. Nate isn't a foster parent or his new best friend; he's an English speaker offering help with math.

"Good evening," Emilio replies, taking Nate's hand. "I'm pleased to meet you."

He is a perfect gentleman in every way.

Nate tells Emilio's mother that they'll be fine and asks both of them permission to exit the building and study in a coffee shop around the corner. "Will that be better?" he asks.

Her nod suggests that – just like in high school – it will be better if they leave the building to a place where nobody will see them.

Catherine *Writing on the Wall*

Two more people lost their jobs today. Tim Nicosia was an activist Catherine counted on, but Alexandra Samuels had never so much as marched in one of their public actions. Indeed, Alexandra once said that she supported the campaign in principle but couldn't afford to take a risk of any kind.

Today when Alexandra arrived at work she had a hard time finding her time card. Even as she was looking for it, the two looming security officers figured out who she was. They'd been briefed on why certain people wouldn't be able to find their time cards and what to do when it happened. One officer grabbed each of Alexandra's arms, and escorted her off the premises. She was in tears by the time she reached Catherine at the UCW office.

Alexandra wasn't empty handed, though. The officers passed her a copy of a flyer that was hanging on the wall by the timeclock and copied in a stack by the door, an official announcement on Pac-Shoppe letterhead.

> It is with deep regret that we inform you that it has become necessary for us to reduce workforce at this Pac-Shoppe location. We have done everything possible to avoid this recourse, but unfortunately it is necessary as a result of diminished sales and site-based instability.
>
> Anybody who loses their position as a result of this trimming will be welcome to reapply when business returns to normal. We appreciate your patience and your continued commitment to Pac-Shoppe excellence.

Nate *Variable Sunshine*

"You can buy anything you want," Nate tells Emilio. "It's on me."

They are in Peet's Coffee shop around the corner from Nate's office, which he chose because people in Fitzgerald Financials generally use the Starbucks. "No, thank you," Emilio replies, his eyes on the floor.

"Please, go ahead," Nate insists.

Emilio is staring like it's a new life experience and Nate realizes he might never have been in a store like this. Peet's walls are painted in swirling colors of bright acrylics, with papier mache mobiles hanging from the ceiling. One wall is covered with dragon paintings for sale by a local artist.

Emilio stares in wonder at the pastries under the countertop, a parade of cupcakes, cherries and swirls that look too beautiful to eat. Then his attention moves upward to the menu on the wall, a bewildering catalog of lattes, mochas and drinks. He seems equal parts astonished and confused. A whole panel is dedicated to *Javiva Espressso* and *Dolce Frappuccino*, a language he probably does not speak. To Nate this is an ordinary coffee shop, but to Emilio it's a rocket ship. "Really?" he asks.

"How about hot chocolate?" Nate replies.

"Thank you," Emilio says, eyes back to his shoes.

Nate doesn't usually drink coffee in places like this – the common pot in the office suits him fine when he needs some caffeine – but he's going all out for the cause.

While Nate settles up, Emilio finds them a seat. He has brought spoons and napkins for both by the time Nate arrives.

"Here you go," Nate says, passing Emilio his hot chocolate.

"Thank you," Emilio says with a smile but quickly returns his eyes to the table top.

"What grade are you in?" Nate asks. He'd prepared that question in advance, remembering that he always used to start with questions with clear, simple answers, to start the ball rolling before heading uphill

"Eleventh," Emilio replies. "At Huguenot High School."

Eleventh grade? Nate feels like he's caught in some infinite time loop, somewhere between Groundhog Day and Doctor Who, stuck in eleventh grade with different people and different maths.

Nate doesn't know Huguenot High School but he remembers eleventh grade. "Ouch," he says. "Eleventh grade is hard. If math was ever easy, it isn't any more."

"Math was never easy," Emilio says. "I worked for my Bs in algebra, but this year it needs to be an A."

"Why's that?" Emilio sounds like he has something in mind, not math for its own sake or the purity of good grades.

"The Latino Leadership Fund," Emilio explains. "A local businessman, a Puerto Rican, created a fund to send kids to college. Any Latino who gets straight As in his junior year gets $5,000 toward his freshman year."

Now Nate understands Emilio's and his mother's alarm. These aren't just grades. This is a whole future taking shape. And trigonometry is hard. "How's it going?" he asks.

"All my other classes are As. Math is just barely hovering between an A and a B. Now it's the end of the year and I failed yesterday's quiz." He shakes his head, eyes down on the table. "I just don't understand trigonometry."

"Not much time to bring the average back up," Nate agrees.

"The fourth quarter counts the most," Emilio says.

Nate nods agreement. "What's the name of your math teacher?" he asks. He doesn't expect to know and it doesn't matter. He just wants to change the subject and ask something easy. Hopefully it won't be Mr. Leibniz, the same name as his and Catherine's calculus teacher. He'd need to call the Time Police.

"Mrs. Weaver," Emilio replies, not noticing Nate's grateful gasp. He takes a cautious sip of his cocoa, which is probably too hot to drink.

"Well, let's get to work," says Nate. "We're going to teach Mrs. Weaver how to spell the letter A."

Twenty minutes later Nate is enchanted by Emilio but infuriated with Mrs. Weaver. Emilio is bright and willing, and not as bad at math as he thinks he is. His confusion seems to reflect more on her than on him.

"Look at the word," he says, going back to the beginning. "*Trigonometry*. Take it apart. It means the 'measure of triangles.' The 'trig' is the triangle and the 'metry' is the measurement."

"Medida," Emilio replies, recognizing the root in Spanish.

"Nice job," Nate says with a smile. "Now picture a triangle. Take a doorstop, for example." He draws a triangle on a piece of paper and writes "doorstop" underneath. It's a right triangle with the bottom side much longer than the vertical one, a narrow angle at the end.

"El tope in Spanish," Emilio offers. "Tope."

"What?"

"Doorstop. In Spanish it's 'tope.'"

"Hey!" Nate exclaims in jest. "Who's teaching who around here?!" But then he concedes, "Gracias. Let's look at a tope."

Now is the serious part. Nate points to his picture. "Does it surprise you that if we know the length of this side" – he points to the bottom of the doorstop that touches the floor – "and the measure of this angle" – he points to the skinny angle on the end – "then you can calculate the height of this side" – he points to the short vertical side that goes from the floor to the door.

"That seems right," Emilio replies. "You know two of the three."

"Bingo," says Nate. "That's the *sine*."

Emilio looks up like Nate is trying to fool him. Nate decides to go on rather than repeat himself. "What's the name of this long leg, the side that wedges up against the door."

"The hypotenuse."

"Bingo. If you know the measure of this skinny angle and the length of the side on the floor, then you can calculate the length of the hypotenuse. That's the *cosine*."

"You're kidding me," Emilio says.

"Two out of three," Nate replies. "Trigonometry is just measuring triangles. It's the mathematical relationship between the angles and the lengths of the sides. All you have to do is remember which function solves which combination."

As Emilio looks on in wonder Nate slows down, repeat himself, and turns it into practice problems.

Catherine is at the office with her head in her hands, wondering whether she can live with herself. She is doubting how she does it, why she does it, or how much longer she can keep doing it. Maybe it's just too much.

Today Catherine filed six new complaints of unfair labor practices at the local office of the National Labor Relations Board. Alexandra Samuels' was the weakest of them all.

Everyone at Pac-Shoppe is an at-will employee. They all have the same contract, and they can be fired at any time, with or without cause. They have no legal protection at all.

For Deb Little, Catherine can make the case that she was fired for workplace or union activism. The UCW's complaint says Deb was "wrongfully fired for exercising her legally protected right to free association, self-organization, and designation of representatives for the purpose of negotiating the terms of employment." It's boilerplate language, but for Deb it's true. In addition to the boilerplate, Catherine highlights the role Deb played in workplace activism and paints her firing as retaliation.

But poor Alexandra Samuels was pure collateral damage. Pac-Shoppe fired non-activists like her just so the activists like Deborah Little won't appear to have been targeted. Firing Alexandra makes it look like routine downsizing, not personal targeting of people like Deborah.

Or that's what Pac-Shoppe will argue if it ever gets to court, which it won't.

UCW's legal defense is a giant charade. Catherine knows it, and so do Pac-Shoppe and Theresa Staedtler.

"What will happen?" Alexandra asks in despair. She has three children, and her ex-husband pays child support occasionally when he's sober.

"Our complaint will be assessed by a review board," Catherine replies.

"How long will that take?"

"Six months, on average."

"Six months? What am I supposed to do in the meantime?"

"Probably you should find a new job." Catherine keeps a straight face as she says it.

"Then what?"

Catherine explains that a contested hearing can take as long as two years. "Don't worry," she says, as if offering reassurance. "We'll be with you every step of the way. We'll be your lawyer. You don't need to hire someone else."

"What am I supposed to do in the meantime? My rent is due on the thirtieth, same as next payday."

"If you win, Pac-Shoppe has to pay the difference between what you actually earned and what you would have earned if you'd still been at Pac-Shoppe."

"That's two years from now!" Alexandra's voice is cracking by now.

Catherine is having a hard time taking herself seriously.

"Keep a brave face," Catherine says. "Pac-Shoppe can't keep this up forever." Catherine explains that Alexandra is among the few who sacrificed for the good of the many. Catherine says she's sorry.

She's been saying that a lot recently. "I'm sorry."

"What will I tell my landlord?" Alexandra is almost crying by now. She's trying to keep a brave face. She knows exactly how much that's worth to her landlord.

"I'm sorry," Catherine says again. "I wish I could help."

Last week Alexandra had a job. Not a great job, to be sure, but it was a steady job with a paycheck. Last week she could buy food and clothing for her children. Last week she knew how she was going to pay her rent.

Now she doesn't. If she ends up evicted and homeless it feels like Catherine's fault.

Is that okay because in the long run the survivors might be better off?

Catherine isn't so sure.

How long can she keep convincing herself? How long can she keep fooling her people? Are they better off if she does?

Deb and Alexandra are out of work. Stephanie and Jasmina are working the graveyard and missing their children.

Is Catherine actually doing any good? She doesn't know.

And she's wondering how much longer she can live with herself.

Maybe they'd all be better off if she quit.

Nate *Discovery*

The archeology is behind him and he's back into Pac-Shoppe.

Nate wastes no time looking for efficiencies. He's been postponing Theresa Staedtler for days, gainfully procrastinating while his eagerness to investigate her – and implicitly Catherine Campbell – has intensified in the background. This morning, again bright and early, he begins his detour as soon as he has enough files open and what looks like productive work on his screens.

He starts with accounts payable and receivable, old friends since the hellfire confidential flash drives where he first met them. If Pac-Shoppe made payments to Theresa Staedtler for those alleged illegal activities, they'd be in there.

But there are no such payments. Nate sees no evidence of Theresa Staedtler nor any likely alternative spelling he can devise.

Next he checks a few of the company names Catherine mentioned. "Ultimate Employer Solutions" yields nothing, nor does the acronym UES. He searches Pac-Shoppe records for another name she suggested, "Ultimate Union Solutions," along with the acronym UUS. Neither turns up anything. No payments were made nor invoices received from any such company.

Part of him wants to give it up as a bad idea. Catherine Campbell turned out to be crazy after all. But part of him doesn't want to give up so quickly, if only to retain his idealization of Catherine Campbell and his childhood daydreams.

He turns genuine attention back to his real work while it percolates. He's tracking how much time certain Pac-Shoppe products spend in inventory, paid for but not yet sold.

"How goes?" asks Dan Daniels, walking in unannounced. "Anything new?"

"Nothing since that semiconductor distraction," Nate replies, reminding him whose fault it is if he's been unproductive these last few days.

"Keep it up," says Mr. Daniels as he walks away.

Now Nate realizes he was limiting himself by searching with too much precision. Catherine suggested that Staedtler always uses the word "Ultimate," but everything else was a guess. He searches again, looking only for the word "Ultimate."

Unsurprisingly it turns up impossibly large numbers of entries. Ultimate Health provided some health care services. Ultimate Design installed shelving. Ultimate Windows repaired windows, and Ultimate Plumbing repaired some pipes. Ultimate Events catered a series of meetings last October.

But it's not impossibly many, really. Nate routinely deals with bigger numbers. It's not so many that he can't scroll through them looking for something plausible. He sorts the search results alphabetically, and Googles any name whose meaning – like Ultimate Windows – is not self-evident.

Checks were written to "Ultimate Business." Was that her? No. "Ultimate Business" prints business cards.

How about "Ultimate Beyond?" No. "Ultimate Beyond" facilitated those meetings last October.

"Ultimate Classica?" No.

After a while he finds a rhythm, cutting and pasting the name and address into Google in one window, and opening the company web pages in another.

A company called "Ultimate Efficacy," however, does not have a web page.

Nor does a company called "Ultimate Engagement."

Nate tries looking up their addresses but they appear in neither the white pages nor the yellow pages nor any business directory in Richmond. He closes his door and telephones the city's main post office.

He waits through a long hold time and several transfers, but eventually a helpful post office employee tells him that "Ultimate Efficacy" is registered to a PO Box at the Brooks Square post office on the north side of Richmond. Next she tells him that "Ultimate Engagement" is registered to the very same PO box.

"Wait!" Nate says. "How can that be? How can two business be registered to the same PO Box?"

"None of our business," she replies. "But it happens all the time. Businesses often share a single PO Box or the same office mailing address. Efficiency, I suppose. One guy can check both PO Boxes in one trip to the post office. Both businesses might be run by the same guy. Who knows? We just make sure the mail gets in the box."

"Thanks," Nate says.

He reopens his door and returns to his browser. Who are these companies? No search of news or the web yields anything relevant.

Next he checks the payment histories. It's exactly what Catherine suggested. "Ultimate Efficacy" received a payment of $18,975 in April. Three weeks later "Ultimate Engagement" received a check of $22,425, and the following week "Ultimate Efficacy" received another $19,455. Both companies have UE acronyms, just like Catherine said to expect.

None of these payments warrants attention on its own. But together they start to become meaningful amounts of money, especially since the purpose is utterly opaque.

Nate isn't yet convinced, though.

He exits the accounts and turn toward files of correspondence. These tend to be less complete, as they don't include emails, text messages or incoming letters that Pac-Shoppe never possessed electronically. But they're better than nothing. Over time, files like this can indicate the overall contour of a relationship.

By now he's not surprised that searching for Theresa Staedtler produces nothing, nor do searches for "Ultimate Efficiency." But his first examination of "Ultimate Engagement" strikes gold.

"Dear Ms. Staedtler," begins the letter dated April 12. "It was a pleasure to meet you. I look forward to working together under the terms we discussed."

It is signed by Tom Grillo, the vice president of operations for Pac-Shoppe.

Clearly it does not discuss what they would be "working together" to do, nor does it itemize the terms they "discussed," making it useless and irrelevant as correspondence.

But as a piece of evidence it's priceless, consistent in every way with the story Catherine Campbell told, from the illegal activities to the off-the-record cloak-and-dagger operations. Poor Tom Grillo made one small mistake early in the relationship, and the automated bureaucracy of Pac-Shoppe captured it for posterity.

That only leaves on question, but it's a big one.

Now he's found something important. What should he do with it?

THREE

It's just as obvious that Nate can't possibly copy this document as it's imperative that he do so. Just thinking about sneaking client financial material out of the office feels like committing a felony. He can't possibly share confidential internal records with someone else. He has no honest reason even to be looking at them.

At the same time, it's only a letter. It isn't a mathematically important document like a budget that shows how much a person is paid or how prices are calculated. Plus it's a letter that might demonstrate intent to perform illegal activity. Surely, Nate ought to turn it in. Maybe it's a felony not to. If he purposefully hides evidence of a crime, is he committing a crime of his own?

He minimizes the letter and hides it behind other work on his screen, then closes the door and walks down the hall for a cup of coffee. He doesn't close the file, though. Somehow it feels like if he puts it away it might disappear forever.

"Good morning" says Mr. Daniels. "Even the ascetic sometimes requires caffeine?"

"How are you?" Nate replies.

"Better than you, from the look of it," Mr. Daniels says. "Did someone run over your dog?"

Nate figures he must not be wearing his poker face. He hardens his eyes, straightens his shoulders and stands up taller. "All better now," he says. "Thanks."

Then Nate does something he rarely does. He goes to an unused conference room and sits at the big table by himself. He alternates between sipping his coffee and setting it down. Up and down; down and up; nothing changes. He sits there looking at the empty wall and blank tabletop, his mind spinning in circles, concluding first that he can't possibly share the document, then concluding for legal and moral reasons that he must.

No, he should not sacrifice his job, his ethics and his honor because a few people are arguably underpaid. Of course he shouldn't violate client confidentiality or embezzle information. It seems easy when he considers it like that.

But who's really wrong? Who's the lawbreaker? The behavior Pac-Shoppe contracted out is illegal for a reason. If Nate doesn't turn over what he knows, maybe he's covering up a crime. Maybe he becomes some kind of accessory-after-the-fact. Pac-Shoppe is hurting people, and using investor money – Nate's money – to do it.

The only thing Nate knows for sure is he wishes he'd never looked.

Thankfully, nobody walks in on him. Nobody asks what he's working on or thinking about, sitting in a conference room by himself, with neither phone nor notebook open before him. Nobody stops in to say good morning or talk about a baseball game. For better or for worse, he is left alone with his thoughts.

He considers going for a walk to stretch the time, hoping that a nice spring day might show things differently, but he knows it won't. This is not a problem fresh air can solve. Besides, leaving the office would leave those documents unprotected at his desk. It's already been a while since he left them alone and unguarded.

He returns to his desk to find everything as he left it, as it should be of, course. Nothing looks disturbed, and his computer wakes up in exactly the same place.

Taking care that nobody is looking, he again maximizes the document so it fills his screen. "I look forward to working together," it still says, bright as day. Nate dares not copy the document or "save as" something new. He doesn't know what security is built into these electronic files nor what usage history can be extracted from them later. Mr. Daniels called them hellfire confidential and warned him not to test it. Nate would just as soon take him at his word.

Then Shaolin forces descend miraculously from the cosmos. Divine inspiration tells Nate what to do.

He takes his cell phone from his pocket and snaps a picture of the illicit document on the screen. There. Done. Just like that. As the Staples commercial says, "That was easy." It isn't the original but it's no worse than a photocopy.

Even as he plays with fire he is cautious. He checks that the photo came out properly, and takes another to be sure.

Both photos are fine. Nate tests them carefully, zooming in and reading them on the screen. “I look forward to working together under the terms we discussed,” it says quite clearly, followed by Tom Grillo’s signature at the bottom. What’s the use of confirming something if you don’t restate the terms? To Nate, it’s practically an admission of guilt.

He closes the files, shuts down the programs that were running them, and returns his cell phone to his pocket. But now the Shaolin forces stop talking to him.

Okay, then. Now what?

Catherine *Like a Million Pieces*

This time at least Catherine knows where she's going. She parks in the visitors' lot of Saint Mary's Hospital and heads straight to Orthopedics. She called in advance to make sure Elena was still there and confirmed the visiting hours.

Catherine shouldn't be surprised that the hospital is filled with sick people but it upsets her anyway. As she walks past people dressed in nightgowns or pushed in wheelchairs and connected to IV bottles, she thinks back to places she's worked. Garbage trucks. Sewerage plants. A fishing trawler.

The hospital is worse than any of that. The odor of antiseptic and terminal illness slaps her with morbidity and mortality. She worries that her glass must be half empty, since she sees herself surrounded by sickness and death, when she is equally surrounded by vitality and healing. One young man with a purple leg cast practically dances past her on crutches, accompanied by his friend carrying a basketball, talking about a victory in overtime.

Maya spots her before she's fully entered the room. "Catherine!" she exclaims, and runs over for a hug.

Catherine kneels down to her height but this time she's clutching more desperately than Maya. They stay together for several heartbeats, a sincere hug not a passing courtesy.

"Mommy is comminuted," Maya declares as they break. She makes this sound like good news. Elena is sitting on the bed that Maya just vacated.

"Comminuted?" Catherine asks, hoping she got the word right. Doubtless Maya learned this one recently.

"It means her leg is broken into like a million pieces," Maya explains. But still she sounds happy about it.

"That's good?" Catherine asks.

"One hundred percent recovery," Maya continues. "Come look!"

Maya tugs Catherine toward her mother like she might get away. "Mommy! Look who's here!"

“I see,” Elena says. She looks like a whole new person. She’s sitting on the edge of the bed, face made up, hair brushed to cover stitches and shaving. She’s connected by tubes and wires to an apparatus in the corner of the bed but the jungle gym framework has been dismantled and disappeared.

Elena brightens when Catherine turns her way. “God bless you,” she announces. “I was getting bored.”

“What’s the news?” Catherine asks. “I guess it’s pretty good ... or better than it might have been?”

“Mommy’s a dinosaur!” Maya interrupts. She pulls from the side of the bed a picture that started as a diagram of a femur, but the round ball of the thigh bone that goes into the hip socket has been turned into a dinosaur head, with sharp teeth and pinprick eyes. “She’s a trochantesaurus,” Maya explains.

Catherine must not be the only one falling in love with Maya. Some doctor, nurse or medical resident explained this injury to Maya’s complete satisfaction.

Elena says, “It’s an *intertrochanteric* fracture, if that helps.” Doubtless she’s learning new words as well. “The head of the femur broke off completely from the thigh part.”

“That’s what makes it *comminuted*,” Maya interjects. “Broken into more than one piece.”

“But they taped and screwed and made some magic ... and now it’s back together again.” Elena continues. “They estimate sixteen weeks to full functionality.”

“She has a wheelchair,” Maya adds.

“Only for a short while,” Elena says. “As it heals I’ll advance to crutches then a cane and eventually ...” she shakes Maya by the shoulder “... to freeze tag.”

Elena goes on to explain that surgery was the day before yesterday, after her head injury had stabilized, and that everything went smoothly. Today she is resting and eating. Tomorrow she’ll go home.

“Can I beg a ride?” she asks.

“Of course,” replies Catherine. “And your insurance is okay? No problems with that?” Good news or not, Catherine is worried.

"No problem. Not for me anyway. They know who hit me. Now it's all his problem ... and his insurance company's. Ricardo's company made sure of that. They don't want me on their plan. Whatever therapy or after-care I need ... it's all on the other guy." Elena leans her weight backward into her hands, and carefully raises one leg straight out from the bed, moving slowly, obviously in pain, but like a patient testing her limits not a lifeless cripple on oxygen.

When she's moved to her satisfaction she turns back to Catherine. "We found a lawyer," Elena declares.

"For the car accident?"

"No, for Ricardo's injury."

Catherine cocks her head in puzzlement.

"We learned what happened. We learned about the burn." Elena looks like she's about to turn angry, so she slows herself down by repeating the exercise with her leg, lifting it straight out from the bed, then returning it slowly until it hangs down against the mattress. Finally she continues, "Ricardo didn't make any mistakes. Somebody else turned on the steam. Without warning."

"That sounds bad."

"You think?" she says sarcastically. "It's a fundamental rule. Ricardo calls them 'safety protocols.' Even I know it, and I don't even work there. You're supposed to tell people before you turn on the steam. Always, always, always. You announce you're turning on the steam, and you don't do it until everyone says okay." She tells the story of Ricardo climbing the ladder and reaching the joint. It's a regular workday until thousand degree heat comes blasting into his face. "He's lucky he didn't break a leg jumping off the ladder," she concludes.

"Lucky or skilled," Catherine agrees. "Good thing you have a lawyer."

"Ricardo got him through his doctor's office." Elena repeats the exercise with her leg, up and down slowly. She's straining against the pain, but Catherine detects satisfaction in the background. Vindication will come. "Now tell me about Pac-Shoppe. I understand it's not going so well."

"Honestly, I don't know what to do."

Catherine surprises even herself with her sudden candor. Something in the setting brings her despair to the surface. Maybe it's Elena straining against the pain, trusting that justice will be done, or the hospital filled with injury and death. Catherine treats Elena like her spiritual advisor and confesses what's on her mind. Elena is in no hurry. With nothing to do but wait and heal, she's happy to listen.

"They win by doing nothing," Catherine says. "They have plenty of money to cover any small inconvenience we can cause. We're fleas on an elephant, and we're losing people left and right."

"Losing people?"

"Deb Little and Tim Nicosia were fired outright. Stephanie and Jasmina were moved to the graveyard shift. Everybody's work is harder in one way or another. Pac-Shoppe is making sure everyone knows who's the boss. Frankly, I'm astonished anyone is sticking with us at all."

"Everybody wants to help," Elena says.

"I'm worried about our partners, too. If we keep marching in front of the store entrance, eventually we'll tick off the customers. If we keep blocking traffic, we'll lose the commuters. We just don't have any leverage."

"The bad press?"

"It costs Pac-Shoppe a penny in sales and a nickel in public image – which investors don't like – but it's not enough to matter. Or it doesn't seem to be."

Now Elena, too, appears defeated. She looks down at her leg injury and engages in the same painful exercise of straightening it out from the bed, then returning it to a seated position. It looks like she's somehow following doctor's orders. Clearly this hurts and her attention is internal. When she's done she adjusts the tubes in her arm and disentangles them from the sheets. "What's Plan B?" she asks.

The question is so straightforward Catherine is almost ashamed to answer it. "There is no Plan B," she admits. To cover her embarrassment she steps to the corner of the bed and adjusts Elena's tubes in a way that looks like it might be more comfortable. "We fight as long and as hard as we can. Either we succeed or we lose. Plan B is accepting a tiny wage concession and giving up on the union." Catherine dares not wonder what will happen if Pac-Shoppe offers no concession at all.

Elena seems less troubled. She stretches out her arm, now less encumbered by the tubes and wires. "Then we need to hit them harder," she proclaims. "More pickets, more protests. More traffic stops. We need to hit them until they feel it. Fleas are a bummer. Have you ever had them in your house? We can't give up on the union."

"Five people have been fired. I can't keep asking for sacrifices with nothing to show for it."

"Or what?"

"Or people will stop coming to meetings. I'll ask for volunteers and everyone will have something else to do. I'll schedule a protest and three people will come, then they'll leave rather than embarrass themselves." Catherine shrugs her shoulders. "By next year this will barely be a memory. Like rain on a picnic, bad but forgotten. People who lose their jobs will move on. People who stay will be happy if they get a raise, or just keep plugging away if they don't. Honestly, I'm ready to give up."

"No!" cries Elena, with surprising strength. "You can't give up. We need you. Everyone is counting on you." Elena pushes forward from the edge of the bed and keeps going until she is standing. The pain is palpable but her face holds firm. The tubes in her arm stretch menacingly but she doesn't back off. Supporting herself with one arm on the bedrail for balance she grabs Catherine's hand.

"What's the old slogan? *No se puede?* Is that how it goes? It's too hard. We can't do it. *No se puede?*"

Catherine shakes her head. She's almost ashamed of herself.

"Please don't give up," she implores. "We need you to hold us together. Together we can. *Si se puede*, please. Without you, we're peons on our own. All together we're something to reckon with."

She takes the step backward and collapses onto the bed, sitting as she was when Catherine entered. "Strength in numbers," she says. "That's what you tell us. You are the glue that holds us together."

"Thank you," Catherine mutters, eyes on her feet.

"What do you need me to do?"

"Elena! You're in the hospital! All I need you to do is get better."

"I'll do whatever it takes. The car didn't kill me. But if you give up the fight to live ... that's when you start to die."

"We're from Peru," says Emilio as his next trigonometry lesson begins, two days later. He and Nate are back in Peet's coffee shop. This time Emilio declines the offer of hot chocolate but accepts a plastic cup of tap water as Nate buys the coffee that entitles them to use the space. "My mother thought you might like to know."

"Thanks," says Nate. "Were you born there?"

"I was born here," Emilio says. "Both my parents and my big brother were born in Peru. They came here together when he was a baby."

They chat about the immigrant experience and Nate is amazed by how differently he understands it. To Nate, this is a success story about seeking opportunity and making a better life. To Emilio it is a story about searching for work permits and green cards, with high fees, long waiting periods and the dangers of imperfect documentation.

"Did class make more sense yesterday?" Nate asks. Probably it's better just to stick with trigonometry.

"It was amazing," Emilio replies. "Now that I understand we're just measuring triangles."

"All you need is two out of three, and the right trig function."

"Bingo," Emilio replies, using Nate's word from their first lesson together. "So what's the point of a unit circle?"

Now it's becoming serious trigonometry. Emilio's questions suggest insight and understanding far better than the confusion of only Tuesday. They spend ten minutes going over yesterday's homework, then they talk about unit circles. Once it all seems clear, Emilio starts his night's homework while Nate sits quietly and answers the occasional question.

"I'm going to college," Emilio declares after puzzling out a tricky problem, sounding like a pilot who found a hole in the clouds.

"You surely will," Nate replies.

"I want to be an engineer," Emilio says. "I want to build bridges and dams and cool things like that."

"Then you better learn your trigonometry."

"After my mom cleans your building, the next building is some kind of engineering firm. I go sometimes if someone on mom's team is sick or needs a substitute. I get paid." He looks directly at Nate. "I have a work permit," he says as if Nate has challenged him. "The firm keeps pictures on the walls of things they build. Sometimes a man there explains them to me. He's from Bolivia," Emilio adds with pride.

Nate realizes that Emilio has probably been in his office too, though without Nate noticing. Emilio would have been one of the nameless bodies pushing a vacuum cleaner or wiping the countertops. He starts to feel guilty for not noticing, as if he's done something wrong.

"How many buildings does your mother clean?" Nate asks.

"Three buildings at night. From roughly six to ten o'clock. During the day she works at Safeway."

"Safeway? The supermarket? Cleaning?"

"No, at Safeway they rotate all the jobs. Sometimes she works in the freezer, sometimes restocking the floor, sometimes at the cash register. That's her favorite, the cash register. Freezer is the worst." He drains his little cup of water. "A different company comes to clean at night."

Nate nods as if he knows what Emilio's talking about. "Now to work," he says. He pushes Emilio's homework toward him and goes to refill his little water cup.

Nate doesn't know what her hours are at Safeway but he imagines it's something like all day long. Then she works from six to ten at night. *That poor woman*, Nate thinks. *Is this what she came to America for? Is this what she expected?* He truly doesn't know. Surely, it must be better than what she left ... but for no reason Nate starts to wonder.

"What's your mother's name?" Nate interrupts Emilio's homework like a naughty boy, but it seems like something he ought to know.

"Martina," Emilio replies.

"Has she ever worked at Pac-Shoppe?"

"She used to work at Pac-Shoppe. She left. She says Safeway treats people better. It has a union."

On the legal front, there is nothing more Catherine can do without additional proof. She wants to connect Pac-Shoppe to Theresa Staedtler, and connect Theresa Staedtler to the illegal threats. But she can't wait for Nathaniel Hawley of Frank Cox High School, even if he ended up at Fitzgerald Financials. This battle won't be won in the courts, anyway.

Catherine is equal parts chastened and emboldened by Elena. Most importantly, Elena has clarified what Catherine needs to do. The first truism of union organizing is that the union can't organize the workplace; only the workers can organize the workplace. The workers are truly in it together. They have the same boss, the same paycheck and the same risks. Only they have the credibility to balance the stakes, call the shots and forge the bonds of collective action. Professional organizers can offer tips, tricks and experience – but they only help. The workers have to do the heavy lifting themselves.

So Catherine goes back to the people. She doesn't attempt a big meeting. She decides to talk one-on-one with the crucial allies – people who work day shifts, people who work overnight, and people whose kids' schedules make meetings inconvenient. There is no other way. Catherine needs to see how they feel, learn what risks they're willing to take, and listen for new ideas.

Nate is forgetting all about his regular job. Accounting? Whatever. Shark? That's a fish.

He finds no joy in making two plus two equal four, even when the digits are hidden in multiple subaccounts and it takes sleuthing genius to put them all together. The highlight of his day is meeting with Emilio. Last week they met on Tuesday and Thursday, and they agreed to meet this week again on Tuesday and Thursday, maybe more if needed.

Dare Nate think that he'll be sad that Emilio will soon be fine and won't need him anymore?

Now it's Tuesday and he spends his day looking forward to it.

"Does Grasshopper have a date?" Mr. Daniels inquires midway through the day. "I see him checking his watch and living life impatiently."

Nate wonders how Mr. Daniels sees through him so. Is he equally transparent to everyone else?

"No, master," Nate replies. "I am tutoring a boy in mathematics. We are meeting this evening. I care only for his success."

Today Mr. Daniels has diversified his appearance to the point of a handkerchief in his pocket, white, the color of his shirt. He is carrying files but he doesn't pass them to Nate, just breezes onward. Nate spends the next few hours checking balance sheets, trying to care about the ratio between operating income and the contribution margin.

When Emilo walks in he is glowing. He's early today, a quarter to six, and they come quickly to Nate's office before he hears the telltale vacuums. He is wearing brand new jeans and a striped polo shirt.

"I got an A," Emilio announces.

"In what?" If he had a trig test Nate would have known.

"We had a pop quiz in trigonometry. Everything made sense. I used the trig functions and calculated the unknown side, just like you showed me."

"Tell him more," his mother prompts him. "Tell him the rest." Her hands are empty. She must have parked her cleaning supplies before she entered his office.

Now Emilio looks at his feet, and Nate sees the bashful little boy sipping hot chocolate. "I got a plus," Emilio says. "Not a plain old A, but an A plus. Mrs. Weaver gave me extra credit. She wrote a note that said 'Well done. You figured it out.'" Now he brightens and the little boy becomes the confident young man. "Her note said, 'I knew you could.'"

Nate steps forward to shake Emilio's hand like he won the Nobel prize. "I knew it, too."

"I'm going to college. Just you watch."

His mother is looking at him like he can fly.

Catherine *Nuclear Guidance*

Catherine wishes she could start with Deb Little, whose role in the campaign was to track internal sentiment. But she can't because Deb's been fired. Next she would talk to Jasmina, and she still might, but Jasmina is barely surviving on the graveyard shift and she's admitted she's looking for work. Asking advice might be like rubbing it in.

Instead Catherine turns first to Stephanie Lerner, who was the star of their Saturday shopping action and whose son, David, has earned the nickname, "Cheeky." Stephanie is also working overnight but in some ways it makes her easier to catch.

They meet by arrangement at a gas station near the Pac-Shoppe. Catherine can't possibly go into the store without attracting attention. Management knows who she is, and anyone she talks to gets a target on their head. Even the parking lot is too close for comfort.

But they decide against someplace comfortable – a coffee shop or someone's home. They only need a few minutes anyway. They work out the timing with precision and Catherine is sure to arrive a few minutes early – which is easy, because Stephanie's shift starts at 1:00 am and it's not as if Catherine has anything else to do at that hour.

Besides, she's low on gas. She's legitimate in every way.

"How are you doing?" she asks when Stephanie arrives. Stephanie is a little late but Catherine's windows need washing and it's been a while since she checked the tires. "How's David? How's the graveyard shift?"

Stephanie is wearing a green turtleneck and a bright red woolen vest, looking almost like Santa's elf on this cool April evening. "At least someone is happy about the graveyard shift," she replies.

Catherine looks up puzzled.

"David loves being a latchkey kid," Stephanie explains. "Loves it, loves it, loves it." She says it was different in the earlier years. Kids need lots of hugging in pre-school, and someone to come home to in the early grades. "But he's in high school now. He's making butt jokes on television! Not only doesn't he need me at home, he appreciates the independence. I can trust him to do his homework, and I wake up from my 'nights' sleep around seven in the evening. We cook a nice dinner together – though for me it's breakfast."

"So the graveyard is okay, after all?"

"I wouldn't go that far. I definitely miss the daylight. David says the days are getting longer, but I can't tell. But the problem was never the hours, it was the attitude."

"Attitude?" Catherine asks. She can guess what Stephanie means but needs to hear it from her.

"The attitude," Stephanie affirms. "If they asked me if I wanted to work the graveyard shift, I might have said yes. In some ways it's easier. It's slower. With fewer customers and more re-stocking. If they offered an extra dollar an hour I might be happy to work overnight."

"But they made you do it."

"Forced it on me like punishment."

That brings them to the heart of the matter. "What do you want to do?" Catherine asks.

Now it's Stephanie's turn to look puzzled. "What do you mean?"

"They're punishing you. They've banished you to the overnight shift forever. Jasmina is even worse. They keep changing her shift, on and off the graveyard, so her body never knows when to sleep. Some people they fired outright. And you know this business about the timeclock ..."

Stephanie scowls at the mention of the timeclock.

"... they're punishing everybody. What do you think we should do? Should we back off? How would you feel if we gave up on the union?"

Catherine pauses because she knows this is unexpected and she can see Stephanie's mind starting to turn. "Maybe we went too far. Maybe we're asking for too much." She makes the case as strongly as she can. "Maybe we should ask for one simple thing. More money. A modest raise. Everyone can understand that. If we can get that, it's good for everybody immediately. What do you think about that? Should we forget the union and just ask for a raise?"

The light is dim. The night is dark, and the street lights and station lights together are barely enough to fill a tank. But the anger on Stephanie's face is as bright as day. "Are you out of your fucking mind?" Her voice is quiet like the night, but intense enough to ignite the gas in the tanks under their feet.

"We didn't come all this way and put up with all this bull-shit – pardon my French – all of this punishment, just to quit. Suppose we give up on the union. Suppose we ask only for a raise. Suppose we get one. Suppose it's a good one. What then?"

She is asking but this is not a question.

"What about next year? How do we get next year's raise? And the year after that? Even if I'm gone by then, what about the people after me?" Stephanie stops to shake her head. "Forget about the people after me. I don't even need to go that far. How about control over our shift schedules? What about my incentive for working graveyard? What about that bull-shit at the timeclock? To get some respect we need a union."

Before Catherine can reply, Stephanie adds, "No, ma'am. I'm not giving up now. We'd be starting all over. We need to do this. We need a union. We need it now. I'm sorry. We need it yesterday. Pardon my fucking language."

Nate *Sorry, but No*

Nate wants to tell Catherine about Emilio. He wants to brag about giving up evenings and buying treats to help a young man make it college. He wants to tell her how much he's learning about the immigrant experience and life at the bottom of the pay scale.

Maybe she'll be impressed. Maybe she'll appreciate that he's finding new meaning in life, helping the dispossessed.

Hah! He scoffs at himself even for thinking along these lines. *What are you doing to help their dispossession?* she'll ask, and rightly so.

Sure, helping Emilio is terrific. Catherine will give Nate a gold star then ask about the payments to the union buster. *You want to help the dispossessed?* she'll say. *I showed you what they need. What are you doing about it?*

No, he can't contact Catherine Campbell. Not until he knows what to say about that letter.

Catherine *No Mistake*

Catherine talks next with Ramona of the communications committee. Again she considers it an indicator – Ramona speaking for herself, and also judging the temperature on site. Does everyone share Stephanie's level of commitment? Or is that only the activist core? Catherine can't survey everybody; she needs to trust her team.

She also wants to test some new theories – what actions they might take, what disruption they might cause, everything informed by how far people are willing to go.

"What if we tried to slow down their work?" Catherine inquires. "Maybe we could re-stock merchandise onto the wrong shelf or unload it into the wrong category. What do you think? Would it cause inconvenience?"

"Interesting," Ramona replies. They are in a side room of the UCW office with an old poster of Cesar Chavez on the wall and a nice collection of empty pizza boxes on the floor.

"We'd need to pick mistakes that couldn't be tracked back to any particular individual. We want to slow Pac-Shoppe down without getting anyone in trouble." Catherine has been thinking about the old factory sit-down strikes or slow-down strikes. Operations were interrupted – or at least slowed down – by workers acting in protest. But workers couldn't be replaced or bypassed because they were physically in the plant. Operations couldn't go on around them.

Ramona shakes her head in opposition. "It won't work. Or at least it wouldn't work in public. If Pac-Shoppe weren't giving us bathroom breaks and we insisted on taking them, that would inconvenience Pac-Shoppe and keep the public on our side. People understand we need bathroom breaks.

"But messing up the merchandise would tick off the customers. Pac-Shoppe will come after us for not doing our jobs. I'll have a hard time defending my right to put shampoo where customers expect baby food. It might mess up Pac-Shoppe but it will mess us up even more."

She's right. Catherine realizes that if she were in charge herself, she might have done it out of spite. Good thing she's not in charge. She thinks of an old saying, *If you want to go fast, travel alone. If you want to go far, travel together*. Her team is properly slowing her down.

"What do you recommend?" she asks.

"Those subsidies piss people off," Ramona replies. "Remember, yesterday I was interviewed on talk radio? Callers kept asking about those subsidies. They almost couldn't believe it."

Catherine nods in encouragement. She's not sure where this train is heading but she doesn't want to get in its way.

"Let's get it out of the building. Let's keep it in the streets. We're not slowing down Pac-Shoppe. We're working hard for Pac-Shoppe's customers."

"That's for sure," Catherine agrees.

"And we're protecting taxpayers," Ramona affirms. "First, we need to keep working with our external partners to make sure we have all of their support. Then we need to block traffic like it's never been blocked before. This isn't just our problem. It's a city problem. We need to get the whole city involved in making it go away."

"The police have been cutting us some slack," Catherine warns. "Next time they'll bring out the handcuffs. We can't handle a mass arrest."

"Why not?"

"Does a mass arrest get you your raise?"

"A union and a raise. We're going to get all of it. Just you watch."

Nate *Windfall*

It's been a while since Nate made himself a nice dinner, so tonight he pulls out all the stops. He sautés a beautiful chicken marsala, with his favorite shape bowtie noodles on the side. He steams fresh brocolli he picked up on sale.

The telephone rings as he sits down. The caller isn't identified but the number looks familiar so he answers.

"Hey, Nate," says the voice on the other side. "It's Ethan. Ethan Blumenauer."

"Hey there. What's up?" It's Ethan, of all people. Nate is sharing his magnificent dinner with the guy whose concert tickets torpedoed his marriage.

They talk a minute about sports and the weather, then Ethan cuts to what's really on his mind. "I have a date for you."

"A date?" Having wrecked Nate's last marriage, Ethan is arranging his next one? What, does he get a finder's fee?

"She's perfect. She's attractive, intelligent and athletic. She's new to the office and new in town. I know she's single because I heard her talking to some of the other women."

"If she's perfect, why is she single?" By this time in life, people without problems have paired, including Ethan.

"Because she's been waiting for you."

That gets a smile, at least. "But I'm not really looking to date," Nate protests. Okay, maybe he is, but he wouldn't start with Ethan.

"Yes, you are. You just don't know it yet. Come on. Do you plan to stay single forevermore?"

He's right about that, too. Nate isn't hoping to stay single forever, certainly not forevermore. And for someone who's not looking to date he seems to be disproportionately smitten by a woman who appears to consider him nothing more than the potential procurer of rare and illicit documents.

Why, then, does it feel like a betrayal to think about someone else? Catherine Campbell is a daydream, not a mutual commitment. He is not two-timing her if he spends an evening with someone who is "attractive, intelligent and athletic."

Athletic? Nate wonders what sport she plays. There's one way to find out. "Let's give it a try," he says at last.

"I'll send a three-way email. I'll get you connected then leave you to it."

"Um. Thanks?"

"Someday you'll say that for real."

Her appointment is with Harmon Wright, Methodist minister and volunteer leader of the campaign's faith outreach committee. Catherine thought the appointment was with Harmon alone, so she's surprised when his office is filled with people. She wasn't planning for a community rally; she wanted a quiet meeting to explore Harmon's private opinion on priorities and tactics.

They are in Harmon's church, Calvary United, a modest brick building with a short steeple and pretty stained glass windows. Harmon's office looks more fit for a university than a church, with his desk, and four chairs around a coffee table. One wall is covered by books ranging from dignified hardback tomes to tattered paperbacks. Another wall has a small window to the outside but the only decoration is an abstract expressionist painting, bold colors darting upward with a swoosh. No Christs, crucifixes or overt religion is on display.

Harmon starts the introductions as soon as Catherine enters, gesturing toward people around the room. "Of course, you know Annie Burke who has brought many large and enthusiastic crowds to your actions."

"Of course," Catherine replies. "Hi, Annie." Annie is a small gray-haired woman in a blue blouse with her hair tied up in a white kerchief that always reminds Catherine of an Amish farmer or Little House on the Prairie. But she's seen Annie at any number of actions and planning meetings, and knows that a shrewd tactician lurks behind that wholesome simplicity.

"You can't survive on $7.85," Annie replies. "You really can't."

Catherine almost blushes as she remembers that Annie was present on the day of the *All Cheek Panties* at Victoria's Secret, but Harmon is already moving on, indicating the large African American man beside Annie. "This is Bishop Donald Perry of the Bible Way Baptist Church," Harmon says.

If Annie looks like a farm girl, Bishop Perry looks like a banker in his gray pinstriped suit with a red bow tie. He has impressive shoulders and shakes Catherine's hand with a powerful grip that lasts a long time. "Good to meet you," he says in a voice she can imagine thundering from the heavens.

The last man Catherine already recognizes as a Catholic priest, dressed as he is in white shirt and black vest with a clerical collar. Now that she looks she's struck by how cute he is, with short blonde hair and dreamy blue eyes, the vintage All-American boyfriend from the movies. Quickly she reminds herself that he's probably gay and likely a child molester — though she probably deserves a lightning bolt just for thinking such thoughts.

She settles by concluding that he really is cute and realizing how long it's been since she's been on a date.

Oh my God. Here in church and looking at a priest, she's starting to think like her mother. Probably this isn't what she had in mind for her birthday present.

Even as Catherine is distracting herself, Harmon is starting the introduction. "This is John from the St. Francis of Assisi Catholic Church on Franklin Street. John is a radical Catholic."

Catherine manages not to laugh as Harmon uses two words she's never considered using together. She forces herself to focus.

"Thou shalt not kill," says John as he takes her hand.

That brings her back to attention. "I hope not. I wasn't planning to."

John continues quietly, as if this is what they're talking about. "Nearly every tradition has a version of that edict. For Christians and Jews it is in the Ten Commandments. In Islam, the Koran forbids the taking of souls, with the exception of the death penalty imposed by the state. All faiths condemn murder."

"I understand," Catherine says.

He shakes his head as if to suggest she might not. He asks, "What does *thou shalt not kill* mean in a world where a tiny fraction of the population consumes so much and wastes so much it challenges the very survival of everyone else? What is *thou shalt not kill* in a country that denies life-saving health care to millions of its citizens, and where homeless people die in the street?"

Wow, Catherine thinks to herself. *That's pretty radical.*

"Poverty makes a mockery of God's creation. Widespread poverty, hunger and despair are a crime. You are working to end it." He bends in a sincere bow. "I am at your service."

"Thank you," Catherine replies. She bows back but fears her gesture appears awkward and imitative in comparison.

Harmon motions for everyone to be seated and offers them cups of water or coffee. Among them, only John accepts a cup of water.

"My people are weary," Catherine confesses, as people look to her to explain why they are here. "Pac-Shoppe has been firing people, reducing hours or changing people's shift schedules so they can't see their children." She almost feels bad, playing the child-card in a room full of faith leaders, but they appear neither troubled nor motivated by the reference. She goes on to explain how Pac-Shoppe can wait them out, their limited leverage, and how they need more support in the community.

"Or we can quit," Catherine concludes. "Failure is, in fact, an option. We could reduce our demands to something they might pay just to shut us up, and maybe we can try again next year." She tries to read the tenor in room but their expressions are impenetrable; she is making confession on the other side of a screen. "If we go on, we will need more support in the community. I came to discuss with Harmon what seems feasible."

They are silent for what seems far too long. Nobody seems to be fidgeting but nor are they waiting for someone else to speak first. Catherine leans back in her chair and wonders if maybe she needs to say something more.

Eventually Bishop Perry takes the stage. He rises from his chair and stands behind it, reaching down to touch the back but towering over Annie and John beside him. When he finally speaks it is to ask a question.

"Do you know how Martin Luther King died?" He is looking only at Catherine.

"He was shot." Catherine is sure she's right but equally sure she's missing the point.

"Do you know what he was doing when he was shot? Where was he on that fateful day that changed so many lives?" Catherine fears a sermon coming on, but Bishop Perry goes straight to the point. "Reverend King was shot at a *union* march. He wasn't marching for civil rights or equal justice under law, he was marching with the Memphis sanitation workers. One of their members had been crushed to death in a trash truck. The janitors' union wanted more money and safer working conditions. In today's terms, we might call it 'Justice for Janitors.'"

He looks Catherine straight in the eye. "Are any of your workers black?" he asks.

"Of course."

"Latino?"

"Of course."

"White?"

"Some of them."

"I don't care about any of that. Your workers need a raise. I don't care about the color of their skin or the content of their character. All I know is that as a black man and a member of the clergy, I need to help. What is it you're thinking to do?"

Catherine was expecting to talk to Harmon alone. It turns out Harmon knew better than she did what she needed.

Nate *Face Time*

"How about the Virginia Museum of Fine Arts?" A week of email and phone tag after Ethan established the connection, Kristin Cooper is talking to Nate on the telephone.

"I've never been there," he replies.

"Then you'll find out what you've been missing." She explains that it's open late on Thursdays and Fridays, with a pretty little restaurant on the deck upstairs. They settle on next Thursday at six.

"Meet me at the face," she concludes.

"The face?"

"It will be obvious when you arrive."

Press Release.
For more information contact:

Harmon Wright, Calvary United Methodist Church

Father John O'Connell, St. Francis of Assisi Catholic Church

An Open Letter from Richmond's Faith Community "We Stand with Pac-Shoppe Workers"

To the good people of Richmond:

As faith leaders in our community we are writing to show our support for the workers of Pac-Shoppe as they struggle to gain a "living wage." This is a struggle about what kind of a city we want to be – a city where all people can live with dignity, or a city of stagnation and poverty, where only a small percentage of our residents have access to the resources they need to grow and thrive.

We are standing up for fair pay and decent benefits for ALL working people, starting with Pac-Shoppe. We call on Pac-Shoppe leadership to do their part to keep Richmond families out of poverty. The economy of Richmond is strong yet workers in our commercial sector remain underpaid, and workers in Pac-Shoppe are paid least of all.

We call on ALL business leaders to do their part by creating good jobs, raising wages and providing affordable health care to their employees. We ask our city government NOT to support companies that don't pay their fair share of the social contract. Together we can restore balance to our economy, improve our community and create opportunity for future generations.

Signed by:

Harmon Wright, Calvary United Methodist Church

Father John O'Connell, St. Francis of Assisi Catholic Church

Bishop Donald Perry, Bible Way Baptist Church

Reverend Joseph Fiorello, Bishop Emeritus, Archdiocese of Henrico

Rabbi Barry Isserow, Beth El Reform Congregation

Bishop Gabriel Lawson, Piedmond Synod, Evangelical Lutheran Church in America

Reverend Glenda Mah, United Methodist Church

Reverend Lisa Trover, St. Stephens Episcopal Church

Reverend Marty Graves, Richmond Mennonite Church

Reverend Wilke Woodward, First Congregational Church of Richmond

Sister Cecily Zangas, Dominican Sisters of Richmond

Imam Shaker Jackson-Bey, Dar Al-Hijrah Islamic Center

Reverend James Feldspar, First Shiloh Missionary Baptist Church

Rabbi Aaron Black, Congregation Or Ami

Reverend Lila Fithian, Webster Presbyterian Church

Father Alberto Zanetto, Assumption Parish, Richmond

Sister Margaret Blumenauer, Sisters of Charity of the Incarnate Word

Bishop Maya Kaine-Barrett, Nichiren Buddhist Sangha of Virginia

Father Ricardo Wall, Basilian Fathers

Imam Abdul Azeem, Masjid Al-Islam

Rabbi Lloyd Grossman, Temple Beth Torah

Reverend Anabel Atkins, Trinity Episcopal Church

Minister DeWayne Webster, Visions Fellowship Church

Reverend Ronnie Lassiter, Virginia Center for Spiritual Activism

Father Gerry O'Keefe, Maryknoll Fathers and Brothers

Nate *Seeing, Hearing, Listening*

The face is indeed obvious when Nate arrives, overlooking the grassy lawn by the front door, a giant spectral presence over two stories tall. The face belongs to a woman, pale and lunar, not quite two-dimensional, like she's made from paper, with just enough curve and depth to support the structure and make her interesting from any angle. She is resting and peaceful, eyes closed in a quiet contemplation that spreads throughout the garden. The placard calls her *Chloe*, a recent installation by a "world-renowned" Spanish artist, Jaume Plensa, who Nate has never heard of.

He walks a few laps around Chloe, appreciating her restful countenance from the front, her braided hair from behind. She is alabaster and marble, all one color, not quite white. The placard says she was made for this space and installed in 2017.

The grass underfoot is deep and green and so soft he wishes he were barefoot. A pond with water lilies stands between Chloe and the building, though in early May there are not yet flowers on the lily pads. Stunning red reeds of sculpted glass erupt between the lilies, another work of art that the plaque says was designed by American artist Dale Chihuly in 2013.

The pond is fed by a stream that cascades gently down a stairway leading from a plaza that overlooks both Cloe and the museum itself. At the top of the stairs stands another large outdoor sculpture, probably in bronze.

Nate wonders if he has time to climb the stairs and check out the bronze, sightsee Chloe from above. Probably not. He is a few minutes early but he'd rather his date find him as agreed than have him trickle in after she's been waiting. They can tour the plaza together after she arrives.

He is wearing the same red sweater he wore for Catherine Campbell. It's one of his favorites and easy to spot, though this time he needn't worry it will be misconstrued as strike support.

Kristin Cooper arrives as he starts another lap around Chloe. Kristin is wearing blue as promised, and she's pretty enough to have caught his attention even if Ethan hadn't told him what to look for. “No problem finding it?” Kristin inquires, skipping the part where she makes sure he’s the right guy.

“Chloe is beautiful,” Nate replies. “Thanks for taking me out to see her.” Kristin nods agreement and he continues. “Can we go up the stairs?” He gestures toward the stairwell of falling water and the plaza above.

“Later,” she replies. “I’m starving.”

He consoles himself that the overlook will still be there after dinner, or maybe next weekend if necessary. Then Kristin walks him to the front door like she’s a tour guide. “The face is by Jaume Plensa, a renowned Spanish artist,” she says, repeating what Nate already read on the plaque. “The red reeds are made from glass by Dale Chihuly, an American artist, and acquired by the museum in 2013.” She tells him the history of the sculpture gardens and that the water pond is intended to create a feeling of peace. She goes on to explain that the museum was established during the great depression, “to demonstrate faith in the future during the depths of despair.” This building is new, opened in 2010.

She is not uninteresting but the tour-guide monologue soon becomes tedious. Kristin offers no opportunity to greet her or ask her any questions. He can’t ask where she lives, where she’s from or what she does for a living – or even what artwork she likes and why she likes it. When they reach the front door she points to ink drawings of water lilies by Van Gogh and starts to recite information that he can read for himself on the accompanying plaque.

Unable to stand it anymore he dares to interrupt the monologue. “Why did Van Gogh become a painter?” he inquires.

She seems perplexed by the question.

“Because he didn’t have an ear for music.”

First she looks simply puzzled, then she replies tersely. “That joke’s not very sensitive to people with disabilities.”

Now it’s Nate’s turn to consider carefully before he answers. He wants to say, “I didn’t hear it that way.” He settles for “Sorry,” then points to a nearby glass sculpture that looks like the red reeds in the lilies outside. “Look at that one.”

Press Release.
For more information contact:
Ramona McNamara (757) 573-0124
Elena Perez (804) 555-0115
Catherine Campbell (804) 555-0191

UCW Calls on Mayor Jefferson to Stop Subsidizing Pac-Shoppe
Mayor and Pac-Shoppe have Both Broken Promises

RICHMOND. Today the United Commercial Workers Local 429 called on Mayor Bill Jefferson to stop subsidizing Pac-Shoppe until it agrees to pay its workers a living wage. In the past three years, Pac-Shoppe has received $2.5 million in property tax abatements, $1.4 million in tax increment financing and $600,000 in Enterprise Zone Financing, totaling $4.5 million paid by Richmond city taxpayers.

UCW erected a scale in front of City Hall. One side of the scale holds stacks of bricks painted gold, representing $4.5 million in public subsidies. The other side is empty, representing promises made by Pac-Shoppe and Mayor Jefferson for good jobs in return.

Paul Spaft, who served two tours of duty in Iraq, roundly condemns the public subsidy payments. “When Iraq funnels government money to friends in industry we call it corruption. Here we call it economic development. This is the very definition of something for nothing.”

Elena Perez who works at Pac-Shoppe talks about the effect of poverty wages. “I already have two jobs,” she says. “My husband was injured on his job so he can’t work for a while. An extra forty cents an hour might not sound like a lot but it would make a big difference for me and my family.”

Mayor Bill Jefferson strongly supports the subsidies. He championed them against resistance in the City Council when they were first enacted. "It's an investment," he said at the time. "It costs money up front but it will more than pay for itself in the future."

Yet analysis of Pac-Shoppe tax payments by Citizens for Tax Justice, an independent non-profit research institute, reveals that Pac-Shoppe paid zero tax in any of the past three years.

Confronted by such criticism in the past, the Mayor Jefferson has said that Pac-Shoppe workers still pay personal income taxes and they spend their earnings in the area, more than recovering the cost of the subsidy. However, most Pac-Shoppe workers are paid so little many qualify for Earned Income Tax Credit, Medicaid and often food stamps — so the government is subsidizing Pac-Shoppe's low pay at both ends.

Catherine Campbell of UCW called on the City of Richmond to stop the payments immediately. "All Pac-Shoppe workers want is a living wage, a decent home for their families, and a union to help them achieve it. Mayor Jefferson needs to show whose side he's on."

Sources: Good Jobs First (link), Citizens for Tax Justice (link)

Nate *Too Cold or Not Too Cold*

The interior atrium of the Virginia Museum of Fine Arts is sunny and spacious, the length and height of the building, criss-crossed with skyways and stairways that connect wings dedicated to American art, European art, and pre-Columbian art of the Americas. Kristin guides them with laser focus toward the Amuse Restaurant and Café, visible on the third floor in the rear. A sculpture of a leaping rabbit bounds from a post beside its door.

"Would you like to be seated inside or on the porch?" asks the maître d' as they arrive.

Amuse is a tidy boutique restaurant with high ceilings, spherical hanging lamps and colorful abstract artwork on the walls. Through glass doors Nate can see tables on a porch overlooking Chloe's lawn.

He says to Kristin, "The porch looks nice."

She says to Nate, "It will be too cold later." To the maître d' she says, "Inside."

They are escorted to a table for two, a glazed black tabletop with comfortable gray chairs. Each place is set with an orange napkin and a ceramic plate that looks like it came from the pre-Columbian exhibition, with geometric shapes painted in Earth tones. Two yellow daffodils in a tall slender vase mark the center of the table.

Nate considers the menu fabulous but somehow beyond him. Slow roasted duck breast. Pulled pork croquettes. Chestnut polenta. He flashes back to dates with Rose, eating hotdogs on the third base line of minor league baseball games, so close they could hear the footsteps of players running for home. Both tickets together cost less than lobster thermidor here at the Amuse café.

"Do you come here often?" he asks Kristin, attempting conversation. "I will happily accept recommendations on the menu."

"It's my first choice for dates," she replies.

Nate's happy that she doesn't specify a number and he doesn't follow up. Ethan did suggest that she's dating pretty hard. Instead he changes the subject. "Ethan said you just moved here. Where from?"

That gets her going. She explains that she moved from Chapel Hill after "finally ditching a dead-end boyfriend," and she's eager to start over in Ethan's design firm.

"What do you do in Ethan's firm?" Nate asks.

"I do the fun parts. The parts with colors and carpets, the parts where we make it pretty."

"What does Ethan do?"

"Ethan does the architecture stuff. He designs the space. He calculates angles and makes sure it doesn't fall down. I hate that part. Numbers! Yuck!"

"You don't like numbers?"

"Hate them! Ever since grade school. Numbers always give me the wrong answer."

"Maybe you aren't asking them nicely."

Fortunately, the waitress comes by at that moment to take their orders. Kristin orders the duck and a glass of white wine, with the "local greens salad" to start. Nate opts for a chicken dish because he likes the sound of the "rosemary garlic fingerling potatoes" on the side, which sound like French fries dressed up for dinner. He would have skipped the appetizer at $9 per plate but he, too, orders the salad so he doesn't throw off their timing. "Just water to drink" he adds.

"Sparkling or flat?" the waiter needs to know.

"Tap water," says Nate. He and Kristin haven't established who's paying, but he guesses they'll cut it in half, which means he's subsidizing her wine. He doesn't need to stack up the total.

They sit there silently for a while, neither of them starting the conversation. Then Kristin brings them back to where they are. "Look around. What do you see?"

"A pretty little restaurant," Nate replies, not knowing where she's going, hoping that's the right answer.

"Exactly!" she declares.

Thanks goodness. He got it right. No secret Shaolin allusions.

"Start with the windows," Kristin declares. "They look like large rectangular windows and a sliding glass door."

"That seems right." Nate is still hedging his bets.

"Now notice how the rectangular windows contrast with the round columns that support the ceiling." She pauses for him to look around, and when he turns back she continues. "Now notice how the round columns relate to the spherical light fixtures." She gestures up to lights and across to the columns in one fluid motion. "See how it all works together?"

Now that she points it out, he does. He says so.

"Now for the *piece de resistance.* Notice how the side walls are white but the back wall – opposite the windows – is tinged with pink.

"I see."

"The windows face west. The setting sun is spectacular. Half an hour from now that back wall will pick up the pink from the sunset." She is points to the wall like it's about to hit a home run. "That little tinge pushes it over the top. It will be glorious."

Nate wants to say, *It's a shame we're not sitting outside.* Instead he says, "And an interior decorator made that happen."

"Nothing is coincidence. Every wall could have been painted a different color. Every lighting fixture is a choice from a catalog."

"Interesting," he says.

"That's why I took this job. I get to do the fun part of interior design. I get to play with colors, textures and shapes to make people happy."

"Congratulations," Nate responds. Her enthusiasm almost has him caring about lighting fixtures.

"A job needs to be morally meaningful," she continues. "Some people find meaning by doing social work, or by teaching children or helping the homeless. I make people happy through interior design. It's just the same! I find joy by spreading joy." She declares it like a moral triumph over grift and sloth.

Nate is happy to learn about design and not unwilling to share her enthusiasm for it, but positioning herself with

Mother Theresa seems excessive. It also makes him worry about how to describe his job when the time comes. She hasn't asked yet – maybe Ethan briefed her in advance – but he's trying to figure out how his work means anything to anybody, including himself. Moral meaning in work? Her moral imagination plus the price of dinner takes him someplace else entirely. He asks, "Does your firm by chance have photographs of dams and bridges on the walls? Are there pictures of things they've built?"

She looks at him like he's asking about colonies on Mars. "No nothing like that," she replies. "We don't do dams or bridges, and pictures never do justice anyway." She gestures around the room as if she's exhibiting dimensions beyond photography. "Why do you ask?"

"A kid who cleans my office was mentioning an architecture firm with dams and bridges."

"Kids clean your office?"

"His mom, actually. Sometimes her son substitutes for a grown-up on the team. He said the next office they clean has dams and bridges on the walls. Pictures, I mean." He looks around the Amuse Café but sees only abstract art with ambiguous swirls and curves. Searching for common ground he asks, "Does a cleaning crew come to clean your office after hours?"

"Of course. But I don't actually *talk* to them. Do you?" Again she looks at Nate like he's speaking Martian.

He tries to make it sound as normal as it has now become. "This kid is a teenager. He's in high school. His mom works like three jobs just to put food on the table." Maybe Nate's overstating the number of jobs, though probably not the number of hours. "Dad works, too," he adds, to cut off any accusations. "A dinner like this probably costs more than they make in a day."

"They're only cleaners! Of course they can't afford a place like this."

"Or hardly anyplace else."

"Are you suggesting they should be paid more?"

"Why not?"

"Okay, guys," says Catherine. "This will be the mother of all actions."

The central meeting room at UCW Local 429 is filled to capacity. If the fire marshal were to come tonight, they could be in trouble. Tonight along with the activist core are Pac-Shoppe employees with a wide range of commitment plus diverse representation from the wider community. Ramona McNamara has been throwing verbal firebombs all evening. Paul Spaft is wearing combat fatigues. Father John O'Connell, standing wordlessly near the front, signals his blessing with the silent presence of his clerical collar.

"Pac-Shoppe puts profits over people," says Ramona.

The crowd cheers its agreement.

"I think we have the logistics down," Catherine declares. "Now for the hard part."

She pauses for people to appreciate her sarcasm because the logistics have been impossibly hard already. This action is designed to bring their opponents to the table, or at least prove that the campaign is not backing down. This action will show both Pac-Shoppe and Mayor Jefferson what it will cost them to win. More than they are willing to pay, Catherine hopes.

"First, we need two teams," she says. "Who here wants a raise?"

Everyone hollers affirmation.

"Who here wants a union?"

Catherine is thrilled that affirmation for the union is even louder than for the raise. Crystal Steele, standing in the back, raises her baby high over her head, spinning him around for all to see. It's great that Crystal was able to make it tonight.

"Who here is willing to go to jail?"

Crystal brings her baby back to her chest. Many people look at their feet, but a smaller number shouts louder than ever.

"You're team number one," Catherine declares. "You're the *arrestables*. You can give your team a new name if you want, but you're the people who are willing to take an arrest. Thank you for your commitment."

Again the room breaks out in affirmation, supporting Catherine, supporting the cause, supporting those who are willing to risk an arrest. Before they came here tonight they knew where this was heading, the decision they would be called to make.

"As you know, this will get messy," Catherine continues. "The police have been tolerant so far but we are poking the bear. We don't know what it will do." Catherine sees David "Cheeky" Lerner tugging on his mother's arm. She can imagine what they've been arguing about, which team his mom is keeping him off. "The police might bring us tea and cupcakes ... but they might taser us into handcuffs and haul us off to jail. We must be ready for anything."

Someone yells from the side, "Bring it on!"

"Thank you," Catherine replies, turning in the direction of the voice. "We need you."

"Those who are *not* willing to risk an arrest, you are doing nothing wrong. You don't need to explain yourself or justify yourself in any way. You might have family responsibilities—" she looks directly at Crystal in the back with her baby. "Or it might be your prior record, your citizenship status, your health, or just plain nerves. It's all okay and it's your business alone. Don't worry. We love you just as much. We need you just as much.

"We need you watching the arrest, filming the arrest, and filming the police. Most importantly, we need you to fill the crowd. We need you waving banners, shouting slogans and showing support. We want *all* of you, we want *more* of you, and we want you to bring your friends."

Ramona yells, "No justice, no peace!" and the crowd takes up the chant. "*No justice, no peace!*" reverberates through the room.

Catherine lets it fly for a while before bringing them back to business. "Those who are willing to take an arrest, please come to this side of the room." She points to a wall where two women and a man with notebooks have been standing all evening.

"These are lawyers from the National Lawyers' Guild. They've promised to help us legally. I want everyone to know that whatever happens you will have the highest quality lawyers on your side, at no cost to you personally. UCW and the National Lawyers' Guild will do anything and everything to keep all of us safe. The Guild lawyers will discuss the downside risks and what to expect. Later you can let us know what you plan to do.

"Folks who aren't willing to risk an arrest, come to this side and talk to me. And just remember, the arrests mean nothing without our side of the room. They might be the heroes who are willing to go to jail ... but our crowd will turn their sacrifice from lawbreaking into a movement for change."

As the room reorganizes itself into teams, Catherine pulls Crystal to the side. "Does your baby have twenty minutes left in him? Join me over here, and let's turn up the heat."

"Sure," says Kristin. "The cleaning crew could be paid more. But money isn't free, you know. Where would it come from?"

"Loads of places," Nate replies. "From the company who hires them, from the building that hires the company, from the people who rent the space. Between them there's a lot of money floating around."

"Or from us," she responds. "Ultimately that cost gets passed to our employers, which means less money for us."

The waitress comes by with their salads, elegant little bowls of red leaf lettuce with almond slivers, orange slices and what looks like watercress. "Dressing is on the side," she explains. The bowls are wooden and somehow make Nate think of little boats floating outside in Chloe's lily pond.

"Our side might end up paying," Nate says to Kristin. "But why do you assume the payment comes from worker bees like us? Why not from our bosses? Or from profits or shareholders or whatever? There's plenty of money in the system. The question is who gets it." Nate starts to wonder if this is him talking, or Catherine Campbell? "Whether the employee is at our professional level or the cleaners' bottom-most level, we are only one part of the cost structure. Cuts can come from elsewhere, too. Why not from higher up?"

Now the waitress comes by to refresh their water and offer Kristin more wine. Her acceptance of a second glass infuriates Nate even more. Does she assume he's paying for this? If so, then by Kristin's own reasoning the money that's buying her wine could just as easily have gone to Emilio's mom. Or the people who clean Kristin's office at night. Or the secretaries. Nate finds her assumptions so disagreeable he digs in on the other side. "What if we hold the line and our bosses take the cut?"

He's speaking Martian yet still she fights back. "It's a fantasy," she says. "Everybody wants the money. You want the money. Your boss wants the money. The kid cleaning crew wants the money. Everyone can't have more. Somebody has to get less."

The ghost of his former self makes an appearance. "I guess the cleaners could go back to school," he suggests. "Get a better job."

"Exactly."

But he finds himself unconvincing. "Who pays for school?" he inquires.

"They can take out a loan. They can take another job."

"Who will lend it to them? How can they add more work to a sixteen hour work day?" He's thinking out loud as much as he's arguing.

Kristin shows no such loss in confidence. "People do it all the time," she declares. "People lift themselves up by their bootstraps, work hard to get ahead ... all that stuff. It's the American Dream. People have been doing it for generations."

"A generation ago wages rose faster than the cost of living. Now it's the other way around. Costs rise faster than wages. By a lot."

"Look, I said I don't do numbers. I just know that I work my tail off. If the cleaning crew wants a better dinner then they can get a better job. I can't keep everybody happy, you know." She closes with a scowl.

Nate decides to give up. "If you can keep yourself happy and your design clients happy, I guess that's enough," he concedes. "In fact, you're doing pretty good."

"Now you're talking," she says with a smile.

He scores more points by noticing that the sun is coming down, and turning to appreciate the color on the wall behind. Magnificent would be an overstatement but it's pretty for sure. Does the pink paint in the wall enhance the pink in the sky ... or is that cheating? He doesn't ask.

Nate's chicken is very good, especially the French fries. He's happy that both of them decline coffee and dessert, which he can't help but judge on Emilio's pay scale. When the moment comes, he accepts Kristin's suggestion to split the check.

Nate realizes as soon as he steps outside afterward that it's perfectly warm. A person sitting on the porch wouldn't even need a sweater. Not until he's halfway home does he realize that neither of them even mentioned a second date.

The next morning Elena catches Catherine on the telephone. "I'm sorry I couldn't make it last night," she says.

"Heavens!" Catherine replies. "You're doing more than enough. What's going on?"

"It's Ricardo."

"Is he okay?" Catherine worries that Elena's husband has lost his vision permanently. What if Ricardo has seen the doctor, failed some tests or given up hope? Then she realizes it could be worse. He could have fallen down, been hit by a car or suffered some new catastrophic accident. He could be crippled or injured or dead. "Oh my God," Catherine says out loud. She didn't mean to.

Elena seems to know what Catherine is thinking and rushes to comfort her. "It's not that," Elena says, and starts to cry.

Above all else, Catherine wishes she could see her. She wants to hold Elena's hand or wrap an arm around her shoulder. She just listens to Elena crying by herself on the other end of the telephone line. But why did she call? A few times Catherine tries to insert a question and decides simply to wait.

At last Elena continues. "I don't know what to do."

"What happened?" Catherine replies. "What changed?"

"We saw the lawyer. That's what happened."

Something's gone wrong. The lawyer was supposed to vindicate the accident that wasn't Ricardo's fault. Elena starts weeping again, and Catherine has no choice but to wait.

When Elena speaks again her voice is gentle and reassuring, saccharine sweet. "Remember how good the company was to us? Remember how they kept Ricardo on the health plan? Remember we thought they were being nice?" Catherine hears Elena mocking herself with her dulcet tones, hears a trap being laid. "The company paid some wages and helped apply for workers compensation. The company sped us along so the workers compensation came quickly. They got us workers comp nice and fast."

As Elena talks about speed Catherine senses a wall ahead.

"The lawyer said that as soon as we cashed the check for workers compensation we gave up any and all other claims for money damages," Elena declares. "That's how the lawyer says it. *Any and all other claims.*"

Catherine is starting to understand. It all makes sense. She wishes she'd figured this out herself.

"It has to be one or the other," Elena continues. "Workers comp, or a lawsuit. Not both. That's what the lawyer said. As soon as you accept the workers comp you 'forfeit your right of action' against the company. Those are the legal words. That's why the company helped us so much. The company got us paid before we learned what happened. Before we found a lawyer." By now her tears are turning into anger. "Before we knew."

It all fits together. Of course the company wasn't nice. The company is never nice. It's Ricardo's first major injury but not the company's. They've done this before. They know the drill.

"I don't know what to do," Elena says.

Again Catherine wants to hug her close and reassure her. She wants to tell her friend and partner that everything is going to be okay.

But it's not. Everything isn't going to be okay. Catherine can't lie and won't make promises based on dreams. She has no choice but to put her head down and say what she's been saying a lot lately. "I don't know, either."

FOUR

Nate *Sun and Clouds*

Catherine asks Nate quietly and politely, "I assume you want to remain anonymous? I doubt anyone here knows you, and you might prefer to keep it that way."

They are in her office, the UCW headquarters in a low-rent part of town. Catherine agreed to meet as soon as Nate said he had something for her. But he didn't want to say what it was over the phone and she seemed too busy to drive across town on a guess – so he came to her.

As soon as he arrives he understands why she didn't want to drive across town without good reason. The office is filled with people intensely focused and obviously on deadline. Some people hunch over laptops while others confer in small groups or stride purposefully from one room to another. A map of the city covers one wall, with routes sketched out in colors and post-it notes at intersections where color lines cross. The adjacent wall is racked with paint, poster boards and art supplies lined up neatly in rows. Nate can't tell what's afoot but it's big and it's complicated.

Catherine turns him around as soon as he arrives.

"What's going on?" he asks as she all but pushes him out the door, back into the parking lot. Maybe it's her own secret and she's protecting information in more than one direction.

"We're planning for tomorrow," she says. "I can give you a tour if you're curious. I like to think you'll see it on the news. Otherwise it will be easier for everyone if we talk out here." She stops him in an empty space between two blue minivans. "How's this?"

"Perfect," he replies. It's getting warm, but with a light breeze and thin cloud cover that makes it bright but not sunny. Nobody is in view and nobody seems to be paying attention to him.

"You said you have something?" Clearly, Catherine doesn't have time for good morning.

"I went ahead and looked," Nate replies, following her focus on business. It seems unwise to linger with her, whether indoors or in the parking lot, and eventually he'll be missed in his own office. "I can't believe I did it. I checked Pac-Shoppe records for Theresa Staedtler. I looked for variations of 'ultimate' and 'UES,' just like you said. At first I was just curious, but then ..."

"... but then you found something." She finishes his thought. "Thank you. Truly. I understand that just looking was no small thing. Telling me is even more. I appreciate what you're doing. I really do."

She seems sincere, and Nate appreciates her appreciation. "I found a letter," he says.

He already had her full attention but the letter doubles it. It's like he claimed to hold the winning lottery ticket. Nate sees optimism mixed with skepticism, like she wants to believe him but doesn't want to raise her hopes prematurely.

"And I found checks," he continues. "Just like you said. They are in odd amounts with eccentric timing. Payments were to *Ultimate Efficacy* and *Ultimate Engagement.*"

Catherine permits herself a low whistle. Optimism is winning. "For how much?" she asks.

"Roughly $20,000 each."

"What do you have? Copies of the checks?"

Nate shakes his head. Neither checks nor check copies are in his system, just the record of them. He doesn't even know where the checks would be. "I have a letter," he says again.

He pulls his telephone from his pocket before she can ask. It only takes a moment to log on and find the image. He passes her the phone. The sun is perfect for viewing.

Catherine is silent. She looks quickly at the screen, showing no hesitancy with someone else's phone, rotating it to look from different angles. She uses her fingertips to zoom in and zoom out, studying with increasing attention and care until there is an almost physical bond between her eyes and the screen. "This is worth its weight in gold."

"It's digital. It doesn't weigh anything." He immediately regrets saying it. Why pretend to be clever and modest? Why can't he simply accept her congratulations? Twenty years in prison doesn't weigh anything, either.

Catherine blows right past his humility. "The key is the date," she explains. She zooms in and shows him the date at the top of the letter. "April 12 is the date Pac-Shoppe committed to 'working together,'" she declares. "April 13 is the day strangers started threatening our workers at night. April 14 is when hooligans started to visit the Pac-Shoppe parking lot between shifts, when our workers were coming and going. May 6 is when the firing started."

Nate thought the key was the signature that shows Pac-Shoppe's vice president of operations confirming his intent to "work together" with union-buster Theresa Staedtler. But Catherine keeps her eye on the date.

"This letter defines the chronology," she explains.

Now Nate understands. "Pac-Shoppe signed this letter ... and then bad things started to happen."

"The very next day," she agrees. "This letter supports our charges of unfair labor practices orchestrated by Pac-Shoppe. This letter gives our lawyers the good faith belief they need to file a TRO – a temporary restraining order – against further dealings with Theresa Staedtler. Pac-Shoppe will challenge the TRO, of course, but their challenge will entitle us to discovery we can use to get the original letter, the checks, and everything else."

Nate has the winning lottery ticket, after all.

"Everything follows from that good faith belief," Catherine proclaims. "Pac-Shoppe can accept a TRO and be held in contempt if they violate its terms ... or they can challenge its issuance. But even a challenge is good for us. As litigation stretches on we'll get information in discovery that we can't get any other way. And we'll have a judge looking over their shoulder for unfair labor practices."

Nate can barely follow what she's saying but he sees her mapping a chess match ten moves ahead. "This letter is pivotal," Catherine concludes. "Thank you so much for this."

"I guess you're welcome," says Nate. Will he lose his job, his license and his self-respect? At least it wasn't for nothing.

"Do you have the original letter?" She waves the digital image in the air. "How can this be shared?"

"That's all I have. An electronic copy. I can email it to you."

"No!" she cries, like he's about to step into traffic. "Email creates trails that lead back to you and your phone. You don't want trouble like that."

Nate nods his head in agreement.

"Come on in. We'll plug in your phone and drag the files onto one of our computers. We'll take a picture of your picture and anonymize it completely." Then she looks up like she sees more traffic coming from a different direction.

"Is this your personal phone?" she asks. "Or is this a company phone."

"It's a company phone."

Catherine looks worried. The traffic is upon them. "When did you take this picture? How often do they back up?"

"I don't know." Nate doesn't like where this is going. Suddenly he's thinking differently about the free phone he casually accepted when it came his way.

She starts clicking and scrolling around the phone again. Nate sees her in the settings menu but can't track what she's trying to do. She understands the inner workings far better than he does. "This is bad," she says at last.

"What?" He is feeling sick to his stomach.

Catherine shows him the screen as she explains what it says. "Photos taken on your phone are automatically uploaded to the cloud. They go into your company's data account, which is backed up every night." She puts the phone back in his hand. "Please tell me you took this photo this morning." She is worried like a mother wondering whether her daughter drank the fresh lemonade or the poisoned lemonade intended for her husband.

Nate stares into the dirt. "It's been a week," he says. "More than that." All that time when he was waiting, wondering, and cautiously stewing over what to do. That's the time that killed him.

If he didn't know how bad it was, Catherine's expression would have told him. Her daughter drank the poison lemonade. "Let's delete the photo, then delete it from the trash," she says. "That's the best we can do. I'm sorry. Your company's photo archives will show that you took this picture. It's a long away around ... but you're trackable."

Catherine feels terrible but never changes her stride. She walks into her office with Nate's phone still in her hand, and plugs it into the computer with her own cord. The closest they come to reconsideration is Catherine's declaratory, "You're okay with this?" during the few seconds it takes for the file to move.

Nate nods noncommittally. Catherine interprets it as consent. The rock is rolling down the hill. Strength and determination would be needed to turn it around.

Her only hesitation is in actually deleting the file from his phone. Might deletion suggest a guilty conscience, like he is purposefully hiding something? Does it foreclose the possibility of someday claiming it was an accident? But momentum carries her right past this small and unlikely calculation. She deletes the file according to plan and gives Nate his phone back.

"Thank you again," she says. "This will help hundreds of people. Maybe more."

He nods affirmation and puts the phone in his pocket.

"Do you want to look around? I can show you how we operate."

He shakes his head like he's lost all interest.

"Thank you again."

"I need to get back to the office."

She walks him past the campaign bustle to the door. "Hey!" she calls after he's stepped outside.

But he doesn't turn around. Mentally he's already left or else he can't hear her over the noise of a car pulling in. But Catherine feels a moment of guilt. She hoped for some help. She hoped for a tip or two, a rug to look under, or a rumor she could chase down for herself. She didn't intend to end Nate's career or get him indicted.

He deserves far more than a causal thank you. She would hug him – if he let her – and offer "I'm sorry" from the bottom of her heart. She's been saying that a lot lately but this time at least something good can come from it. Catherine deeply appreciates what he's done and will make sure it's used to the fullest extent. His risk deserves nothing less.

Above all else, she feels bad. Is this sweet, gentle Nathaniel Hawley more collateral damage in her quest for justice? Catherine hopes not. She underestimated him. She's been underestimating him since eleventh grade. This was far more than holding a door open. Nate just did more for her cause than she could reasonably have asked. If she hasn't killed him, she could learn to like this guy.

Nate *Watching and Waiting*

Sitting in his car, before he starts the engine, Nate takes his phone out of his pocket and simply stares at it. He doesn't even turn it on. He just looks at it in disbelief, like it's a pet that bit him. His telephone was a fun toy that moved from affordable to free when his company was acquired. But what else can it do? What else is it doing to him?

Is Fitzgerald Financials reading his emails to his mother? Does Mr. Daniels know that Kristin Cooper invited him to a first date but not a second? His life isn't that scandalous but it might be embarrassing. Does his phone have a location tracker that knows he just went to the UCW headquarters? Is he suddenly scandalous after all?

Nate fears he is only beginning to imagine the possibilities. As he drives back to the office he wonders what settings are fixed and what he can change. But how would he learn how? And would they know he's done it?

Only now he realizes he could ask Catherine Campbell to delete the file he just gave her. Kill the information and hope it goes away. If the letter isn't used against Pac-Shoppe in court, nobody will ever wonder who else has seen it or where they got it. As Catherine said, it's a long way from a TRO filed by UCW against Pac-Shoppe to an accountant at Fitzgerald Financials. Who would ever look for those tracks? Why would they bother?

But it's done. The ship has sailed. The photo has been taken and its presence registered. Nothing can take that back. Even if Catherine might have agreed, that conversation has closed as well. Nate can't call her back and ask her to pretend it never happened. She gets her prize, and he gets his ... well, he'll find out.

He turns Rose's cool jazz back on and listens to easy melodies while he drives back to the office. The traffic is easy and the lights are green. By the time he arrives he's convinced himself that he'll be okay.

He even checks the Pac-Shoppe stock price. It's stopped falling. It's even a hair up today. Maybe he bought at the perfect rock bottom after all.

Catherine *Drinking Problems*

Today is the day they lay it all on the line. Either this brings Pac-Shoppe to the table or Catherine needs to admit that it can't be done.

Pac-Shoppe can't know that, obviously. Pac-Shoppe needs to think this is merely the campaign's next step and to worry what more might be coming.

Of course it's hot. Richmond always turns hot in May, but today might break the record. Catherine worries that her walkers will have all the water they need and whether any pedestrians will be on the streets to see their show at all – or whether everyone will be hunkered inside with air conditioning. She worries whether the news will even notice them, or maybe it will be all personal interest stories about the weather. Kids playing in sprinklers. A dog locked in a car.

Catherine is in the parking lot at UCW with a crowd far exceeding what any Fire Marshall would allow. She rented porta-potties for the day and asked her neighbors if her people could overflow into their lots. The campaign will be shuttling people around town all day in an array of private cars, church vans and a decommissioned school bus.

"Good morning!" she calls to the crowd. Hundreds of people wearing red and carrying banners look back at her. Catherine sees familiar faces from Pac-Shoppe, including employees and family members. She sees Father John O'Connell backed by two vans of followers from his church. She sees Annie Burke from Harmon's ministry, hair tied up in her old-school bun, with more minions of her own, though she doesn't see Harmon. Catherine sees UCW members from other UCW locals in the region and a constellation of brother and sister unions who have answered the call to support prospective members and better wages for everybody. She sees students from VCU whose black and gold stands out in the sea of red, a deliberate show of both separate identity and solidarity with the cause.

Lawyers and interns from the National Lawyers' Guild are sprinkled through the crowd, wearing distinctive yellow baseball caps, identifying them as lawyers or witnesses for those who know the code.

Best of all, Catherine sees people she's never seen before. The parking lot is filled with people wearing caps from the animal clubs, the Moose Lodge and the Elks. The campaign's networks have spread through their networks to bring in people whose purpose is purely to support the cause. A living wage. Justice for the poor and powerless.

She is standing on a makeshift stage created from old wooden pallets with a sound system rigged up by workers from Communications Workers of America Local 2201, which is always up for a fight.

"Are you ready?" Catherine shouts.

People erupt with applause and cheers, with the occasional "Yes!" or "Ready!" rising above the din.

"Want to have some fun?"

That gets more applause and generous chuckles. She sees Loren Ibsen smiling like he's ready for anything. Usually Loren makes himself invisible in the crowd or skulks separately around the edges. Today he stands near the front with Catherine, like a security officer, distant enough to be inconspicuous but on hand should need arise.

She reviews the plan for the day, emphasizing the need to spread out so more people see them. They want the density that looks like a crowd and the range that makes them look like they're everywhere. "Know your routes and follow your captains," Catherine says.

Loren chimes in from the sideline, "And mess up the police!" which gets him some laughs of his own.

Catherine uses his invitation to turn her attention to one wing of the crowd, dressed more modestly, without red, slogans or visible banner of any kind. "You all are the arrestables"? she inquires.

They nod and applaud in affirmation. Now she sees Harmon Wright, the Methodist minister, among the arrestables. She didn't realize he volunteered for that.

The mood among the arrestables is notably different. More somber and serious, they are soldiers on their way to battle not fans outside the concert hall. Their sobriety gives them power.

“As you know we will be marching in an orderly fashion with permits issued by the police. But we will also be pushing boundaries into civil disobedience. We intend to provoke. We don’t know how the police will react. I trust you’re all set, and ready for anything.”

The crowd murmurs affirmation. A few people applaud.

“The National Lawyer’s Guild should have everyone’s information. Most important are your emergency contacts. If you’re arrested, Guild staff will call them. Your family will know why you aren’t home for dinner. Your boss can be alerted before you don’t show up for work.

“Second is bail information. The Guild should know your ties to the community – your home address, your local family and where you work. Everything the judge will use in deciding whether you can be released pending trial. The more we know the easier it will be to get you released. It will also speed things up. If we are a crowd, hopefully the judge will agree to hear us all together at the front of the line.”

Catherine sees Guild lawyer Annette Wilcox stepping to the front while fumbling to turn on her handheld megaphone. Catherine gestures for her to come onto the stage and use the microphone. Once Anette is set up she turns her attention to the arrestables. “A point of personal privilege, if I may?”

Catherine gestures for her to continue.

“This is none of my business and it’s kind of personal,” Annette says, like she’s testing both the microphone and the limits of propriety. “It’s hot today. Has anybody noticed?”

The crowd signals appreciation. The arrestables are paying particular attention. “If you are arrested – and again you might not be – but if you are arrested you will likely be placed into police vans for transport for booking.”

Surely, they know this but everyone is listening. “The police might drive the van straight to processing, quick and easy. Or they might leave you in the van all afternoon ... just to teach you a lesson. They might run the air conditioning because it’s hot. Or they might *not* run the air conditioning ... because it’s hot. Windows will be locked shut so the van turns into an oven. The police will have total control. They’ll keep busy with something else while you wait, wonder and roast.”

Some people start to look uneasy. Theoretical heroism is running into real world nervousness.

"Now the personal part," says Annette. "You might choose to be well hydrated. It's wise to drink a lot ... because of the heat. Drink all day, starting now. But know that the van does not have a bathroom. Nor can you expect the police to release you to use one." She pauses to be sure everyone understands the implications. People start looking at each other, left and right, as if to see what each other is thinking.

"I leave it to you and your bladder how you choose to manage your hydration. Drink well and be hydrated. Or drink minimally so you won't need a bathroom. We probably won't be able to help." She passes the microphone back to Catherine.

"Thank you, Annette" Catherine says. To the crowd of arrestables she says, "If anyone wants to change your mind, we have plenty of room in the crowd. If you're still willing to risk the arrest, know that we are with you and your bladder ... whatever you decide."

A voice calls from the middle of the arrestables, "I'm in!"

Another voice echoes, louder. "I'm in, too!"

Harmon Wright of the Calvary United Methodist Church calls out, "Christ on the cross didn't take bathroom breaks!"

"Shall we do it, then?" Catherine cries to the crowd.

The cheers are fearsome and humbling. People raise their banners and shout their support. Someone starts clapping in a rhythmic beat, and soon everyone is stomping and clapping in unison. Catherine is as excited by the uproar as everyone else. She can't wait for this to begin.

Loren Ibsen cries over the tumult, "Let's go put the F in union."

Nate *In and Out*

Nate catches Mr. Daniels while he's making a cup of coffee in the morning. "Why don't we just give them a raise?" Nate asks. "As you say, it's trivial money. Why not just give them a raise and be done with it?"

Nate's not really a coffee drinker, but he makes a cup now because it gives him an excuse to extend the conversation. Later he can drink it or not.

"They want two things," Mr. Daniels replies. "A union and a raise. A raise might be fine but unions can be pretty damn annoying. Union rules will slow down a workplace worse than a raise ever does."

Nate hadn't really thought of that. He's never really worked with unions but the mythology is forbidding. Catherine never mentioned that.

"Second, we're not in it for the long haul. It doesn't matter to us how Pac-Shoppe labor costs change or whether it makes money in the long run."

That's puzzling. "I thought we were in it for the money," Nate replies. "We're investors looking for a return." He rests his coffee cup on the countertop beside him to suggest that he's not in a hurry.

Mr. Daniels accepts the invitation. "Our theory is that next week the stock price will rebound. Maybe because the union gave up and went home. Or maybe because they signed a contract and resumed normal operations. We don't care either way. As soon as the stock price returns we're outta here."

"Oh." Nate hopes he doesn't sound as innocent and naïve as he fears.

"On a different day we might come in just to break a union, sell off a few properties or slash the research budget. If Wall Street likes the short-term look, our work is done. We sell on the spike and we're outta there!" He says it like he won a baseball game on a triple. "Once I bought ten percent of a firm. Then I borrowed money against the workers' pension fund, used the money to buy another twenty percent, and used the high debt payments to force cuts in the pension benefits. When the stock price soared on the cuts I sold the whole thing. I made a mint! Or at least the firm did. Nowadays I, myself, am closer to the gold."

Mr. Daniels must see how uncomfortable Nate feels because he throws him a bone. "Fear not, young Grasshopper. You'll get there. You, too, shall have your turn at the meat."

Catherine *Compass Call*

"Welcome," says the mechanical voice on the other end of the line. "This service is provided by FreeConferenceCall.com. Please enter your access code followed by the pound or hash sign."

Catherine enters the digits from her calendar as she marches with a crowd of protestors toward the capitol plaza.

The mechanical voice continues, "You are the ninth caller on the line."

"Hello, everybody," Catherine says, after a few clicking sounds. "Sorry I'm late." She's wearing red and so is her crowd. Most of them are carrying banners and trying to engage passersby, but that's difficult because they're surrounded by police. Armed officers clear pedestrians from the path before them, and chase people back into stores. The adjoining street has been shut down and two police cruisers creep alongside, matching their pace while they walk.

On the phone line Catherine hears a babble of voices and the remnants of the conversation she interrupted. Even as she's getting oriented a new chime indicates that someone else has joined the call.

"Let's count off," Catherine says. "Start on the east side, team number one." She imposes order so everybody doesn't talk at once.

After a moment of silence she hears quite clearly. "This is Richard. We're on Broad Avenue. We started at Robert E. Lee. Now we're approaching first street."

"Perfect! Thank you. Right on schedule." The site of the controversial Robert E. Lee monument is almost two miles from city hall, farther than most people wanted to walk, and too far – Catherine thought – to keep a demonstration intact. But Richard's crew wanted to start with slavery and insisted they could go the distance. Catherine decided that if Richard's crew wanted the symbolism and could manage the work, she shouldn't get in the way. "Did you get any police?"

"Loads of them."

"Terrific. Team number two?"

"This is Melanie. We're on Cary Street approaching third."

"Police?"

"Plenty of 'em."

"Crowds?"

"Got them, too."

"Spirits?"

"Awesome."

"Terrific. Next?"

"This is Jaime Quinteros. We're on seventh street, approaching Canal." Catherine loses him to noise for a moment, then he comes back loud and clear. "I don't know how Richard and Melanie can have any police – because it looks to me like we have all of them."

Jaime can't hear her, but Catherine actually laughs out loud. She says, "You might need to slow down a little. You should meet Melanie at Cary Street, and she's only at third."

"I noticed that," Jaime replies. "We'll have a donut with the police. We have loads of media, too. TV, print, radio ... the whole roadshow."

"Go, team," Catherine replies. "Now let's hear from the west side, north to south. Check in. Who's where?"

Nate *Surprise, Surprise*

"Don't go downtown," Mr. Daniels warns someone who seemed to be heading out for lunch.

"What's up?" Nate hears someone say. He's at his desk pretending to work. On his screen statements of account and balance sheets appear in orderly columns. Outside in the hallway, people are talking.

"Something about the union. It's a mess."

A different voice chimes in, Mr. Daniels' secretary. "It's Pac-Shoppe again. Police are shutting down the streets."

"Which ones?" That's the first person speaking again, a junior analyst Nate doesn't know very well.

"All of them, from the sound of it. It's like spontaneous protests all over town. Each protest is marching from a different direction. They seem set to converge at City Hall. Apparently, they have a permit for that. City Hall, I mean."

"They don't have permits for the rest of it?" Mr. Daniels wants to know.

"How would I know?" his secretary replies. "I'm just telling what I hear. Don't go downtown for lunch."

Catherine *Dance Steps*

Catherine Campbell is having too much fun. Her crew has reached their permitted demonstration on the plaza of the state capitol. To one side is the state capitol building with its marble columns and grand staircase. To the other side is the old city hall with its baroque spires and intricate stonework, magnificence from a bygone era. Behind them rises the new city hall, a white rectangular skyscraper, looking like the corporate office tower that government has become.

The march brought its own band, and it is playing on the concrete plaza – guitar, bass, trumpet and drums. In front of the band people are dancing. Tents for shade dot the plaza while the campaign's crowds mill about under the hot hot sun, showcasing banners and breaking into spontaneous cheers. "Hey hey! Ho ho! Corporate welfare has got to go!" They are celebrating while the rest of the city is tied up in knots.

The police tied it up, not the campaign. Roughly an hour ago the campaign started marches from six different locations, each with its own route and its own staggered start time, all scheduled to meet at the plaza at noon. Each march had enough people to feel like a crowd but few enough that the campaign could stretch its numbers across six different routes. Each crowd marched its own route, led by captains who had practiced it many times. While people walked they shouted their slogans, displayed their banners and solicited bystanders. "Want to come to the rally at the capitol? Here's a flyer."

But everyone was careful to stay on the sidewalks and stop at red lights, even when the cross street had been closed to traffic. They had determined to be cautious, law-abiding pedestrians. They didn't want to risk a ticket, even for jaywalking.

The police chief fell for it perfectly. Within minutes of each march starting, troopers arrived to divert traffic away from its path. Squadrons were deployed in numbers that clearly didn't anticipate a new march starting fifteen minutes later.

By the time the last march started, the chief must have called every off-duty officer in the metro area, and maybe used up some favors with colleagues in neighboring towns. Without planning, one step at a time, the chief had shut down traffic throughout the city. All the campaign was doing was taking a walk.

Catherine wonders what Mayor Jefferson will say about this one. Will he give the chief another hug?

How about later when he gets the bill for police overtime?

Catherine marches on a route from the west with Stephanie and David "Cheeky" Lerner. As they arrive at the capitol plaza the crowd greets them with applause. The plaza had a base-camp protest of its own, plus three march routes that arrived ahead of Catherine and David. The band starts, "When the Saints Come Marching in" as they come into view. Catherine takes David by the hand and starts to dance.

The band is ad-hoc, made up by the incredible talent that lives all around them. Ramona had the idea of asking around for music. Some people play an instrument at home, or flirt with a garage band on the weekends. Might they play at the rally? The word went out. Sure, came the replies. The band created itself, picked the music and found time to practice. The version of "Born to Run" she heard a few minutes ago would have made Bruce Springsteen proud. Ramona wanted it festive, not angry. With the music it feels more like a birthday party than a political protest.

"Good morning, Miss Catherine," says little Maya, as she comes dancing alongside. She's wearing green shorts and a red tank top, with her hair tied up in red ponytails. Catherine suspects that her mother, Elena, helped choose her outfit.

"Good morning," says Catherine. "Hey! Shouldn't you be in school?" Catherine knows the answer, though.

"Mom and Dad said I could take the day off," Maya replies. "We walked the Seventh Street route."

"We'll call it a late May Day," says Catherine as Maya scampers off.

Catherine follows the applause to what must be the fifth team arriving, and shares in the hugs and high-fives all around. The logistics of this action were extraordinary, but the campaign managed them perfectly, a message that hopefully won't be missed by Pac-Shoppe or the city. Flying overhead are both a news helicopter and a police helicopter. Here on the plaza news crews are set up with cameras, and just ahead Catherine sees a print journalist interviewing Elena Perez, who is parked in her wheelchair in the middle of the fracas like a rock that breaks the waves at high tide. Catherine tries to catch Elena's eye, but Elena is fully focused on the journalist who's taking notes in his spiral binder.

A cohort of VCU students walks past, wearing yellow and red, carrying posters with pictures of an alarm clock that says, "Poverty Wages are Alarming."

"Thanks for coming out," Catherine says to a VCU student she's never met, a young woman carrying leaflets not a banner.

"I worked at Pac-Shoppe when I was in high school," says the student. "They paid me bean-squat. My co-workers were parents and grandparents. We were like three generations in poverty at the same time. We need to do something!"

As if to prove her point, the band begins to play "We're Not Gonna Take it!" The driving rhythm makes Catherine want to dance, and the VCU crowd goes ahead and does it. Catherine would join them but she knows this is the last song before the band turns over the stage, and she's the first speaker. She sashays her way toward the stage, stopping to swing a few steps and receive another hug from Maya. Next thing she knows she's standing on the stage looking over a crowd of people she has mostly never seen before. Plenty are from the original crew, of course. But more of them are from the expanded network or simply people who saw something was going on and followed the marchers or came out to see what was happening or show support.

Up here by the stage the campaign is giving out water and ice. On this hot day Catherine appreciates Ramona's proposal to put the water near the stage, not banished to the back as originally planned. They want the water to support their focus, not distract from it.

Catherine takes the microphone and starts with her favorite cheer. "Show me what Democracy looks like!"

The crowd thunders back, "This is what Democracy looks like!"

They go around a few times then gets to business. "Some of you wonder what unions are, and what unions do. *Now you know!*"

The Communications Workers of America who set up the stage cheer loudest of all, and even the VCU students join in. They might find poverty wages alarming, but their generation is still learning about the connection between low wages and worker organizing. Catherine congratulates everyone on the day well done and thanks people for coming out, then she does a familiar riff about how much Pac-Shoppe makes, how much its CEO makes, and how much the city pays Pac-Shoppe to keep its workers in poverty.

Catherine uses her allotted three minutes, careful to demonstrate staying on schedule, then she turns the microphone over to Dale Anderson from the Loyal Order of the Moose. The campaign planned six speakers at three minutes each with a musical intermission by the band at midpoint.

Catherine doesn't stay to listen, though. She hurries off for the masterstroke conceived by Loren Ibsen. By now the campaign looks to be happy, concluded and well-established in the central plaza. By now the police have settled into a maintenance presence here in their midst, and likely released some extra hands back to their assigned duties or their days off. By now, traffic throughout the city is returning to normal, though here by the downtown plaza traffic has been stopped and diverted away.

Catherine sidles toward the arrestables, all disguised as regular citizen participants. They are not wearing red, not carrying banners, and don't look distinctive in any way. Catherine is a lightning rod, so she can't join them at this time. She just nods farewell as they leave the plaza, heading toward the newly busy intersection at 14th and Broad Street where the police have redirected traffic to avoid the central plaza.

It's a ten minute walk. The arrestables leave in small groups by different routes, each individual having one final cup of water or not, as they wish.

Nate *Danger Danger*

Nate can't stand it anymore. He's barely even pretending to work. He's watching the news feed and getting every update he can find. Eventually he admits to himself that he's wasting time and maybe becoming dangerous. When balance sheets don't add up in the future, it will have been Nathaniel Hawley who made two plus two equal three.

He heads for the door, checking his watch as if he's going somewhere.

"I have an errand," he says. "Don't worry. I'll avoid the downtown."

Catherine *First and Second Wave*

Catherine joins the conference call as she walks down the street, though she's not involved in the logistics on this part.

"Who joined us?" Stephanie Lerner asks as Catherine chimes in.

"Catherine Campbell, UCW. I'm just curious and listening in. Don't let me slow you down."

"Come on in," Stephanie says. "Your timing is perfect. Just watch."

Catherine is approaching the intersection of Fourteenth and Broad Streets. It's generally a busy intersection, but now it's backed up in all directions, with its own traffic plus the overflow directed from the capitol plaza. Cars are lined up as far as Catherine can see, each waiting its turn at the light. A lone police cruiser is parked in front of a VCU building that happens to be at this intersection. The officer appears to be dozing in his seat.

Also strange is the pedestrian traffic. The adjacent streets are mostly empty, yet here at Fourteenth and Broad, the sidewalks on all four corners are filled with people. Why would that be?

"Counting down," says Stephanie on the telephone. "Next cycle."

Catherine knows she means the cycle of the lights. Right now, Broad Street is green and Fourteenth is red. They'll change at the cycle.

"If any arrestables are on the phone, disconnect and give your phone to a friend. From here on, you're empty handed."

At the intersection Catherine can see the "next cycle" warning being passed around, but nothing else. Hands must already be empty. They know what they're doing.

People start to move as the green light turns yellow. By the time it's red people are dashing from all four corners. During the heartbeat when both lights are red – Broad Street has stopped but Fourteenth hasn't started yet – pedestrians occupy the intersection completely. Now when the light turns green there is no place for cars to go. Fourteenth Street has the right of way but nobody can move. The cars are trapped in place.

After a moment the cars behind, who can see the green light but not the people in the intersection, start to honk. *Why aren't we moving?* they honk in frustration. Catherine watches the police officer leap out of his car. He is on his feet shouting into his radio.

The car in front creeps incrementally closer but the driver can already see the truth. There isn't enough room to pass, and the people in the middle of the intersection aren't moving to make way.

All of a sudden, the people occupying the intersection start to disrobe. Overshirts come off. Red UCW T-shirts come into view underneath. The arrestables puff out their chests and whirl the extra clothing overhead, showing off who they are and why they're here. At the same time, more people come pouring into the intersection from the sidewalks. Some of the second wave collect the extra clothing into empty tote bags. Others pass out signs and banners then hurry back to safety on the sideline.

As horns start to honk, the crowd in the middle makes its intentions clear, sitting down in a large circle. *We aren't going anywhere!* Their arms are high and their clothes are red. They raise the newly distributed signs for all to see.

"End Corporate Welfare."

"America Needs a Raise."

"Pac-Shoppe is Winning the Race to the Bottom"

By now a chorus of honking fills the air. The officer is shouting frantically into his radio but looks basically helpless. Cars are stopped in every direction, and half of them must be leaning on their horns.

The people in the intersection begin to cheer, "The people united with never be defeated!"

The people safely and legally on the sidewalks join them, chanting and unfurling banners of their own. "The people united with never be defeated!" They sing in unison. Catherine sees and hears the excitement everywhere she looks.

Overhead the news helicopter swoops so low Catherine can feel the downblast and smell the exhaust. She imagines footage being collected and beamed to newsrooms everywhere, even as reporters at the Capitol plaza are being directed out this way.

They will need to travel on foot. No way they're getting here by car.

The chants continue. "Hey hey! Ho ho! Corporate welfare has got to go!" The crowd in the center of the intersection calls and echoes with the crowd on the sidewalk. "Hey hey! Ho ho! Corporate welfare has got to go!"

Catherine stands on the sidelines to watch. She can hear some directions being said over the phone but the time for coordination is over. The most important people are off the phone anyway. They are sitting in the intersection, hands joined, blocking traffic, pockets empty of valuables, wondering what will happen next.

They didn't just poke the bear. They hit it with a sledgehammer.

Nate *Disaster Tourism*

Nate approaches the Capitol from the east, parking his car far from the plaza, long before any signs of disturbance. He figures it's maybe a fifteen minute walk down Broad street, but after five minutes he can already see something happening ahead.

News and police helicopters start circling overhead, swooping up and down, in and out as if changing views or investigating different angles. When they're high enough or far enough away to reduce their engine noise, the sound of car horns takes its place. Whatever is happening, it's producing a racket.

Nate picks up his pace, far more curious than afraid. He suspects this is UCW and Pac-Shoppe, not terrorists and bombs. He wants to see the show. He catches up to cars lined up along Broad Street, frozen in a queue even as other cars add to it from behind. A few cars up ahead tangle themselves as they U-turn or seek to escape on the cross streets. Then police squad cars power in, traveling the wrong direction on Broad street, speeding inbound on the outbound lanes, lights blazing, sirens blaring. One cruiser nearly hits a car in the middle of a U-turn.

The epicenter comes into view as Nate traverses the overpass over highway I-95. Above him, helicopters spin in circles. Below him, cars on I-95 are moving at speed. Ahead of him, at the intersection where Broad Street crosses Fourteenth, cars are stopped, backed up on both streets in both directions. Now he can see the problem. UCW protestors are in the middle of the intersection, not letting traffic move in either way. As a pedestrian he can walk straight through the frustration and din. In no time at all he's close enough to read the protest signs under the traffic lights.

"End Corporate Welfare."

"America Needs a Raise."

"Pac-Shoppe is Winning the Race to the Bottom"

He pauses like a sightseer to read the signs and appreciate the energy. People of every race and age are chanting and swirling. Between the sirens and the helicopters he can hear the cheers.

"What do we want?"

"A raise!"

"When do we want it?"

"Now!"

Then he sees her. Catherine Campbell. Of course she's in the thick of it. She's on one corner, watching the melee, talking into her telephone, hand pressed against her other ear as she tries to listen on the line.

Nate walks up to greet her. He doesn't expect much attention and doesn't want to distract her, but he wants her to see he's here.

Catherine *Then They Hatch*

Catherine surveys the chaos feeling like a demigod, lord of her domain. What was it she said to Loren Ibsen those weeks ago? *No injuries, no property damage, maximum distress.* She thinks they hit it again this time, at the cost of a few porta potties, water bottles, and a continued investment in art supplies.

It's too early to count her chickens but she feels pretty good about their risks, their calculations and above all else, their execution. More police are pouring in now, though they're mostly standing and watching, unsure what to do. Meanwhile more protestors are arriving from the plaza, filling the sidewalks with cheers, enthusiasm and support. The campaign has taken over the city. It will be tonight's story, for sure. Catherine imagines news anchors making jokes about feeling the heat.

Okay, Mayor. Are you listening now?

End those subsidies ... or tell Pac-Shoppe to give us our money's worth.

But that is neither the mayor nor his chief of staff striding so purposefully toward Catherine. That man is not part of the plan, neither carrying a sign nor shouting a slogan. As he nears, Catherine gets a better look.

"Hi, Nate," she says. "What's a nice guy like you doing in a place like this?"

He flashes her an innocent grin. "You, on the other hand, look like you were born here." He surveys the chaos and the police. "What's new with you?"

At this instant she's not very busy. Her people are in place and the next move belongs to the police. Will they make the arrests?

How could they not?

Catherine and the team have calculated this many times. If the arrestables leave the intersection now and disperse back into the crowd, the damage would have already been inflicted

… and nobody would be left to arrest. They might get away with it.

But they collectively concluded that arrests would move them beyond this single news cycle. They don't just want a news hit. They want a raise. A union and a raise. That will take a longer story and more shared sacrifice.

"Wait a second," Catherine says to Nate as she turns her attention back to the telephone, intending only to check out for a moment. "And here. Hold this."

She passes Nate the *Union! Now!* placard Maya put in her hand a little while ago. She couldn't say no to Maya but she prefers to keep her hands free. Nate seems like a perfect recipient for Maya's gift.

Suddenly, a powerful hand grabs Catherine's shoulder, turns her around.

"This one," a voice says.

A uniformed officer twists back her arm. "She's in charge or something. Don't let her get away."

A second officer grabs Nate and swings open a pair of handcuffs. "Him, too."

Nate

Nate can't believe this is happening.

Is this for real?

The police officer twists Nate's arms behind his back. Nate feels the officer's breath on his neck, smells the tobacco as he maneuvers the handcuffs into place. Nate feels hot metal against his wrists. He hears the clinking of chains and the snap as they shut.

He tries to move his arms, testing the trap.

It is absolute. It is secure. Nate's arms are tied uselessly behind his back.

He is helpless.

He is in a crowd of protestors surrounded by sirens.

A police helicopter is whirling overhead.

The officer pats him down.

He is under arrest.

Catherine

"No!" Catherine cries. "He's innocent!"

She ignores the officer pulling her hands behind her back. All she cares about is the officer who's grabbing Nate. "He had nothing to do with anything!"

She reaches toward Nate's officer, trying to get his attention.

That gets her a hard twist as her officer makes clear where he wants her arms.

"Really, please," she pleads. "Let him go. Book me." She puts her hands behind her back and offers complete submission. "I know everything."

Nate

They sit Nate down in the middle of the intersection with the other protestors.

Do they not notice that he's the only one not wearing red?

All Nate knows is that he doesn't belong here. He's a tourist! He came to sightsee. "I don't even know the chants," he says as if someone is listening.

Nearby protestors look just as puzzled as the police slam him down in their midst.

"Who's this guy?" the man beside Nate asks the officer.

The police give him no attention, either.

Most people don't notice Nate at all, busy as they are with their cheers and their chants. The crowd in the middle of the intersection is having a great time playing with the crowd on the sidewalk.

"What do we want?" booms the middle, going nowhere as cars honk and helicopters whirl overhead.

"A union!" replies the sidewalk, waving banners, hands held high.

"When do we want it?"

"Now!"

But Nate's officer isn't done with him. He jerks him back to his feet and starts working on his handcuffs.

Nate thinks he is being set free. *By now they've realized their mistake.*

Then he notices the officer is carrying a fistful of nylon twist ties, like for garbage bags, where one end slides into the other and locks in place, but thicker and stronger. The officer gets behind him and locks the twist tie into place around Nate's wrists, hauling it shut tighter even than the handcuffs. Now his wrists are bound so tightly it hurts.

When the officer is satisfied he takes off the handcuffs and puts them back on his belt.

What? They must not have enough handcuffs for everybody.

The officer shoves Nate back down to the pavement, back into his place in the middle of the protestors. This time it hurts because his hands are locked so tight behind him he can't organize the way he hits the ground.

"What do we want?" the sideline asks.

"A raise!"

"When do we want it?"

"Now!"

Catherine

Catherine tries to catch the attention of the lawyers from the National Lawyers' Guild.

She wasn't supposed to be arrested. She wasn't in the plan.

They'll figure that out quick enough, she supposes. Someone saw her getting cuffed or will notice her in the middle. Probably she's being discussed right now on the conference line. Her team knows enough about her to fill in the blanks for the bail hearing. And she likes to think they can carry on without her.

But what about Nate? They don't know anything about him. *They don't even know he's one of us.*

Nate

Nate's been sitting with his hands cuffed for what seems like two hours by now. The temperature is a hundred degrees and the black tar pavement is a hundred degrees hotter than that. The sun is relentless. Nate figures it's the least of his problems, but the skin on his face is starting to burn.

For whatever reason the police leave them smack in the middle of the intersection. They could have walked everyone to the sidelines so traffic could flow back to normal. Instead they treat the protest like a permanent fixture and redirect traffic all around it. Hundreds of cars U-turn, K-turn, or turn down the adjacent blocks, sometimes seeking escape on their own, sometimes coordinated by officers on duty. At some point the helicopters give up and head off to whatever happens next.

Nate wonders about the people back at Fitzgerald Financials. *Have they given up on him ever coming back?*

Or maybe they know exactly where he is.

Maybe they've seen him on TV.

How will Nate explain that to Mr. Daniels?

Catherine

There is nothing to do but wait. Catherine tries to maneuver herself closer to Nate but all she gets is a poke in the belly and a shove back down to the pavement.

She remembers what the National Lawyers' Guild said during the training. A blow to the belly leaves no mark, not even with a wooden police baton. Until it's strong enough to rupture a kidney, nobody will know you took the hit.

The protestors learned that in their training. The police already know.

Nate

The man next to Nate tries to tell him that he'll be fine. He says he'll be released on bail and win his innocence at trial. Everyone in the circle will testify on Nate's behalf. He wasn't involved, and everyone knows it.

He tells Nate what he knows about the process of bail. He says bail is all about making sure you come back to court. The bail decision factors are about ties to the community and risk of flight. Not the crime itself.

"Look, you're married with kids, right?" the protestors says, sizing Nate up by his looks, a middle-aged office worker in slacks and a collar shirt. "That's a dead certainty that you'll come back for your next court date."

"Um, no" Nate replies. "Not married. No kids."

"You own your home?"

"Sorry, but no."

"How long have you had your current job?"

"That depends."

"The court defines employer by paystubs. How long since you got paychecks from the same place?"

Nate thinks about the acquisition. "About six weeks."

"Oh, my," the man replies.

Catherine

Sitting on the hot pavement with her hands tied behind her back is a lot of work. Catherine is basically fit and sometimes does sit-ups in the morning, but even she is struggling.

The man next to her seems truly to be suffering, though. He's an older African American man, considerably overweight. Catherine can't imagine the last time he did sit-ups, if ever. Yet here he is, locked on the tarmac for hours, trying to hold a sitting position with his arms tied behind his back.

At one point Catherine watches him try to lie down, but it's impossible to lie back with your arms behind you, and he utterly fails to maneuver himself onto his side. When he finally muscles himself back to a sitting position he seems worse off for having tried anything else.

Catherine hears him beside her, holding his position, wheezing with strain. The man is trying and succeeding at maintaining his dignity, not crying out for help. To a casual onlooker, he's just one of the crowd, holding a place in the circle with people half his age and half his weight. But Catherine is close enough to know what it's costing him. She can hear his breathing and, every now and then, a groan.

She considers calling for help on his behalf but decides not to. Asking for help is the assault on dignity he's working so hard to avoid. It would be even worse if someone else did it for him.

All around them police are on patrol. There are far more cops than are needed now that the whole crowd is all seated and trussed, especially since most of the police are just standing around like they have nothing better to do.

Catherine sees an officer on the far side of the circle look her way and snap to alert. He's a strong young African American man, good looking like a hero on TV. He starts moving toward Catherine. She can tell that he's purposefully slow, camouflaging his intent, acting like he's milling around like the rest of the force, but he is deliberately moving her way, watching her closely. She watches and waits, wondering what's on his mind.

But he's not looking at Catherine after all. He stops when he reaches the struggling, overweight African American man beside her.

The police officer leans down and whispers something in the older man's ear, and is told something back.

From his pocket the officer takes a twist tie.

He fastens the new twist tie around the man's wrist, but Catherine can tell from where she sits that he doesn't pull it tight. Then the officer cuts the original band away and drops it on the pavement. Finally he stands up behind the man, mission apparently accomplished.

But the officer doesn't leave. In fact, he's standing so close that the older man is leaning against his legs, treating him like a backrest for a moment of relief. Catherine hears the old man's breathing change, can almost feel his gratitude as he leans against the brace, like a timeout in a long, hot, painful day.

A minute later the officer needs to move along, but first he reaches down to touch the older man's shoulder.

"You going to be okay?" he asks.

The older man nods in affirmation.

As the police officer moves along for his duties, Catherine hears his final farewell. "You guys need a raise."

Nate

Everyone in the circle is passed a placard with a number on it. First it just sits face up in their laps. Eventually, one-by-one around the circle, an officer comes around to hold the placard in front of each person's chest while another officer takes a picture that includes their face. There. Done. Nate is now arrest number 052356. He is official. He is in the books.

Is this Nate's new identity? Is he 052356 forevermore? The placard goes back in his lap, face down.

Nate only came to sightsee! He was curious what was happening, and hoped maybe to score a point with Catherine at the same time.

It might serve him right if they caught him for stealing Pac-Shoppe's letter to Theresa Staedtler. Maybe they could arrest him for that. *But this?*

Nate realizes that now that he's number 052356, someone might make the connection. An analyst at Fitzgerald Financials was arrested at the Pac-Shoppe demonstration. The same analyst has access to the letter. How long will it take them to go from one to the other? It's all over, he begins to think. *He's doomed.*

Catherine

As expected, vans arrive to bring them in for processing. Will they take them to the jail, to the court, or to the police precinct? Catherine doesn't know. The Lawyer's Guild said it could be any of the three.

She hopes that as they move around and reorganize she can find people to send her messages. She needs to tell the Lawyer's Guild that Nate is one of them. She needs to tell them what she knows and alert them to include Nate in their petition for bail.

She also needs to tell Nate what to expect. He needs to recognize the Guild lawyers in their yellow hats, and that he can trust them. Above all else, she wants to greet him. He deserves a smile or an apology. He needs some human touch so he knows he's not on his own. She owes him that, at least.

Nate

They are commanded to rise from the pavement to be loaded into vans. Nate hopes during the shuffle that maybe he can find a chance to talk to Catherine. The guy next to him is trying to be nice, but Nate needs to learn what's happening for real.

Catherine isn't more than ten steps away. There are no obstacles or even protestors in between. Nate takes one step in her direction when the orders are announced.

"Males in this van, females in that one."

Catherine

The only good news is that they let people use the bathroom as soon as they arrive. Catherine hadn't done the personal calculation the Guild recommended but she realized during the long wait in the circle it was a good thing she'd fallen behind in her hydration during the earlier hot and busy part of the day. She's about to burst by the time they arrive.

The female van went to the police precinct. She doesn't know what happened to Nate or the male van. Most of her time in the van she could think about only one thing, especially when they hit a bump.

Nate

Nate is being fingerprinted. Some kind of police forensic lab tech in a white jacket is slapping his hands and telling him to relax.

"Let me control them," the man says. "Trust me." He is white-haired like a grandfather, so it's easy.

Nate finds a way to relax his hands as the man takes his first finger, rolls it onto a black ink pad, then rolls it onto a paper pre-filled with his identifying information, including 052356.

"See," he says gently, like a teacher to a toddler. "We roll the whole finger from edge to edge ... and don't miss the fingertip. There! That's a nice fingerprint." Nate can almost hear the smiley face emoji in his voice.

Nate understands why it's taking so long, as each person gets the same loving attention in turn.

"Now fold that finger underneath, and let's get to the next one. Easy! Relax. I'm in charge."

After the careful rolling of eight fingertips the man does both thumbs simultaneously, and commends Nate for a job well done. Next he guides Nate to a booth across the room. "Mug shot," he explains.

Mug shot?

If Nate had any doubt whether he's a criminal, this erases it.

The officer in charge of the mug shot doesn't even pretend to be courteous. He gives Nate the placard with his number and shoves him against a wall with height marks at every inch. Then he walks a few steps to a camera on the other side of a screen.

"Smile for the camera," he commands.

Nate doesn't smile.

Catherine

Now for the first time Catherine's crew is mixed with other people who happened to have been arrested at the same time. As she advances through processing the woman behind her is in tears. "I'm so stupid!" she exclaims again and again. "What have I done? What will happen to my daughters! My two little girls! I'm so stupid!"

She is an African American woman who looks to be roughly thirty, not far in age or size from Catherine, her hair short and straight. Catherine learns in installments that the woman took a turn with the marijuana when it came her way with friends last week. "I'm so stupid! What was I thinking?" She'd been clean for five years and out of prison for three. Now a moment of carelessness showed up in a random urinalysis, and her probation officer won't cut her any slack.

The girls' father is in prison. They're with grandmom right now, but the woman isn't sure how long that can last. She's more afraid of foster care for her kids than prison for herself. "Three years!" she says again and again. "I'm so stupid."

Nate

Nothing prepared Nate for the terrifying reality of the cell door being shut.

He remembers touring Alcatraz with his parents when he was a kid. Like thousands of kids before him he stood in the cell while his parents clanged the door shut. They took a picture. Told a joke about being a good boy.

He remembers how scary it was, the door being shut, even for pretend, even make believe in a tourist attraction. Being locked in a cage is a primal fear, but this time it's real. He turns and grabs the bars. He shakes them but they don't move. His terror is raw and absolute. He fights panic.

He is not alone in the cell. Two men are locked in with him.

The door clanks shut, then clanks again as the lock turns home.

The guard walks off.

Nate's never been so frightened in his life. Is it the memory of his family at Alcatraz? He wants to cry for his Mommy.

Catherine

Catherine is put in a holding pen with the eight other women arrested in her crew plus three other women, including the mortified young mother from processing.

The pen is the size of the central conference room at UCW. Three walls are concrete. The fourth wall, the front, is steel bars. The only way in or out is the barred gate in the front.

Catherine was proud that they had thirty-two volunteers willing to be arrested, enough for eight people on each corner. Thirty-two was enough to fill the intersection and claim the space.

But from the point of the view of the police, thirty-two is probably no more than a busy Saturday night. They might arrest twice as many on July Fourth or New Year's Eve. The pen into which they unload the women could hold all thirty-two of them, but after waiting an hour for the men to arrive Catherine concludes that the men have been taken to the jail. The police seem to be keeping them as divided as possible.

It's nice hanging out with the women, though.

Catherine wouldn't call it festive but their mood is pretty good. Although everyone is nervous, at least they have each other. They brag about their success on the day, compare highlights, and dare Pac-Shoppe not to give them a raise. They are stronger together.

Annette Wilcox from the Lawyer's Guild succeeds in getting an interview. It is limited to five minutes and only for one of them. The crew nominates Catherine, which makes her happy.

She updates Annette on the status in her pen, and learns that the men have indeed been taken to the jail. Most importantly she can tell Annette about Nate. She tells her to look out for him along with the rest of their crew. He's an ally, not a stranger who happened to be arrested at the same time.

She gives Annette the best information she can for his bail hearing.

Catherine knows his name.

She knows where he works. Fitzgerald Financials is a major firm in the city with a reputation to protect.

She doesn't know his home address.

"Is it inside city limits?" Annette asks. "That matters a lot for a bail decision."

Catherine truly doesn't know, but Nate doesn't seem like someone who wants a long commute, nor someone in a house with a yard. She remembers where they had that dinner, and suspects it was in his neighborhood. "Probably," she ventures. "I think so."

"Is he single or married?"

Catherine hasn't asked him but on this she has perfect confidence. "Single," she declares.

Unaccountably, that makes her happy.

She even catches herself smiling.

Nate

Nate's cell has two bunk beds, one on each side.

It is the size of a walk-in closet, barely wide enough for the two narrow beds and space for a person to walk in between. The walls are cinderblock and the door is barred. At the far end, opposite the door, is a metal fixture that obviously serves as both a toilet and a sink. There is no lid or seat of any kind. The tank of the toilet has a basin and a spigot on top. This is the sink.

The operation of the toilet is self-evident. The edges of the toilet bowl, wide enough to sit on, are spattered with liquid.

The beds are metal shelves on a two-level frame, with thin matts on each shelf. The men appear to be sleeping when Nate arrives, one on the top left bunk and one on the bottom right bunk. Nate is more frightened than he can ever remember. At some point the men will become more than inert bodies, but he's glad that time isn't now.

The two remaining bunks each have a sheet folded on top. Apparently, Nate gets to pick which bunk he wants.

The next person will get the bunk he leaves, the last-choice space.

Nate decides on the top right because the top seems somehow farther away, but before he climbs he empties his bladder. He stands to use the toilet, his stream of urine at most a foot away from the head of the man on the bottom bunk. Nate is scared to death that the man will wake up and treat Nate like he's pissing on his head. But the man doesn't wake up. Or at least he pretends not to.

Nate wonders if he will be released before he needs to sit on the toilet with his pants at his ankles.

If only he knew.

Catherine

Around five in the evening the call sounds down the hall. "Chow time. Dinner. Come 'n get it."

Catherine has been moved from their social holding pen to a double cell with a woman who speaks only Spanish. They're kind to each other, exchanging *Hola, Excuse me* and *Permiso* as they navigate the narrow cell, but surely it is no accident that Catherine is incarcerated with nobody from her team. Doubtless they have been distributed among as many cells as possible, with the smallest possible overlap or ability to coordinate.

This isn't the first time Catherine wishes she spoke Spanish.

She misses her telephone. She wonders what's happening out there.

She's not hungry but probably it is best to eat.

The cell door snaps open and she steps outside. She can see and hear that she's in a line of cells that all snap open at the same time. A line of women is stepping out, taking their places. Several people are in Catherine's UCW family. The woman with the two daughters and the probation violation is just behind her.

Uniformed officers stand at both ends of their line. Both are men.

"Hey, Lisa," Catherine calls to one of their arrestables just ahead of her in line.

"No talking," commands the officer in what seems to be the front of Catherine's line, based on which way most of them are facing.

A moment later they all start walking in that direction. Enough people have eaten meals here that everyone understands which way to walk.

Single file they proceed to a room that would look like a high school cafeteria if there weren't so many bars and uniformed officers. Four arrestables appear to be in this meal shift, and nobody stops them from sitting at a table together. They are not, however, permitted to talk.

Nate

The jail is timeless. Nate's watch was taken with the rest of his personal possessions, and there is no clock in view.

In real life he lives by the clock. Now he doesn't even know what time it is.

That's not quite true. At the end of the hallway Nate can see what looks like a window, with enough light coming through that he can tell the sun set a short while ago. He guesses it's around eight o'clock. A voice over the intercom announces, "Lights out in ten minutes."

Nate has barely more than grunted with the people in his cell, neither in the cell nor over the small meatlike patty they were served at dinner.

Nate discovers again what he noticed this afternoon when he first lay down. The bed is tiny. Nate isn't very big, but he fills the whole thing. His head hits the wall at one end and his feet reach the edge at the other. It's wide enough for Nate's shoulders, but a larger man wouldn't fit at all.

What did they think at Fitzgerald Financials when Nate never came back from his errand? Did they try to call him? Did they try his home? His cell? It's too soon for them to think he's quit, but how long before *that* happens?

Earlier today he pretended he was working. Now he pretends he's going to sleep. Will he go to work tomorrow morning?

The man at the protest talked about bail. When does that happen?

Nate wonders about a telephone. Isn't he supposed to be allowed a call?

His head is starting to itch. Is that coincidence or lice? So far it hasn't been cold enough that he spread his sheet, using it instead as a pillow.

The itching is getting worse.

Who would he call? Probably a lawyer. But who? Nate doesn't have a lawyer.

Would he call his mother? Mr. Daniels? What would Nate tell him?

The man in the bottom bunk gets up and uses the toilet and then – what manners! – washes his hands in the sink.

Nate can't believe he's here.

He knows there isn't any soap.

He's going to spend the night in jail. He's going to spend the night in jail.

Nate has never spent a night in jail. He didn't get drunk in high school. He engaged in no prankster hijinks in college. He's seen enough movies and TV to know what happens in a locked cell when the lights go out.

Where the hell is Catherine Campbell?

He is going to spend the night in jail.

Catherine

Catherine's cell is much quieter overnight than she expected, and much quieter than other cells where she's spent time.

Nobody is talking. No music is playing. There is no shared rec room with a television down the hall. There are no social sounds at all.

The only sound is the building. Cell doors clanging open and shut.

The creaking and whirring of ventilation.

Toilets that flush with a vicious vacuum rush like on an airplane.

Every hour or so a voice comes over the intercom.

"Garnett, cell three."

"Papadopoulos, 211."

"Washington, 426."

Often announcements are followed by the sound of a door opening or closing, but not always.

Catherine worries about her team and wonders how their action played on the evening news. Above all else, she worries about Nate. Catherine has been incarcerated before, and the arrestables all know what they signed up for. They've been fully briefed and trained on what to expect.

Nate doesn't know any of that. He must be terrified.

Nate

Nate lay in his bunk listening to the sounds of other men.

The man below him seems to be asleep, his breath loud and rasping, a bronchial infection he's sharing generously with Nate and everyone else. Once when he is coughing in great liquid bursts, officers arrive and pull him from the cell, replacing him with someone new. The new man takes his place in the coughing man's bunk and covers himself with the same sheet.

The breathing of the man across from Nate is shallow and steady. Nate suspects that he, too, is awake. Every time the man rolls over Nate is certain he's coming after him – but he just curls up and returns to breathing. Once, he sneezes.

All night long there is traffic. The new man in the bunk below Nate is replaced with someone else. In the cell across the hall, one man is muscled out and three men are put in his place. Maybe an hour later one of them is taken somewhere else.

Nate's head itches more and more. He scratches and slaps at himself. Is it nerves or is it lice? What does the man next to him think of his racket? Eventually Nate gets cold and decides to use the sheet as a blanket. He unfolds it and spreads it over himself. Maybe he's spreading the lice but at least he's not so cold. He loses his pillow, though. He lies with his head flat on the mat.

At one point the entire unit is awakened and they are all told to stand by their bunks for a headcount. Officers walk the tier and point flashlights in everyone's faces as they count them off, although the lights are all on and the flashlight only makes Nate squint and his eyes flash.

"All present and accounted for," comes the call when the officers reach the end of the line. A moment later the cell lights go out, though the hall lights stay on all night.

At some point Nate must have fallen asleep because he is awakened when the lights snap on and the call comes out. "Five AM. Get a move on."

Catherine

Watery porridge is served for breakfast. Catherine removes a fly and a hair, and pours in a packet of sugar.

A different group of people is brought in for breakfast, although three UCW arrestables are still with Catherine. She sits with the arrestables at a table and they stare sleepily at each other.

"How are you holding up?" Catherine asks, but she's slapped in the head from behind. *No Talking* is still in effect.

Midway through the meal, Catherine and the UCW arrestables are marched out. They stand in the hallway next to the cafeteria for nearly an hour, far longer than it would have taken to slurp down the rest of their porridge. The regular arrestees bus their dishes and are marched away, presumably back to their cells. Catherine's UCW team stands in the hallway until the next shift arrives for breakfast. The UCW arrestables are lined up outside with the earlier set, no food or drink offered, while the regular arrestees are shepherded into the mess hall.

The UCW crew stands outside the mess hall, wordlessly in line, until the second shift has eaten and been escorted away. Then they are marched wordlessly back to the vans.

Nate

Like cattle in a line, they are herded into moving vans. They aren't allowed to speak, nor are they spoken to. Nate follows the people in front of him, and other people follow him from behind. Any divergence is poked or prodded back into place. If Nate were in a better mood he would moo.

He can still read, however. As the van parks after a short ride he spots a sign that says Richmond General District Court. Is this the bail hearing? Is this where he'll see a lawyer at last?

Security is especially heavy as they unload, armed guards with big, conspicuous guns watching every move. Once they enter the building it gets more casual. Nate and his contingent walk several hallways in straight line in perfect order – moo! – then each of them steps through a door, held open by the person ahead of him, holding it open for the person behind. Now they are unmistakably in a courtroom.

The judge sits up front on the dais, a young woman with curly red hair and large hoop earrings who, other than the black robe, looks nothing like Nate expects of a judge. She is surrounded by administrative support staff, uniformed bailiffs and flags of both Virginia and the United States.

In front of her are two desks that Nate thinks from TV shows are called counsel tables. Immediately he recognizes Catherine Campbell at one table, in hushed conversation with two people he supposes must be lawyers. At the other table sit three people that must be lawyers for the other side.

The audience portion of the courtroom is rows of benches. The first three rows are filled when Nate arrives, maybe twenty people. His herd fills the next two rows, roughly a dozen people more.

Other than Catherine Campbell, the only other familiar face is the young man who sat next to Nate in handcuffs and tried to reassure him about bail. They are generally young, a mix of races and genders. They look like the crowd of protestors from the intersection, all wearing red T-shirts from yesterday.

Soon Nate recognize someone else, an older, heavier African American man who was also in the intersection.

Nate figures this must be progress. Or it's better than jail, anyway. The courtroom even has a clock. It's a few minutes after nine. He is now officially late for work.

After Nate's load has filled its benches Catherine Campbell turns around and spots him where he sits. She touches the people she's been talking to, and points him out. One of them makes notations in her notebook, turns to examine him some more, then adds another notation.

Nate tries to catch Catherine's eye. Hello! He wants desperately to talk to her. *What the hell is going on here?* He has so much to ask and so much to say. What's happening? What's going to happen next?

Catherine stands up and looks like she's starting in Nate's direction, but one of the people she'd been talking to pulls her back.

The judge addresses her audience. "It is 9:09 AM on May 24. We are now in session. Good morning, everyone."

She pauses as if people might say "good morning" back, but she doesn't wait for an answer she surely doesn't expect.

"Today is a procedurally unusual day," the judge continues. "Each of you will receive the individualized justice that your case deserves and the constitution requires. But you are all charged with the same offense and represented by the same counsel so I will sometimes address you in bulk and save time by not saying the same thing thirty-four separate and individual times. If this is not acceptable to any of you, you may object at any time and other arrangements will be made."

This time her pause is sincere, giving the audience a legitimate opportunity to object or for people to separate themselves.

All Nate really hears is the word *counsel.* So he seems to have a lawyer after all. Is he better off *en masse* or with one of his own? At this point he has no alternative so he stays silent in the herd.

The judge resumes. "You are charged with Obstructing Free Passage of Others under Virginia Code section 18.2-404, a Class One misdemeanor punishable with confinement in jail up to twelve months and/or a fine of up to $2,500."

After that Nate hears nothing else. *He could go to jail for a year for this?* How much worse does it get? For doing a favor and wanting the pretty girl to see him doing it?

The judge hasn't stopped. "All of you will be represented by Attorneys Annette Wilcox and Miriam Sennett from the National Lawyers' Guild. If any of you have alternative counsel or if alternative counsel are present I invite you to make an appearance."

Her pause is again sincere. By now Nate can see that she is doing something genuinely unusual and difficult, and she is trying to be careful.

"Now for what you most want to hear," she continues. "Every one of you is being released on your own recognizance. Every one of you will be free to leave this courtroom when the proceedings have concluded."

A collective wave of relief reverberates through the courtroom. Apparently, Nate wasn't the only one worried about this. Underpaid or not, everyone wants to go home.

"During your release you will be subject to standard conditions, including restrictions on alcohol and drug use, with enforcement subject to the Department of Pretrial Services. Most importantly, you will return to court on June 22 for a preliminary hearing. If any of you does not return to court on June 22 a warrant will be issued for your arrest and the United Commercial Workers will forfeit the $20,000 cash bond it has offered on your collective behalf. Paper orders will be provided to each of you individually before you exit this courtroom. Copies will be mailed to your address of record."

Nate sees people looking around the room, and looking at each other, as if to make sure this is okay. Catherine and the two lawyers survey the room with care.

Nate is caught between resentment that he is here and appreciation of the care people seem to be taking so that – whatever is going on – it all goes smoothly.

What the hell was Catherine thinking when she put that poster in his hand? *Was that an accident? Was that a trap?*

If Nate didn't have a protest poster, would he have been arrested at all? Will it be used against him at trial? $2,500 and a year in jail?! For a piece of cardboard?

"If there are no further questions we will proceed." The judge motions to the bailiffs, and counsel all stand to attention. "Defendant number one, step forward and state your plea."

Catherine

But for two extra arrests, Catherine would be pleased at how smoothly everything is going. All thirty-two of their arrestables went the whole distance, and the police took the bait. They tied up traffic and she's sure they dominated the news. Now the group representation is going exactly as they hoped and planned.

If she didn't need a night's sleep, a toothbrush and a shower, she'd be delighted. As it is, she muscles through the proceedings – though she is now both a criminal defendant and the Guild's legal assistant at the same time.

Catherine is deeply concerned about Nathaniel Hawley. He doesn't deserve this. Last night was far more than anything he signed up for.

She knows he wasn't in her van. When he doesn't appear on the next two vans, she worries even more. She hopes he hasn't been separated from the UCW crowd and processed with the rest of the arrests. When he finally unloads she doesn't even get a chance to talk to him. She wants to reach out – turn and smile, at least! – but the judge keeps them moving like a freight train has been added to her regular workload. The judge wants nothing but to get it done, and the Guild lawyers are matching her pace. Soon enough, she too, has forgotten Nathaniel Hawley in a hard slog of careful bookkeeping.

Defendant number one is Wendy Stott. As she steps forward from the benches, the Guild lawyer steps into the aisle to greet her and walk her into the well of the court.

Clearly, they know each other. They are all but hugging and congratulating each other.

The judge asks Wendy Stott to restate her full name for the record, and recites the charges against her, Obstructing Free Passage of Others under section 18.2-404, but now it ends differently. "You can be punished by up to twelve months in jail and a fine of up to $2,500. How do you plead?"

Wendy Stott turns to look at the lawyer beside her. Receiving a signal, she turns back to the judge. "I plead not-guilty, your honor."

The judge nods in agreement. "Do you promise to abide by all conditions of your release and return to court on June 22?"

"I do."

"You may proceed. Defendant number two."

After Wendy Stott comes Jonathan Adler, followed by Peter Rickman and Colin Flory. Nate can do nothing but wait. Every time he thinks maybe he'll be next. Every time he's not. Finally Nate gives up and just lets the names roll past like the tide.

Ronald Ruggiero. "Not guilty."

Kristin Johnson. "Not guilty."

Nathan Kleinman. "Not guilty."

It doesn't take long to learn the drill, and it never varies.

Step forward when the name is called.

Listen to the charges.

Enter the plea of not-guilty.

Promise to abide by the conditions or release.

Promise to come back to court on June 22.

By number twelve Nate is getting tired and barely listening. When the guards woke them up before dawn Nate flirted with the idea of heroically getting into the office so early nobody would miss him.

Gretchen Donart. "Not guilty."

Tim Rosario. "Not guilty."

He has long since given up on that idea.

After each defendant pleads not guilty and accepts the conditions, they exit through a side door and generally don't come back, though one or two have returned until they leave again with a friend. No doubt they'll all go home for a shower, out for breakfast or even back to work. Nate doesn't know. But he can understand why they don't want to stay. By defendant twenty-two – still not Nate! – he wants to be anywhere but here.

He keeps trying to catch Catherine's eye, but she doesn't even look his way. He wants to walk up and pull, childlike, on her arm but that won't get him anywhere. She talks to the lawyers before and after each case is called. She is being productive, he assumes, in some legally important way. She's too busy for him.

Lila Fithian. "Not guilty."

Jawair Culbreath. "Not guilty."

Thomas Quinn. "Not guilty."

Nate needs to figure out what happens between today and when he returns to court on June 22. Catherine Campbell surely has an opinion, and those lawyers likely have ideas of their own. Probably the lawyers are okay, or at least good enough for Pac-Shoppe workers, but probably Nate needs a lawyer of his own. A real lawyer, not some public interest lawyer who probably couldn't get a real job out of law school. The National Lawyers' Guild? What is that? Some eighteenth century barrister's union?

"Defendant number thirty. Harmon Wright."

"Not guilty."

Harmon Wright isn't Nate, either.

Defendant thirty-two is Larry Cohen, then the audience is empty. Nate is the only person in six rows of vacant benches. Surely he's next.

"Defendant thirty-three, Catherine Campbell."

Nate forgot Catherine had been arrested too. She's not just busy at counsel table, she's a defendant like everyone else.

"Catherine Emily Campbell," she says. "Present." She steps away from her work table and into the well of the court. Neither lawyer accompanies her.

"How do you plead?"

"Not guilty."

"Do you promise to abide by all conditions of your release and return to court on June 22 as ordered?"

"I do."

When Catherine is finished she returns to counsel table and – goddam it! – she doesn't even look Nate's way. By now he doesn't care how busy she is. Surely she can at least acknowledge his existence. She got him into this!

"Defendant number thirty-four, Nathaniel Hawley. Step forward and state your full name for the record."

"Nathaniel Jonathan Hawley," he replies. Surely his mother never meant his name to be stated like this.

"You are charged with Obstructing Free Passage of Others under Virginia Code 18.2-404, a Class One misdemeanor, punishable by up to one year in jail and a fine of $2,500. How do you plead?"

"I plead not guilty," Nate replies, but he doesn't leave it there. "I'm really not guilty, your honor. I didn't do it. I didn't obstruct traffic. I just happened to be – "

The judge cuts him off. "You can present a defense at trial, if you choose. Discuss it with your lawyer. Do you accept the conditions of release?"

What conditions of release?! Nobody has told him. As Nate hesitates, one of the court staff puts a piece of paper into his hand.

"Do you accept the conditions?"

Nate wants to read them. He doesn't even know what they are.

The judge isn't waiting. "Will you return to court on June 22, as is ordered in the paper in your hand? Along with all of the conditions."

Everybody is looking at him. It doesn't matter what the conditions are. Nate knows he is going to accept them, just like everyone else. "Yes, your honor," he says.

"Yes, what?"

"Yes, I accept the conditions."

"And?"

"Yes, I will return to court on June 22."

The judge stands. "This session is now in recess. We will reopen in one hour for regular arraignments."

The support staff surrounding the judge leap into action, moving paper files, passing electronic tablets and opening doors. Nate is suddenly irrelevant.

Catherine Campbell hurries to his side. She looks like she spent the night in jail. "Are you okay?" she asks, reaching for his hand. "Can I buy you breakfast?"

Nate snatches his hand back, and answers like she tried to slap him. "Yeah, right."

FIVE

Catherine *Informed Consent*

Catherine feels guilty. Nathaniel Hawley went through far more than she ever expected him to. She wouldn't have asked for that much as a favor, let alone expect him to volunteer for it.

But he didn't volunteer, of course. He got caught in the crossfire.

I'm sorry can only go so far. She wonders if there is some way to make it up to him. How can she help someone who has good reason to be angry? How does she apologize to someone who wants nothing to do with her – and he's right?

Then she remembers that temporary restraining order. That, too, was a risk that went too far. Nate seemed to think he could pass her Pac-Shoppe's letter anonymously. He was willing to sneak a look and pass her the truth. But he thought he'd be an invisible helper, a confidential informant, not a champion for open records. That's fair. She should be grateful for what he offered, as far as it went.

That's the answer to what she can do.

Catherine will contact Nate and ask his permission to use the letter. Now that he has learned it's trackable. Now that he knows it can come back to hurt him. If the letter sits unused on Catherine's shelf, nobody will ever wonder where she got it. After it's filed in court Pac-Shoppe will investigate where it came from. With his eyes open and implications fully understood, Nathaniel Hawley deserves a chance to stop it before it starts.

She'd be happy for his heroism, of course, if that's what he chose. But future risks must be assumed by agreement. After what Nate's been through, he deserves a chance to say No.

As soon as she gets back to the office, she'll tell her lawyers to press the pause button.

Nate *Lather, rinse,*

Nate takes a long, hot shower, scrubbing every inch of his body and scrubbing it again, working feverishly to scour the residue off his skin.

Scrub, scrub, scrub. It doesn't help. He still feels dirty.

He steps out of the shower, but toweling dry feels like rubbing leftover filth into fresh clean linen. He returns to the shower to scrub some more. *Out out, damned spot!* Lather, rinse, repeat. He is Lady Macbeth, scrubbing and scrubbing, never coming clean.

He wishes he could boil himself. He wants to dunk his body into a flaming cauldron, and stay there until he's sterilized at last. He can come out like a lobster, boiled and red, ready to eat. He wants to immerse himself in acid, floss the pneumonia out his lungs. Chinese laundrymen can scour him with steel wool until they reach the bone.

Would that help? Nate scrubs and scrubs and he's not so sure. He's trying to wash the bedsheet off his skin and the not-guilty plea out of his hair. He wants to eradicate the experience, rub it away until it never happened.

Catherine Campbell? *How could she have done that to me!* That's what he wants to know. *What the hell was she thinking?* She lured Nate into her riot, passed him a poster and locked him up. Then she has the nerve to invite him to breakfast, as if that might make it okay?

Eventually he knows he needs to give up. He even starts thinking about his water bill.

Nate lathers rinses and repeats one last time. He dries off with a fresh towel and tosses the first one into the laundry.

Then he makes himself a sandwich and heads to the office.

Catherine *Well Done*

The lawyers are thrilled. They too went a night without sleep, and they too pulled off a heroic legal and logistical accomplishment. Thirty-two – no! – thirty-four people arrested, arraigned and released.

When Catherine reaches the office they're at the hugging and high-fiving part of the adventure. Annette Wilcox of the Lawyers' Guild is locking files in the cabinet while co-counsel Mariam Sennett is rinsing old coffee down the sink. The Guild was in charge of the criminal proceedings but Catherine's own UCW lawyers also race over like puppies for a reward.

"We did it!" cries UCW's lead counsel, Mira Laney. Her assistant alongside, Steve Worceski, looks like a kid who spent the day at the circus, exhausted and excited. He's a young lawyer and thrilled to be in the big leagues.

"Did what?"

Steve steps up to the plate. "We filed the TRO," he replies. "We connected Pac-Shoppe to Theresa Staedtler and the illegal nighttime harassment. We asked the court to order Pac-Shoppe to stop payments and preserve the status quo."

"You filed it?" Catherine asks. "Or you finished drafting it?" She fears that she heard him correctly.

"Both," Steve announces. "We finished drafting, and polished it to perfection. Exhibits and all. We filed last night, minutes before the court closed."

Catherine feels sick in her stomach.

"Is everything okay?" Steve asks.

"Everything is fine," she replies, covering quickly. The card has been played, there's nothing to do. "It's been a long night. Well done."

Steve puts a legal filing in her hand.

PLAINTIFF'S EMERGENCY MOTION FOR A TEMPORARY RESTRAINING ORDER
AND PRELIMINARY INJUNCTION

He points to the date stamp where the filing was submitted to court, May 23, 4:52 pm, yesterday. "We wanted Pac-Shoppe to feel pressure from every direction," he explains. "The courts *and* the streets. When they meet to discuss their next move, they'll have the TRO to deal with, too."

Catherine doesn't really hear him. She's turning pages in the file. Exhibit A is Nate's letter. Tom Grillo of Pac-Shoppe writes Theresa Staedtler that he looks forward "to working together under the terms we discussed."

Steve sees where she's looking and finishes her off. "Now they know what we know. They need to deal with it."

Nate *Study in Contrasts*

Nate reaches Fitzgerald Financials on the late side of lunchtime, resolving to act as if everything is normal.

"Nice sunburn!" says the receptionist as he arrives. "Don't tell us you got stuck in traffic."

That answers whether he was missed.

Mr. Daniels detects his arrival and wanders over to say hello, looks Nate over from top to bottom. "I won't ask," he declares. "What happens in Vegas, stays in Vegas."

"Thanks," mutters Nate. He feels like a high schooler busted by his parents trying to slip in after bedtime.

"Stay out of Pac-Shoppe for a minute," Mr. Daniels advises. "Remember Phoenix Semiconductor? New problems arise."

Nate is still in the waiting room; he hasn't even reached his desk. Nonetheless, Mr. Daniels descends from the Shaolin heavens to spread accounting tables across the couch, calling Nate's attention to certain charts, pointing to one figure and then another. Mr. Daniels is describing what seems to be wrong but Nate has a hard time following.

All he sees is how the charts clash with the floral designs in the couch. Spreadsheets and flowers just don't mix.

Afternoon is for housecleaning. All balls are in other people's courts, and the UCW office is a disaster. It's quiet. Most people are back at work or resting after the long exertion. Catherine finds peace picking up trash, scrubbing tabletops, and putting away supplies for future use. The simple tasks are both useful and relaxing.

The mayor's chief of staff reaches Catherine's cell phone while she's scrubbing paint residue out of the bathroom sink. "What the hell are you trying to do?" he hollers.

He doesn't even introduce himself. He assumes that her cell phone knows his number or that she'll recognize this voice. Catherine takes the time to dry her hands before answering him. "We're trying to make sure the taxpayers of Richmond get their money's worth."

"By clogging our courts and bankrupting our police contingency fund?"

"I take no position on how the police choose to use their contingency fund," she replies, "though we were delighted for their company yesterday while we went for our walk."

"You sat down in traffic."

"A few people seemed to get tired late in the day. It was hot, you know. Did we end up breaking that heat record?" Catherine is enjoying herself. She never did hear how that heat record turned out.

"I don't know what you want from us. This is a dispute between private actors. You want a raise, and Pac-Shoppe doesn't want give you one. As you say with regard to the police contingency fund, we take no position on it." He isn't hollering anymore, but his anger is palpable through the cell phone.

"What do we want from you?" She aims his words back at him. "We want you to stop the corporate subsidies unless and until Pac-Shoppe keeps its end of the bargain. I'll send you a draft letter I want the mayor to sign. If he signs it, I'll ask my people to stand down. If he doesn't … well, they had a good time yesterday. They might want more exercise tomorrow."

"Are you threatening me?"

She picks up the sponge she was using when he called. "I'm offering you a peace accord."

Nate is happy to have something, anything else to do. He's glad not to be looking for "efficiencies" in Pac-Shoppe, not to be examining its balance sheets and, above all else, not to be questioning its contractors. He is in a different company's spreadsheets. He is solving a math problem. He has immersed himself not in boiling acid but in numbers and calculations. He is putting Pac-Shoppe behind him.

What's better, it's easy.

Not only is Nate up to the challenge, but he sees notes he left in the file mere weeks ago. He detected these problems last time, and left notes for himself or some future self suggesting the resolution if it ever became necessary.

He was right last time, under pressure of deadline, not to go further than needed.

He was right to anticipate this problem might arise.

He was smart to leave notes to make it easier. The observations he recorded when he was previously immersed give him a head start now.

In short, he was a star. He appreciates why Mr. Daniels likes him.

Now he's going to do it again.

Nate's clarity is stunning and his energy unbounded. Last night has passed into the distance. He feels better now than ever before. Is it because he stood up to his fears when the door slammed shut? Is it relief that the worst didn't happen or pride that he didn't let it? No matter. He is tearing through the work, computing differences and measuring alternatives. He tears through the semiconductor accounts with vigor as if after a long holiday.

He is happy.

And why shouldn't he be? Phoenix Semiconductor needs something, and he is giving them what they need.

Forget his bad date at the museum and Kristin Cooper's moral measure of work. Nate is happy where he is. He solves puzzles and helps people settle their accounts. That's good in and of itself. He is at peace.

Nate also thinks of Emilio. If Nate's moral measure is short, he can volunteer as a math tutor or do something useful for schoolchildren. If he wants to go full Mother Theresa, he can volunteer at a homeless shelter. Rose sometimes arranged social evenings preparing meals at the food pantry,

But Nate is happy doing math. People bring him problems and he gives them back solutions. That's a good life. It's what he needs. It's all he needs.

Before Catherine goes home for the night, she emails the mayor and chief of staff a proposed draft letter for the mayor to send to the regional director of Pac-Shoppe. It seems as efficient a way as any to explain her proposal and make her demands. Besides, she wants to make it easy for him to do the right thing. Adapting her draft letter is far easier than starting from scratch. Her subject line is, *Let us know how this works for you.*

Dear Mr. McDonnell:

As you know, we are happy that Pac-Shoppe has chosen Richmond as a base of operations. We invested in this partnership and we look forward to working together for many years.

Unfortunately, disputes between Pac-Shoppe and its workforce are causing concern to our city, our residents and our police. For weeks I have maintained neutrality in the face of this private dispute between private actors. The difficulties, however, have not dissipated. Pac-Shoppe appears unable to manage its operations to the satisfaction of our community. Citizens including students, unionists and clergy have voiced their concerns about low-pay, inadequate benefits and lack of representation. As mayor, I am responsible for keeping the peace.

I would be delighted to hear your view of these matters. I invite you to a meeting at my office along with concerned citizens and representatives of the United Commercial Workers next week [insert date and time of your choice]. I need to better understand the situation before I can recommend continuing our subsidy program. I look forward to hearing from you.

Sincerely,
Bill Jefferson
Mayor of Richmond

In the text of the email she invites the mayor to pick a time that works for him. Obviously her team will accommodate his schedule. She also invites Mayor Jefferson's input on how many people should attend the meeting. Ten seems about right to her, though they could grow or shrink as needed. She imagines two people from the mayor's side and two from Pac-Shoppe, along with Pac-Shoppe workers like Elena and herself from UCW. They would add community members like students from VCU and clergy like Harmon Wright or cute John the radical Catholic. Paul from Iraq might want to meet the mayor.

For good measure, she includes a bullet list of statements made by Mayor Jefferson when he was seeking the subsidies and defending them against critics, each statement hyperlinked to the original. The mayor's own research and personal memory will inform him that her list is merely representative, not complete:

- "This is an investment in good jobs," *Richmond Times-Dispatch*, March 17, 2017.
- "Pac-Shoppe will bring us the kind of jobs we always wanted," *NBC News 12 WWBT*, April 3, 2017.
- "This investment will pay for itself before the first year," *Richmond Free Press*, April 5, 2017.
- "Our community needs dignified work that pays a living wage. Our community needs Pac-Shoppe," *ABC News 8, WRIC*, April 6, 2017.
- "Pac-Shoppe is a good corporate partner and a good corporate citizen," *ABC News 8, WRIC*, April 22, 2017.
- "I am working hard to bring good jobs to Richmond. I stand by Pac-Shoppe," *Richmond Times-Dispatch*, March 22, 2017.

Catherine doesn't actually care if the mayor ends the subsidies or not. It's small money in the city budget, and small for Pac-Shoppe as well. But the subsidies work well in the press, and they give the mayor an excuse to express his disappointment. Pac-Shoppe can keep the subsidy, as far as Catherine is concerned. She would happily trade it for a raise. Let Pac-Shoppe become the "good corporate partner" Mayor Jefferson promised.

As if on cue, Emilio's mother knocks on Nate's door.

It's late by now. He's focused on the Phoenix accounts and he knows he started late today, to say nothing of lost time yesterday. He is cranking along, and he needs to crank. Like in the old days, he barely notices when the sound of vacuuming starts.

"Hello?" The tiny Latina woman ventures timidly through his open door, with far more caution than she would have used to empty his wastebasket. She is wearing the blue overalls of her cleaning company, her hair pulled back with a red ribbon. "May I to trouble you?"

"Of course," Nate says. Now he feels bad that he didn't greet her when her company first appeared. "How's Emilio? Please come in."

"Emilio is very well, thank you. The trigonometry is no longer a problem. Thank you." She is barely in the room, all but hiding behind the doorframe. For perhaps the first time Nate appreciates how pretty she is, with a fine-featured face on a tiny body made strong by work.

He wishes he could increase her confidence, somehow convince her that helping Emilio was more of a privilege than an inconvenience. Hopefully time will tell. "What's going on? How can I help you?"

"I'm sorry, sir. I need some more favor." She seems to shrink even more, despite his effort to encourage exactly such a question.

"How can I help?"

"It is the Science Fair. Emilio is working on a project. It is a very big project. It has big signs he made from the boxes."

"That sounds cool." Nate remembers Science Fair from his own high school days. He made big displays with three sides of cardboard folded like a stage.

"He needs some ride. It is too big for the bus, his project. We are not having a car." She is working so hard with her English. He can see her embarrassment at mistakes even as he understands perfectly what she is asking. Even her accent is pretty good.

"Of course!" Nate replies. "I'm happy to help." He stands up and walks to where she stands in the doorway. He meant standing to show respect, but unfortunately the difference in their heights now has Nate looking down on her. "I have a car. It will be easy to do. Just tell me *when* and *where*." He talks slowly and enunciates carefully.

She looks at her feet in a way that reminds him of Emilio during their first day together, overwhelmed in Peet's Coffee shop. Now he knows where he got it from.

"Truly," Nate says again. "I am happy to help." He grabs a nearby notepad and writes *date, time, place* on the first page. "Tell Emilio to write down the date, time and location," he says as he passes her the page. "Tell me where to pick him up. Can you do that? I will be happy to help."

She seems to understand perfectly. She even takes the paper, though surely Emilio has paper of his own. "Gracias, senor," she concludes. "May I to empty your trash?"

She walks toward the trash can but he reaches down to pass it over to her.

"I'm an idiot," says Ramona. "And I've also invented a new rule."

She and Catherine are in the parking lot of the north side Pac-Shoppe, which has become a de-facto campaign office these past few weeks. Catherine hangs out there during shift changes, greeting people as they come and go, answering questions and offering reassurance. Even with their outreach committee structures, she likes to keep in touch with as many people as possible, and be available if they want to talk. Often she ends up giving someone a ride somewhere, since her personal car has become a public utility, featuring a private meeting room and portable closet of posters, flyers and storage for the campaign.

Ramona keeps going. "Hopefully my new rule will prevent such idiocy in the future."

"Do tell," Catherine replies. She has time, and Ramona has a story.

"I was in the loading dock. I noticed that the clipboard with the daily *What goes Where* was showing the notice from the wrong day."

"And?"

"So I fixed it. I thumbed through the pages and put the right day on top."

"So?"

"So I'm an idiot!" Ramona exclaims. "Somebody would have noticed it eventually. Worst case scenario, some boxes would have been unloaded to the wrong zone. What do I care? Nobody would suffer but Pac-Shoppe. Let Pac-Shoppe figure it out on its own sweet time. They can pay us to set it right. Or they can pay me enough to care."

A car drives past with a Pac-Shoppe assistant manager, who is also starting her new shift and who looks at them suspiciously out the window. Catherine pauses the conversation until she's gone. "So why did you fix it?" she asks at last.

"Because I'm a good little girl," replies Ramona after the car is gone. "I saw something wrong, so I fixed it. I did the company a favor."

"What's wrong with that?"

"Would Pac-Shoppe have done me a similar favor? Would Pac-Shoppe have paid me if I submitted a time card for the wrong day? Or if I forgot to punch the timeclock."

"Probably not."

"That's my new rule. Remember the Golden Rule we were all raised with?"

"Do unto others as you would have others do unto you — or something like that."

"Exactly," says Ramona. "My new Golden Rule for the Workplace is exactly the opposite of the Golden Rule we grew up with."

"I'm ready."

"Don't treat your employer better than your employer treats you." Ramona pronounces her rule like Moses declaring the eleventh commandment. "The Golden Rule for the Workplace. We should hold them to the same standard we hold ourselves. If they treat us well ... then we do them favors. If they treat us like shit ... then we shit them back. Why should I do my best for someone couldn't care less if I live or die?"

"The Golden Rule for the Workplace," Catherine acknowledges. "I love it."

Nate *Science Experiment*

Emilio's Science Fair project is indeed large. All three of them – Nate, Emilio and his mom – load it into Nate's car. They start by maneuvering the main display into the trunk, cardboard moving boxes cut and taped into a three-sided stage that barely fits inside. Unfortunately for Nate, it's folded with the front facing inward so he can't read what the project's about. They also carry a big black garbage bag filled with something light, like empty milk jugs, and a paper shopping bag filled with rags of many colors.

"What's your project?" asks Nate.

"Cleaning," Emilio replies.

He's worked his mom's night-job into his Science Fair experiment?

Emilio holds up the garbage bag and sticks to business. "Is it easier to work this into the trunk or keep it in the back seat with me?"

"Keep it with you," Nate replies. "There's plenty of room." He notices that Emilio assigned himself to the back seat, and put his mother up front with Nate. "Pretend it's a friend riding with you."

"I'll call him Tony," says Emilio as he sets the bag into the seat behind the driver. "There now, Tony. Are you comfortable? Are you ready to go?"

Emilio mocks a different voice and answers himself, "All set, thanks. Let's go."

Soon enough they are on their way, with Emilio and his mom both seatbelted in place. They collectively decide it's okay to leave Tony unbelted because it's a long reach for the seatbelt and they're willing to take the risk with him. Nate's phone could give directions but Emilio saves him the trouble. He also explains that his mom can take the city bus from school to her shift at Safeway. "School starts the very early so no problem," she interjects, following the trajectory of their conversation.

Nate checks his watch. School's early start is good for him, too. He can deliver Emilio and reach Fitzgerald Financials roughly on-time for a regular workday – later than his usual, but probably before the secretaries. He can stay late if he finds himself behind.

He considers offering Emilio's mother a ride to work but that seems premature. They can see how the timing works out when they're done. He also doesn't want to look like he's crowding her and doesn't know the situation with Emilo's father – her husband? Nate knows that her name is Martina from his first session with Emilio, but he's deliberately never used it with her. They haven't formally been introduced.

They reach Huguenot High School a short ride later, and with it come Nate's memories from childhood. Huguenot is a broad sprawling building of light brick on the outskirts of town. Rows of yellow school buses disgorge students dressed in bright colors and carrying backpacks, lunch boxes and instrument cases. Nate lines up for entry into the parking lot along with other students and families muscling in their own Science Fair projects, extra traffic during what is doubtless already a busy time of day.

The Science Fair is in the gym and Emilio has been assigned table number 41. The three of them carry everything in from the parking lot in a single trip but as soon as they're finished Emilio's mom kisses him goodbye and hurries off. Nate doesn't even try to offer her a ride, but Emilio sees him thinking. "You can go, too, if you need to," says Emilio. "Thank you so much for the lift."

"I'm happy to help set up if you'd like," Nate replies. He's curious to see the inside of the display and a few extra minutes won't change his day.

"That would be great, thanks."

Step one is unfolding the three-sided stage, more easily achieved with someone on each end. Nate can read the exhibit as it unfolds. *GET CLEAN!* It says in big letters across the top. *BUT HOW?*

Emilio explains that he tested commonly used laundry detergents to see what works best and at what cost. He got samples to test and empty bottles to display from of his classmates and friends. The big bag is filled with empty jugs of Tide, Downy, Kirkland, Value Corner and Gain.

Emilio points to charts taped onto the three-sided stage so Nate can read the data while Emilio sets up the bottles and rags in a design that adds artistry to the numbers. He explains that he tested rags with coffee stains, ketchup stains and a "nasty odor" he got by putting an old t-shirt at the bottom of a friend's kitty litter for two weeks before cutting it up for testing.

"How does it turn out?" Nate inquires. "What's best?" He is curious about the Science Fair project and also – to be honest – for himself as well. Nate buys laundry detergent, after all. Why not get the best wash at the lowest cost?"

"Tide is best," Emilio replies. "Kirkland is pretty good, too, and better for the price." He points to the table labeled *Most Clean* and another table called *Cleanest per Penny* that divides the cleanliness score by the cost per ounce.

"Nice math," Nate says. "Did you think you'd be doing that when you learned division in third grade?"

Emilio responds, "All I thought about in third grade was that Jennifer Peachy sat on one side of me and Bruno Alverez sat on the other."

"I won't ask," says Nate.

"Please don't."

By now it's getting late. Emilio's luggage is delivered and his display is in place. Nate accepts his generous thank-you's and tours the Science Fair presentations on his way to the door. He is happy to relive his own Science Fair memories with no interest in dredging up his equivalent of Jennifer Peachy or Bruno Alverez from grade school. Nate notices that most kids here are minorities but the projects look just like in his own high school which was mostly white. He walks slowly past displays of plants growing upside down and investigations into how long batteries last at different temperatures. One especially impressive exhibit shows the moon in phases and asks how it can be seen during the daytime. At the next table a family is struggling to set up the display because what looks like mom is in a wheelchair, the other adult is confused, and the kid is getting frustrated with both of them.

Nate doesn't even know what language they speak, but from his view he can see exactly where the corner of the display needs to go and why that other adult is confused. He risks stepping in to help, and the confused woman looks back at him.

No mistake. It's Catherine Campbell.

What the hell is Nathaniel Hawley doing here?

Catherine is beyond surprised. Nate is both someone she wants to see and the last person she expects to see setting up the Science Fair in Huguenot High School. He, too, doesn't know what to do.

"Um, hello?" Nate says. He manages to go first but he sounds like he lost both his English and his sense of direction.

"Right, hi," Catherine replies, barely surpassing his delivery but plowing ahead. "What are you doing here?"

Nate gestures back toward the crowd. "Helping someone load. You?"

"Helping someone load," she says, using his same words. But instead of gesturing emptily into the crowd, she makes her introductions.

"Elena, I'd like you to meet Nathaniel Hawley," she says. "Nate is a rock-star financial analyst at Fitzgerald Financials." She doesn't explain why she knows him or how Fitzgerald Financials connects to their work.

"Nathaniel Hawley, I'd like you to meet Elena Perez. Elena was injured in a Pac-Shoppe action a few weeks ago. You might even recognize her." Elena has already wheeled herself in front of them.

Will Nate know or remember the incident? Elena is a fellow traveler in involuntary sacrifice on the Pac-Shoppe campaign. They may be on opposite sides but they have a lot in common.

"In the parking lot?" Nate exclaims with perfect recollection. He points to his head, reflecting the news focus on her coma. "Are you okay?"

Elena sees that he understands. "My head is all better, thank you. I am learning to walk." The wheelchair makes this obviously an overstatement, but her optimism shines through.

By now Malva has had enough. She pushes back to the front of her Science Fair display, the corner still out of place. "Hello buenos dias Science Fair project," she says to Catherine like it's all one word. "Are you helping or not?"

"And this is Elena's daughter, Malva," says Catherine as if she's just finishing the introductions. Elena's younger daughter, six-year old Maya, may be in Catherine's sweet-spot for kids, but tweenaged Malva is not. Stress about the science fair doesn't make it easier.

Nate seems to understand perfectly. He nods acknowledgement to Malva, then maneuvers the stray corner of her display effortlessly into place, implicitly demonstrating both what Malva wanted Catherine to do and why she was frustrated that Catherine didn't see it.

In true tweenage form, Malva thanks Nate with perfect manners. Then she turns to Catherine and says quickly in all one word, "Thank you for the ride you're done dismissed."

Catherine smiles at Elena to signal that everything is fine. Probably Elena will thank her again later, though it won't be necessary. Most importantly Catherine turns to Nate, who hasn't gone anywhere.

"I owe you a big fat *I'm sorry,*" she says. "Do you have a minute?"

Does he have a minute? Hasn't Nate dreamed that someday Catherine Campbell might ask a question like that?

Probably he has that minute, but then he'll be late. Not just late, but late *again*.

She said she was sorry.

Can Nate believe her? Is this for real? What is up with this Catherine Campbell? There's only one way to find out.

"Only a few," he says. "Can you promise I won't spend the night in jail?"

"Sure," she says with a smile. "But I can't promise the police will listen to me."

The anger he expects is nowhere to be found. Is it the promised apology, the ironic smile, or simply the bubble of good will surrounding Emilio's Science Fair? He doesn't know. But he finds himself agreeing to coffee and concluding together that it's easier to stay where they are than drive somewhere separately and park two cars, or for one car to shuttle back and forth between the school and a coffee shop.

Thus Nate finds himself sitting with Catherine Campbell on a bench in the side yard of Huguenot High School. It is another hot day in May, and they are sitting under a tree. Yellow school buses pull in and out of the driveway. Children hurry around in organized chaos.

"I'm sorry," Catherine says again. "I didn't mean for you to be arrested. I truly didn't."

She sounds utterly sincere, almost despondent. Nate has no choice but to shake his head and tell her it was okay, as if he's the one who's comforting her. She asks, "Did you get in trouble? At work, I mean."

Again he shakes his head in reassurance.

Now it's Nate's turn and he asks what's truly on his mind. "You're a union organizer, right?"

She nods back at him.

"Why? Why do you do what you do?"

Catherine is astonished. She is flabbergasted. Speechless. Never in a million years did she expect Nate to ask her that, or anything even close to that.

Taken by surprise she does what she always does. She tells the truth.

"I don't know," she says.

That's true, as far as it goes. She didn't grow up dreaming to become a union organizer. But it's not good enough for today and it's not good enough for Nathaniel Hawley – who smuggled information and went to jail – so she digs deeper.

"Later I will tell you about the X-charts," she says. "You're good at math so don't let me forget to tell you about the X-charts. But since you want to know *why* I'll tell you about my father."

He gestures toward the school like there is no better place to dredge up old memories.

"My father's real job was in manufacturing," Catherine says. "He worked in a plant that made O-rings in Racine, Wisconsin. They made O-rings for anything and everything. Any diameter, any-thickness, any material. I remember when I was a little girl my father would walk around town pointing to things – lawn mowers, gas pumps, Cadillacs, all kinds of things – and he would brag how they were using his O-rings.

"He loved his job and he loved his factory. They hired him out of high school. They trained him for his first job, and trained him up for his next job after that. By the time it all fell apart he was a shift supervisor.

"Manufacturing had changed a lot by then. It was much more automated. There were fewer people on each shift. But even automation requires human intelligence. People are the controllers, programmers and operating engineers. To him, "automation" just meant troubleshooting different problems. He loved his job and he had loyalty to the plant."

"What happened?" Nate asks.

"You guessed it. You already know," she replies. "The factory closed down. They moved operations to Indonesia."

"Cheaper labor," Nate declares.

"No, not cheaper labor," says Catherine, shaking her head. "Automation, remember? Labor is only a small cost in modern manufacturing."

He cocks his head like he's really listening. He understands numbers and he probably pays attention to labor costs.

"The Indonesian government subsidized the move. They offered free land and covered transition costs. Most importantly, they freed the factory from cumbersome regulations – you know, like limiting what they can dump in the river or spew into the air. Factories in Indonesia are disgusting. That's where the savings come from. Wastewater and air pollution. Oh, and safety. Indonesia doesn't have the same tort lawyers, safety standards or workers compensation programs. More people get hurt ... but more money is saved.

"And taxes?" Nate asks. "I'm new around here but aren't there rules about taxes?"

"Thank you, and taxes," Catherine agrees. "If you offshore your profits you can defer tax payments forever. So at the same time Indonesia is subsidizing the creation with development grants, the United States is subsidizing the exit with tax breaks. My father's company did what made sense. They moved the plant to Indonesia, set up a paper subsidiary in the Cayman Islands, and acted as if all the profit came from the Cayman subsidiary."

"With a zero tax rate," Nate adds. He knows that much. "So what did your father do?"

"He found a new job. Then another job. Then another. We even moved to Virginia Beach for what looked like a decent opportunity but it didn't work out. As you know, we left within the year. My father always worked and always earned a living. My mom, too. But he never found another job that paid as well, had full health-benefits, or the same esprit de corps as the plant job staffed by people who stayed together for years." She points again to the school building, as if to indicate the passage of time. "Those guys grew up together. They went to each other's weddings. I used to babysit his co-workers' kids."

Two children walk past, looking to Catherine like sisters late for school. They aren't carrying science fair projects but each has a lunch box and what looks like the older sister is holding a volleyball. "Mom says to be careful at Lily's house," the older child says. "And don't climb that tree!"

Tree climbing. Catherine remembers how she used to love climbing trees, and how her mother hated when she did. It took years for Catherine to appreciate her mother's dread when Catherine called, "look how high I am!" The cancer was mostly gone by the time Catherine started climbing trees but not the fear that tomorrow they might not have a doctor. Catherine's mother and father spent the beginning of their professional lives worried about illness, and the rest worried about health insurance.

Catherine continues her story. "It wasn't until the non-union jobs that my father realized how important the union was in creating and maintaining that esprit de corps. It created the baseline security like health care but it also created a path to longevity."

"Because of guaranteed pay raises?"

"No. Not even close. Because the union got people trained for the next job rather than replaced by someone who already knew it. Because the union forced downsizing to happen by attrition and reassignment whenever possible. Making people more than replaceable widgets is as important to union members as the raise. When my father left the union to become a manager, he sometimes complained about union rules but he was still part of a big team with a common goal. Not until he worked in non-union jobs did he realize the importance of the union up and down the workplace."

"I never thought of it that way," Nate confesses. The accountant is looking beyond his spreadsheets.

"There's more," Catherine replies. "Workers are loaded with experience and ideas. The people closest to the work – people on the factory floor, school teachers, janitors, anything, whatever – they understand it differently. They see what works and what doesn't work, and they have ideas about how to make it better. Workers aren't just costs. They're resources.

"People treat new equipment and advanced polymers like they're progress. But factory workers who see how things move across the floor and remember something that didn't work five years ago, nobody asks *them*. Floor workers might have ideas about how to make something safer or quieter, but nobody asks them. Unions force management to do the right thing."

"You don't read that in the newspaper," Nate observes.

"Germany has strong unions," Catherine replies. "Germany has high wages and great benefits. And Germany is kicking our butt at manufacturing."

A robin red breast drops from the sky and hops around in front of them, looking one way and another, then flies off like it got the message which way to go. Another robin lands in its place, hops around a while, then flies off in the same direction.

"Somewhere along the line I went to college," Catherine continues. "I went to the University of Wisconsin in Madison. Then I got a first job and a second job. They weren't union jobs, obviously. Hardly anything is, these days. But when union organizers came to town, I signed a membership card and .... Well, you can see how it goes after that."

Nate does more than just nod. He stands and moves in front of Catherine, as if the news is too important to take sitting down. Like the robins, he looks one way and another before focusing on the last bus pulling away. He checks his watch, but instead of flying away he returns to sit next to her.

"Now it's your turn," Catherine says. "What about you? Why did you choose to become an accountant?"

The word that stumps him is *choice*. If Catherine had simply asked Nate why he became an accountant it might have been easy. But choice is too much.

"I don't know," he replies.

They realize together that's the same answer she gave him about becoming a union organizer. He elaborates before she makes a joke of it. "In my family, college was career training. No soft talk about self-exploration or personal discovery."

"No classes in African literature or Existential philosophy," she says like it's a path that's familiar to her.

"You know I'm good at math. My advisor suggested I become a CPA. 'It's portable and pays well,' he said. 'People who like math will always be rare. You can get a job anywhere.'"

"Good advice," Catherine agrees.

"*Very* good advice. It was so good that next thing I knew I was studying to be a CPA and the next thing after that I had a good job that paid well."

"Congratulations," Catherine replies without sounding congratulatory. "Well done. But you don't love it."

"I wouldn't say that," he says. She's a little too sarcastic for him. He does like getting paid to solve puzzles and make balances add up. "For sure I don't hate it. But I do sometimes ask the *why* questions." More than ever he is appreciating that he arrived here by momentum, not by choice. Until the takeover by Fitzgerald Financials, he'd never even tried to do anything else with his math.

This isn't a therapy session, though, even if he is paying for it with every minute it makes him late to work. Instead he tells her about the takeover and his new different role.

"That explains a lot," she says.

The school bell rings before he can ask her what she means. They simultaneously look at their watches.

"It's time," Catherine declares.

Nate stands in agreement but the moon catches his attention. It is nearly full, even in full daylight, the middle of a bright blue sky, just like in that Science Fair exhibit. "Look at the moon," he replies.

Catherine just plain stares at the moon for so long Nate wonders what's happening. "I always think it's cool when it's out during the daytime," she says at last.

Catherine *Making the Call*

Stephanie Lerner catches Catherine as soon as she steps into the office. It's a few minutes past nine in the morning, a little late for Catherine, but Stephanie would have just finished her overnight shift. "Call the Labor Relations Board," she declares like a referee announcing a goal. "It's time for a vote." Overnight or not, Stephanie looks no more tired than Catherine does after a regular workday – which to her, this is.

The UCW campaign long ago met the preconditions set by the NLRB to vote for union recognition. They can request a vote anytime after thirty percent of employees sign a pledge card. Thirty percent is suicide, though. Catherine wouldn't call a vote until she hit at least seventy percent. You need a majority to win the election, minus people drop off or don't show up to vote, and the boss always has new tricks up his sleeve.

Stephanie plunks a pile of pledge cards on the table. "They've been piling in since our big action and our mass release," she says. "I got signatures from people I never expected. People want the raise ... and now they see what a union can do."

"Get people fired?" Catherine's inner cynic defends itself.

"Get people out of jail," declares Elena Perez, who has wheeled over to join them. Elena has bonded and made peace with her wheelchair. The old dynamo is back, wearing a pink sweatshirt with a purple headband, zipping around the office, radiating energy.

Elena picks up the pile of pledge cards, starts thumbing through them. "Vicky Rivera," she declares, reading names in the stack. "Nick Collins. Amjat Eman. Look at that! We got Alberto Ferrera! I never thought he'd come around. Call the vote. If we can get Alberto Ferrera we can get anybody."

"Alberto and I had a nice long talk last night in the shoe section," Stephanie says, "Technically, we were making sure the shoes in the display boxes were correctly paired after the customers got through with them. In reality, I was explaining what UCW stands for and why we are doing this. Alberto gets it. Stop waiting. Call the NLRB. Schedule the vote."

They're right, of course. They created a rough numerical threshold they wanted to cross, but more important is the spirit of the movement. Morale skyrocketed the day they shut down the city. Catherine wasn't so much waiting for the numerical threshold as this kind of certainty.

"Does one of you want to call the NLRB?" she asks Stephanie and Elena. "Or shall I?"

Nate *Making the Call*

Call and ask her out, call and ask her out, call and ask her out.

It's pretty much all Nate thinks about all day.

He arrives around nine, later than usual but not late enough to be conspicuous. Mr. Daniels usually arrives after ten, though he often has meetings in the morning.

Nate does spreadsheets to warm up. That's as easy as falling off a log. The hard part is calling to ask her out. He wants to call. He knows he should call. He doesn't quite have the nerve to call.

If he doesn't ask her out, he might never see her again. Probably their paths will cross at the court date in June. Nate still needs legal advice and Catherine might ask more about Theresa Staedtler – but that's all business. Nate wants to talk to the little girl whose father made O-rings. He wants to meet the Catherine he never met in Virginia Beach. They got along so well under the tree by the school buses. She even liked the moon. If he wants to talk to her again, he'll need to call.

Ask her out, ask her out, ask her out.

It's a long day at his desk. Hopefully he didn't make any mistakes. He doesn't think he did, but people never do. He double checks every five minutes.

Ask her out, ask her out, ask her out.

Catherine *Decision*

The email arrives from the mayor's chief of staff. It is to *mitch.fowler@pacshoppe.com.* Catherine knows that Fowler is in Pac-Shoppe's management structure, though she doesn't know what he does. She's never met him. She is cc'd on the email.

> Hey, Mitch. It's been a while. I just want to check in about this union business. These days I'm paying as much in police overtime as I spend on your EO grant. Catherine Campbell wants to arrange some kind of summit meeting. I am willing if it becomes necessary but I'd rather you all just work it out.

EO is the Economic Opportunity grant program that gives Pac-Shoppe its subsidies. Mayor Jefferson came through, after all.

Nate *Lost and Found*

Although Nate never manages to make the phone call, he seems to have turned the corner that it's time to start dating. He goes through his mental contact list. Work, softball, friends of friends. It's no surprise that nobody's there. If someone were available, it would have come up long ago.

By now most of them are married. Some of them have kids.

What has he been doing while their lives have moved on?

Is he in eleventh grade, too scared to make a phone call?

He shouldn't put all his eggs in one basket, anyway. He should consider his options and see what's out there, learn how desperate he needs to be. On his computer at home he starts clicking around dating sites to explore a new world.

Immediately he is presented by photos of gorgeous young men and women. Every one of them is young, healthy, vibrant and attractive. They are fashion models, Olympic athletes or adorable nerds. *They don't need a dating service*, he says to himself. *People probably line up to say hello.*

But it isn't like that, he knows. The world is full of lonely people, barely putting their best photo forward. Even those gorgeous young women have trouble finding a decent guy, he is sure. So much youth and beauty, but people still can't find what they want.

They're also a decade younger than he is.

His exploration soon hits a dead-end anyway. He discovers that he can't move beyond the home page or promotional photos without creating a log in and user ID.

That he's not ready to do. He doesn't want to use his personal email and he's not ready to create a new one just for this. What might it be? *Divorcedsolventaccountant@gmail.com*?

Actually that's probably taken. He'd need to be *Divorcedsolventaccountant1001.*

More curious than deterred, he searches for web pages dedicated to divorcees and people in their thirties. That's Nate, after all. Thirty-something and divorced. Sure enough, there are web pages for people like him. At least he doesn't have kids. That's probably worth a point in someone's book.

The web sites for divorcees show tragedy of a different kind. Their photos aren't gorgeous sunny models from a Nike commercial on TV. These are grown-ups. They have moved beyond the sunshine phase. They are not unattractive but they are so much more than their looks. You can see the souls in their eyes, the experience behind their smiles. These people made promises in good faith. Something went wrong and stayed wrong. Now they are trying again. They're even willing to advertise on a web page. Just looking at them makes Nate sad.

He leaves without creating a log in, though he's found his community. Tragic and worn. He's one of them.

Catherine *Calls and Calls*

"Ricardo will join us today," says Elena. "My husband."

Catherine recognizes Ricardo, of course, though she's surprised to see him at the UCW office before Pac-Shoppe's first shift in the morning. "Good morning," Catherine replies. "We're happy to have you. How are you?"

He looks far better than when Catherine first saw him at the hospital. Gone is the zombie mask of dead and peeling skin. In fact, the fresh new skin gives him youthful vigor to match his natural athleticism and the strength in his shoulders. He moves and stands with more assurance, too. If his vision is still gone at least he's gotten used to it.

Catherine is curious about his vision but hasn't asked Elena about it. Partly they're busy doing other things and partly she's afraid to call it out directly. If the news is bad, why make her think about it?

Ricardo seems to guess what she's wondering, or maybe he hears it hidden in "How are you?"

He responds, "I'm getting better every day. I can tell that the lights are on. I can see light and dark, and big shapes in my way."

Elena adds, "The doctor says that's the first sign of healing. It might keep getting better."

"Let's hope so." Catherine hopes she doesn't jinx anything by saying it out loud.

Now Elena takes control. "Today we deliver the petitions to the NLRB," she declares. "Ricardo will do a final count and bundle them into groups of ten. We will both spend most of the day on the telephone."

"Perfect," Catherine agrees. "Let me know if I can help. Otherwise I'll stay out of your way."

"Bring Ricardo rubber bands for each group of ten," Elena calls over her shoulder as she guides Ricardo to a table where he can work.

After she delivers rubber bands, Catherine sits at a table

in the middle of the room while people bustle all around her. Ricardo is counting the petitions that need to be delivered to the local office of the NLRB to justify the vote. The NLRB will do its own count, of course, and verify each petition card, though Catherine has no doubt they're far over the legal thirty percent threshold.

Her work now is to fill out the federal 502-RC form to officially request NLRB supervision of an election. The form must be accompanied by proof that she formally notified the employer of the request, which she did yesterday with a court-certified process server.

The fight is now on, officially and legally, though of course it's been in the background for months. Catherine is happy because officially requesting the vote increases both their legal protections and Pac-Shoppe's difficulty in getting away with violations. They seem to have backed off lately – no signs of Theresa Staedtler – but they might also be lying in wait or have contracted with a different Theresa Staedtler.

Elena scoots herself over in her wheelchair. "Anything different on the phones today?" she inquires. "Do I say anything new?"

"Yes, please," says Catherine. "Ask people if they want to join our bargaining committee."

"Our what?"

"Our bargaining committee. We'll be making a lot of decisions – about the vote and ultimately our new employment contract. We'll need a team of smart people to sit in the middle of it. By the way, you're nominated." Catherine touches her on the elbow.

Elena bobs her head noncommittally and returns to her original question. "How about today's calls. Just like the others?"

"Basically," Catherine replies. "Make sure people know that we've asked the NLRB for an official vote. The timing and details of the actual vote are being worked out. Probably it will be in about a week but we'll tell them the exact date as soon as the bargaining committee works it out." She stresses the committee name to help show what's being asked of her.

"Otherwise it's the same script. Ask and answer questions. Make sure people are still on board."

"How does the vote take place?"

"Probably ballot boxes in the locker room ... but we'll see."

"More work for the bargaining committee?'"

"Exactly. Try to defer questions about the mechanics of voting. Focus on promises and threats. We need to know if threats are being made against people who vote *yes,* or if promises are being made for people to vote *no.* As always, our lawyers await." Catherine points to a door behind which staff counsel is hard at work."

"Gotcha, boss. Promises and threats."

"And reassurance," Catherine adds. "People will be nervous."

Catherine has filled out these 502s many times before. Employer name and address. Applicant name and address. Number of workers. Definition of bargaining unit. It's the basic *name, rank and serial number* of an election to certify a union.

But what appears straightforward can still be tricky. Is the "Employer address" the two locations in Richmond or the corporate headquarters in Seattle. Is the "Applicant address" the UCW office where Catherine sits or the national office in Washington, DC? The company will argue about the number of workers and who counts in the bargaining unit. Part time workers? People who technically work someplace else, and are temporarily deployed to this location? Offsite employees make sense to exclude ... until the corporation reassigns the entire workforce to a different location and acts as if the Richmond stores are temporary deployments. Negotiations can be tricky.

Elena wheels around with a phone in her ear and a clipboard in her lap. "Is it the same mailing?" she asks the person on the other end of her line. "With the tombstone? *You'd think they could make a new one by now!* How about the phone calls? If they threaten you personally, tell us right away. UCW lawyers are on call at any time."

Around ten Ricardo delivers the petitions grouped into sets of ten, then retreats with Elena into a side room to make phone calls. In addition to their UCW organizing calls, they both have new jobs as telemarketers. They are paid microscopically by the hour but get commissions for making sales, and Elena reports – truthfully, Catherine has no doubt – that they're both pretty good at it. Ricardo controls his phone by voice command and works his magic with the customer, then reports the results to his phone and advances it to the next number.

"Telemarketers need a union, too," Elena says as she settles Ricardo into the room. "Including commissions, some people make less than minimum wage."

"We'll get them next," Catherine replies. "America needs a raise."

Early in the afternoon Catherine's telephone rings. That's not surprising, people call her all the time with worries, doubts, questions and fears.

"Hi, it's Catherine," she says.

On the other side is a long wait. She gives them time. Maybe they've lost their nerve or maybe someone has come into earshot that prevents them from saying what they called for. She hopes it's not a telemarketer. Plenty of them have her number, and the long lag is a telltale sign. At last a voice comes over the line, strong like as though the delay was for an actual reason not a failure of nerves. "This is Nate Hawley from Fitzgerald Financials," he declares. "How are you?"

Catherine can't imagine why Nate is calling. She worries that maybe he's gotten in trouble at work. But at the same time she wonders if maybe he's found something new in their files. "What's up?"

Now comes another long pause, and this time Nate sounds more cautious, almost timid. "Remember we were talking on the bench at school?"

He pauses again so she cues him to continue. "Sure. It was nice to chat." She doesn't want to sound impatient but she is busy and holding a lot in her mind. "What's up?"

"The weather is beautiful these days," he replies. "It was hot on the bench. Now it's cooler. Still sunny, but not as hot. It's nice."

Surely, he isn't calling to talk about the weather. He has something on his mind. He found another payment? The FBI is on his trail? Catherine can feel it trying to come out. "The weather is perfect," she agrees. "I wish I could enjoy it more. I'm just too busy." Was that too strong? She is trying to politely move him along.

"I was wondering if maybe we could talk again sometime."

"Sure. What's it about? Do you want to make an appointment?" Hint, hint, hint.

Again there's a long pause. "Um, no. I thought maybe we could do it nicely..." his voice trickles off.

Catherine tries to add reassurance into the breach. "We should *definitely* do it nicely," she agrees, a statement with no cost and no meaning.

"Like dinner," he says, then blurts out as if he might have said something wrong, "Or lunch. Or coffee. Or whatever works for you." He is all but stammering by now. "It's not about work."

Finally Catherine puts it all together – her certainty that he's single and his willingness to give her so much time and attention. It all comes together in a way that would have happened a lot faster if she were still in high school.

She exclaims so loudly the people around her look up. She even catches Elena and Ricardo's attention in the other room. At what must be top of her lungs she exclaims in surprise. "Are you asking me out?"

Nate can tell he caught Catherine by surprise. It is obvious now, if it wasn't before, that she wasn't thinking of him in that way.

But she doesn't say no. In fact, she says yes.

She tells him it will be tricky during the final stretch of this campaign, and they might need to wait a while. She does sound sincere. Like it's just about scheduling, not punting him into the infinite *maybe someday*.

"After the vote," she says.

"How long will that be?"

"Less than fifteen days."

"I can wait that long."

"Maybe our paths will cross before then," she says.

"Not in court, I hope." He meant it as a joke but creates an inadvertent chill.

"I'll see you soon," she concludes. "I'm looking forward to it."

Nate is exhilarated. Excited like he hasn't been for years. Not only did he do it, but she said yes – or at least it sounded that way. She even said she was looking forward to it.

He soars through his day and stops on the way home for fresh vegetables for dinner, and ice cream because he hates to run out.

Maybe it's a bad habit but he checks his Fitzgerald Financials email after he's home and unloaded but before he starts cooking in earnest.

A message from Dan Daniels is at the top of his inbox. It is marked urgent and the subject line is all caps, "WHAT IS THIS?"

Inside is an attachment and three capital letters, "WTF."

Nate clicks on the attachment as he considers the possibilities, afraid of what Mr. Daniels might be talking about.

The file takes forever to load. The cell phone on his home wifi isn't as fast as a real computer, but eventually it opens and resolves.

It's the photograph he took of Pac-Shoppe's letter to Theresa Staedtler, the photo he gave Catherine Campbell from their confidential archives. On his screen is the letter from Pac-Shoppe's vice president of operations, Tom Grillo, telling Theresa Staedtler that he looks forward to working together "under the terms we discussed."

Today is Saturday. It will be another busy day at the phones. Ricardo stays home but Elena brings in Maya for the morning. Catherine is happy to see her and delighted to receive a nice long hug.

"I made daddy cry last night," Maya announces. She is all but dancing. "I made daddy cry!"

She's happy she made her father cry? Catherine must be missing something.

Maya keeps singing, "I didn't even know daddies could cry! I never see grownups cry." She's smiling with her whole body.

"Okay," says Catherine. "What happened?"

"I asked him how many fingers I was holding up." Maya holds up her hand with five fingers open. "He looked right at me and said, '*I see your hand!*' He didn't know how many fingers I was holding up but he kept on saying, 'I see your hand! I see your hand!' Then he walked right over, with nobody helping. He reached out and touched my hand with his own. He pressed his hand right up against mine."

She presses her palms together, first in front of her, like she's giving herself a high-five, then moving them below her chin as if in prayer. "He held my hand for like a whole minute. Then he started to cry."

For an instant Maya is still dancing, but then she starts crying herself. First sniffles, then true sobs pour out of this little girl, a tangled mess of happiness and sorrow and strain.

This time Catherine initiates the hug. She kneels down to Maya who burrows into her shoulder. Catherine can feel Maya shaking and feel her ragged breath between the sobs. Soon Catherine is fighting her own tears, struggling to steady her own body against Maya's. The faith of Maya's father seems finally to be paying off.

Catherine's phone rings while she's on her knees.

She goes ahead and checks the screen. It's Nate Hawley. Really? Now? Hopefully it isn't about that date.

Catherine stays on her knees and holds Maya with one hand while she answers with the other.

"Talk fast," she says.

"I need a lawyer."

Nate doesn't sleep. He lay in bed cursing his idiocy, his bad luck and misguided chivalry. What was the thinking when he gave her that letter? Nate's usually so practical. His sense of self-worth is wrapped up in his accountant's precision and care. Half the reason Rose left him was his insistence on slowing down, thinking things through and considering the long-term consequences.

What happened to him? He could forgive himself a little carelessness. Sometimes people lose their car keys, but *this*? At the very least, he'll lose his job. Likely, he'll lose his accountancy license. He could go to jail.

No, not *to* jail. *Back* to jail. Once was enough. Nate lay in bed, tossing and turning, everything but slapping at lice. What was he thinking when he gave her that letter?

His thinking becomes more and more fantastical . Maybe he should flee the jurisdiction. He has a passport. He can move to Mexico and never come back. He can dodge criminal court and the wrath of Dan Daniels with a one-way plane ticket. All he has to do is learn Spanish and find a job. But wait! What's he thinking? Why Mexico? How about England? He can find a small town in the countryside that needs someone who's good at math.

But deep down he knows he's just playing with ideas. Nate's an accountant down to his bones, and he's sticking with his calculations. He didn't commit a crime. He uncovered someone else's. Besides, fleeing the country would violate his bail conditions and probably jeopardize everyone who went to jail with him. That's not fair.

Above all else, Nate has work to do. He has to admit that he hasn't been at his best lately, sometimes distracted or otherwise engaged. He can do better. He has to do better.

Nate falls asleep resolving to stick to business. Get to work. Turn in quietly excellent performance until Mr. Daniels calms down. Tomorrow he will report early to work and crank out another day of stunning productivity. He'll remind Mr.

Daniels why Nate is his favorite, his devoted Grasshopper who lives only to serve.

That's better than proving his guilt by buying a plane ticket. Isn't it?

So Nate blasts into the office on Saturday morning. He drives fast, the lights are green and traffic is low.

Oddly, Mr. Daniels has beaten him in. Mr. Daniels often works on Saturday but rarely so early, and Nate feels like he would know if deadlines were looming. If it were urgent enough to bring Mr. Daniels in early on a Saturday, he would have built a team, and Nate would probably be on it.

Equally odd, Mr. Daniels' door is closed. He keeps his door open in spirit and in practice.

It's just as well, Nate concludes. Nate wouldn't know what to say, anyway. He doesn't want to fake an awkward good morning, and the hard questions can stay unspoken between them. He goes straight to work, with his door open. Accounts out of balance await his attention.

An hour later Nate's computer freezes. The files he's working on close suddenly and won't reopen. He clicks and clicks to no avail. He tries restart, control-alt-delete and every home-remedy he can imagine. The programs seem to work but the files still don't open. The only thing that seems normal is his email, which now has a new message from Mr. Daniels, right at the top.

The subject line is simple, in all capital letters, "YOU'RE FIRED."

There is no attachment but the message screen shows a photograph. Nate. His mugshot. The photo taken of him in the police precinct the day of the Pac-Shoppe action, holding his intake number against his chest.

He races straight to Mr. Daniel's office. His door is still closed but Nate knocks forcefully. Receiving no answer he knocks again and walks straight in. Mr. Daniels is alone.

He whirls around in his great leather chair, looking surprisingly sad and old, but in no way surprised to see Nate. Mr. Daniels is wearing a blue suit with a red tie.

"I can explain," Nate says. "It was a mistake."

Mr. Daniels replies, "Give me your phone. Don't bother to clean out your belongings."

"I wasn't part of the protest! I was just walking by! I got swept up in the proceedings."

"You need to leave right away," Mr. Daniels says.

"It was a mistake!"

"We will send you your things."

"Let me explain."

"I'm going to call the police."

Catherine *Bargaining Time*

The UCW bargaining committee starts with Elena and Ramona. Catherine wants Stephanie Lerner to join but that creates a logistical inconvenience because Stephanie works overnight.

All of them are able to meet on Saturday, though. Stephanie takes every other Saturday off so she can watch at least a little of David's soccer season. This Saturday David doesn't even have a game, so they all meet at UCW for lunch. Catherine orders pizza and brings a head of iceberg lettuce, which she chops into pieces and sets on a plate in the center. She even finds little packets of dressing leftover from somebody's take-out, probably within the year.

Catherine says to Stephanie, "I'll tell Pac-Shoppe that you're vital to this committee. I'll ask them to change your shift."

"That would be nice," Stephanie replies. "It would be easier for all of us."

Ramona chimes in with a mouth full of pizza. "Better idea. Propose negotiations at midnight to accommodate Stephanie's schedule."

"I love it," Catherine replies. "If Pac-Shoppe doesn't want to meet at midnight, we can graciously accept their counter-offer to move Stephanie off the graveyard shift. How's that for a concession we're willing to make?"

Everyone laughs. Stephanie says, "I hear there's still a sun in the sky."

Catherine refills their water pitcher and tops off everyone who's empty, then sets the pitcher in the middle of the table. "Who else do we want on the committee?" she asks. "How about Alberto Ferrera?"

"Alberto?!" Ramona exclaims. "Why him? We barely got him to sign the petition ... and I, for one, don't even trust that he'll vote *yes* when the time comes. Why do we want him on the committee?"

"It's good to include skeptics," Catherine replies. "He might see something we miss. And if he comes around he'll bring his allies with him."

They kick around names for a while, and eventually settle on what seems like a feasible brain trust to make a committee. Next they discuss who will reach out to each of them and invite them to join.

"More pizza?" Catherine asks the team. It's been nearly an hour since they started.

Ramona replies, "What?! No ice cream?"

Catherine responds by gathering the used lunch plates, fitting them in the empty pizza box, and setting it by the door for the next trip to the dumpster. Two unused packets of salad dressing go back in the drawer by the microwave, then Catherine declares like a government formalist, "Lunch concluded, let us advance to the next item on the agenda."

"Timing," says Ramona, who remembers the agenda from advance.

"Pac-Shoppe has proposed a date for the vote," Catherine replies. "At the end of next month."

"Why so long?" Stephanie inquires.

Ramona replies, "They want more time. Right now our energy is high and our morale is good. We would win an election held tomorrow. In a few weeks, our energy will drop. They'll fire a few people and scare the rest. Momentum will shift ...."

Elena jumps in, "We need to move as fast as we can." She holds up her cell phone to show off a photo they've all seen many times, the mailing with the tombstone and the warning, *Who wants to be the next Deb Little?* "It's not as if they didn't know this was coming."

Nate *Wanted and Unwanted*

Nate leaves the office humiliated and in despair.

He's never been fired before. He hasn't had that many jobs but he's always been the star. Even working in the cafeteria in college Nate was the guy who always showed up on time and cleaned up afterward. Nate's bosses always wished everyone else could be like him. During his time in their little accounting firm – before the Fitzgerald acquisition – Nate saw only one other person fired, and he had a serious drinking problem. Even so, Mr. Daniels gave him plenty of time and indulged many mistakes before sending him off with a generous severance and sincere wishes for a speedy recovery.

But Nate? Cut loose by email. Because he wanted to impress a pretty girl. First he wanted to show off what he found, then to show up for her march. Serves him right for being an idiot.

He wants to walk home, or at least go for a walk, but then his car would be left in the parking lot at Fitzgerald Financials. Would they let him back in to retrieve it? When? With his tail between his legs Nate takes his last trip to the basement garage to retrieve his car.

Of course there's no traffic. He cruises straight home, accelerating away from Fitzgerald Financials like cosmic forces are pulling him forward, or maybe because Fitzgerald Financials can't get rid of him fast enough.

He notices that his car is low on gas. Should he fill it up? He calculates whether it's better to spend money now or defer it until later, but he can't even pretend to find a difference. Gas is but one of many expenses he'll be paying when no money is coming in. Gas. And rent. And food. Probably he should cut back on ice cream. He skips the gas and goes straight home.

What about that $25,000 dollars he threw into the shark tank? Half of his life savings is unusable, sitting in some Vanguard investment account on the fantasy that Pac-Shoppe stock price will rebound. If he needs it sooner to pay rent he'll have to sell at a loss. He wonders what the hell he was thinking. He realizes he isn't a shark. He's the chum they throw overboard to bait the frenzy.

Nate parks at home, leaves his briefcase in the car and takes that walk. The day is sunny and warm, a perfect spring day, cooler than it has been, with a light breeze.

He needed a lawyer before, and now he needs a lawyer on a whole new level. He was sticking with the Lawyers' Guild on that criminal case, convinced that his case was better off with all the rest. But Catherine suggested the Lawyers' Guild again when Nate called yesterday about the stolen letter. She said the issues were all related and one lawyer would be best – though she invited him to ask the Lawyers' Guild to send him onward with a better recommendation if they wished.

Not only does Nate need a lawyer of a whole new level, but now he doubts whether it is safe to trust Catherine, the UCW or her Lawyers' Guild recommendation at all. They might not want to do Nate wrong, but their interests and attention are elsewhere. Nate is totally on his own.

But if not Catherine's recommendation, then whose? Who can Nate ask?

He misses the diversity of friends from back in the days of Rose. Nowadays Nate isn't only lonely, he's helpless. His universe has shrunk, and he is bumping into the walls. The best he can think of is Ethan Blumenauer of the ruinous free concert tickets. Ethan, at least, is polished, skilled and connected. He hangs out with lawyers and doctors as well as loser accountants like Nate. *Ethan, Ethan, Ethan.* Why does Nate's life keep coming back to Ethan? Is Ethan the sun he orbits around? Nate is the lost and lonely child in his big brother's shadow?

Nonetheless, Ethan is what Nate has and the best he can do. Nate decides to call him.

He'll have to report on his catastrophic date with Kristin, though. He never really did.

Ethan probably heard it from her anyway. Nate might as well tell his side.

It's not much of a plan but at least it's something. When he gets home he'll call Ethan and find his own lawyer.

And pay the lawyer how? He parks that question for later.

Everything is forgotten when Nate arrives home. His mailbox is filled with solicitations. Arrest records must be public, and his has apparently been discovered by the hungry sharks who swim in that tank. Today must be the number of days it takes for records to be found and mailings to be created and delivered because they all arrive at the same time.

Top-Flight Bail Bonding, says the notice on top of the stack. The picture is a man in a suit holding the bars to his cell. "Bail for all misdemeanor and felony charges. Bonding at competitive rates." The records must show that he's been arrested but not that he's been bonded out.

Old Dominion Bail Bonds comes next. *A family owned and operated leader since 2011.* The back of the mailer offers "a variety of financing options to get your loved one out of jail and back into your loving arms."

Apparently Old Dominion Bail Bonds thinks more people may live at this address. People who love Nate and want to see him home.

Sorry, Old Dominion, Nate thinks to himself. It's only me. Nobody loves me except maybe my mother and she doesn't know about any of this – yet. Hopefully the sharks won't find her. What if her mail has advertisements like this, offering to help bail her son out? That's a nice way for mom to find out what he's been doing lately.

He flips as quickly as he can through notices from *Henrico Bail Bonds, TJ Best Bail* and *Affordable Issue.* He is torn between not wanting even to read the promises they offer and a morbid fascination with pledges to "buy your freedom on terms you can afford."

Beneath the advertisements from bail bondsmen come ads from lawyers. "Don't leave your future to chance," advises Cornyn and Leachy. "Take control of your life. Financing options available."

"Find hope," says Stewart and Grassley over a photograph of handcuffs and a list of likely charges: *DUI/DWI, Drug possession/sale, Assault, Violent crimes, Larceny/theft.* The back side says, "Call us now. We'll beat your charge or beat it down." It lists an 800 number for a free consultation.

Nate must really be a criminal now. If he didn't know before, the evidence has reached him where he lives. *Need a lawyer? Here's a lawyer!* What could be easier?

He is reminded of an old Groucho Marx joke. "Any club that would have me, I wouldn't want to join."

It's the same here. Any lawyer who sends him mailings based on his arrest record is a lawyer Nate doesn't want.

Yeah, that's nice. But what are his options?

Catherine *Soda Machine*

Their meeting on Sunday is more like church revival than a business meeting. Indeed, plenty of people just came from church, dressed in literally their Sunday bests. Others look ready for a picnic in their shorts and sneakers. Little kids are watching from grown-up shoulders and big kids are throwing a football on the margins. Catherine correctly trusted the weather predictions and planned to be outside in the UCW parking lot. Again she alerted their neighbors and again she rented some porta potties. Their friends at the Communications Workers of America lent their makeshift stage and set up a sound system. Now they have a big crowd fired up and ready to go.

"What do we want?"

"A union!

"When do we want it?"

"Now!"

Every round increases their collective energy. Posters and signs from past demonstrations are held high in the air. Catherine didn't ask for red for this meeting, since it's internal business not a public demonstration, but still the crowd has learned to red themselves together as a team. Catherine, too, is wearing a red t-shirt as she leads the chant.

"What do we want?"

"A raise!

"When do we want it?"

"Now!"

She tells them the vote is nearing and emphasizes the importance of sticking together. She urges them to stay strong and not to be nervous. "Management can make up stories about how unions will destroy all that is good and holy in America – starting with Pac-Shoppe – but they cannot fire you. Revenge firing is illegal, and we have lawyers on hand." She points to their legal team, who stands and waves so people can see they're real or pull them aside to talk to them later.

Catherine wishes she had the whole bargaining committee with her, but Stephanie and Ramona both have to work at this time. Alberto Ferrera, however, agreed both to join the committee and attend their meeting this afternoon. He is standing up front on the edge of the stage, an imposing figure, better than six feet tall and considerably overweight, a man of Peruvian origin with a black goatee beard. While Catherine invites anyone else who wants to join the committee to come and find them, Alberto waves "come on up" to the stage. The bargaining committee could fit several more before becoming inconveniently large, and more people brings more ideas to the discussion and more legitimacy to the conclusion. Catherine wants every piece of this to be as inclusive and public as possible. She is grateful, therefore, when someone calls an important question from the audience.

"What if we get a raise ... but our union dues cost just as much?"

It's a fair question. Catherine spends most of her time debunking the myth that raises will drive the company out of business, and explaining that the question is not whether there is enough money but who gets it. But the question of dues also comes up regularly, in private conversation and in group meetings. This time she tries a new approach she learned from a colleague in Minnesota.

"Unions are not a soda machine," she declares, a purposefully perplexing response. When people look up in confusion Catherine knows they're primed to listen.

"With a soda machine, you put money in and get soda out. That's how it works. Money goes in. Soda comes out. If the soda doesn't come out ... then something went wrong, and you can complain about it.

"Unions aren't like that. Dues go in and raises come out ... complain if you don't get what you want. That's not how unions work."

People are looking closely at Catherine. Some even seem to be uncomfortable. Isn't a raise the point?

"A union is like a gym membership," Catherine explains. "Paying your dues lets you use the gym. Paying your dues means you can lift weights or run on the treadmill. But actually lifting the weights or running the miles ...that's up to you.

If you're not in better shape at the end of the month, you can't blame the gym."

Heads start nodding. People are making the connection.

"Your union is your tool. Creating a union enables you to take your complaints and demands to management. With your union, you can complain about how things are, and suggest ways to make things better. The union puts you in position to bargain together for higher wages or better benefits.

"But that doesn't happen because Alberto and Stephanie and the bargaining committee wave magic wands. It happens because all of us band together to be taken seriously. Like we're doing now." She raises her voice and shouts her conclusion, "*You get in shape by using the gym, not by paying your membership dues.*"

Somebody in back hollers one of Catherine's favorite slogans, "Pac-Shoppe works because we do!"

"That's right," she agrees. "Pac-Shoppe works because we do. And your union will work because you do." She gestures around the crowd, hoping that they appreciate their size and can see in themselves the collective power they've acquired in the past few weeks. "We are going to win this vote. We are going to get a contract. We are going to get a raise."

Catherine is thrilled by the level of applause that comes back to her. She pauses to let the enthusiasm roll, and so people can look around and see each other clapping. Technically they can win an NLRB election for union recognition with 51% of the vote ... but that would mean 49% of the people are against them. That's no way to start a union. Catherine wants to win with an overwhelming majority. She wants to build something that will last long after she's gone.

Monday morning and today Nate is really out of work. Today is the first day he doesn't report for duty.

Last night he didn't even turn his alarm on.

Today he wakes up at his ordinary time anyway. He's programmed. Programmed for work.

Except it is Monday morning and Nate is not only out of work, he is disgraced. He will be looking for work without a reference or recommendation.

"Why are you leaving?" prospective employers will ask.

"Oh, I stole confidential client information. My boss had to fire me."

Not great for a job interview.

Will Nate's reputation follow him, even without a formal reference or background check? Mr. Daniels is widely known and respected in Richmond. He might talk about Nate informally at lunch, or people will feel free to ask.

Mr. Daniels won't lie to protect him. He wouldn't lie at all.

Unlike Nate, apparently.

Nate rests in bed staring at the ceiling, thinking thoughts that cannot possibly be useful to anyone for anything, until finally he kicks himself out of bed.

Breakfast. He can plan that far in advance, at least. Make breakfast. Eat it. What next? *Shut up and make breakfast.*

So he makes a fabulous breakfast, way too nice for a work day. He turns stale bread into French Toast, and adds a side of sliced fruit with almonds. Of course, he cleans as he goes so even the kitchen is beautiful when he's done. All that's missing is someone to share it with.

Everyone in Richmond knows Mr. Daniels and his little firm that's now part of Fitzgerald Financials. A Mr. Daniels recommendation would be gold and its absence might be noteworthy. His reputation extends as far as the eye can see.

But *only* as far as the eye can see. Mr. Daniels isn't the President or the Pope. Maybe it's time to put that portability to work. Maybe it's time for Nate to uproot his useless little life here in Richmond – no job, no house, no girlfriend, no prospects. He can be an accountant anywhere. Maybe that's where he should go next.

Or maybe he should find a lawyer. Maybe that's what God and yesterday's junk mail are telling him. "Hey, Nate! I gave you the day off. Go find a lawyer!"

He almost hears God whispering in the background, "You jerk."

He still hasn't called Ethan. He can guess what the Lawyers' Guild will say, telling him to stick with the team and that they have it all under control. He is pondering his next steps – for his day, for his case, for his life – when the doorbell rings.

Oh, good, he thinks. *A distraction.* Maybe it's the Mormons or Jehovah's Witness here to save his soul. What if it's a Girl Scout? Can he afford to buy her cookies?

At the door is a uniformed police officer. "Nathaniel Jonathan Hawley?" he says.

"Yes."

The officer doesn't say another word. He just puts a notice in Nate's hand.

WARRANT OF ARREST – FELONY
COMMONWEATLH OF VIRGINIA. Va. Code § 19.2-71,-72
Henrico County, General District Court

TO ANY AUTHORIZED OFFICER:
You are hereby commanded in the name of the Commonwealth of Virginia forthwith to arrest and bring the Accused before this Court to answer the charge that the Accused did unlawfully and feloniously __________________________

Handwritten into the blank space in big letters in blue ink it says §18.2-95. Grand Larceny.

Underneath the handwriting is a text box pre-printed with Nate's personal information: His full name, age and date of birth, along with the street address where he lives and is presently standing. A separate text box is pre-printed with his race and gender, and a pretty close estimate of his height and weight.

"What am I supposed to do with this?" Nate asks the officer. The officer is white, like Nate, and not far from Nate's height and weight.

"Do you live here?" The officer politely confirms Nate's answer against his copy of the form.

"Yes, sir."

He asks Nate's date of birth, and checks it against the form in his hand.

"I didn't expect you to be home," the officer says as if this is a normal conversation. "I figured you'd be at work."

Thanks for pointing that out, Nate thinks to himself. To the officer he says, "What does this mean? What am I supposed to do with this?" He still wants to be polite even as he is getting confused and a little angry.

"It's just what it says. It's a warrant for your arrest."

"What?" says Nate. He is having a hard time processing this. "I was eating."

"Sorry about that."

"Can I finish breakfast?"

"No, sir," the officer answers politely. He is a professional who has done this many times before. "You are under arrest."

Back at work on Monday, barely cleaned up from the weekend, and Catherine's telephone rings with a number she doesn't recognize. "You've reached Catherine Campbell," she states formally for the stranger.

"This is Mitch Fowler from Pac-Shoppe," replies the voice on the other side. "Director of Virginia operations."

"Nice to meet you," Catherine says at once, stepping into one of their private rooms and closing the door behind her. She can open it if she wants to make this public, but right now she doesn't want any distractions.

"You know we got the message from the mayor a few days ago," says Mitch Fowler. "I figured this would be better than email. I told the mayor I was planning to call."

"I am happy to hear from you. Yes, I agree" says Catherine. "Talking is better than email." She doesn't need the reminder about the mayor. It's amazing what a few words from a powerful person can do. She finds a blank sheet of paper and pulls a pen from her pocket.

While Catherine makes herself a desk, Mitch Fowler launches into a monologue about Pac-Shoppe's history, telling how it grew from a single storefront in Seattle to nationwide chain thanks to its "visionary leadership, hard working staff and commitment to its customers." Soon Catherine is barely listening. Mitch Fowler sounds like TV commercial she would have turned off, or a puff-piece magazine article she would never read.

"How can I help you?" she asks when he pauses long enough for her to interrupt.

That gets her another soliloquy about Pac-Shoppe's commitment to staff and its desire for a "smooth, well-functioning workplace."

"Have you considered increasing pay for the overnight shift?" Catherine suggests, launching from his own stated desire. "Little things like that would matter a lot. In addition to a raise across-the-board," she adds to remind him who he's talking to.

"That's just it," he says. "I am prepared to offer you a raise."

"Terrific," Catherine replies. "I am happy to hear that. Is this something you are going to do over the phone right now? Or is this something you will do next week when you're negotiating a new contract with your new union?" She deliberately compresses the time frame to remind him what else is going on.

Mitch Fowler follows her tone away from soft marketing into business. "I can offer you $8.10 an hour right now," he says sharply. "Across the board. Everyone now getting $7.85 will move up to $8.10 at the next paycheck, with proportionate increases up the scale. How does that sound to you? Pretty good, eh?"

Catherine does the math in her head. "Sound like three percent," she replies. "Maybe higher than inflation, maybe enough to cover the cost of gas." She is happy to see movement but doesn't want him to think she's fooled. "If you'd offered that when this started, people might have taken it and run."

"I'm offering it to you now."

"But we've come a long way since we started," Catherine observes. "To begin, I can't do anything without asking our negotiating team, and probably the entire union."

"You don't have a union."

"Next week I will. Shall I bring them your current offer ... or perhaps you have a better one?"

"I'll get back to you."

"It's been nice to talk. Thank you for calling."

Sadly, Nate knows how to get his fingerprints taken. He relaxes his muscles and lets the technician roll them one at a time over the ink pad and the fingerprint form, eight little boxes, labelled clearly, one for each finger and another box for both thumbs.

Again the officer tells him to smile for the mugshot. Again he doesn't. He's not happy to be here, and he's not smiling. Someone else might even see it later. *Hello, Mr. Daniels.*

This is new. He is given three minutes in a telephone booth with a telephone book. The sign above the phone says "Free. Domestic only." He looks up the National Lawyer's Guild, and calls the only lawyer he knows. Annette Wilcox isn't in but he leaves a message with a live receptionist. At least it wasn't voicemail. He uses his last minute to look up the local office of the United Commercial Workers to see if he can get Catherine Campbell, but the door opens and an officer escorts him out before he can dial. "I need more time," Nate pleads.

The officer doesn't say a word, just gestures toward the line of people who also want the phone.

The officer brings Nate to a holding pen that's both new and familiar. It's new because he hasn't been here before. It's familiar because it looks like other places he's been spending time recently.

The pen is large enough for maybe thirty people, with ten people in it now, all men. The floor and walls are concrete. The front wall with the gate is barred with vertical steel bars, just like his jail cell and in the movies. The concrete back wall has a steel bench bolted in, with a few men sitting down. The side walls don't have benches, but several men sit on the floor and lean their backs against the bare cement. Two men are standing in the center of the room and talking quietly. Another man is lying on the floor, head in the corner, flat on his back, apparently asleep, legs pointing toward the center of the room, spread more widely than he would probably want them if he were awake.

The two uniformed officers standing outside are both white. Inside the pen Nate is the only white person.

There is a familiar uncovered steel can toilet at each end of the cell. Nate winces as the cell door slams shut, though not as badly as the first time it happened. Nate soon learns that the door opens and closes regularly as inmates come and go, shoved in by police officers or escorted away to whatever happens to each of them next.

Catherine *Accepting Rejection*

Catherine knows she shouldn't have rejected the offer without discussing it with the bargaining committee first. That's why she created the committee and why she wanted to have group determination of every decision. After all, it's not her life, not her wage and not her private negotiation.

It's also dangerous. Pac-Shopped might take the offer directly to the workers and tell them to take it with no union, or get nothing at all. How long before they make a move like that? What if they do? Some workers will want to take the money and run.

She steps out of her newly private room to make sure nothing needs attention in the main office, then she closes the door and telephones the bargaining committee.

She reaches Ramona first. Ramona quickly calculates it was a 25 cent raise and exclaims, "They offered us a quarter? That's a quarter of what we should accept. Well done, chief. Keep the pressure on."

Stephanie is more complicated. "You were right to reject, but I'm not sure it's right without asking us first."

They discuss the role of the bargaining committee and the importance of negotiating as a team. Catherine concludes equal parts chastened because Stephanie is right that Catherine shouldn't have rejected anything without consultation, and thrilled because Stephanie is really taking ownership of her role and her union team. "I'll talk to Al Ferrera myself," she advises. "He might be tricky."

Together they decide to risk not telling everyone about the 25 cent offer. Everything can't be done as a giant group; that's why they formed the committee. They're happy that Pac-Shoppe is making concessions before negotiations even start. But they fully agree that if they accept a raise now it will reduce the resolve for the union, which will make people worse off in the long run.

"That's why they're doing it," Stephanie observes.

"But they're too late," Catherine agrees. "We've come too far to turn back now."

By the time Catherine is finished in her little room the main office has filled up with workers making outreach calls. Elena is in charge. She is making sure everyone has lists of people to call that line up with their own work schedules and don't overlap each other's. Catherine can tell just by listening in that it's going well. Nobody wonders why they're being called, and they seem to want the union as much as they want a raise.

Ricardo has joined them, too. "I'm just telemarketing," he confesses. "But why sit at home by myself?"

"It's nice in the middle," Catherine replies.

"My eyesight is getting better every day." He adds with a smile, "It's because of the union."

"Obviously. It couldn't be anything else."

They're interrupted by a call her phone doesn't recognize. "This is Sharon Brown at the NLRB," the person declares. "I'm calling to schedule the vote."

Nate *Voice of Experience*

When the door opens this time it's for Nate, and minutes later he's back in a transport van. Somebody is already on board when he's loaded, a tiny woman who is desperately nervous but doesn't speak any English. Nate doesn't know what language she is speaking. Maybe Vietnamese? She looks to be from Southeast Asia, an older woman, maybe sixty, wearing a pretty floral print shirt. Nate can only imagine how frightened she must be, not even understanding the language that took her under arrest. She might have no idea where she is going, or why.

Soon they are parking in the same back lot of the Richmond General District Court. Nate sees the sign, and recognizes the loading bay.

The tiny Asian woman is pulled away as soon as they open the door. The officers don't bother to explain in any language what they are doing or where they are going. They just pull her down a long and narrow hallway.

Nate is escorted courteously and professionally through broader halls back to the same courtroom where he was arraigned just days ago.

The courtroom is busy and crowded with strangers. People are sitting in the benches and standing in the aisles. Court is in session, though the judge up front is not the one with red hair and hoop earrings. This judge is also a woman, though older, African American, and looking more ministerial in her black robes. Court clerks extend beside her on both sides of the bench, while uniformed bailiffs hover behind her and beside every door. Lawyers sit at counsel table in the well of the court, in the middle of something with their laptops open. Nate is shepherded into a group of chairs off to one side, separated from the rest by a low bannister rail.

As he scans the room looking for a familiar face, Annette Wilcox of the Lawyers' Guild puts her hand on his shoulder. "You're going to be fine," she says.

Catherine *Next*

Nate is in the jury box when Catherine arrives. He spots her as soon as she walks in and he brightens up in surprise. His joy is pure, sweet and unadulterated. He doesn't even try to keep a poker face. He is a two-year old spotting his momma.

"Thank you," he mouths in her direction.

"Good morning," she mouths back.

That gets a wry grin and a shake of his head. He's had better mornings.

Catherine arrived in time for only a short wait. Nate's name is called soon after she finds a place. He steps expertly to the well of the court. "State your name," commands the judge.

"Nathaniel Jonathan Hawley," he replies.

"You are charged with one count of Grand Larceny under Virginia code section 18.2-95, punishable by imprisonment in a state correctional facility for not less than one nor more than twenty years. How do you plead?"

"Not-guilty, your honor."

He sounds more composed and less surprised than Catherine is. The judge continues, "The commonwealth has agreed to defense petition that you be released on your own recognizance. I am willing to accept this recommendation on your verbal assurance that you'll return to court for preliminary hearing on July 12. Can you make that commitment?"

"Yes, your honor."

"And you will abide by the conditions of your release, including commitment not to leave the commonwealth of Virginia."

"Yes, your honor."

"Next."

Nate *1 + 1 = 1*

Attorney Annette Wilcox of the National Lawyers' Guild escorts Nate out a side door and into the adjacent hallway. It is broad and tiled, a public courtroom corridor crowded with lawyers, clients and families finding space for private conversations. She walks him down the hall, looking for a space big enough to talk, and finds an unused courtroom in an adjacent corridor.

They aren't the only people in it, but the far corner is empty. Annette Wilcox treats it like a private conference room she's used many times before. "I'm sorry you got caught like that," she begins. She has light brown hair mingled with gray, cut short with a gentle curl. She wears big brown tortoise shell eyeglasses that would have gotten her teased in grade school but somehow suit a middle-aged lawyer who probably splits her time between the computer and the court. Wilcox looks roughly forty years old, but Nate suspects she is pushing fifty and looks young, not thirty-six and looking old.

"Thank you for coming," he replies. "I'm sure you had something else to do."

"I'm glad I was able to," she says. "In fact, this is the case I was working on."

"But this is a whole new case," Nate protests. "This is felony larceny, not misdemeanor obstruction of traffic. And I'm charged by myself, not as one of a crowd. The judge said I could get twenty years." Nate is pleased with his concise and legalistic explanation, emphasis on the ending. He needs her to understand where he's coming from. Twenty years is approximately forever.

Annette is having none of it. "This is Pac-Shoppe attacking UCW from a different angle. They're using you to get at Catherine."

"I don't need a different lawyer of my own?"

"You can get your own lawyer if you want. I'd be happy to work with them. Do you have someone in mind, or do you want suggestions?"

She makes it sound so easy, so matter of fact. Asking for a different lawyer isn't some great betrayal or crucial parting of the ways. It's just details of administration. As an accountant, Nate gives and receives references all the time.

He realizes he's weighted it too much. And she's right that Pac-Shoppe is the ultimate party in interest. Maybe one lawyer, the same lawyer, is what he needs.

Wilcox says, "Give me a day to read the complaint and the police report. I'll let you know if it looks like you can benefit from someone else."

Before Nate can reply, Catherine peers through the door and spots them in the corner. Only now it occurs to Nate that they've been running away from her. Catherine had no idea where he and Wilcox went when they left the courtroom, and she might not have found them. Catherine is wearing a yellow sun dress that's no doubt practical around the office but makes her look pretty in a wholesome country way here in a municipal courtroom.

"Why did the belt get arrested?" she asks as she joins them.

Nate knows this one, and its familiarity makes it even funnier. "Because it held up a pair of pants."

The joke changes everything. It's ridiculous that Nate's been arrested on some grand theft scheme. He is willing to confess mea culpa on the ethics of accounting, but it's preposterous for Pac-Shoppe to have Nate arrested for not helping hide evidence of Pac-Shoppe's own crimes. Surely, they can't get away with that.

Catherine *Language Trouble*

"I know I owe you lunch," Catherine tells Nate when the lawyering is finished ...

"... but you're busy and you need to postpone until later," he finishes her thought. He seems surprisingly relaxed, considering how he spent his morning.

"I'm in the middle of negotiating the date of the vote and the exact language on the ballot," she explains. "Check this out." She opens her phone to show him what Pac-Shoppe proposed for the ballot, which arrived while he was in court. "The vote is Yes or No."

> *I agree to give United Commercial Workers the exclusive power to negotiate all conditions of my employment and that I shall have no rights other than those afforded to me by the United Commercial Workers under my contract with them.*

"Pretty unfriendly," Nate says.

"Phrased like that, even I might not vote to join the union," Catherine replies.

"Go make your counteroffer," he says. "I'll walk home. It's a beautiful day."

"I can give you a ride." Catherine knows he arrived in a police van.

"I am made of time."

By the time Nate gets home he is starving. Breakfast was interrupted and he was too cheap to buy lunch while he was out. As soon as he steps in the door he is reminded of what's good in life. His table is all set, with French toast sitting uneaten on a platter and a lovely fruit salad that hardly looks worse for a few hours unattended.

He puts the French toast in the microwave with maple syrup and heats them together, chewing on almonds and pear slices while he waits. "Whoever made this breakfast was really smart," he says to the open air.

When the microwave chimes he answers back, "He's a catch, too. Some lucky woman should snatch him up."

That ends the dialogue, though. Sitting down to eat, he realizes that he is unemployed and has two criminal cases pending against him, one of them a felony. Maybe he's not such a catch, after all.

At least he has a lawyer. He is convinced that he should keep Annette Wilcox for both cases together. She even said that this case fits in UCW's retainer so he needn't pay her more. That matters more than it used to. He can't complain about a free lawyer.

Then comes another knock on the door. What now? Girl Scout cookies, he hopes. Maybe he can find a few dollars for Thin Mints.

It isn't the Girl Scouts, but at least it isn't the police. This time it is a young woman from UPS, dressed in the distinctive brown uniform. She passes Nate an envelope labeled UPS Express, boldly colored in red and black, with a gold UPS logo in one corner.

As he turns it over to see who it's from she hands him a digital notebook. "Sign that you've received it."

Nate scrawls a passing resemblance of his signature onto the touch screen and hands it back. "Thank you," he replies, with no clue what he's thanking her for.

He doesn't examine the envelope until she's gone and he's back at his breakfast. "Let's see," he asks the envelope. "Who are you from?"

The envelope doesn't answer. The return address is simply a street in Charlottesville that means nothing to him. He pulls the tab that unzips the envelope along one side.

Inside is a one-page letter. It is addressed to Nate and from the law firm of Drewry and Danziger in Charlottesville. In bold capital letters across the top it says, NOTICE OF INTENT TO SUE.

Dear Mr. Hawley,

> It is with deepest regret that we write to inform you that it has become necessary for Pac-Shoppe, Inc. to consider legal proceedings regarding your theft of intellectual property from Fitzgerald Financials, specifically a letter dated April 12 between Pac-Shoppe and Ms. Theresa Staedtler of Ultimate Engagement, Inc.

The letter goes on to itemize $6.5 million in actual damages for increased payroll costs associated with unauthorized release of the letter, plus $8 million in damage to "reputation, goodwill and other intangible assets" and an additional $5 million in punitive damages for "willful and wanton disregard" of standard practices regarding confidentiality.

The total damage claim is $19.5 million. Pac-Shoppe gives Nate seven days to respond with a plan for satisfaction or they will "commence legal action to recover the debt without further notice."

Nate can hardly believe this is real. Pac-Shoppe wants to sue him for $19.5 million? Annette Wilcox is way out of her league.

A second page alerts him that a collateral action will be initiated against Fitzgerald Financials, should he fail to offer an acceptable remedy within the seven-day window. The action against Fitzgerald Financials will be based on negligent supervision, including a "grossly reckless level of indifference" to security and confidentiality. Should Nate not be able to make Pac-Shoppe whole, they will seek the same remedy from Fitzgerald Financials.

So Pac-Shoppe will sue Mr. Daniels if Nate doesn't pay up? That's ridiculous.

Nate is sure Mr. Daniels has all the lawyers he needs. Nate will be embarrassed even to look at him.

Pac-Shoppe overplayed its hand. The NLRB mediator looked at Pac-Shoppe's proposed ballot language and concluded that they were not bargaining in good faith. Catherine ended up with an expedited vote and ballot language that the mediator will draft herself. Catherine hasn't seen it yet.

Alberto Ferrera requires extra attention, though. "Aren't unions corrupt and inefficient?" he asks.

He and Catherine are in the parking lot at UCW making plans for the vote. The weather is perfect, sunny and still. Alberto suggested they carry the table outside, and he couldn't have been more right. Now they are sitting outside as if at a picnic, though Alberto overwhelms his little folding chair and in his big blue t-shirt he looks like the Smurfs Catherine watched when she was a kid.

Catherine is always happy for questions like Alberto's. It's better to kick around those longstanding myths than live with them in silence. "I don't know where Jimmy Hoffa is buried," she replies. "If there was corruption back then, there isn't much now. I mean, there are millions of union members and employees in thousands of local affiliates. If the occasional jerk steals from the union cookie jar, it pales in comparison to what banks, mortgage companies and Wall Street get away with. Unions generally want to do right by their members."

"What about the inefficiency?" Alberto continues. "Don't unions slow things down?" He looks so sincere and concerned, Catherine thinks of a father talking to his child. She sees that he's wearing a wedding ring, though she doesn't know about kids.

"Inefficiency can be real," she confesses. "But mostly it's about the relationship with the employer. If the employer chooses to tap the staff for ideas, efficiencies or expertise, then everybody can come out ahead. If the relationship is adversarial and about nothing but rules, timeclocks and sick days, then employees tend to work to the rule... and probably not much more. That doesn't serve anybody very well."

Alberto rubs his goatee beard. "I never really thought about it that way." Colored paint on his forearms suggests maybe he has young children, after all.

"Take Pac-Shoppe. Do you have any ideas for how to make things run more smoothly?"

"I don't know anything about running a giant corporation," Alberto replies.

"I mean little things about your store. Do you have ideas about how to make things faster, safer or easier?"

"Of course," he declares. He launches into stories about pallet jacks rolling around the loading bay, and how merchandise is unloaded according to its brand of origin rather than the aisle it ends up in. "I have to go back and forth like a hundred times a day," he concludes. "It's a huge waste of time for no good reason." Catherine hardly understands what he's talking about, not knowing how stock moves inside Pac-Shoppe, but it sounds sensible and Alberto is in position to think about it everyday, day after day.

"Has anybody ever asked you for ideas like that?" Catherine asks.

"Are you kidding me?"

"Why do you say that? Management should ask you questions like that all the time."

"That would be better for everyone," he says.

"That's why you need a union."

Nate *Busy and Fruity*

The office of the National Lawyers' Guild is on Marshall street near the courthouse and the capitol. It turns out to be a beautiful old townhouse in a pricey neighborhood, with gabled windows and a sunporch of white columns with Corinthian crowns. The door is similarly columned and crowned, with a bronze knocker in the center. This is not the dilapidated shack Nathan expected, but a plaque beside the door answers the obvious question, thanking a generous donor for the bequest of what was once his private residence.

Nate knocks with his hand, not the bronze knocker, and pushes the door open without waiting for reply, the way he would enter an office building, not someone's home.

Inside it is obvious that the bequest covered the property but not the upkeep. The wallpaper is peeling from the walls and the beige carpet is threadbare and stained. By the entry it's so bad the Lawyer's Guild covers it with a welcome mat.

They've also turned the beautiful entry foyer into a crowded reception area. At the base of a staircase with carved handrail sits an old woman at a crooked desk. Folding chairs suggest what she would offer if Nate wanted to sit. In the living room to the side, a window that must be broken is boarded over and covered with a poster of Martin Luther King. Three people are working at a table in their own folding chairs, notebooks and laptops open before them.

"I'm here for Annette Wilcox," Nate says to the old woman. "I have an appointment."

The woman looks like she might have been here since the bequest, wearing an old white head scarf and thick mother-of-pearl eyeglasses. On her desk is a calendar notebook and a digital device that looks like an intercom. The woman turns away from Nate and calls up the stairs, "Annie, someone's here to see you."

A familiar voice comes from upstairs, "Send him up."

Nate steps past the old woman and climbs the stairs, receiving barely a glance from the people working in the living room.

Clearly this level was once bedrooms, with three doors visible from the landing. Annette steps out of the far door as Nate reaches the top stair. "Come in," she says. A poster of Bruce Springsteen on the wall beside her door is hung so it almost looks like she's talking to Bruce, not Nate.

Annette's office shows the same blend of vintage grandeur and modern practicality. The walls are lined with bookshelves, some classic and some Ikea, all filled with books. The windows have Corinthian frames consistent with the porch, and curtains of faded paisley. But her desk is modern with technology. A desktop computer is connected to dual monitors and a laptop is also open and playing classical music. A carved wood end table has become a printer stand.

"This isn't urgent," Annette says as he enters. "There is no emergency and you aren't being chased by the police."

"What does that mean?" Nate replies. "That's good, right?"

"That means we can take our time. Come in, have a seat." She gestures to a pair of old wooden armchairs with paisley cushions that match the window treatments. "Would you like some tea?" She points to a Pyrex water boiler on a sideboard, beside an array of tea bags.

"No, thanks." Nate replies reflexively, then corrects himself. "Sorry. Tea might be nice."

She flips a switch on the water boiler. As she pulls out mugs, the boiler hisses and the water begins to bubble. "Rooibos?" she inquires.

Nate doesn't know what rooibos means, but he guesses it's a type of tea.

"Sounds good," he replies.

A moment later they are sitting together in the armchairs, each of them holding a mug of hot water that's steeping tea.

"All news is good," she begins, then she too corrects herself. "Okay, maybe *all* news isn't good. But regarding your cases, all news is good."

Good news is better than bad news, of course, but Nate notices that *cases* is pluralized. He has a whole rap sheet by now.

"Start with misdemeanor obstruction of traffic," Annette goes on. "On June 22 everyone else will appear in court and plead guilty to time served. That one night in custody will suffice to satisfy their sentences. Your case, however, will be dismissed in its entirety."

"Dismissed?" Nate echoes.

"You weren't wearing red. You don't appear in any of the earlier protest photos. You don't work at Pac-Shoppe and you aren't on any list of community members who attended planning meetings."

Nate nods his head as Annette itemizes his innocence.

"The police report states that you were on the sidewalk when the police officer confronted and apprehended you, and he subsequently sat you with everyone else in the intersection."

She asks rhetorically, "How can you be prosecuted for Obstruction of Traffic when you were on the sidewalk until the officer moved you into the intersection?"

Nate nods agreement with her rhetorical question.

"It was too much even for the prosecutors. They recognize that you got swept up by mistake, and they will voluntarily dismiss the charge against you at the June 22 court date. You do need to attend, however."

Nate replies, "Is this where I say 'thank you'?"

"You can if you want," she says. "Though it shouldn't be extraordinary for prosecutors to do the right thing."

"So I need to show up in court," Nate confirms, "but that case is finished? Gone? Goodbye?" Nate doesn't know if he should be sad or thankful that he probably won't be missing work on that day.

"Gone, goodbye. But it's still America. You owe $130 in court costs plus $80 to the victim fund and something-or-other in processing fees. All told, the cost of being innocent was your night in jail plus not quite $250 in related costs."

"Oh."

"But don't worry. UCW will pay for that, along with everyone else's. After June 22 you'll be free to leave on the Obstruction case. Just don't worry if you receive receipts or payment orders in the mail. I alert you so you know to disregard them."

Nate remembers the bail bonds advertising, and has no doubt that a warning would have been useful. But he also hears in her tone that they aren't finished yet. She steps past the water boiler, throws her tea bag into a trashcan, and carries the can over for Nate to deposit his own used tea bag.

He manages the transaction without dripping, and tests a sip before she sits down but it is still too hot to drink.

"Now about the felony," she continues. "They claim that you stole that letter."

"Correct. But this time I actually did it." He explains with more detail what he told her hastily in the empty courtroom, and Annette says she has discussed the matter with Catherine Campbell.

"Still," she goes on, "the complaint alleges that you stole the letter from Pac-Shoppe."

"It was Pac-Shoppe's letter."

"No," she corrects him. "It was *Theresa Staedtler's* letter. The letter was addressed to Theresa Staedtler, and mailed to her. Theresa Staedtler might step up as the complaining witness and the complaint could be amended accordingly, but the complaint as-is does not correctly allege the violation it claims."

"I see." Nate is starting to understand what lawyers do all day.

"The letter was taken from the files of Fitzgerald Financials. They, too, could complain about wrongful conversion of property..."

Nate finishes the thought for her. "But they, too, are not properly identified in the complaint."

"You're getting the hang of this. Now I don't know the details of your departure. Do you think Fitzgerald Financials would come after you, attack-style, like Pac-Shoppe did?"

They discuss for a while the circumstances of his departure. Mr. Daniels clearly feels betrayed but Nate doesn't think Mr. Daniels would come after him like this. He would probably let it go. Annette goes on to explain that Pac-Shoppe has an ownership interest in the thoughts expressed in the letter, along the lines of a copyright, even after the letter is mailed. "But such ownership interest is not stated in the complaint with sufficient precision to constitute notice."

"So what happens next?"

"I'll file a motion. They'll file a motion back, maybe amend the complaint. Theresa Staedtler will probably be helpful to them, but Fitzgerald Financials probably has better things to do. I'll go back and forth with Pac-Shoppe like that, except that we probably won't even go back and forth because Catherine is discussing this in the context of the union negotiations and Pac-Shoppe will eventually drop the whole thing ... but until then, we'll act like it's real and we lawyers will keep each other busy."

Nate thinks he's following her, including her contradiction about whether they actually go back and forth. The real news is that Catherine considers him part of her negotiations. Essential, not a distraction. He also discovers that his tea is cool enough to drink, and that Rooibus tea is tasty, fruity and sweet without sugar. He resolves to remember the name even though he's not much of a tea drinker. "May I tell you my favorite lawyer joke?" he asks.

"The world needs more lawyer jokes," Annette replies.

"A town that's too small to support one lawyer can support two."

She smiles as she, too, sips her tea. "Too true. The world needs more lawyer jokes but not more lawyers."

From her point of view they might be coasting to completion but Nate isn't finished yet. "There are other developments," he says. "Remember when you said 'all news isn't good'? I have more of the other kind."

"Lay it on me."

Nate pulls out the envelope that was delivered yesterday when he got back from court, Pac-Shoppe's multi-million dollar lawsuit for theft of intellectual property. "Maybe this is too much and I need a separate lawyer," he says, "but it seems related so I should at least ask you what you think."

She's barely listening as she manipulates the NOTICE OF INTENT TO SUE out of the envelope. As she reviews it she starts to smile, and when she reaches itemized damages she actually laughs out loud.

"I'm sorry," she says. "I shouldn't laugh. You probably think this is serious."

Nate nods his head earnestly to signal how right she is.

"Catherine tells me you're a whiz at math," Annette says. "And you've examined Pac-Shoppe's books. Tell me, then. How much do you think is Pac-Shoppe's payroll at these Virginia locations? How much will a twenty-five cent raise set them back?"

Nate has looked at this many times from many different directions. He knows a dollar raise would cost roughly a million dollars a year. So he cuts that by a quarter and announces his results.

"Right," she says. "That's the joke."

She pauses like she expects Nate to get it.

But Nate looks helpless enough that she goes ahead and explains. "The lawsuit claims $6.5 million in 'actual damages.' You just estimated the actual damages potentially credited to your misconduct in the $250,000 range. Now let me ask you this. I know you were only estimating. But are your estimates off by a factor of twenty?"

"Actually it would be twenty-six."

"It's not anything," Anette says. "It's a joke. $6.5 million in actual damages is a joke. Add another $8 million in pain and suffering, then $5 million more in punitive damages?" She raises her cup of tea like she's hoisting a trophy into the air. "$5 million punitive damages is what Bayer gets if it accidentally puts cyanide in its aspirin jars. $5 million in punitives is what the bus company gets when its blind, drunk, unlicensed driver plows into a school bus at the end of a 36 hour shift. Pac-Shoppe is not getting $5 million in punitive damages because you snuck into someone's files."

Nate is convinced, but he is not as entertained as she is. "What about the Mr. Daniels part? What about the threat to sue Fitzgerald Financials?

"Pac-Shoppe is going to sue its majority shareholder?" she asks him back.

He understands the irony but he is not as optimistic as she is. "So what should I do?"

"I'll talk to Catherine. You should just keep drinking your tea."

Catherine *Shift and Change*

The first round of voting begins at 8:00 AM and closes at 10:00 AM, an hour on either side of the 9:00 AM shift change. Another two-hour window will open before and after the 5:00 PM shift change, so everyone should get at least one chance at the vote today. They designed it to make it easy to vote, though people who aren't working today would need to make a trip.

Catherine and Elena are the official observers for the union side. They will monitor both voting periods, along with their counterparts from Pac-Shoppe and the NLRB, looking for signs of threats, promises or intimidation. They are in the north side Pac-Shoppe, though similar arrangements have been made to the East. Voting takes place in the locker room with the timeclock. Elena shows Catherine the rack of time cards on the wall and where the poster that said *Who wants to be the next Deb Little?* has been taken down.

Stephanie Lerner shows up sharply at 7:59 AM, a minute before the polls open. "I wanted to be first," she says. She is nearing the end of her overnight shift, and it's easy for her to slip into the locker room for a minute. "Is this the ballot?"

A stack of paper ballots and pens are set beside cardboard ballot boxes. The technology is the same as a vote for class president in elementary school. People mark their ballots, fold them up and put them in the box. The language on the ballot was drafted by the NLRB and comes straight from the text book:

> *Do you agree that the United Commercial Workers should be recognized by Pac-Shoppe for purposes of collective bargaining in current locations in metropolitan Richmond?*

The teams will count the ballots manually at six o'clock after the evening shift change.

Pac-Shoppe did, in fact, offer to move Stephanie off the graveyard shift to facilitate participation on their committee, but she declined the offer. "I'd feel bad that somebody got stuck with it instead of me," she explains. "Unless someone actually wants the graveyard shift. I'll change shifts after we win an incentive for working overnight. Then I'll give it to someone who wants it – unless the incentive is so good I decide to keep it myself."

Right now the NLRB monitor is watching and they aren't supposed to chat. "ID?" the monitor says to Stephanie, holding out her hand.

Stephanie hands over her drivers license.

The NLRB monitor compares it to names on a print-out, checks off Stephanie's name and hands her card back.

Catherine looks over her shoulder to make sure that Stephanie is checked off correctly and that only one single name has been checked. Stephanie has now voted ... and she can't vote again.

If Stephanie didn't have a drivers license or other official ID, she could show a Pac-Shoppe paystub. Those were the terms negotiated by the bargaining committee.

Stephanie is all business as she takes her ballot and a pen and finds a private place to mark it up. Catherine wishes she could join her to share the moment, but she properly and respectfully leaves her alone to vote in secret. Stephanie is smiling as she folds the paper, and by the time she puts it in the box she is glowing. She turns to Catherine with pride like she's just birthed a baby or bought a new car. This was *her* vote. She worked for it, she made it happen, and – if things go as expected – this will be her union.

But she doesn't venture over to talk or even shake Catherine's hand. Her moment elapsed, she hurries back to work.

By now a second person has found his way in. "Is this where we vote?"

Nate Moonrise

Nate is feeling sorrier for himself than he probably should. Okay, he is out of work and devoid of purpose. But he's not in jail and his legal problems seem to have lifted. He should be happy, right?

He makes himself yet another nice dinner from simple ingredients and goes for a walk. It is early on a beautiful spring evening. Families are out with children and couples are out holding hands. He walks a familiar route past restaurants he likes to a little park with swing sets and a creek.

As he turns into the park the moon takes his breath away. It is gigantic, full, and low on the horizon. Somehow it's magnified, probably by the angle through the atmosphere, and glowing orange, probably from the sunset. Nate has spent enough time outside to know it will be full but he wasn't expecting a scene like this. He sees a dad pointing it out to his child, and a woman working to take a picture from her cell phone. The moon is simply magnificent, but Nate has nobody to share it with.

No, he thinks. He can do better than that.

He takes out his phone and texts Catherine. "Are you busy? Look outside to the East. Look at the moon."

He regrets sending it as soon as it's gone.

The spectacle might be different from wherever Catherine is, or gone by whenever she looks. *Look at the moon*? She might think he's an idiot.

Catherine At rest

Catherine and her crew are at the UCW office finishing off the evening. Between administrative procedures with the NLRB, cleaning up Pac-Shoppe's locker room , and storing and sealing ballots, there is more than enough to do. In the middle of this she receives a text message from Nate.

"Are you busy?"

Of course!

"Look at the moon."

He has to be friggin kidding me. She sympathizes that he's out of work, but everyone doesn't have free time like he does.

Nonetheless, as she walks down the hall she looks through the window that she knows points to the East. Just visible through the slats of the venetian blind is what must be the moon. The glimpse is enough to make her stop to open the blind.

"Wow," she says, as it comes fully into view. The moon is huge and swollen and orange, an oversized vision from myth and legend.

Catherine's exclamation plus her unusual move with the blind catches the attention of other people. In a moment a small crowd has gathered around her. Looking together at the moon, the world comes to rest.

Ramona whispers, "Give us bread, and give us roses."

They stand together in solidarity, gazing at the moon like nothing else matters in the world.

But soon this, too, must come to an end. Catherine lowers the blind and ushers everyone back to work.

Last thing before she sits at her desk she texts back to Nathaniel, "Thanks."

Nate *Promises*

The front page of the Richmond Times Dispatch makes the outcome clear. *Union Scores Decisive Win in Pac-Shoppe Campaign*, it says across the top.

Nate turns the pages, looking for quotes by Catherine Campbell, maybe a picture. But she isn't reported at all. A Ramona McNamara calls it "a win for workers," and one Alberto Ferrera says, "we'll finally get paid what we're worth." Pac-Shoppe worker Stephanie Lerner is less celebratory, though. "We wanted a union and a raise. We're halfway there."

Elena Perez merits a story of her own, a whole sidebar that goes from her coma to her wheelchair. A picture shows her with her husband, who is recovering from his own workplace injury.

Nate turns on his computer to see how it's reported elsewhere, but first he checks his email, and his eye goes straight to Catherine Campbell in the middle of his inbox. It is a single message with the subject line, *X-charts*.

The message contains no text but one big image. It isn't her toasting with her friends or celebrating victory. The message doesn't contain vote counts or even – dare he dream? – a proposed date for dinner. Instead it is the promised chart in the shape of an X. It's a graph with the time scale starting in the year 1970 and counting up to 2017. The ascending line is red, labeled *Top 1% Share of National Income*. It wiggles a bit but rises distinctly over the years.

The descending line is blue and labeled *Union Density*. It, too, wiggles as it goes but declines prominently over the same period. Together the two lines make an X. The caption at the bottom reads, *Inequality Rises as Union Density Declines*.

Correlation isn't causation and Nate doesn't know these data series, but the message is pretty clear. As unions shrink, the top gets more of the money. That's probably why the big guys go after the unions. If he wants more, Catherine provides a link to the underlying data.

Nate replies not with a comment but with a question.

The farmer has 38 sheep. Why did the sheep dog bring back 40?

Catherine answers within the minute: *The farmer said to round them up.*

SIX

Negotiations will take a while. Pac-Shoppe's first offer is a thirty-five cent increase to the hourly rate at the bottom end, better than the twenty-five they offered over the telephone, plus an extra sixty cents for people who work overnight.

Catherine's bargaining committee is pleased but hardly overwhelmed.

"Why don't they just give us the non-economic issues?" Stephanie asks. "Better control over our shifts, regular schedules, things like that?"

Catherine doesn't have a good answer to that. It does seem that they should make concessions that don't cost them anything, to show good will if nothing else.

"It's about control," Ramona offers. "If we know our schedules then we can make other plans. If we're always waiting to see what they give us, it keeps us dependent and subservient."

"What will UCW dues cost?" Alberto wants to know.

"It depends on people's pay and how many hours they work. Something in the range of ten cents an hour for people who work full time."

"They offered us thirty-five cents already?" he confirms.

"Including the dues deduction, that moves your wage from $7.85 to $8.10, and we've only gotten started."

"Sign me up," Alberto says.

"Hold out for more," Ramona replies.

As they discuss pros and cons, Catherine points out that any agreement the committee reaches with management has to be ratified by the full membership.

"We should take the thirty-five now and ask for more again next year," Alberto says.

Catherine hears in that an adult looking to the future, not a child grabbing the candy now. "Here's a caution," she adds. "Next year people will see union dues taken from every paycheck but they won't get a weekly reminder of how much smaller their paychecks used to be – and still would be –without the union. Even if we succeed at negotiating improved schedules or other soft goods, people will forget how that happened. But they'll see union dues taken from their paychecks, and they'll start to resent us."

"Our opponents will use it to create division," Ramona observes.

"Exactly," Catherine replies. "Don't fall for it. Not next week. Not next year. The union is yours. It's your partnership and your tool. It works because you do. But it's not a soda machine."

"Will you still be with us next year?" Elena asks.

"If you want me," Catherine replies. "I work for UCW, and UCW is your union. So I work for you now. Literally."

The day the union contract is announced, Pac-Shoppe stock rockets back to where it was before this all began. Mr. Daniels was right, investors didn't care about the wages, what they disliked was the noise and uncertainty.

So Fitzgerald Financials made a boatload of money for doing no work. Hundreds of millions of dollars magically appeared on its balance sheets, though no new goods were produced, nothing was invented or improved, and no additional sales were made. Money came literally from nowhere and for nothing.

Of course, Nate made a little himself. His $25,000 risk suddenly seems like a shrewd investment. He watches the stock price climb straight back to where it started, then creep up a little more in the next few days. When it starts to drop back down he sells it all.

He doesn't have the stomach for this. He doesn't want to watch his gains disappear, no matter how ill-gotten and unnatural they feel. He takes the first $25,000 and puts it back in his nice, safe, diversified Vanguard mutual fund. He intends to forget this ever happened, and see it again at retirement. That leaves him with not quite $6,000 profit, money that he was never supposed to have, a souvenir, if you will.

That profit goes straight into his checking account.

He needs it right now, of course. He'll be without income for a while, but still paying for food, rent and all the rest. He fears his little reserve fund will run out before he knows it.

But looking at the new money in his bank account doesn't give him the pride he expected and hoped for. He doesn't feel like a shark enjoying his feast. He feels like he won a scam. Like he came out ahead in a confidence game. That money simply wasn't earned. Or if it was earned, it was earned on the backs of people he sat with in handcuffs. People who risked incarceration for a raise and who treated a stranger like one of their own. That money isn't a triumph, it's an embarrassment.

He decides to divide it into thirds.

One-third is his, he concludes. $2,000 should cover the additional taxes and other expenses of this misadventure.

The next $2,000 becomes a check for Emilio. It won't pay for college but it's an honest beginning. Let Nate's unearned gains accrue to someone else, he decides. He still has Emilio's home address from the day of the science fair.

He imagines driving it to his place and seeing the joy on his and his mother's face as he passes them the surprise ... but then what? An awkward conversation with a woman who doesn't quite speak English and a father who won't know what to make of him? Nate decides it is enough simply to write the check and address the envelope. On the card he says, *For your sophomore year. But you still need to get your A's.*

He doesn't truly know that they'll spend it on college, but if he can't trust Emilio, he can't trust anyone.

The last $2,000 of his ill-gotten gains goes to the National Lawyers' Guild, a non-profit that survives on charitable gifts and modest fees from clients who can pay. The Lawyers' Guild helped Nate plenty and never asked for anything in return. He barely even said thank you. His gift isn't a town house on Marshall Street, but maybe it can fix that window – or if they prefer to leave the window and spend it on the poor and powerless, that's okay too. He addresses the envelope to Annette Wilcox. On the card he writes, *Here's the money I don't owe you.*

Catherine *The Art of Agreement*

Catherine agrees to lunch on Saturday but she can't possibly date him for real. At work people call her Catherine but her family and old friends still call her Cate. Nate and Cate?

Someone will figure that out. What next? *On a date with my mate?* She needs to stop that before it begins. *In a crate?*

Nate is thankful that Pac-Shoppe agreed not to sue him or Fitzgerald Financials, a small condition that Catherine included in negotiations and that the Pac-Shoppe bargaining team considered as much a distraction as she did.

"Let's meet at the art museum," he proposes. "The Virginia Museum of Fine Arts," he adds as if maybe there's another one in town.

"I've never been there," Catherine replies. She's driven past it enough times, and often wished she could fit it in.

"It's free," he adds, and that seals the deal. "Meet me at the face."

Chloe still haunts the Museum garden by the front door, peaceful and serene. Catherine and Nate walk a few laps around her, appreciating her fine features and the lily pond that borders the museum.

Catherine notices how the lily pond is filled by a stream from above. "Let's go up there," she says. "We'll check out Chloe from above, and see how that stream works."

"Great idea."

The stream turns out to be pretty cool. They climb a flight of stairs to the plateau above, while the water descends its own staircase alongside. The steps on their respective staircases are different sizes, heights and colors. The pairing is subtle and magical.

It's another beautiful day in June, though now instead of being unseasonably warm it is seasonably hot. The sun is fierce, and Nate is sweating when he reaches the top.

"Terrific," says Catherine, as she joins him to look back over Chloe, the museum and gardens. "This is great. Thanks for bringing me."

"Thanks for coming," Nate replies. "I want to look at that one." He gestures toward the sculpture that intrigued him since his doomed date with Ethan's colleague, the sculpture in view from Chloe that she wouldn't let him climb to see.

So they check out the sculpture, which doesn't prove to be very interesting after all: a seated man who is wearing a superb collection of pigeons on his head and shoulders.

Together they enjoy the cooing pigeons and gurgling water until they agree that it's too hot and it's time to go inside. "I think you helped turn the corner," Catherine says as they descend.

"What do you mean?"

"Pac-Shoppe was in full-tilt union opposition, hiring Theresa Staedtler and all the rest. Then they kind of backed off."

"You think that letter helped?"

"I'm sure it did. The letter, plus blocking traffic, pressure from the mayor, unity from our workers, support from the community, stupidity from the police chief, sell-offs in the stock market, and maybe a million other things. But Pac-Shoppe moved pretty fast from hostile to compliant."

"So you got your raise."

"Sure did. The big shareholders were leaning on management to just get it settled. The money men wanted them to sign the union contract and move on. But even before the raise, Pac-Shoppe let us move quickly to a vote,"

Nate has little doubt Mr. Daniels was involved. Daniels always cared more about labor peace and better headlines than the nickel in payroll. At some point that moved from the prediction of an observer to the position of a majority shareholder. Pressure was doubtless applied. Nate's only question is whether the letter he found – or at least its illicit disclosure – helped focus Mr. Daniels' attention in that way, or how it played inside of Fitzgerald Financials.

He'll never know.

Maybe next year Mr. Daniels will have a cup of coffee with him. Maybe he can ask.

Nate likes to think that by then he'll be in a position to tell Mr. Daniels about his new job. But right now he's with Catherine Campbell, on the date he's always wanted. He barely tunes back in as she asks, "Tell me more about Virginia Beach. Tell me about your family."

"Wow, this is incredible," Catherine says as she enters the museum, and sees the broad atrium, filled with artwork and sunshine. A Calder mobile hangs by the door and a beautiful oil landscape makes it like they never came inside. "I want to be a billionaire philanthropist and build places like this. Is it too late?"

"You might consider a career change," Nate says.

"Would the other career get me arrested?"

"Probably not. But not because you wouldn't deserve it."

As they walk in farther Catherine hears music, the unmistakable sound of a string quartet. She races in deeper and finds in the center of the atrium a string quartet, four musicians on simple wooden chairs, nearing the end of a masterpiece.

"That's Dvorak," she says. "The American quartet. How perfect. Can we sit?"

Catherine would sit on the floor to listen to this, maybe even on nails, but a bench is only a few steps away. Most people are ambling around, treating the quartet like background as they visit with each other and look at the real art, but for her the music is center stage. She is inches from a live performance of musical genius. Nate sits with her on the bench for the five, maybe ten minutes, before Dvorak reaches his conclusion. She wants to burst into applause as the musicians look over at them and smile. Surely they noticed how Catherine and Nate sat to listen while everyone else kept walking and talking.

Catherine wants to visit with the musicians, but that would be rude to Nate. She offers a few words of polite appreciation as she notices that they don't have a hat out for tips she would happily give. "Thank you," she says to Nate, who implicitly understood that you can talk while you look at a garden but not while listening to music.

"You used to play viola," he declares.

Catherine doesn't ask how he knows. She imagines that at some point he did some due-diligence background research on her, and it's not that deep a secret.

"In grade school I wanted to play violin but the orchestra didn't need more violinists. They assigned me viola. I was no virtuoso, but violists turn out always to be in demand. I messed around in a quartet all the way through college." She points to the violist, who hasn't yet vacated her space between the violin and cello. "Turned out I liked viola best after all. You get to sit in the middle."

Nate looks at her like clouds have parted. "You like being in the thick of things."

"Exactly," she replies, "Shall we?"

As the musicians close their music and put away their instruments, Nate and Catherine walk back toward the museum entrance, as if to start again from the beginning. The exhibit by the door is labeled pre-Columbian, and is filled with ceramic cups and plates painted in vivid black and orange. They are walking simultaneously through artwork and history.

"That's more than a thousand years old," Nate declares, pointing to a vase decorated with shapes, stripes and colored monkey heads.

"It's amazing," Catherine replies. She wonders how any of this was found or restored, considering its age and condition. Unfortunately, the rack of informative *Free Take One* pamphlets is empty.

"Refill with pamphlets!" she commands.

Nate looks at her like she's speaking some ancient pre-Columbian tongue.

"It's a game I learned from a six-year-old. It's about imaginary superpowers."

She starts to explain Maya's game, worried about embarrassing both Maya and herself, but she doesn't get far before Nate reaches for his shirt pocket and declares, "Put my pencil back!"

"Exactly." Catherine pulls her cell phone from her pocket and waves it around. "Fix my reception!"

They amble around a while, looking at artifacts and artwork, and imaging superpowers as needed. "Remove her hat!" they whisper simultaneously to each other, as they approach a beautiful Cezanne whose view is blocked by the woman in front of them.

They move at the same pace, which is nice. Catherine is neither bored when she wants to move along nor pulled when she wants to linger. Together they look at ancient art, contemporary art, and an amazing exhibition by students of the museum's associated studio school. When they are both hungry and dead-legged, Catherine points out the Amuse café on the third floor, visible from almost anywhere in the museum. "Let's look at the menu," she suggests.

But the menu is beyond her, with celery bisque and mint raita. She points out a pretentious-sounding chicken dish with fingerling potatoes.

"Those are French Fries, right?" she asks.

"Pretty much."

"Then let's stay stay hungry until we can find someplace where both of us can eat for the cost of one appetizer here. How's that?"

"Suits me fine," he says, smiling in a way that makes her suspect there's more going on behind the scenes. "I won't starve before we find a food truck."

On the way out they cruise through the section on European Romantics. Nate spends a long time studying an oil painting of a feast that's not very interesting to Catherine. The table in the painting is sumptuously set, with lacey tablecloth, silver wine goblets, and bowls of fruit piled high. Ladies in silks mingle with men in cravats.

Nate seems to be looking especially at the ham on a silver tray being delivered to the head of the table by a serving girl. He doesn't mention anything about brush strokes or lighting, observations they've shared over other paintings. Catherine almost wonders if he's hungrier than he's let on, fixated on the dinner scene and staring at the girl carrying ham. Finally, she asks, “What is it?”

He points to the serving girl. “I’m just wondering how much she’s paid,” he replies. “Compared to the cost of the ham, I mean, to say nothing of the tray.”

Catherine steps between him and the painting. “Unions need people who like numbers, you know. We hire accountants. We lead contract negotiations. We study the employer financials.” She kisses him gently on the lips. “Want to come work for the good guys, Nathaniel?”

THE END

ACKNOWLEDGEMENTS

Some old friends did me the kindness of reading parts or versions and telling me what they thought. Thanks to Joan K., Heather A. and Sylvie M.

The good folks at the Arlington Writers Group offered support, community and helpful edits. Thanks especially to Michael Klein and Fran Dattilo.

In the spirit of organized labor, my day job at the National Education Association gives me weekends off, which gives me time to write. Thank you to the millions of educators – from classroom teachers to aides, librarians and bus drivers – who collectively care for our children in the great public schools that are a cornerstone of our democracy.

Master organizers Secky Fascione and Stephen Lerner offered history, tips and tricks. Thanks especially to Secky for making sure drafts reflected reality.

Thanks to Tim Sheard at Hardball Press, who took the risk and offered some sharp-eyed edits of his own.

Thank you to the people who matter most. My parents, my children and my lovely bride get credit for everything, at least the good stuff.

Just one more thing: Thank you, Micaela Pond, for the F.

ABOUT THE AUTHOR

Eric Lotke has worked for, with and against labor unions. Early in his career he did advocacy in the criminal legal system, researching problems and proposing solutions that all reached the same conclusion – we lock up too many people (especially people of color) and don't do enough to keep people safe. His work includes the book, *The Real War on Crime*, and the studies such as *Hobbling a Generation, The Tipping Point* and *Prisoners of the Census*. An attorney, Lotke sued private prison companies and departments of corrections over the high price of prison phone calls and other conditions of confinement. During this time, police and corrections unions were usually on the other side.

He spent the next several years as research director of a think tank, the Campaign for America's Future in Washington DC, researching and writing about kitchen table economics – including health care, manufacturing and clean energy. Now he often found himself on the union side – the folks who brought us the weekend. Eventually he decided to join the union team. He worked first for the Service Employees International Union (SEIU, "Justice for Janitors") and most recently the National Education Association. He spends most of his time fighting against the privatization of public education and in favor of higher pay for educators everywhere.

Lotke is the author of two novels, *Making Manna* and *2044: The Problem isn't Big Brother, it's Big Brother, Inc.*

TITLES FROM HARD BALL PRESS

A Great Vision: A Militant Family's Journey Through the Twentieth Century, Richard March
Caring: 1199 Nursing Home Workers Tell Their Story, Tim Sheard, ed.
Fight For Your Long Day, Classroom Edition, by Alex Kudera
Good Trouble: A Shoeleather History of Nonviolent Direct Action, Steve Thornton
I Just Got Elected, Now What? A New Union Officer's Handbook, 3rd Edtion, Bill Barry
I Still Can't Fly: Confessions of a Lifelong Troublemaker, Kevin John Carroll
In Hiding – A Thriller, Timothy Sheard
Justice Is Our Love In Action: Poetry & Art for the Resistance, Steward Acuff (author), Mitch Klein (Artist)
Legacy Costs: The Story of a Factory Town, Richard Hudelson
Love Dies – A Thriller, Timothy Sheard
The Man Who Fell From the Sky – Bill Fletcher, Jr.
Murder of a Post Office Manager – A Legal Thriller, Paul Felton
My Open Heart: 1199 Nursing Home Workers Tell Their Story
New York Hustle: Pool Rooms, School Rooms and Street Corner, A Memoir, Stan Maron
The Secrets of the Snow –Poetry, Hiva Panahi
Sixteen Tons – A Novel, Kevin Corley
Throw Out the Water – Sequel to Sixteen Tons, Kevin Corley
The Union Member's Complete Guide, 2nd Edition, Updated & Revised, Michael Mauer
Welcome to the Union (pamphlet), Michael Mauer
What Did You Learn at Work Today? The Forbidden Lessons of Labor Education, Helena Worthen
Winning Richmond: How a Progressive Alliance Won City Hall – Gayle McLaughlin
With Our Loving Hands: 1199 Nursing Home Workers Tell Their Story, Timothy Sheard, ed.
Woman Missing – A Mill Town Mystery, Linda Nordquist

The Lenny Moss Mysteries (in order of release) – Timothy Sheard

This Won't Hurt A Bit

Some Cuts Never Heal

A Race Against Death

Slim To None

No Place To Be Sick

A Bitter Pill

Someone Has To Die

One Foot in the Grave

All Bleeding Stops Eventually (2020 release)

Children's & Young Adult Books

The Cabbage That Came Back, Stephen Pearl (author), Sara Pearl (translator), Rafael Pearl (Illustrator)

Freedom Soldiers, a YA novel, Katherine Williams

Good Guy Jake, Mark Torres (Author), Yana Muraskho (Illustrator), Madelin Arroyo (Transslator)

Hats Off For Gabbie!, Marivir Montebon (author), Yana Murashko (Illustrator), Laura Flores (Translotor)

Jimmy's Carwash Adventure, Victor Narro (author), Yana Murashko (Illulstrator), Madelin Arroyo (Translator)

Joelito's Big Decision, Ann Berlak (Author), Daniel Camacho (Illustrator), Jose Antonio Galloso (Translator)

Manny & the Mango Tree, Ali Bustamante (Author), Monica Lunot-Kuker (Illustrator), Mauricio Niebla (Translator)

Margarito's Forest, Andy Carter (author), Allison Havens (illustrator) Omar Majeia (translator)

Polar Bear Pete's Ice Is Melting! (A 2020 release) Timothy Sheard (author), Kayla Fils-Aime (Illustrator), Madelin Arroyo (Translator)

Trailer Park, JC Dillard (Author), Anna Usacheva (Illustrator), Madelin Arroyo (Translator)